tumultus

The Chronicles of Fate and Choice
Book Two

τumulτus

K. S. TURNER

RUBY BLAZE PUBLISHING

Published in Great Britain in 2010 by Ruby Blaze Publishing

Copyright © 2010 by K S Turner

The moral right of the author has been asserted

A CIP catalogue record for this book is available from the British Library.

ISBN 978-0-9562242-1-7

Typeset by Hewer Text UK Ltd, Edinburgh
Printed by Cromwell Press Group, Trowbridge, Wiltshire

Ruby Blaze Publishing
Ruby Blaze Ltd
Somerset, UK

www.rubyblaze.com

For you, who remember.

Acknowledgements

My heartfelt love and thanks go to my mum, Stefania, my step-dad, Tonka, my brother, James, and my sister, Jenny. Thank you for being inspirational yet grounded, brilliant yet humble, caring yet carefree, thinkers and doers, and for the limitless love and support you've given me.

A huge thank you to my editor, Jeremy, whose guidance, understanding, and genius are an honour to work with.

A big heap of thanks and love to my friends, especially to Zoe and Amanda: two beautiful, brilliant and very different, rare gems. To Niko, Blade and Mong from Switchblade, for their inspiring creativity, and to all my friends, for their encouragement and enthusiasm for the story.

Thank you to my agent, and to all those in the literary world who have been part of this path – the list is long, so I will simply thank you all.

And a special thank you to my readers, whose imaginations really bring these stories to life.

I have heard they've done many things:
Controlled and liberated, destroyed and created.
Remember, the balance of greatness can be tipped either way.
Sometimes it is not a case of good and evil.
Sometimes it is just a matter of choice.
And sometimes, choice is all that we have.

PROLOGUE

Before the Beginning . . .

In a time before time, when there was no such thing as time, and there was no such thing as right or wrong, everything was nothing, and nothing was everything. All universes had a timeless consciousness. Consciousness naturally expanded, and universes enveloped each other, one rolling into another, one consciousness merging into the next. Growing and merging. Growing and merging. It was a natural fusion, until the last two consciousnesses remained. The last two universal consciousnesses kept growing. Their course would be that they would become one.

At the moment they touched, realisation was born.

At the moment realisation was born, time was created.

Time and realisation created choice.

The smaller of the consciousnesses realised that its end was close and did not want to lose its self awareness. The larger consciousness realised that it did not want to envelop the smaller one, knowing that they were the last. But it was inevitable. What they were could not stop it from happening.

In that split moment of newly created time and newly created choice, the smaller consciousness chose not to merge with the other, and so fragmented, pulling itself into millions of pieces. The explosive fragmentation flung these pieces to distant galaxies; some pulled by the power of light, and some by the strength of darkness. Each fragment was too incomplete for the larger one to merge with, yet complete within itself, and no two pieces were the same.

Those fragmented remains of the penultimate universal consciousness were many. Each piece was aware of time, realisation and choice. Each piece was conscious of itself. These pieces became a new race of beings. They became known as the kutu.

The Shaa-kutu were those drawn to the light. The Nigh-kutu were those drawn to the shadow. They inhabited opposite sides of existence.

Feeling the fragmentation of the lesser consciousness, the last remaining universal consciousness discovered sadness. It realised that it was now the last and the most it would ever be. Knowing that it now filled all universes and could touch all times, it centred its consciousness here, in this planet, Earth, where it now sleeps, because it is as good a place as any.

The last universal consciousness has many names.

I simply call him the Old One.

I am Tachra.

I was born second-generation human. My parents are both of the originals. The originals were created by the Shaa-kutu and placed here on this planet, Earth, along with other young adults. They were prearranged in male-female pairs, designed to harvest energies, living and reproducing to sustain themselves and naturally fulfil their purpose. My parents seem happy with who they are. I don't understand such contentment and I fret watching them grow old. I do not accept the inevitability of death.

The Shaa-kutu made us. These kutu are beautiful, intelligent and strong. They exist in a state of energy and matter, and able to live in any combination of the two. They thrive on change and are constantly moving, seeking to be the best that they can be.

The kutu feel and think much as humans do, only more, much more. They are capable of great things, great thoughts and great acts. They can fly like birds when they wish, using their energy wings. I've seen them. They can eat as we eat, when in flesh. I have feasted with them. And when they laugh, it lights up the air with the most beautiful colours: fluid, luminous and glittering colours that reflect their very nature. I see their condensed power; it swirls around them in colours that we have no name for. I see their thoughts. All thoughts have intent, complex or simple, and theirs share aspects of both. And I can see inside their souls. Like a map of three-dimensional shapes their essences are clear to me, if I look.

I choose not to look.

I was eighteen when I first discovered the Shaa-kutu. I'd travelled from my home in the idyllic village of Threetops to find answers. I'd walked through deserts, mountains and villages, until my body had almost broken. I'd found refuge in an isolated, beautiful valley, my valley. And then I'd found the kutu.

I hadn't been looking for the kutu. At that time I didn't even know of their existence. But the kutu had been looking for me. They'd seen the link between the Old One and me, but they had not understood it. They'd thought the Old One was a potent new energy to harvest and that I was the one human who could harvest it for them. But that was before they truly knew what I was. I am nothing. It is the Old One who is everything. My link to the Old One was born into me and is the foundation of who I am. The Old One is not an energy that can be harvested.

Nevertheless, believing that they had discovered a potent new energy, the kutu had gone to great extremes to locate me. They took the form of flesh and set up a base here on earth, and they even kidnapped my loved ones in order to discover my whereabouts. When our paths did eventually cross, they tried to take me away from my beloved planet to use me as a harvesting tool. It didn't matter to them whether I was alive or dead. I did not want to be their tool. So, I chose death.

In choosing death, I found many answers. I also found Jychanumun, the black-eyed kutu who could walk on the death paths. It was Jychanumun who convinced me to live.

With Jychanumun's guidance, I chose life. By choosing life, I also chose to know the kutu.

The Shaa-kutu makers had been shocked to learn the truth of what the Old One was, and of their own origins. They had thought that they were eternal beings. They discovered that they too had beginnings, albeit thousands of millennia ago. That small group of kutu, who had travelled to Earth to discover a new energy, discovered instead that they had much to relearn. Now, all Shaa-kutu dedicate time to learning of the Old One and of their own origins. I am privileged to consider some of them friends.

Orion is the kutu with raggedy red hair, wild red eyes, and even wilder imagination. He is the embodiment of wonderment. Orion's love is to produce three-dimensional music, music that creates meaning, thoughts and ideas. I've never heard anything else like it. He has the perfect mix of theory and passion that creates artistic genius. Orion is highly respected as a kutu of prominence here on Earth, as well as on Eden1, the Shaa-kutu home-world. He is much loved.

And there's my friend Chia, the only kutu I have met who has chosen to shave off all his hair. Chia is a sensitive and has pure violet energy. He senses energy and intentions. He's predominantly a loner, proud, focussed, and has so much integrity and poise. In a strange way, he reminds me of my beloved cat, Meah.

Kraniel is the kutu with such a fast and active mind. He can never hold less than a dozen thoughts at once, and each one could create a debate to last for millennia. Kraniel would like to be thought of as the greatest analytical thinker, and he is, but I also see in him a great passion for the arts. I managed to get him painting once. He says he hasn't forgiven me, but I know he has that painting on the wall of his room.

And there's Stanze, noble Stanze, the gentle giant. He is one of the leaders of the kutu Anumi warriors: tall, broad and rippling with strength. Stanze can be a fearsome sight to those who do not know him, but his appearance is deceptive. He is honourable, brave, trustworthy and with the kindest heart. His energy is as golden as his hair.

And then there is Jychanumun, my black-eyed one. Jychanumun is the one kutu for whom it says more about him to say nothing at all. Jychanumun is not from the Shaa-kutu race. He is a Nigh-kutu, one who was originally drawn to exist within the shadow. But Jychanumun chose a different path, leaving his own kind and discovering the Shaa-kutu. He is complex, silent and resolute, with a combination of pure black and white energy. This precise blend of opposites gives him great understanding and unique skills. One of those skills is that he can walk the paths between life and death. Another is that he can sense the Old One. Because of that, we can share thoughts.

The kutu have given me the formal title 'Iastha.' It means 'I am three.' The kutu designed my form. I am of the human species. I have been shaped by the Old One. Iastha is an apt title.

The Old One has a name too, but one that cannot be spoken by kutu or human. The Old One is everything and nothing, and all things in-between. He is all our yesterdays and tomorrows. He is past, present and future. He is timeless. His consciousness is everywhere and he understands all things. He is both wonderful and terrible, and knowing his vastness would fill any other with such dread that death or madness would follow. The Old One is the last universal consciousness. He now fills all universes, everywhere. He shaped me.

It has been five years since I first found the kutu. It's also been five years since my Shaa-kutu friends made the shocking discovery of the existence of their Nigh-kutu brothers. In the beginning, long before memory, the Shaa-kutu had followed the light and the Nigh-kutu the shadow. For many millennia they both existed, each unaware of the other. But things changed, as they always do, and now this change is centred here on this little planet, Earth.

Five years ago the kutu warred, fighting over what they thought was a potent new energy to be harvested. It has also been five years since I found the Voice of the Old One to stop that war.

The war between the kutu was short but terrible, filled with a power the likes of which I never thought possible. It was potent aggression against protective might, each equal and opposite in its strength, and both equally deadly. These kutu have the ability to accomplish great things, so for kutu to war is potentially catastrophic.

"The potential of greatness can be tipped either way," Jychanumun once said. He was right. The kutu war could have finished all humanity, such is their ability.

I was almost killed in that war. I was caught in the crossfire by a relatively small kutu weapon. A bolt of energy had made a hole straight through me, dripping my life's blood from my flesh to the earth. I had not wanted to die. I had not chosen to die. The Old One healed me. He understood the value of my choices. The Old One stopped time and made me whole again.

As the Old One stopped time and healed me, the war between the Nigh-kutu and Shaa-kutu also stopped. They were motionless in the midst of its slaughter. They froze, poised in battle charges and bloody combat, as static as statues. I moved among them, awakening my friends and looking into the hearts of every kutu present in order to know whom to waken.

Most of the Nigh-kutu were already too corrupt to be saved. Their hearts were too consumed by the desire for power and war, no matter what or who stood in their way. Still, I could not harm them. Choice is sacred. Life is sacred. So, instead of waking the Nigh-kutu, my kutu friends put forgetfulness in their minds, and then sent them back to their home-world, far on the opposite side of existence. Those Nigh-kutu would not remember this place, or that fight, or any of us. When they awoke, they would have simply lost the memory.

After the war, the Temple of Learning was presented to me. It was a gift, from the Anumi warriors of the Shaa-kutu, to honour my bravery. The kutu had built the temple in the place I considered my home, my valley; the beautiful desert oasis I had found on my travels and had happily lived in with Meah, my cat. The kutu had taken care not to disturb the valley's natural beauty, and the huge, golden temple now stands monumentally tall against a backdrop of green trees. Its expansive walls step upwards, topped by a huge crystal dome that glitters in the sunlight. At its centre is a doorway that a hundred men could pass through without faltering. Either side of the doorway stands a colossal statue, a representation of an Anumi warrior, fully dressed in battle armour. It is a spectacular structure.

I had initially feared the Temple of Learning. The very same structure had plagued my sleep with nightmares before it was built. My nightmares had shown me that it was filled with unknown horrors. I dream those nightmares still. They scare me with a fear that seems displaced from the harmony that I now live in. I've learnt enough about my skills to know that my dreams have relevance, so it scares me that perhaps those dreams are yet to come true. I push such horrors from my conscious mind and strive to accept the temple as the place of peace it was designed to be. I should have no need for nightmares now. It's been five years since the war. The world is at peace.

The Old One now sleeps contentedly, centring his consciousness here, deep within planet Earth, dreaming once again his endless dreams from infinity to eternity. One day, I will join him in eternal slumbers. It fills me with neither dread nor joy. It is merely what I am and what will be.

My fellow humans flourish. They expand and progress, living and loving in contentment. I see my family regularly; they are well, living in Threetops. One summer my father even came here, to the temple, to learn. It felt both strange and wonderful to have the man who had taught me so much sit attentively in my classes. My good friend, Soul, comes here often and brings her daughter, Iris, with her. I love Soul like a sister. She's wilful, honest, passionate, and renowned as one of the fastest learners here. I knew she would be.

The Temple of Learning also thrives. It's filled to capacity at all times with both kutu and humans learning of the Old One and their own origins. I now teach alongside my kutu friends, here in the temple. I teach kutu and humans what I understand of the Old One.

To the kutu, the temple is my home. To my human family, my home will always be with them in Threetops. To the Old One, I will never be at home until I join him in eternal slumbers. And as for me? I have only truly felt at home in the forest, in my valley, sleeping outside, curled up with Meah. In the forest, I am free; we are free.

The world and the Old One are at peace.

To most, it is a beautiful and contented time.

ONE

Knowing that I'm going to die a long and painful death isn't the easiest thing to live with. But I'll do just that: live with it. But, knowing that the ones I love will die trying to save me, I can't accept. To prevent that, I'd change the course of everything. I just had to discover what I needed to change.

I pulled my light robe closer around my shoulders. It wasn't cold. In fact, the morning sunlight filled my room with its warm spring brightness. But a chill ran through me nonetheless.

There was nothing in my life to give me such macabre thoughts. Far from it, everything seemed at ease and I should be happy. My parents were both in excellent health and content with life. My friend, Soul, was well and her child blossomed. And here was I, living a comfortable life, with every need attended to in the Temple of Learning. Here I saw the wonders of kutu and humans working alongside each other in harmony. And this magnificent building? This temple was built by the kutu, in my name, in my honour.

My honour, I thought. *How ironic. I'm nothing, yet these great and noble beings, the makers of humans, the kutu, have built something in **my** honour.*

It made me feel ashamed of myself: ashamed to be standing in this beautiful room, in this beautiful building, surrounded by luxury. I had done nothing honourable. I had gifts, yes, but they were not of my doing. I simply could not help what I was.

A quiet knock interrupted my thoughts. I should have expected it. There was one kutu with whom I shared a connection. He was like a shadow companion, constantly in the back of my mind, aware of my presence no matter how far away I was. He could always sense what I was thinking. He would know when I was blocking my thoughts from him.

"Come in, Jychanumun," I spoke without turning.

The door silently opened and I felt Jychanumun enter the room.

Jychanumun's shoeless footsteps were as light as a cat's. The gentle flurry of air told me that his wings were fully extended. He walked closer, until his proximity made my flesh dance with the colours of our combined energy. Little sparks of black and white energy bounced from my skin, moving between us like tiny sunbeams flickering with shadows, subtly rippling with the multicoloured light of my own energy. I had thought I wanted to be alone, but I was suddenly glad of his company.

Jychanumun was a mix of pure black and white energy: introverted, intense and complex. He instinctively knew many things that were never said. Some kutu thought he was a prophet, but Jychanumun did not like speaking of such things. In fact, he did not like speaking at all.

Jychanumun continued to stand behind me, silently sharing the view from my chamber window. I had the distinct impression that he was observing me far more than he was the landscape.

Despite the early hour, it was already a bright day. This was my valley, an oasis of green amidst barren land. The kutu named this place Elysium, as they say it was made from a great bolt of lightning, long ago. Now, the huge Pine and Gera trees along one side of the valley spanned as far as the eye could see, their thick foliage the darkest green, appearing black against the pale morning sky. The central lake in front of the temple glittered with sunlight as well as its natural radiance. And the flowers around the lake blossomed with colours of every spectrum, dotted amongst the grasses like tiny jewels. It was breathtaking.

I tried to keep focussed, preventing Jychanumun from feeling my mind. I concentrated on the sight of a kutu taking a morning stroll outside. The long-robed student walked past a flowering Punni berry bush and paused, clearly relishing the sweet scent of the abundant white blossoms. I pushed out my senses to that kutu and felt his raw joy as if it was my own. It gladdened my heart to sense such a thing.

Recently, I had struggled to see this wonderful place with the same appreciative eyes. This was still my valley, my refuge, my safe place, and the place that I considered home. But, before the temple was built, this valley had never seen another human, or any kutu. Now the solitude was gone and thousands travelled here every year. Most came to learn, some came to see the temple, and others just came to catch a glimpse the 'other' species. As a result, what had once been my place of solace and peace was now a very public place.

"Are you well, Tachra?" Jychanumun eventually broke the silence. By the tone of his voice, he had detected that my thoughts were heavy, despite my efforts to conceal them.

I bowed my head, feeling a pang of guilt. This kutu, who felt such discomfort in talking aloud, had no choice if he wished to converse with me right now.

"I'm fine," I eventually replied.

"Your troubled face says otherwise."

"You cannot see my face."

"I do not need to. Why do you shield your thoughts from me?"

I wanted to tell Jychanumun that I didn't wish to shield my thoughts from him, that I'd grown accustomed to him being a constant companion in my mind, and that closing myself to him was like losing the best part of myself. I wanted to tell him about the recent terrible things that plagued my imaginings, and that those terrible things included him. But I didn't tell him. I couldn't. Because to tell him would be the undoing of the only possible chance I might have to save him.

Instead of allowing Jychanumun to sense my thoughts, I turned to look at him and mustered a smile.

Jychanumun was observing me. His all-black eyes, usually so expressionless, like dark pools of water, were full of concern. His pale skin and long black hair rippled with the intensity of his energy. He had his arms crossed and was standing perfectly still, as he always did when he contemplated.

Jychanumun stood a good two heads taller than me, wearing his usual black inscribed armlets, long black skirt, and no footwear. His uniform was plain in comparison to most of the kutu. But, with his energy wings fully extended like radiant black shadows spanning out behind him, as they were now, his starkness was striking and potent. As much as I tried to block him from my thoughts, I could still feel his anxiety.

"Jychanumun," I began, looking into his eyes, "can you teach me how to shut out the thoughts and sensations of others, in a way that's not a constant effort? If you could teach me that, perhaps I could control all the rest of the chaos that invades my mind."

"I cannot," Jychanumun shook his head. "I do not choose the way I am. I do not hear all thoughts, only loud ones. But you Tachra, your mind is part of mine. I cannot close myself to you. It is your link to the Old One that enables you to sense many things. No kutu can teach you how to control that."

No kutu? It was not the reply that I hoped for. I felt as if I wanted to slump down on the floor and cry. I was so tired. I hadn't slept properly for days. I just wanted my mind clear of everything except my own thoughts. I needed a long peaceful sleep, uninterrupted by dreams, notions or horrible chaotic images.

My dismay must have been obvious.

"Teach yourself," Jychanumun's tone was stern. "You taught yourself how to switch between your true vision from the Old One and your eyesight as a human. Is that not the same principle?"

It was, but the thought of learning anything new and filling my mind with more information was not a good one. Nevertheless, Jychanumun was right. I should be able to teach myself how to shut out the thoughts of others. It was just a case of discovering how. The main problem was that without a mentor to help me, teaching myself could take weeks, months, or even years. By then I would probably be huddled in a corner with exhaustion, unable to focus on any single thing.

But, my exhaustion wasn't Jychanumun's problem. I shouldn't concern him with it.

"I'll find a way," I replied determinedly. "And please, Jychanumun, don't be concerned if I sometimes shield my mind from you. My head is filled with so much information some days. It all overlaps until it's one big, chaotic mess. I must find a way to decipher or block it, or I will cease of sleeplessness. Are these thoughts mine or someone else's? Are they present, future or past? And why does it seem that the loudest thoughts and dreams are always the most unpleasant ones?"

"You and I could discuss such things."

I shrugged, feeling helpless. "If I could clarify my thoughts, I would. But a muddle of images and notions without substance are no good to either of us."

Jychanumun said nothing and just stood, watching intently, waiting for me to continue.

I sighed, finally relaxing some of the mental barriers I'd put up. Holding them all against Jychanumun, when I was already exhausted, was just too difficult. I could no longer completely fight against the natural link that we had. And, although I could still conceal the darkest of notions from him, Jychanumun could now sense some of my inner turmoil.

Jychanumun didn't flinch, but a frown did spread across his brow and his black eyes shone within their darkness against his ivory skin.

"I don't understand my own mind," I shook my head, not knowing quite where to start. "Everything is so perfect. Look at it all: The valley flourishes. The Old One rests peacefully. The Temple of Learning thrives. Kutu and humans exist in harmony. But if everything is so perfect, why does my mind torture me with the possibilities of terrible things? I desire nothing but peace, I see it all around me, yet it still eludes me."

And? Jychanumun prompted. He spoke silently with his mind now that my guard was dropped.

"Please speak aloud," I insisted. "Just for now. I must keep clarity. I know that spoken words are less efficient, but at least I know they're real."

Jychanumun simply nodded.

"I still dream of this temple, as well as other things," I admitted. "Those nightmares have never gone away. I've learnt to shield them from you when I sleep, but they're still there."

"Are they always the same?" Jychanumun questioned.

"Mostly," I nodded. "The nightmare of the temple never changes. I dream that I'm outside, it's dark, and all I can hear are heartbreaking screams coming from inside. The screams seem to touch the very core of me. They're terrible. They fill me with dread."

"This gives me disquiet," Jychanumun quietly considered. "I thought those nightmares had stopped."

Without waiting for a reply, Jychanumun silently knelt and placed both palms flat on the stone floor. As he closed his eyes the colours of our combined energy ran through him. The iridescence of my energy, colours of a pale rainbow on a grey day, danced through his sleek black hair, reminding me of the feathers of a raven, and his translucent skin looked like the moon breathing in flecks of colours from sunbeams.

Jychanumun was concentrating. I knew that he was going to use his energy to search the temple for any signs of discord that may be causing my nightmares. As he knelt, his luminescence faded and the vibrant light drained from his body, moving down his arms and towards his hands. The floor beneath Jychanumun's hands seemed to absorb his energy and now shimmered, as if lit by a thousand tiny lights that flickered on and off. The shimmering expanded outwards, reaching my feet, and I felt his essence touch me as it passed. His energy continued expanding until it covered the entirety of the floor, walls and ceiling, and then it moved beyond the boundaries of my room. And Jychanumun? He knelt, devoid of any sign of life, his colours now flat and lifeless rather than radiant. He looked like a perfectly poised, stone statue.

I watched Jychanumun as he worked, tentatively studying his motionless form for any sign of change. I'd never seen him do this before now and it made me realise that I'd never know the entirety of his skills. I was lucky to have such a bond to him. I did not ask for it, nor did I choose it, but if I had had to choose any kutu, I would have chosen him.

Jychanumun finally opened his eyes. In an instant his energy returned, as if a mere thought had pulled it back. He flexed, rolling his shoulders, pushing his energy back through his body to form his wings once again, and then stood up.

"I sense joy, anticipation and anxiety, but only from those with deadlines, nothing untoward. Mostly I sense peacefulness," he surmised. "I sense nothing to dread."

"I sense mainly peace here too," I agreed, although still not convinced. "But," I paused, "I fear that one day something terrible will happen here."

"Then if wrongness does occur, we will prevent or solve it as it reveals itself," Jychanumun said decisively.

Jychanumun's voice was resolute, although I still sensed his concern. I did not like seeing such a strong being feeling anxious because of me. If a being cannot help to solve a problem, I realised, surely sharing that problem is increasing its effects. Suddenly, I knew my decision not to reveal my darkest thoughts to Jychanumun, at least not yet, was the right one. I had no right to give him concerns that he could do nothing about.

"Perhaps my dreams are just a random mixture of many things jumbled together. Perhaps they're just nonsense." I tried to adopt a reassuring tone. "Perhaps it will just take me more than five years to get used to such happy perfection as we all have now."

"Perhaps," Jychanumun nodded, although the frown never left his brow. "Yet you still shield many thoughts from me. How would I know if you were in trouble?"

"I can look after myself," I replied, a little too quickly. "Never put yourself in jeopardy to help me. Promise me that you'll never risk yourself."

Jychanumun just looked at me, the corner of his mouth bending into a rare, mild smile.

"Exasperating," I shook my head.

But I didn't argue, because there was no point. And I didn't need to read his thoughts, because they were obvious. We had both risked our lives many times on the paths that led here. Risk was something we were both well accustomed to before we attained this idyllic life. And although neither of us took risk needlessly, neither of us avoided it either.

Perhaps, I considered, *that is my problem. Perhaps a bit of me yearns for adventure, change, or growth. I know so little, yet here I am, teaching creatures who are far superior to my mortal flesh. What about all the things I still have to learn? Yes, I'm the link to the Old One, but I am still a girl with a mortal life to experience. Perhaps I just need the adventure of life as any human would live it.*

Or perhaps, I reluctantly admitted to myself, I just needed a good night's rest.

Jychanumun looked at me questioningly.

"It will all be alright." I managed a genuine smile this time. "Perhaps the time is soon approaching for me to leave the temple. All kutu and humans have the freedom to come and go as they wish. But me? I am reminded daily of my obligation to stay here. I too need freedom of choice."

"It is a notion I understand," Jychanumun nodded.

I knew that Jychanumun understood. He chose to exist with the Shaa-kutu, the kutu made of light. But before this, he had lived among his own kind, the black-winged Nigh-kutu, on the far side of infinity, his choices pushed by their requests. He had escaped such imprisonment. He had chosen a solitary life of freedom rather than one tied to the demands of others. Jychanumun understood the value of freedom.

"I'll not be leaving yet, though, and perhaps not at all," I smiled. "If I did, I'd be back regularly. We'll see." Just the thought of it was already making me feel better.

"Anyway," I altered my line of thought, "What's tomorrow is always changeable. What's now is now. So, for what reason do I deserve your company so early in the day, my black-eyed one?"

Jychanumun paused for a moment. He knew that I was purposely changing the subject, and that I'd not told him the entirety of my dismal dreams. I really didn't want him to push the subject any further. Not yet.

"I have brought refreshments," Jychanumun conceded, with a small bow.

I glanced at the table behind me. There, next to the impressive crystal Memorite statue that took most of the table space, an ornately carved tray now sat on one side. The tray was neatly filled with an assortment of my favourite fruits, spiced nuts and seeded Junir breads, along with two goblets of water.

I took a seat at the table and picked up a small, plump Punni berry, freshly picked from the valley, popping it into my mouth. It tasted of sunshine and flowers.

"Orion will call for a formal meeting," Jychanumun stated, joining me at the table.

"I've heard nothing from him. When? This morning?"

Jychanumun nodded.

It wasn't unusual for Orion to call unscheduled meetings, but it was unusual for Jychanumun to notify me of one. I could only guess that this meeting must be significant.

"Have you sensed what it's about?" I asked.

"Yes," Jychanumun confirmed. "Orion thinks very loudly."

I waited for Jychanumun to enlighten me further, slowly chewing several more berries.

"And?" I finally prompted, unable to restrain the urge to question him further.

"And I cannot break my honour code by discussing the inner thoughts of another." Jychanumun indicated towards the tray of food. "But I thought you would benefit from sustenance first."

Oh. That sounded ominous. Suddenly I wasn't hungry at all.

I couldn't imagine what Jychanumun would deem it necessary to build up my strength for. I sat in silence, sipping from the goblet of water, deciding that not knowing was much worse than knowing, as all things terrible jumped into my mind. Had I done something wrong? Had something terrible happened to one of my family? Had someone ceased? No, surely not. I would have been notified straight away. And Meah, my wildcat? Was Meah well? I felt for her presence.

Meah must have picked up my thoughts. I sensed her drawing closer. As I turned, the now fully grown wildcat padded into my room from outside, looking rather bored and with tree-bark stuck to her fur. She brushed past me, nudging my hand with her head, and sat down beside the table, her nose the perfect height to inspect the tray of food.

I scratched behind Meah's ear and offered her a piece of bread. She took the bread and dropped it to the floor, sniffing it disinterestedly. She didn't think it smelt edible.

Suddenly, the communication port in my room sent out a loud buzz. It made me jump.

I hurried towards the still bleeping screen on my wall and saw that Orion, kutu overseer of the temple, had left a message. Jychanumun was right; a meeting had been called in the central chamber. Both Jychanumun and I had been requested to attend immediately.

Having propped open the exterior door to my room, with Meah choosing to sit half in and half out of the doorway, Jychanumun and I left our half-eaten breakfast, walking towards the central chamber in silence.

The Temple of Learning had been superbly designed. On all sides of the central chamber ran a wide walkway, its glossy, golden stone intricately inscribed to give a fascinating, readable texture. The walls had recently begun filling with kutu and human works of art, gifts from those who had attended the temple. The variety of art was vast, from flamboyant kutu-made sculptures crafted from ores that changed colour, to modest tiny paintings on papyrus. Each one was a precious memento, given from the heart. They made the walkway a constantly changing pleasure to traverse.

All around the central chamber were doorways to rooms that were dedicated to classes and contemplation. Living accommodation was arranged in a similar layout on the upper levels, and their position on the outer edges gave them all outstanding views of the landscape. My room was the only exception, being situated on the ground floor, privately tucked away so no one would ever pass it, with doors that opened directly onto the valley.

In the middle of the temple was a huge room; simply called the central chamber. The central chamber was spectacular space, designed with a beauty that made me hold my breath every time I walked into it. The floor and walls had been built with large slabs of stone and coated in Uana, so they gave off a warm golden glow. The ceiling reached up to the height of a hundred huts. In the centre of the ceiling was a crystal dome that topped the building like a jewel. The crystal dome cascaded the room with multicoloured beams of light, sparkling over the floor in vivid colours. The light was focussed on the gleaming floor in a rainbow-coloured circle. Within this circle of light, bored deep into the ground, was a well.

The well at the centre of the chamber was not a well like the one in my old village, built for functionality. This well was grand and beautiful, designed as an icon to the purity of Earth-water.

The well bored so deep below the ground that the water at the bottom was merely a faint glimmer, like a single dot of light in the distant darkness, shimmering like a solitary star. The energy from the Earth-water, deep below the ground, was strong, creating a bright pillar of luminous energy that pointed back up towards the dome. It was quite beautiful. And not only was it beautiful, it also filled the chamber with a raw positive energy that enhanced clarity of thought. It felt wonderful too. I always enjoyed coming here.

As Jychanumun and I entered, the chamber smelt wonderful. Concealed funnels of incense burnt fragrant woods, spices and flowers. Most of the chairs that were usually clustered into various alcoves in the chamber were neatly placed to one side, leaving seven chairs arranged into a circle. The chairs were obviously for this meeting. Several kutu were already present.

I was surprised to see that the kutu in the chamber all had their energy wings fully extended, something they only did for formal occasions here on Earth, or when wishing to sense a situation more scrupulously. They also wore their formal attire, indicating that we probably had a guest.

"Orion, Stanze, Chia," I called out in greeting, approaching the group. There was also one kutu whom I didn't recognise.

"Tachra, my dear," Orion strode towards me. His long crimson robe and his ragged, long red hair rippled with his energy, leaving a dissipating trail of red behind him as he walked.

Orion took my hand in both of his and kissed it when he reached me, holding onto my hand and patting it while smiling at me. I couldn't help smiling back. There was something about Orion's energy that was contagiously spirited. His energy felt like a mischievous sunbeam dancing through a forest.

"You all look so radiant," I remarked. "You know I love seeing you all less fleshy and more in your natural state."

"Do you not think it would intimidate other humans?" Orion asked. "Probably not," he answered himself, without giving me time to answer. "Perhaps we should be this way more often. It is certainly more comfortable for us."

Orion steered me towards the unknown kutu. He was particularly tall, even for a kutu, with cascading pale hair, golden skin, and the palest blue wings. His energy gave an essence of shyness, yet he was resolute. He made me think of a calm sea. This one was strongly a gold and pale blue, a good mix of integrity, reserve, kindness and intelligence. I had studied the colours of kutu thoroughly over the last five years, so I knew straight away that I would like this newcomer just fine.

"Tachra, this is Gabriel," Orion introduced me to the newcomer.

"Gabriel," I bowed the customary kutu bow, albeit not as fluidly as the kutu could. "I don't believe I've had the pleasure of meeting you before now."

Gabriel's quiet reserve broke immediately and he smiled a wide, genuine smile. Little sparks of blue light bounced from his skin, falling onto the floor around me.

"Iastha Tachra," Gabriel bowed, calling me by my formal kutu title. "I have been looking forward to meeting you. I have every class and lecture you give, recorded and sent to me. I know them all by heart. I have made records of them so that all the kutu on our home world can study them. To meet you is a great honour."

"The honour is mine," I smiled shyly, self-conscious at the praise. "I hope you will be staying here awhile to partake of, and perhaps hold, some classes of your own."

"I hope so too," Gabriel replied.

I bowed again and moved to one side, allowing space for Orion to introduce Gabriel to Jychanumun, and joined the other two remaining kutu.

"Chia, Stanze, my friends," I smiled. It was always good to see them.

Stanze was one of the biggest kutu I knew: three heads taller than me and almost as wide as he was tall. He was wearing his formal golden uniform of the Anumi warriors, but this time he also bore the official insignia plates down his arm that marked his senior rank. Chia donned his full uniform of the kutu head sensitive. His matt black fitted body-suit, gloves, and the streamlined, opaque eye-ware, were all part of the attire to reduce the extent of energy that he felt. He too bore his official insignia today.

Chia lifted his eye-ware, leaned forward and lightly touched my face with his long, gloved fingers. It felt as though his long, violet eyes were looking straight into me.

"Tachra, you look drained. Are you well?" he asked.

"I'm fine. I'm just tired," I replied. "Is it obvious?"

"Not at all," Chia replied. "If I were not a sensitive I would not notice."

"You look as radiant as always," Stanze declared, with a bow. He spoke in human words, pronouncing each one perfectly.

"Stanze, you learn human! Well done," I beamed. "And thank you for the compliment. It seems that you are getting very skilful in the language."

"Soul has been teaching me," Stanze nodded, speaking in kutu once again. "I have requested that it should be mandatory for all kutu here to learn the human language."

"That's a wonderful idea," I agreed. "It would enhance understanding. It seems that Soul is also a good potential teacher."

Stanze smiled. Was he blushing? Do kutu blush? It certainly looked like it.

I noticed Chia glance towards Orion. Orion, it seemed, was readying to commence the meeting.

"We are a body short," Chia stated, noting the seven chairs.

"Kraniel?" I asked.

"Yes. He is late."

"As usual," I laughed. Kraniel's time-keeping had become predictably terrible recently.

"We will have to commence without him," Orion joined us. "We all have other engagements this morning."

Orion sat down on one of the taller chairs. A smaller, human-sized chair had also been included, for me, but I ignored it and went to the spare kutu chair, climbing on so my feet couldn't touch the ground. I felt like a child, sitting on a chair that was clearly too large for me, but I knew that Kraniel would appreciate my humour at making him sit in a little human chair because he was late.

Orion was leafing though a pile of paper-thin information panels.

"We have our usual list of admissions to the temple to go through," Orion stated casually, opening the meeting. "Most have been here before. Tachra, your friend Soul joins us again next week. I have arranged a pod to collect her and her child."

I nodded. I already knew this. Soul had told me herself during my recent visit.

"Does anyone have any internal matters to consider?" Orion asked.

Orion always asked if there were any internal matters first. Normally, I wouldn't have anything to say. I glanced at the empty chair and thought of Kraniel's continued absence. I couldn't be the only one who noticed how bored he had grown of late.

"I think Kraniel should be reassigned," I suddenly spoke aloud. I hadn't intended on saying anything, but my mouth seemed to vocalize my thoughts anyway.

"Reasons?" Orion asked. "Other than his perpetual lateness."

"It's not his time-keeping," I replied. "I think he must be bored. He's spent five years lecturing humans on the lowest basics of how kutu technology works. Kraniel's a genius; it has to be frustrating for him."

"I thought it would be a good exercise in patience," Orion smiled.

"Surely five years must have taught him all the patience he's capable of."

"Point taken," Orion agreed. "I admit that I have been surprised that he has not complained."

"He keeps himself occupied in other ways."

Orion looked at me questioningly.

"I think he's got a secret place for his inventions," I said slowly, unsure as to whether I should be mentioning it. "I think it's underground somewhere."

The kutu laughed. They all knew Kraniel well. A clandestine underground laboratory was entirely his style. I was relieved that I hadn't just got one of my favourite kutu into trouble.

"Very well," Orion decided. "We will let Kraniel get on with his extra-curricular activities. I am sure he likes his secrecy, but he will be reassigned. He can teach kutu his more complex inventions. That should exercise his mind rather more."

Orion waited a moment to see if anyone else had a comment on the matter, and then began leafing through his agenda pile once again. Suddenly, he stopped what he was doing and pushed all the paper-like panels to one side. He put his hands together on his lap, his face taking on a sterner façade as he looked around at us all.

"Those can all wait," Orion decided. "There is a more sensitive matter that must be considered and I see little point in delaying it. Gabriel here has arrived to discuss that something with us. So, I will pass straight on to Gabriel . . ."

Gabriel nodded to Orion. "Thank you," he smiled. He glanced around the group.

"There is a specific reason for my presence here," Gabriel began. "For the past five years I have been assigned to monitor Shursa's rehabilitation . . ."

Shursa? My mind froze on the name that I'd managed to banish from my thoughts for five years. Shursa was the only Shaa-kutu that I didn't like. He'd been responsible for many terrible things. My mind churned around, highlighting a barrage of unpleasant images from the past and Shursa's face was at the centre of them all. Why would they want to discuss that appalling kutu here and now?

Concentrate! I disciplined myself, struggling to focus on Gabriel's words.

". . . agree that he has done well, especially over this last year," Gabriel was saying. "Una, the Supreme, considers Shursa rebalanced, although he does lack confidence. He has declined to reapply for his old position, saying that he wishes to continue his studies. The Supreme agreed, and Shursa now works with me, translating lessons from the temple. He wishes to come here, to the temple, to study. I think Shursa would be a good student, and so does the Supreme."

Gabriel closed his obviously well-rehearsed speech.

"And here," Orion added, "is Shursa's application." He gestured towards a crystal and information panel on the top of his pile of notes. "Shursa has applied to come here to study."

No one said a word.

Shursa come here? To the temple? The thought horrified me.

My mind raced. Yes, Shursa used to be an esteemed kutu councillor, but he had done terrible things and made terrible choices that caused pain and suffering for many. He had used his position of authority to manipulate Shaa-kutu with lies and treachery. He had singlehandedly introduced deceit into the Shaa-kutu race. He had tried to become kutu Supreme by wrongful means, almost killing Una, the rightful Supreme, in the process. He had made the first contact with the Nigh-kutu and tried to use their strength to control all Shaa-kutu. He had instigated the kutu war.

My thoughts tumbled together, a mixture of fear, shock and horror. What of those who had died because of Shursa? What of the thousands of humans who had accidentally stood in the path of the war he instigated? What of the Anumi warriors, who now wore battle-scars because of him? I had looked into Shursa's mind when he was corrupt, and what I had seen had made me sick. Shursa had wanted to come here, to Earth, to take over and harvest the Old One's energy, and to kill me, if necessary. He had been obsessed with planet Earth and its potent energies. Surely no one could change in such a short time. Here, Earth, was the last place he should be.

"Here?" I finally exclaimed, unable to contain my horror. "But it's only been five years. Could a kutu with such wrongness rebalance in only five years? I think not!"

I halted my outburst, surprised at my own lack of restraint. The kutu remained silent.

"It is true that five years is a short time to heal," Orion agreed, thankfully breaking the silence, "but it took far fewer than five years for Shursa's mind to be corrupted in the first place. Una has personally recommended that he attend the Temple of Learning, and confirms that he has greatly improved. But we who are here must all agree. Tachra, if you have objections then it will not happen."

"Shursa tries very hard to be a better kutu," Gabriel added. "I have seen it myself."

Gabriel looked at me with his long, pale blue eyes, and I saw the sincerity of his words.

"He strives to make better choices," Gabriel added, his gaze fixed on me.

Shursa strives to make better choices? I thought about this. Shursa had chosen a conflicting path five years ago: that had been his choice. But now I was told that he had regained his balance and was making better choices?

'*Choice*,' I sighed inwardly, *that sacred word.*

Perhaps Shursa had indeed now chosen a balanced life. Everyone can change. Surely these kutu were no different to humans in that. Perhaps Shursa truly had rebalanced. If so, surely it would indeed be beneficial for him to come here to the temple. Who was I to say no to such a notion? Who was I to hinder the progress of another being?

Suddenly I felt deflated.

"Has he truly made the choice for a better way of life?" I asked Gabriel.

"I believe he has," Gabriel replied. "He has found a love of learning. That learning has helped him ascend to a better place in his heart. He spends his time in studies, private meditation, or indirectly helping others. He has tried very hard."

I looked around at the others, waiting for someone else to say something.

The kutu were watching me intently. None of them said a word.

"This decision can't be down to me to make," I shook my head. "I only met Shursa for mere moments. Unfortunately, in that short time I only saw the side of him that I'd rather forget. You all know his history far better than I do, so this must be your decision. If you all feel he's rebalanced, and it's truly is in his heart to study here, then I can't deny him that."

Still none of the kutu offered an opinion. They just sat, looking at me. I got the feeling that they were waiting for me to say more.

"What have I missed, anything good?" a voice suddenly came from behind, breaking the silence.

It was Kraniel. He strode forward, beaming, looking unusually bedraggled.

"Oh," Kraniel suddenly stopped, noticing our serious faces and formal attire. "I really have missed something."

Realising that he'd interrupted a grave matter, Kraniel quickly slicked his hair back into a neat ponytail and took a tuning disc from his tunic, placing it on his forehead. Energy immediately began swirling around his flesh in various shades of green and as it did, he seemed to grow in stature, although his size never changed. A shimmering pair of darkest green energy wings formed behind him, the energy tendrils constantly moving as if feeling the air. His eyes now glowed completely green, and his skin lit up with the light-dance of his heightened energy. Kraniel wasn't the tallest or largest of kutu, although he was still two heads taller than I, but he shone with grand intention.

"My friends," Kraniel bowed in a more formal introduction, "apologies for my lateness."

Kraniel moved to sit in the one remaining seat, raising an eyebrow when he noticed he had the small, human-sized chair. He sat, part falling the last few inches as he made contact with the little seat. My intended ironic humour now seemed completely inappropriate.

"We were discussing Shursa's recent request to study here at the temple," Orion stated, ignoring Kraniel's discomfort.

"Very good," Kraniel nodded matter-of-factly. "When is he arriving?"

"We were debating if he should arrive at all," Orion replied. He glanced around at us all. "The notion has Una the Supreme's blessing. But the question is whether it is acceptable to us, and whether his presence will unbalance matters."

The kutu turned to look at me once again. It actually made me feel rather uncomfortable.

I composed myself. This obviously needed clarity of mind.

"It must be your decision," I decided firmly, taking my teaching stance. "The harm Shursa did to me and mine derived from his belief that he could control the power of the Old One. In reality, it wasn't much different from your own initial assumptions, although none of you chose to harm others to achieve your aims. It is all of you that Shursa wished to harm, not I. You've all known Shursa for many millennia; I don't actually know him at all. So, the choice must be yours. If Shursa has changed of his own accord, then I'll be joyous that such a thing is possible. If he comes here to learn, I'll strive to treat him like any other kutu. If he does not, well, then he simply does not. But that choice, as I said, is not mine to make."

I finished my speech, unwilling to offer any more. I had said enough. Who was I to judge Shursa's merit?

"Tachra is right," Orion considered gravely. "The choice should be ours. Studying here is the Supreme's recommendation. Una does have the best perspective on this matter. So, providing there are no objections, then I too would recommend that he comes to the temple to study. Initially he could come for a trial period, accompanied by Gabriel here, to help him settle in. And if, at any point, any one has cause for concern, it must be discussed and dealt with. Do we all agree?"

The other kutu nodded their agreement, albeit hesitantly. I understood. Only Jychanumun did not signal his agreement, but he did not object either.

Orion made some discreet notes on the leaf-thin screen beside him and then tucked the small crystal and Shursa's application to the bottom of the pile. The gesture and his expression of grim relief made me realise that he'd been quite apprehensive about broaching the subject of Shursa. I wasn't surprised. All the kutu now sat in grave contemplation.

Clearly anxious to move along with the meeting and improve the atmosphere in the chamber, Orion skimmed rapidly through the remaining subjects on his agenda, tacking onto the end the issue of Kraniel's reassignment. He sat inspecting his read-out panel as he made the suggestion, as if this were a long-considered matter instead of an impromptu decision. Of course, once it was mentioned, the entire group agreed to Kraniel being allocated more challenging lectures.

Orion had only made a brief mention of Kraniel's 'other' laboratory, but it did not escape Kraniel's notice.

"You know of that?" Kraniel asked, looking rather disconcerted.

"Officially, no," Orion replied. "Although I have known you long enough to expect a degree of unpredictability, so I am not surprised. I assume that you have taken all the necessary safety measures in this laboratory?"

"Yes."

"And you are not doing any experiments that you should not?"

Kraniel hesitated.

"I do not believe so," he cautiously replied.

Orion shot him a questioning glance.

"It is mostly theoretical. There are no rules yet as to these studies," Kraniel shrugged.

Orion raised his eyebrows, waiting for Kraniel to continue.

Kraniel sighed, his shoulders slumping. "Very well," he held up his palms. "Yes, it is experimental. Yes, it can be a little bit dangerous. I am trying to discover the core energies of darkness and light. It is rather, umm, volatile, but the laboratory is deep underground and I do have every safety measure in place. I just wanted somewhere to work uninterrupted."

"An interesting area of research," Orion considered. He tried to hide it, but I could see he was quite impressed. "Nevertheless, I am overseer here. I want you to arrange with Stanze for a full inspection."

Kraniel looked momentarily trounced. I guessed he was concerned his project may now be in jeopardy of interference. Orion noticed the expression too. He waved his hand. "No, do not worry; we will keep this off-record until you are ready to present your findings. I know you do not work so well when you have the council chasing you for results. But at the very least, you must allow Stanze to monitor safety measures."

Kraniel nodded his thanks, his expression now one of relief. Orion just smiled to himself and picked up the pile of screens and crystals. "Meeting adjourned," he simply nodded.

With the meeting over, the kutu began chatting amiably, discussing current events. Their mood had easily rebalanced. It was as if Shursa's application to come here meant nothing to them, as if he were just another student. That surprised me. I however, still felt just as anxious at the thought of Shursa's arrival to the temple as I had when it was first mentioned.

Feeling too muted to hold any superficial conversations, I made my polite excuses and headed back to my room, accompanied by Jychanumun, who never enjoyed conversing anyway.

As we walked, Jychanumun seemed more distant than usual. I knew he had opinions on the matter of Shursa attending the temple – opinions that he did not wish to share. I did not ask him questions, so we walked in silence and I wracked my mind for something that would ease our spirits too.

Meah was still sitting in the doorway of my room when I returned. Jychanumun turned to leave.

Would you like to walk with us? I silently spoke through our mind connection.

I would, Jychanumun replied. *May I join you shortly?*

Of course, I smiled. *We'll be in the heart of the forest.*

Once Jychanumun had left, I removed my robe and opened the trunk in the corner of my room. The trunk was almost empty. Just a few items lay neatly on the bottom; all were remnants of my past life. I moved aside the small carvings I had made, some water pots that had survived my travels, a length of twine I had completed, and my precious knife, and then picked out the fabric at the bottom. It was the one remaining piece of clothing from my old life: my choosing dress. Mother had carefully hand-stitched that dress over many nights. It was very raggedy now, but I still loved it. I gently shook the dress and put it on. Right now, I wanted to feel like the old me again.

Meah looked at me and strolled from my room, pausing as I caught up with her. Human and feline together, we walked out into the bright mid-morning.

It was a beautiful day. The call of birds filled the air as they flitted between bushes, happily feeding on the abundance of early-season fruit, and the lake mirrored the cloudless sky. In the distance, I could just make out a small team of kutu planting shrubs to extend the luscious greenery beyond the valley's natural boundary.

Meah knew exactly where I wanted to go. I followed her as she headed to the edge of the forest. Within moments, we were shaded by the trees.

The darkness of the forest and the smell of warm soil instantly made me feel at home. I felt sad, because I missed being here so much, but also happy to be here once again. I'd spent over a full turn of the seasons living here, alone, before I had found the kutu, and well before the Temple of Learning had been built. The trees felt like old friends welcoming me into their realm, as if they had missed me too.

Out of habit, I touched the tree trunks and branches as I

walked deeper into the forest, feeling their essence and giving them my greetings back. Tiny sunbeams speckled through the dense foliage, making tiny dots of light that danced on the forest floor. It was as if they were greeting me into their world and directing my way in the gloom. But I didn't need light here. I knew this place better than anywhere, even on the darkest of nights. Kutu never came here, unless I invited them. This place was considered *my* forest.

I took off my sandals, leaving them in my path to collect later, and headed to the area that I knew best. In a small clearing, dried leaves and grasses had accumulated from years of my visits and now lay scattered in layers over the soil, making my footsteps crunch pleasantly under my feet.

Meah padded to the centre of the clearing and began rolling contentedly, abandoning all her usual grace. I lay down to join her, wriggling until covered by dried leaves. It was a game that we played. It made me laugh, as if nothing would ever matter. Finally, we would be still, lying contentedly submerged in leaves and dried bracken as if part of the forest floor. Meah let out a long breath, like a sigh, stretching her limbs to touch my face.

This place was my perfection. Here, in this small, dense forest, I felt at one with the earth and at one with myself. The smell of life and growth filled me with peace and strength. Even the dried leaves that now covered me were filled with life and the transition of all life. These were not the discarded, dried remnants of the seasonal change of trees. These leaves were still alive, their essence a gentle and strong energy, flowing in tones from gold to amber to brown. Their energy was similar to their physical forms, yet brighter, bolder, blending with the energy of the trees and the land. Here was the purity of life. Here I felt at one with the Old One.

Meah found a moment of mischief, suddenly leaping up and running over my torso with purpose. She wanted to play. I tussled with her for a moment. She kept starting to run and then coming back to me. She wanted us to run together, as one, joined by minds.

Mind sharing with an animal was not an easy thing. It left my mind feeling quite fragmented for a while, so it was not something that I chose to do very often. But with Meah mind sharing was natural. My bond with her was constant and we'd been connected since she was a cub. Sometimes we would run together in the flesh, tearing through the forest, with my speed and agility never matching up to hers. And sometimes we would join minds and run together. She liked that. She would climb trees as I took a dormant role in her mind, showing me how to stalk, chase creatures or even leaves, knowing that I was with her. This is what she wanted to do now.

"Come then," I said.

I relaxed onto the ground and threaded my consciousness into the back of Meah's mind. She sensed me straight away and was off.

It was wonderful. Meah's energy seemed limitless as she ran through the forest, climbing trees to show me the new places of interest that she'd found, before bounding off to show me something else. She had just finished excavating what she considered to be a particularly troublesome pile of leaves when she stopped. She sensed Jychanumun. She was off again, running to greet him.

Meah found Jychanumun in no time. She stopped to let him notice her, and then led him to the heart of the forest, where my form lay motionless on the leaf-strewn, mossy ground.

I threaded my consciousness back into my body, opened my eyes and smiled. The two creatures I was bonded to were here with me in the place that felt like home, the place where I could be at one with the Old One. I felt a rare wave of contentment.

Show me again, Jychanumun silently spoke, sitting cross-legged at my side.

Jychanumun was referring to the true vision. The true vision was seeing, not just with physical eyes, but also with my mind, using my connection to the Old One. With the true vision I could see the essence of all matter, and the world became filled with even more beauty. It became the beauty of the truth of everything. And although Jychanumun could not see the world as I could, he could feel my thoughts and see through my eyes when we both wished it.

Without a second thought, I opened my true vision.

Suddenly the world around me had an additional dimension. The Old One's energy was now everywhere. Even while the Old One slumbered, his essence was in all places, touching all things, giving everything meaning.

The forest around me now only vaguely resembled the place that I had entered moments before. Now, with the true vision, it was so much more. The air itself had substance, sparkling with tiny specks of light that moved around each other in purposeful dance. The trees emitted their noble and gentle essence. I could hear them singing in their deep fluctuations, merging their songs with one another to create meaning. Each tree held a relationship with the next, and together they were part of the whole, strung together by both intertwining vines of plants and intertwining threads of light.

Along with seeing the truth of all things physical, with the true vision I could see other forms where no physical object existed. Lines criss-crossed randomly above my head, pools of essence hovered in mid air, some shimmering with brightness and others with shadow, like deep pools of understanding. To my side, a pillar of amber light rose far above me from beneath the ground. I instinctively knew that it marked the presence of where a mighty tree would stand in years to come. With the true vision I saw not just a given substance, but its meaning and relativity. And with the true vision, time was irrelevant.

I stood up, walking to one of the large Gera trees. Small saplings surrounded its bough, each vying for its place in the forest. I leaned forward, lightly brushing my fingers against the bark of the tree, allowing my flesh to become one with its energy. The pale green energy of the Gera tree flowed through my fingers, moving up my arm and saturating my flesh until I stood like a statue of glowing jade. It was a young tree, yet strong. I could feel its roots deep in the soil and I enjoyed the awareness of cool moisture as if those roots were my own feet buried far down in the earth. Its upper leaves felt glad to be basking in the sunlight, waiting patiently for the laughter of movement from a breeze. This one tree was part of everything, and everything partook of it.

A push against my legs made me look down. Meah contentedly strolled past, nudging me with her head. Her silver and golden energy wove around me, like a scent that marked that we were bonded. She wandered off further into the forest until only the finest line connected us. That line would always be there.

It is beautiful, Jychanumun smiled.

I turned to face Jychanumun, his containment of form now showing its true state. He was a mass of potent contrasts. The starkness of his black and white energy was more condensed than most, as if he kept it close to him. Within that black and white were multi-coloured specks, my colours, giving him iridescence within his shadow and light.

I pushed out the energy of the young Gera tree towards Jychanumun. The energy snaked through the air, wrapping itself around him and rising up to the top of the forest and down into the soil.

Jychanumun shut his eyes, relishing the understanding of the strong, young tree. In that moment, he looked beautifully serene.

Sensing my observations, Jychanumun smiled. He slowly raised his arms and, as he did, he pushed his energy out around him. His hair moved around his head, his eyes glowed within their blackness, and then, without the aid of any kutu device, his energy wings expanded out behind him until they reached the height of the forest. His force was so strong that it rained shafts of black and white energy around me like tiny droplets of rain.

Before me was Jychanumun in all his glory, a potent mix of pure black and white. This was the side of Jychanumun that was truly free.

Do you see yourself as I do? I asked, smiling.

I do not think that what I see through your vision I recognise as myself at all, Jychanumun laughed. As he laughed, sprinkles of purest white light cascaded from his mouth, falling onto the mossy floor like the morning dew. The laugh sounded like a chorus filled with hope. I had never heard Jychanumun laugh aloud before now.

I tilted my head, hardly able to comprehend what I was hearing or seeing.

"Jychanumun," I said without thinking, "I do believe you're happy."

"A part of me dare not even think such a thing possible," Jychanumun replied.

Seeing this kutu, the one kutu with such a troubled past, actually happy gladdened my heart. Suddenly my own notions seemed irrelevant.

"Come," Jychanumun smiled, holding out his hand. "It may be that your essence can travel to places further than any kutu ever could dream of, but as Tachra you are limited to walk on those two legs of yours. Let me show you what it truly feels like to be kutu."

I walked up to Jychanumun, watching his energy reach out to me. As I drew closer, his energy wound around me like a whirl of water. He put one arm around my waist and effortlessly rose from the ground, gently pushing through the branches of the trees until only the midday sky was above us.

Then he flew, we flew, with a speed and agility that only joy could make. The air rushed past my skin, blowing my hair into raggedy twists behind me, and I was barely able to catch my breath. The valley below us changed from greens and greys to golden, dry land, rushing past, faster and faster until it became green again. We travelled over water, so high that the air tasted of metal, cold and brisk against my skin. But I never felt cold. It was exhilarating. I could stay this way forever.

For that moment, I had no troubles. My mind was free. My flesh was free. Perhaps I too could be happy.

And there, in the empty skies, as the ground rushed past beneath us and the skies beckoned us on, I realised happiness was possible. Perhaps I was happy already.

TWO

Eden1, Shaa-kutu home-world . . .

Inner peace? Contentedness? Happiness? Shursa thought to himself. *How do I contemplate such things?*

From his kneeling position in the middle of his large empty chamber, Shursa lifted his head to check the time. It was past 19.00 already. Personal contemplations certainly did make time fly, yet it still didn't feel as if he'd spent enough time meditating. It never felt enough. He could meditate all day and all night for eternity and it still would not feel as if he had paid his dues for his past errors. His shame never lessened.

As much as Shursa wanted nothing more than to continue his meditations, the Supreme would be calling on him soon. He needed to ensure that he presented himself honourably. He would have to stop, for now.

Shursa stood, stretching his numb limbs.

Outside, the corridors were audibly busy. Tonight was a

feasting night. Here on Eden1, everyone who could would attend the two-moon feasting. Shursa did not want to attend. He wanted to take nourishment here, in his rooms, where he could continue with his studies and stay hidden from the outside world, as he always did. Feasting seemed far too superficial in comparison to the list of tasks he had set himself. But how could he refuse a direct invitation from the Supreme? And, as the Supreme had kindly reminded him, every kutu needed joy in their life.

Joy, Shursa reflected. *I do not deserve such a thing. Not yet.*

He walked across the room, consciously keeping his energy contained, and moved his hand over a panel that looked much like all the others cladding the walls. Instantly, a full set of wash facilities unfolded from the floor. Shursa opted for the section offering a large marble basin.

The cleansing unit displayed a colourful array of luxurious cleansers and fragrant potions. There were multitudes of tall bottles, all bejewelled with crystals and filled with soaps to make the skin opalescent, and there were ornately carved miniature cubes, each containing a single drop of the rarest perfumed essences from galaxies afar.

Shursa looked at the potions, feeling an overwhelming disgust that such things used to enchant him. He picked them up and dumped them unceremoniously in the recycling void. It was the same ritual every day. It would be so easy for him to recalibrate his wash facilities to display only the new items he required, but he chose not to. He chose to remind himself of all his abhorrent past habits. It kept his shame alive. Shame made him strive to do better things.

After undressing, neatly folding his plain grey robe and carefully placing it on the floor to one side, Shursa picked up the one remaining item by the basin: a small, coarse brush. The brush was a replica of those used by the humans on Earth. He wet the small object with plain water and began vigorously scrubbing his naked skin, as if cleanliness could obliterate the dirtiness that he felt inside. As he scrubbed, he chanted his daily mantra.

"Everything is nothing and nothing is everything," he spoke aloud.

This mantra was another of the written sections from Iastha Tachra's teachings. Shursa had vowed to repeat each section daily until he fully understood its meaning. He'd been stuck on this particular section for almost a year. It still didn't make sense. He could not understand how such a concept was logically possible.

If I could study at the Temple of Learning, then I might understand, Shursa thought. The notion entered his head like an unwelcome, taunting guest.

Shursa cursed his wandering mind and scrubbed harder, until his skin nearly blistered, repeating his mantra until it banished such hopes from his head. As much as he might wish to study at the temple, he did not deserve it. He did not deserve anything.

After three continuous cycles of scrubbing his entire body, Shursa finally put down the brush. It did not feel as if it was enough, he still felt dirty, but it would have to do.

He picked up the folded gown from the floor, its fabric now perfectly flattened and cleansed by the invisible nanos embedded in the threads, and pulled it over his head. Its sleeves were to the elbow, the most practical length, requiring no turning up, yet adequately covering his crystal tattoos. Both his arms and his back were adorned with such tattoos: marks of being overseer of the original Earth project, marks of being a councillor, and various marks of achievement and rank. He now wished he'd never accepted the marks of honour. They were a constant reminder of everything he had ruined and everything that he had never deserved to be.

Pulling his long, golden hair together at the back of his neck, and coiling the length into a neat knot, Shursa deactivated the wash facilities as two cleaning droids moved silently around the floor. He had set the cleanliness levels in his room to the highest possible standards. The little droids were virtually a constant companion that he no longer noticed. Apart from them, his living space was empty. He wished for no luxuries to disrupt his studies. Any necessities were neatly folded away into recesses around the room, all invisibly hidden so that he had just one bare space for contemplation.

A quiet bleep told Shursa that he had two minutes before the Supreme arrived to escort him to the feasting. His stomach churned. He had not been to a public feasting for a long time. He had not wanted the humiliation of mixing with so many kutu who would surely still abhor him. He knew he should display his wings for the event; it was protocol. All kutu would be tuned to a state of high energy. But the thought of displaying his energy colours so plainly for all to see appalled him.

Shursa winced inwardly as he corrected himself. *I am not appalled,* he thought. *I am a coward.*

He searched for a good excuse not to retune. Realising his own fear at the prospect of being noticed, Shursa debated the options. Retuning was necessary for the occasion; in addition, if he arrived without his wings he'd most likely be the only one, and even more conspicuous as a result.

Despite his lack of enthusiasm, Shursa fetched a retuning disc from a concealed compartment, placed it on his forehead, closed his eyes and concentrated on the matter in hand. Slowly his bright yellow energy began rippling more intensely though his body until his flesh barely held substance. His skin became luminous, emitting a yellow hue, and shimmers of his colours lit the room. Finally, completing the task, his wings slowly formed behind him, made of his pure force, an extension of who he was. He was now equal parts matter and energy, the perfect balance for a kutu.

The timer announced it was 20.00. The Supreme would here

any moment.

With nothing more needing to be done, Shursa walked up to the entrance to his room and stood in front of the doors, ready for the Supreme's imminent arrival. He gave his gown one last quick check for imperfections and stood straight.

Scrubbed clean, appropriately presented, and adopting the stance of respect, Shursa waited.

And he waited.

And waited.

The moments ticked by. Kutu were always exact with their timing. Had the Supreme forgotten about him? No, surely not.

At exactly eight minutes after the hour, although seemingly an eternity late, the read-out panel to the side of Shursa's door indicated that someone was requesting entrance.

It was the Supreme. At last.

"Come in," Shursa said. The door silently opened as he performed a deep bow.

"Shursa," the Supreme smiled, also performing the customary bow.

"I am honoured that you see fit to accompany me to the feasting," Shursa stated.

The Supreme put a hand on Shursa's shoulder.

"Shursa, please, you can rise from your bow."

The touch felt kind to Shursa. It felt full of compassion and balance. Shursa stood erect.

Una, the Supreme, stood tall in front of him, his pure white hair cascading around his shoulders, becoming almost invisible against his white robe. His eyes shone a silver white against his luminous pale skin. Yet for one so colourless the Supreme did not look enigmatic; rather, he was a vision of extraordinary power without colour. It was Una's colourlessness that gave him such great balance, and it was that equilibrium which united all kutu. It was what had seen him re-elected as Supreme for many millennia.

Shursa bowed again. "I do not deserve your kindness, Supreme," he stated.

"Shursa," the Supreme sighed, "Please stop bowing. Do you forget that we were friends and colleagues for millennia upon millennia? When will you stop punishing yourself? You are trying so hard to make amends. It is obvious to all that you regret your past actions. It is time to move on."

"But I do not forget. Nobody forgets," Shursa spoke quietly.

"Kutu do not hold grudges," the Supreme insisted. "It is good that we do not forget, because by remembering we can ascend, but we must all move on; we have so much to learn and remember. Right now I would just like us to try to be friends again."

Shursa stood, looking the Supreme directly in the eye. Una's honest integrity was almost overwhelming.

"Thank you," Shursa simply stated, not knowing what else he could say.

"Very good," the Supreme smiled. "Now, I know you would much rather stay in your room or visit the great libraries to study, but it will be good for you to socialise. Are you ready to come with me to the feasting?"

Shursa swallowed hard. *I don't want to go*, he wanted to shout.

"Yes, I am ready," he made himself speak aloud, his voice faltering.

Stepping outside his room, Shursa immediately felt intimidated. The corridors were a bustle of activity, with streams of kutu, all dressed in their relaxed finery, heading for the nearest travel points. They were clearly all attending the feasting. Shursa lowered his head, hoping that no kutu would recognise him.

Una touched Shursa's arm reassuringly, and together they wandered along with the crowds. The Supreme chatted casually, keeping the conversation purposely light.

Shursa was soon relieved to be walking alongside the Supreme.

Any passing kutu seemed far too engrossed in acknowledging their Supreme to notice him. But, just before they reached the travel point, Shursa spotted a kutu waiting: a kutu that he used to know well. It was Tarrian, a brown-haired, sturdy kutu of the Anumi warriors, wearing his off-duty armour and an arm insignia indicating that he was now of senior rank. Tarrian had staunchly stood with the other Anumi against Shursa in times past. Of all the kutu Shursa had wanted to avoid, it was the Anumi that he wanted to avoid the most.

Tarrian spotted Shursa immediately. His bright green eyes flashed with recognition.

Shursa expected to see dislike or some sort of warning in the expression on Tarrian's face, but there was none. If anything, Shursa sensed only a mild reserve and slight surprise from the warrior kutu.

"Supreme, Shursa," Tarrian bowed without smiling as they approached.

Shursa nodded briskly, without saying a word. The Supreme made some small-talk with Tarrian as they waited for the travel pod to arrive, before turning back to Shursa. By now, over two dozen kutu were waiting for the pod and Shursa was feeling very uncomfortable.

"I must apologise that I was late for our appointment," the Supreme quietly spoke to Shursa.

"You do not need to apologise, Supreme," Shursa replied. "It was but a few minutes. I know your days are filled with more important things."

"You truly have learnt patience," the Supreme nodded. "The old Shursa would have demanded an explanation for such improper time keeping."

"I am trying to be a better kutu."

"It is something we all aspire to. You are succeeding admirably. Still, do you not wish to know why I was delayed?"

"It would not be appropriate for me to ask," Shursa replied. "Unless it was something you chose to share with me."

"Yes, I think it is," the Supreme paused. "I received a message a short while ago. It was today's mandate from Orion, clarifying that you have been approved to attend the Temple of Learning to continue your studies. You will be on the next ship of scholars, outbound to Earth in seven days. If you still wish it, of course."

For a moment, Shursa could barely dare to believe what he had just heard.

"I have been accepted? To the Temple of Learning?"

"You have indeed," the Supreme confirmed.

"I have been accepted," Shursa whispered to himself, smiling.

A fraction of a moment later, the travel pod arrived. Shursa looked up as the doors opened. The pod was already nearly full and he immediately recognised several faces inside.

I can do this, Shursa thought to himself.

Fighting the desire to turn around and retreat into the confines of his room, Shursa thought about the Temple of Learning. Soon he would be there. Soon he could devote his entire days to his studies. Perhaps one day his fellows would recognize that he was changed for the better. Perhaps one day he would even allow himself to believe he had repented enough.

Shursa forced himself to hold his head high. He even managed nods of acknowledgment to a few kutu that he recognised. Then, walking side by side with the Supreme, he entered the travel pod.

Tonight, Shursa decided, he would allow himself the luxury to celebrate. Just this once.

Over the next seven days, Shursa tried everything he could think of to stay focussed on his studies, although meditation became almost impossible. All his thoughts now churned around in his head, revolving around the next step in his learning programme – attending the Temple of Learning. He had never known time to pass so slowly.

Nevertheless, as much as the seven days dragged, they did eventually pass. On the morning of the seventh day, Shursa left his rooms empty. He had already placed his books in a crate destined for Earth and packed his few meagre possessions into the small satchel that he now carried. He didn't mind that he was early. He didn't even mind that the pod wasn't ready to board when he arrived at the docking station. He didn't mind anything today, because today he was going to Earth.

Shursa entered the docking bays and stood, waiting to board the pod. The little craft destined for Earth was of a new design, the first of its kind to utilise the excess energy that all kutu produced. Such potent energy allowed the ship to travel great distances in mere moments. Its appearance was sleek and grey, without the added texture or surface detail typical of kutu crafts. Its matt appearance seemed to absorb light, rather than reflect it, and there was no sign of any entrance or portals anywhere on its exterior.

The new pod seemed far too small to carry more than one kutu, being not much larger than the individual pods, yet was allocated to carry up to twenty-five kutu, plus their personal necessities. Shursa wasn't quite sure how so many kutu would fit in to such a small craft. Nevertheless, the pod stood, ready to board, in the centre of the docking bay, dwarfed by the other crafts around it. In comparison to the beauty of their standard ships, this little pod was nothing but ugly, but Shursa liked it. It was going to take him to where he wanted to be.

Gabriel was already in the outbound pod when Shursa boarded. It turned out that the kutu had travelled to and from Earth just to escort him. Shursa wasn't offended. He was grateful. He knew someone was going to speak on his behalf in support of his application to attend the temple. He appreciated that it was Gabriel, one of his own tutors.

"What was their reaction?" Shursa asked, squeezing into the small space allocated for him and placing his satchel on his lap.

"They treated your application fairly," Gabriel replied.

"I do not doubt that," Shursa said quietly. "I do not want to cause any discord. Were there any problems?"

"Shursa," Gabriel reassured, him, "it would not be fair of me to pretend that your application was entirely like everyone else's. Yes, they did debate it in more detail than most, but that was to be expected. It would have been wrong of them not to. Remember that they all agreed to grant your application. I am confident that, once they get to know you, everything will go smoothly. Just be yourself."

That didn't make Shursa feel any better. The teachers at the temple were the very same kutu for whom he had caused so much trouble, and he certainly didn't want them to think he was being 'himself'. He had believed he could be a great leader, but now he knew he could never lead: there were kutu far more powerful than him. Orion's talents had almost driven him insane with jealousy. He had hated Chia for reasons that even he no longer remembered. He had betrayed Jychanumun. He had promoted a war. The teachers at the temple would remember his past deeds more than most. They would remember because they had Iastha Tachra, and she had seen into his mind.

"What is she like?" Shursa asked.

"Who? Iastha Tachra?"

Shursa nodded.

"Do you not remember?" Gabriel asked.

Shursa shook his head, as a memory came to him of a pale-skinned female, looking up at him with frightened, yet wilful, wide, green eyes as he angrily picked her up by her hair. He had commanded her to give him her powers. He had believed he was powerful and had acted worse than abhorrently.

"I do not wish to remember that," Shursa told Gabriel.

"Just as well," Gabriel nodded. "Then I would say that Iastha Tachra now is very much like the person we see on the lecture recordings. Although she is much smaller than I had imagined." Gabriel indicated a height just above his waist level. "She is, as most humans are, quite tiny, in fact. But . . ."

Shursa glanced at Gabriel questioningly.

"You will see soon enough," Gabriel smiled. "I do not think she realises how strong her inner presence is."

Shursa nodded. He appreciated having Gabriel to travel to Earth with. More than this, he was thankful that Gabriel was prepared to stand by him during his introduction into the temple, and to Orion, Chia, Jychanumun and Iastha Tachra. He would need all the support he could get if he wasn't to be turned away as soon as he arrived.

"I think we are about to do the distance jump," Gabriel commented, observing the pilots as they relaxed into their seats at the front of the ship. "I closed my eyes last time, but felt nothing unusual. This time I want to observe everything, to see if I can feel anything different."

"I have heard about this," Shursa replied. "The concept of using excess kutu energy to create a travel point is truly a marvel."

Gabriel agreed. "It would be even better if there was enough excess energy to create more than the occasional jump. And better again if the craft were not so small. Such a confined space is not good when one wishes to retune to the flesh."

Suddenly, and very briefly, the colour in the craft seemed to dull. If Shursa had blinked, he was sure he would have missed it. But maybe that was just his imagination.

"No, still did not feel a thing," Gabriel shrugged. "Amazing concept."

"That was it?"

"Yes, that was it," Gabriel confirmed. "It is time to retune, if you wish to do so. The travel point has taken us just beyond the XLS Earth substation. That leaves us eight hours of standard travel to retune and acclimatize."

Gabriel did his best to relax back in the cramped space of his seat, removing a retuner from the pocket in his robe and placing it on the middle of his forehead.

Shursa did the same, taking his own retuner from his satchel and placing the cool disc on his own forehead. Immediately he felt a slight tingle on the skin under the disc. The tingle turned to a more uncomfortable sensation, rather like the prick of tiny pins, and then the familiar heavy tiredness began to ooze through his body as the retuning kicked in. As Shursa retuned to be more physical, and so better suited to Earth's environment, his energy slowly started draining away and his body gained mass, giving his flesh substance. It was not at all a pleasant experience.

Shursa sat in quiet contemplation, trying desperately to concentrate and take his mind off the discomfort of retuning to heightened flesh. But everything he found to focus on just seemed to make the sensations of the body even more unruly. He desperately tried to quell the excitement that mixed with his anxiety as the small pod, carrying twenty-three kutu travellers and two pilots, navigated the final stretch towards Earth.

It was clear which of the kutu on board the pod had previously attended the temple. They sat easily occupying themselves as their bodies took substance. Some talked quietly among themselves. One or two meditated to make the retuning less uncomfortable. The kutu sitting across from Shursa, a senior member of the analysis team, sat taking notes on the physical sensations he was experiencing. Shursa was convinced that nothing could be as bad as what he was feeling.

Shursa had tried to prepare for such extreme retuning. Over the previous days, once he had discovered that he was to attend the Temple of Learning, he had ensured that he spent as much time as possible attuned to the flesh. He wanted nothing to mar his arrival at the temple. In his training he had learned to live quite happily at a three-to-one ratio of matter to energy, well within the tolerance limits that they recommended on Earth. But now, their growing proximity to the little blue planet seemed only to emphasize the heaviness of his limbs and his lurching insides. The discomfort made Shursa wonder if he'd made the right choice. He didn't want to arrive feeling so sick that he couldn't think straight. His stomach was the worst: it flipped and turned of its own accord, whether due to a change in direction or even a mere thought.

Shursa groaned as his stomach performed another flip.

"You will feel better once you are on solid ground," Gabriel spoke consolingly. "You do not have to retune. You know it is now permitted to be in any combination of energy and matter when a kutu is on Earth."

"I know, but I would like to do things properly," Shursa replied.

Gabriel nodded in approval. "I think we all feel the same way," he smiled.

It was true; Shursa had already noticed that most kutu were retuning to the flesh. Only the two pilots and a handful of obviously regular temple attendees were in their natural kutu state. Still, everyone else who was retuning seemed to be dealing with the process without problems.

Shursa stood up to stretch his heavy limbs, hoping the action would help him feel better. The speed of the pod caused a slight vibration in his newly formed flesh which made his head hurt. He began to feel giddy. His head started to spin and a wave of nausea passed through him. He was suddenly hot, very hot – so hot he was sure that he would catch on fire. He reached up with his hand to steady himself.

And then, as if someone had leaned over his shoulder and whispered directly into his ear, he heard a voice.

I remember. I cannot forget.

The voice was deep and smooth.

"Pardon?" Shursa asked Gabriel. The word came out as a slight stammer.

"I did not say anything," Gabriel replied absently.

No, the voice didn't sound like Gabriel's. But Shursa wished it were Gabriel. There was only one alternative; that it was **that** voice; the one that taunted him when he slept and made him question his sanity. But this time he wasn't asleep. He was very much awake. Was this a waking dream?

Shursa went to speak, but couldn't. Something had grabbed his insides and rendered him almost paralysed with dread. He had not heard the words with his ears; they were in his head. Again. But this time he couldn't convince himself that he was dreaming. This time the voice sounded very real indeed.

Go away, Shursa thought, trying to push away the dizziness.

But the sickening feeling and presence in his head did not retreat.

Get out of my head! Shursa directed the thought, concentrating with all his might.

No, the voice replied. *We had an agreement, Shursa of Shaa-kutu. And I do not forget*.

Go away. I'm not listening. Shursa doubled over, clasping his head as if his hands could squeeze out the searing pain. *Please go away! Leave me alone!*

Shursa felt his heart stop beating, as if a hand squeezed it. He felt his legs give way beneath him. *Arrunn, if this is real, if you are real, go away,* he pleaded feebly, with the only strength he had left.

I will not, the voice said. *We had an agreement. Now I claim my dues*.

THREE

I was so excited at the prospect of seeing Soul that fretting about Shursa's coming to the temple faded into the background. I was thankful for that. It was something I would rather not think about, so the distraction was welcome.

Soul was my friend, and had been since the day we'd met. Our initial meeting had been under terrible circumstances: the death of her loved one, Wirrel. But, her inner strength had overcome such a dreadful memory. I was lucky to have such a friend.

Soul was already with child when we met. Iris would be five summers old now, a bright and intelligent child who certainly knew how to find mischief. Soul, Iris and I liked nothing better than finding mischief together. They were the rare times when I remembered what it was to be a girl again. Orion still pretended that he hadn't forgiven us for cutting three inches off the hem of every gown he owned the last time Soul visited. He had arrived to that morning's meeting wearing a gown decidedly shorter than his usual attire, and with a look of startled bewilderment on his face.

He was all in a flurry, stating with utter conviction that something here on Earth must be making him grow taller. I finally had to admit to our misdemeanours when the news sent the entire kutu analysis team into frenzied activity trying to figure it out.

I had just finished preparing my room to make it Iris-proof, moving breakable objects away from her reach, when I suddenly took a fancy for some berry pie. The thought of steaming pastry and hot berries suddenly popped into my head, making my mouth water. I'd never been terribly fond of berry pie, so the sudden desire took me rather by surprise.

It was already growing dark outside. Meah had gone exploring, grown bored with watching me move objects around, and Jychanumun had gone flying. I'd originally planned an early night, but now the desire for berry pie was taunting me. So, despite the fact that I had only eaten supper an hour ago, I left my room and headed for the kitchens, hoping that the cooks had some left-overs that vaguely resembled what I was imagining.

The corridors en route to the kitchens were quiet and smelt of dry stone and sweet incense. As I approached the kitchens they gave off no tempting aromas of food, but, as soon as I opened the large double doors, a wall of heat and smell of cooking greeted me with friendly familiarity. The cooks were all busy, so I didn't disturb them, heading to the area where shelves of surplus food was arrayed in tempting displays. My mouth watered as soon as I saw a platter of fresh Punni berry pie. It was exactly like the one I was imagining. Perfect.

I hurriedly cut a section of delicious-looking pie and put it onto a plate, managing to drop crumbs everywhere. An entourage of cleaning droids sped into motion to sweep the floor around me. Feeling more than a little sheepish at having made rather a mess, I took my bounty and quietly left.

I wandered back towards my room, not in any hurry, happily

savouring my new favourite dessert. As I turned the last corner to the corridor to my room, I noticed someone was lurking in the shadows. It was a dead end here, with only the door to my living quarters. Why would someone just be standing there? I halted in my tracks and stopped chewing.

"Hello?" I cautiously called out.

"Tachra?" the figure replied.

I recognised that voice.

"Soul!" I cried out, happily walking forward as Soul's silhouette emerged from the shadows.

"I didn't sense you! When did you get here? I didn't think you were arriving until tomorrow. Are you well?"

Not waiting for a reply, and still clutching my plate, I hugged her. This was a pleasant surprise.

"I'm well," Soul laughed, "I've only just arrived. I wanted to surprise you."

The doors to my rooms had sensed my proximity and automatically glided open. "Come on in. Make yourself comfortable," I indicated, walking in as Soul followed me.

"I'm anxious that I didn't sense you," I confessed. "Do you think our link is growing weaker?"

"No, don't fret," Soul smiled. "It would seem your senses are stronger, not weaker. I wanted to surprise you, so purposely hid my early arrival." She laughed, pointing at the plate, with now only a few crumbs left on it. "The only thing I could think of to hide my thoughts from you was to concentrate on repeating pie recipes. I've been doing a pie mantra all evening. I didn't think you would sense it so strongly, but I should have known. I just wanted to surprise you. Hello Tachra!"

I saw the funny side of the situation straight away. I was also more than a little relieved to know that the link between Soul and me was as strong as ever.

Soul went over to the materializer in the corner of my room.

"This is new. Is it one of those kutu things that makes things?"

"It is," I nodded. "Although I don't use it a great deal. I don't really have the need to."

"Do you know how to make it work?"

"Yes, it's quite easy," I replied, walking towards the materializer. "The kutu made it especially for me. The kutu ones are more complex, but this one you just speak to."

"You get the stupid-human version," Soul teased. "May I?"

"Be my guest."

Soul leaned forward. "Two very delicious sweet teas please," she asked the machine. "Thank you," she added, remembering her manners.

The 'thank you' made me laugh, but the machine did nothing.

"You have to speak here," I explained, still laughing, pointing to a small symbol at my mouth height. "Although make sure it's in the style that kutu would describe something, or you'll get something strange instead. It's actually more trouble than it's worth."

I leaned towards the machine. "Quantity: two. Item: drinking vessels. Details: prefilled with the human drink, tea, temperature hot. Sub details: sweetened with the apian product, honey."

Soul waited expectantly until I indicated towards the small table by the window. There two ornate goblets filled with steaming sweet tea now waited.

I sat down on the edge of my sleeping recliner and took a long draught from the goblet.

"Iris isn't arriving until next week," Soul said, noticing that I'd moved most items so that they were too high for the child's reach. "She's staying with your parents. I wanted to see you alone first. I've been concerned about you."

"Everything is well," I shrugged. "There's nothing to be concerned about."

"But I've heard Shursa is coming here to study. Is it true?" Soul asked.

"It is," I answered, ignoring the anxious knot in my belly. "He arrives soon. It'll be alright; the kutu say he's changed."

"Maybe," Soul frowned. "But you remember Huru, that beast of a man who murdered Wirrel? He changed too. But even once he was supposedly a better man, I couldn't feel comfortable around him. So do not tell me that you're not fretful about Shursa."

Finally, someone understood.

"I am fretful," I sighed, and the very admission was like lifting a burden from my shoulders. "I feel as if I shouldn't be, yet I can't stop it, so I keep it to myself. I must overcome it. I must tackle it like a kutu would and view this as an opportunity to learn."

"Perhaps," Soul shrugged. "But I decided it would be good if I was here when he arrived anyway," she added matter-of-factly. "Just in case you needed me; even if it's just to have a friend to talk to."

"Thank you," I smiled, feeling distinctly better about it already. Soul's perspective was always refreshing. "So, what of you, my friend? What news from your life?"

Soul began talking, flitting in and out of conversations and subjects with barely a pause. I got the distinct impression that, despite all that she was saying, there was something else that she was trying to avoid. I let her talk, waiting for her to tell me what was truly on her mind. I had learnt that the most important thing was usually the very last thing said.

I was right.

"Tachra," Soul suddenly stopped midway through a detailed description of the current Junir crops. "I must talk to you. You're the only person I can truly speak to. I don't know what to do."

She stood up, clearly anxious about something. Her hands were clasping and unclasping, as if not sure whether to let go of what was on her mind.

I reached out, taking one of her hands, unfurling her clenched fingers, holding them between my hands. I sent her some energy of inner peace until I felt her calm.

"Come," I smiled. "Nothing can be that bad. Speak."

Soul closed her eyes, her face becoming suddenly grave, and she let out a long breath.

"Tachra, I think I've fallen in love," she spoke quietly.

It was strange that she used the kutu word, 'love'. We humans had pairings, some had even developed an inner fire for another, but this love? That was a word that the kutu had introduced to our world.

"But isn't that good news?" I asked cautiously. Soul certainly didn't seem very happy about it. "You are young, beautiful and exceptional; any man would be fortunate to have your love."

"He is not a fortunate man," Soul shook her head. "I have loved Wirrel. Now he's ceased I could never love another man."

I looked at her questioningly.

"It's no man," and as she uttered the words she looked at me, her eyes full of worry. "It's a kutu. I never wanted to care for another. But somehow I have grown to love him."

A kutu? That explained why Soul had used the kutu word, love.

A barrage of images rushed through my mind. Straightaway I thought of Stanze. I knew the kutu warrior regularly visited Soul, but until now I'd assumed Stanze's visits were in friendship, to ensure her well-being.

"Are you taking of *Ish* love, like the love between family, *Ros,* the passionate love, or the love of the mind, like *Lia* love?" I asked.

"I don't know!" Soul shrugged in dismay. "I dream of being

with him, I feel empty without him close, I feel concern for his well-being. Does that have a proper description?"

"Is it Stanze?" I asked.

Soul's silence told me I was right.

"Does he know?"

"No," Soul bowed her head. "I couldn't tell him. It would ruin our friendship. He was due to collect me in the pod tomorrow, to come here. I've avoided him. Tachra, help me. Tell me how to stop the way I'm feeling."

"Is it such a wrong feeling that it needs to be stopped?" I asked.

"It's making me miserable," Soul looked at me beseechingly.

"Is it feeling love that is making you miserable, or is it your fear to tell the one being who should be told?"

"I cannot tell him!" Soul exclaimed in dismay. "It's not right to love a kutu. A human and kutu could never be. It's no more possible than falling in love with a mountain, or a cloud, or a star in the sky. And even if it were possible, how could it work? Kutu live on, we humans live only a hundred short summers, extended to three of four hundred at best with the aid of their kutu machines. Such a match would be doomed to difficulty and heartache, even if it were possible."

"Could such a bond not surpass the ceasing of the flesh?" I asked.

"I don't know what you mean. Please, my friend, talk to me as a girl. Talk to me in a way I'll understand," Soul implored.

"Very well," I nodded. "Come, sit." I took her hands, guiding her to sit back down, and turned to face her.

"Soul," I smiled, "Stanze is your friend. He is constant and true. No matter what, he'll always be those things. The kutu see more than humans do. They see the truth of things as colours, energy and meaning. Stanze will surely have already noticed a change in you. If you talk to him, all you're doing is bringing it out into the open. Whatever happens after that will be the natural course of things, and no matter what that is, you will feel better. Never live a lie. Always be true to yourself and your choices will be the right ones."

"But what if he laughs at me?"

I lightly touched her chin, lifting her face so she looked into my eyes.

"We both know Stanze better than that. He would never laugh at you. And no, before you ask the next question, I can already tell you that you will not hurt or damage him, or your friendship, in any way by speaking with him."

"I feel such a fool. I wish I could have stopped this from happening."

"You're very brave," I corrected. "You could never be a fool."

"Perhaps I will talk to him," Soul considered. "I know it is the right thing, although it fills my stomach with dread."

She slumped back on the sleeping recliner.

"I feel better now, and I'm suddenly very tired," she said, mid yawn.

I leaned back into the pillows. "So am I," I admitted.

"And I don't have a room allocated until tomorrow."

"Then just sleep here tonight."

"Thank you."

There was a moment's silence. I could feel my eyelids wanting to close.

"How old are you, Tachra?"

"Twenty-three summers."

"That's quite old."

"But you're older."

"No. I'm twenty. I just look older."

"I *feel* older," I sighed.

With that, we both went quiet. The comfort of having a

friend to confide in had allowed us both to relax enough to fall asleep.

I dreamt that night. It wasn't the familiar dreams of the temple that haunted my sleep, but something more ambiguous, as if I was not alone. I had dreamt this dream several times over recent days and had just ignored it. It didn't scare me or draw my attention, it was just there. But this night there was one thing different that bothered me: whatever it was seemed to be observing me. The presence was consciously aware of me.

I forced myself awake, glancing automatically to the area of my room where I sensed the presence, but there was nothing. My room looked just the same as always, with shadows upon shadows and an eerily suggestive gloominess that was no more than the normal layout of a room lit by moonlight. Soul slept peacefully on the far side of my sleep recliner. Meah was not in her usual spot, but the outer door was open, as it always was. I sensed she was safely in the forest, contentedly sleeping beside a male wildcat.

I opened my senses to my true vision. My darkened room immediately became a mass of colour and movement. By the corner of my room, where I felt something was watching me, there was nothing. But with the true vision I knew there should be *something*. Everything contained energy. All matter, all empty spaces, even air contained energy. I knew that the absence of anything in that corner was, in actual fact, a confirmation that something was indeed present. And, although there was no distinct spectral figure to focus on, the absence of energy was clearly the size of a tall kutu.

At first, I thought that perhaps I was, or rather wasn't, seeing Jychanumun. The proportions of the body were about the same. But as soon as I thought of it, I knew I couldn't be right. I could sense Jychanumun was still out flying.

With my eyes still open, aligning my eyesight with the vision of my true sight, I looked around my room, searching for any reason for the presence. I expected something, although I didn't know what, but I sensed only agitation, not a reason. The agitation wasn't nice. It made my heart quicken with fear. Was something annoyed with me?

My first instincts were to hide under the covers on my bed or awaken Soul. But I forcefully quelled my fearfulness, knowing that such actions would solve nothing.

"What do you want?" I anxiously chanced a whisper towards the corner of the room.

And then it was gone.

There hadn't been any resonance, or any movement, the presence had simply vanished.

I really didn't like that. Whatever this was had obviously heard me. And it obviously didn't want to make itself known. That made it seem even more ominous. But at least it's gone now, I told myself.

My heart beat as fast as a rodent trying to escape a hunting bird. I slowly counted to ten, relaxing my breathing and stilling my racing pulse with each count. Making myself focus, I forced my mind to scan through the knowledge I had, searching for answers.

This had not been the sensing of energy from past or future. I knew that because the shape had certainly heard my words here and now. It was not the projection of a kutu wishing to talk to me either, because it had vanished once I acknowledged it. My true vision revealed less about who or what it was than usual, so it obviously did not wish to be seen by me. Could I be sensing the dreaming of another? That had happened before, but the images had always left my mind once I awoke. No, those felt like a dream. This had certainly felt real, and whoever it was, they were trying to conceal themselves. I had felt their agitation within me. That had scared me. It made no sense.

Devoid of any answers, there was one place, one being, where I could go to ask questions – to the Old One. I knew he was sleeping deeply, but he had said that he could always hear me. I made the decision to try to reach him in his dreaming.

I shut my eyes, focussing on the place of stillness, and accessed the part of my mind that was always linked to the Old One. The link was almost immediate, like a warm balm, soothing my senses. But then all I knew was the vibration of everything rushing through me, like pain without sensing or noise without hearing. It felt as though I was spinning without direction, until I almost forgot all sense of who I was.

And then I was with him. The Old One was indeed sleeping deeply, his dreams touching everywhere and all times, with a consciousness that threaded through the matter and meaning of everything. I immediately felt his awareness of me. It flooded my entire being with such wholeness that the nothing became everything. A sound spun through my thoughts like a myriad of choruses and vibrations. The sounds merged until they became one, like a beam of light in a dark place, and I understood his voice.

You come to join me now, little one? Join me in eternal slumber. Eternal dreaming for us both?

His voice echoed through my head, consuming every part of me. For a moment I almost forgot why I had come to him, but the vague awareness of my body beyond my consciousness stirred my memory enough to speak.

No. It is not my time to join you, yet, I finally replied.

I sensed no reaction from him. Time meant nothing to him.

I sensed something in my room, watching me. Was it linked to you? I continued.

You know it was not, the Old One sleepily replied.

But I sensed something that I could not fully see.

I felt a slight ripple. He thought my presence unnecessary.

Pointless words, was all he said.

I was hoping you would help me understand. I spoke cautiously.

I felt his dissatisfaction. I thought he was retracting from me. Then the wave passed through me again and I knew that I did not need to ask him such things, but he spoke to me nonetheless.

Why stir my slumbers with questions whose answers you already know? Understand yourself little one. Have you not grown beyond such questions?

I probably had. I should know how to figure things out by now. I knew that if I wasn't finding an answer then it was simply because I'd not found the right method within myself yet. But perhaps I just wanted to ask his opinion. Perhaps I found his presence comforting.

Probably. But perhaps I like speaking to you, I said boldly. I did like speaking to him. He might think it unnecessary, but he knew me, he would already know my every intention and would know that it was part of who I was. *Anyway,* I added, *if we're to spend eternal dreaming together, it might be good for you to get used to it.*

The nothingness around me began to vibrate and a sound pounded through my head, like a thousand horses stampeding around me. I thought my ears were about to explode. He was laughing! It was a beautiful yet almost deafening noise, with wildly oscillating vibrations that made me lose focus.

His laughter finally subsided enough so I could hear myself think.

I accept that you do not give me answers and that I must discover them for myself, I eventually sighed. And although my questions had gone unanswered, it had gladdened my heart to feel his rare laughter.

I felt the Old One's consciousness slowly fade and grow deeper as he relaxed back into dreaming. I stayed a while in his dreaming, just allowing myself the feeling of understanding everything and nothing, a moment of purity. But as much as I found peace at being with him, it was not my time to leave my flesh permanently. Not yet. One day this would be my eternal home, but I, Tachra, still had a mortal life to live. So, regardless of my comfort in his presence, I retreated from his slumbers, knowing that he had not minded my intrusion.

I returned from the Old One's dreaming and centred my consciousness back into my body, on my bed, in my room. I tried again to find a reason for the presence in my room, but true understanding continued to elude me. I searched fruitlessly for any residue of the presence, using every aspect of vision, sight and knowledge that I had, until I was spent with weariness. Finally, with nothing present to try to investigate, I gave up looking. It was pointless. I shut my eyes again, willing myself to find the rest that my body sorely needed.

I must have found sleep because the next thing I knew I was being shaken awake by Soul.

"Tachra, wake up, wake up!"

I sat bolt upright, looking all around me, ready to spring up and face any sign of trouble.

"What's the matter?" I asked quickly.

"You were shouting in your sleep," Soul replied. "Were you having nightmares?"

"Not that I recall."

Something wasn't right. My gown was stuck to my skin with sweat and I was shivering with cold, even though the night was warm. I should have known if I had been shouting in my sleep, but I remembered nothing.

"What was I saying?" I asked.

"I've no idea," Soul shrugged. "It wasn't human words. At first, I thought it was kutu, but it wasn't like any kutu I've heard before. It was deeper, stranger, and somehow angrier. It scared me."

Suddenly I felt sick. Soul's description was almost the same as one I'd used five years ago to describe a language: the language of the Nigh-kutu.

"Did it sound like kutu, only shorter words, more throaty, less fluid?" I slowly asked.

"It did," Soul nodded. "Is everything alright?"

"I don't know," I replied absently.

I was using my senses to locate Jychanumun, but he was still out flying. I would have to talk to him when he returned in the morning. Then another option occurred to me: the crystal in my room might have stored any movement or noise made during the night. Chia would be able to extract recordings of my shouting. If he could do so, then perhaps Jychanumun could tell me if the language was as I feared: Nigh-kutu.

The thought of anything Nigh-kutu scared me, let alone that I was speaking the language. I didn't know how to speak Nigh-kutu. I'd only heard it once. I'd never studied it. And, although I could sense nothing wrong anywhere, my stomach churned with so much anxiety that it almost froze my mind.

"Try to get back to sleep," Soul coaxed, brushing my damp hair from my face and encouraging me to lie down again. "It was just a bad dream. Stanze told me you were overtired. I've been getting enough rest to last a lifetime recently, so I'm going to sit here and watch over you while you sleep. You'll be alright. I won't let you have any more nightmares."

I went to protest, but Soul just held up her hand.

"No, I've decided. I shall sit and watch over you until morning. Meah knows your every move, Jychanumun senses you and I am here. Between us, we'll look after you."

Soul encouraged me to lie back down. It was true: I was exhausted. I was so tired that even my wakeful state felt like dreaming too. I did not need looking after, but just to feel her genuine intent warmed my heart.

"You are a good friend, Soul. And you know I will always watch over you when you need it," I told her. "Sorry I woke you. Let's both try and find sleep."

"Shh," Soul instructed. She stroked my forehead, easing my frown. "Sleep."

I could sense Soul's calming essence directed towards me, and I did not fight the need to relax. Soul continued talking, speaking gently of beautiful places and pleasant things. Her words were like a balm, soothing my spirit. I didn't think I would fall asleep, but it didn't take long until I slipped into a quiet slumber.

I awoke early, feeling heavy-headed and knowing I could sleep for hours more. But Soul's movements around my room seemed to be amplified in my ears. I felt horrid. It was far too early to wake and my body ached nearly as much as my mind. But I was sure I could hear Soul whispering, so I sat up to see who she was talking to.

Soul must have sensed my movement. She spun around to face me, her arms laden with objects and with a mildly guilty look on her face.

"Are you playing with the materializer?" I asked, rubbing my eyes, trying to focus.

"It's so exciting. It made all these," she beamed. "I just tell it to make something, and it does!"

Soul had already changed into clean robes, new colourful silks from the kutu machine that gave her tanned skin a golden glow. They suited her. She put down the items she was carrying and strode forward, holding something out towards me. A familiar smell wafted through the air.

"Is the coffee drink from that thing?" I asked.

Soul nodded.

I took the goblet and put it on the table, not wanting to offend Soul by telling her that the kutu coffee was so bitter and strong that it made my teeth feel as if they were melting.

"I didn't realise you were such a morning person," I commented sleepily. Soul had helped me to sleep and now I just wished to remain sleeping all day.

"I'm not, really. But I thought you had a meeting early today; one to welcome the new admissions, including Shursa."

That woke me up.

I took a long draught of the bitter kutu coffee.

Are you well, I suddenly heard in my head.

I quickly turned around. Jychanumun sat behind me, on a chair, leaning forward with his elbows on his knees, watching me intently.

"Jychanumun," I smiled, feeling immediately calm in his presence. "How long have you been there?"

I sensed your anxiety during the night. I came. I did not wish to wake you.

"Thank you." That also explained why I had slept so soundly through the early hours. "Although, if you don't mind, could we speak aloud? I need some clarity, especially today, especially this morning."

"I did sense something," Jychanumun replied.

"Something is not right," I said bluntly. "Something that I've no name for. I must speak with Chia this morning, and I need you to be there."

Jychanumun just nodded. His face was set into an expression of concern.

I pulled my aching flesh from my recliner. Soul had already laid out my official greeting robe for me. The kutu had made the robe: gossamer fine yet opaque white, which danced with hues of every colour when I moved. The colours made me think of the inside of the sea shells that Orion found so beautiful. The long gown was adorned with intricately woven symbols in white against white that glowed with active nanos. The symbols formed my formal kutu name: Iastha Tachra.

In no time I was scrubbed clean, dressed, and suitably preened. The act of dressing up always felt rather strange, but I had accepted and adopted the kutu formalities of respect whenever they were appropriate. I inspected myself in the kutu reflector. My face looked gaunt and pale, my large, green eyes staring back at me, ringed with dark circles, and the old scar on my forehead was as pale as my dress.

Soul left my room to see if she could locate Stanze. While Jychanumun waited with me, I contacted Chia.

Chia picked up my communication straight away and instructed me not to handle the crystal in my room. He said he would be there immediately.

Chia wasn't exaggerating. Within seconds of closing our communication, he was at the door to my room, requesting entry.

"I do not move that quickly," Chia responded to my remark at his swiftness. "I have been walking the temple to trace an anomaly I felt. It seems I was coming this way anyway."

Chia was clad in his usual matt-black body-skin. It covered him entirely, from neck to feet, and shimmered with nanos with his every move. He nodded his acknowledgement to Jychanumun and then removed his black eye-ware, revealing his long violet eyes, and stood studying me intently for a few moments.

"It is not Tachra," Jychanumun objected.

"I have to check," Chia replied without turning.

A moment later, Chia nodded to himself, as if satisfied with something.

"It is not you," Chia concluded matter-of-factly.

"What's not me?" I asked. "Have you felt it too?"

"I have felt nothing," Chia stated. "But I know you have. Your energy flows like the tides of the sea, invisible yet always there. But recently I have felt waves. This morning, in the early hours, there was a tremendous pulse. Yours is the only energy I do not fully comprehend, so I have learnt to detect energy when it moves around you. Sometimes lack of knowledge can be knowledge in itself. It is you who are sensing something, and that is what I must investigate."

"Although I don't know what," I shrugged. "Something happened last night. Is it possible to extract all last night's events in this room from my crystal?"

"Of course," Chia stated, walking to the small table by my window.

The table had the one item on it that never moved in my room, because it was simply too large and too heavy. The huge black and white crystal, a natural formation of Memorite stone from the kutu home-world, had been a gift from Chia, and its beauty and structure had instantly enchanted me. It didn't look like a natural formation. Its shapes within shapes, like a complex puzzle, seemed too perfect to be natural. It could be disassembled, each piece perfectly formed within itself. Memorite was precious to the kutu, because it naturally stored data. Memorite had memory. Eden1 was the only planet known to have any.

With his gloved hands, Chia tenderly touched the Memorite, as if greeting an old friend, and then took a small bead from a concealed pocket in his body-suit. The bead in the palm of his hand unfolded until it became a glimmering sheet of the finest black fabric. Chia removed the top section of the crystal, picked out a perfectly formed sphere, and then pulled the fabric together to make a small bag around it.

"What do you want extracted, and when?" Chia asked me.

"When: between high moon and sunrise. What: I cannot be exact," I replied. "Apparently, I was shouting in my sleep in an unknown language. I need to hear it. And Jychanumun, I want you to hear it too. I'm concerned it was Nigh-kutu, which should be impossible as I don't speak Nigh-kutu."

"The quickest method of retrieving that information would be if I accessed the Memorite, and then repeated back anything I could hear," Chia nodded. "Either that, or I take this away for translation into images and sound. That would take until about midday."

"The sooner the better. Repeating back is fine. It's hopefully nothing, anyway."

But then I looked at Chia and Jychanumun, and I knew that they did not think this was nothing at all.

Chia sat down on the floor. As he crossed his legs the nanos on his body-suit rippled in response. He peeled off his gloves, revealing his long, pale fingers, and carefully unfolded the cloth covering the Memorite sphere. As his hands moved, they left trails of violet in the air that slowly dissipated, as if they were being absorbed into the stone itself. Chia cupped the Memorite between his palms, without the crystal touching his skin. His hands began to glow an even brighter shade of violet, and the lines of matter that constituted his hands blurred until his fingers were nothing more than tendrils of intense violet light. He lifted his hands, and the Memorite sphere now hovered in mid air, held suspended by his own potent energy. Chia bowed his head, and fell silent.

"I have it," he murmured.

I didn't reply. I didn't want to break his concentration.

"Tachra, wake up, wake up," Chia suddenly stated in a voice that sounded uncannily like Soul's. "You were shouting in your sleep. Were you having nightmares?"

A moment later Chia's body stiffened and his eyes opened, staring directly ahead.

Chia suddenly uttered a kutu word for sleep talk, and then he began saying words that I did not understand. The words were deep and flowing, but with hard, guttural sounds giving occasional emphasis. The words grew angrier. They became dark and more heated, until Chia was almost shouting. The words now all sounded sharp and full of hate. No wonder Soul had been scared. It scared me now, and I was fully awake.

The angry words spewed forth from Chia's mouth, his face contorted. Jychanumun had become motionless beside me, frozen as if in a state of disbelief.

"Enough!" Jychanumun suddenly shouted. He now had anger in his voice.

Chia fell silent, opening his eyes and looking at Jychanumun, with the sphere still poised between his palms.

"I know the words," Jychanumun insisted. "Next will come . . ." and then he spoke several more words in the same guttural language.

"Yes," Chia stated, "that is correct. And then it stops when Soul intervenes and wakes Tachra."

Chia stood up, placing the Memorite sphere back in its place within the crystal formation, and then silently put his gloves back on, patiently waiting for Jychanumun to speak.

"What did I say?" I asked Jychanumun, unable to exercise such patience.

"You spoke in an old dialect of Nigh-kutu. It is not commonly used," said Jychanumun. "The words are a mantra, a curse, although the beginning is missing. The complete curse has sections invoking the attention of the Death-Path-Walker."

"But *you* are the only one who can walk the death paths," I insisted. "I do not need to invoke you. I can just call you. You know that."

"I know," Jychanumun stated flatly. "The curse summons my help. It does not wish me harm."

"What is it then? You said it's a curse invoking your help. Is it some sort of death curse?" I asked. I didn't even know such things existed.

Jychanumun nodded.

"I would not do such a thing!" I protested. "And I would not even know how to. How would I even know of this curse?"

"It was not your voice," Chia reassured me. "You spoke the words, yes, but it was not your voice. Perhaps you were sensing someone else who has this knowledge."

I sat down heavily on my recliner.

"But," I thought aloud, "if it's not me, only a few others here know of Jychanumun's hidden skill. None would 'invoke' him. And all of them I would trust with my life."

"As would I," Chia agreed. He paused a moment, considering something. "We are assuming that only a few of us know of Jychanumun's skill, but who knows what information was left behind after the Nigh-kutu tried to enter this world? Any Shaa-kutu could now know of this power. The one initiating this curse could be no more than a student practicing texts he does not fully understand. Or it could imply a deeper danger."

Chia looked at Jychanumun. "Could one of your kind be trying to locate you again?"

"I do not know," Jychanumun replied gravely. "But that does not concern me; they will not stop looking. But there are other implications."

I looked at Jychanumun, aware of a strange mixture of feelings within him. Immediately I sensed him blocking his thoughts from me. But he wasn't quick enough and what I felt made the blood drain from me. Not only was I something he wished to protect, I had now become something potentially dangerous too.

"What are you insinuating?" Chia asked.

Jychanumun fell silent, looking at Chia, clearly unwilling to say more.

I stood up, feeling a sudden determination. "He is insinuating that there's a possibility that at least one of the Nigh-kutu that we sent away after the war, with forgetfulness in their minds, may not actually have forgotten." I spoke decisively. "And perhaps they are trying to tap into my connection with Jychanumun to locate you all."

"None should be able to remember; we saw to that," Chia objected.

"Am I wrong?" I asked Jychanumun directly.

"It is a possibility," Jychanumun confirmed. "There are many possibilities."

It was a dreadful thought.

"You both know that I must do a full analysis and report on this matter," Chia insisted, once more covering his eyes with his protective eye-ware. "It is an anomaly."

Jychanumun agreed.

"But we must do more than just an analysis," I declared. "We must ensure that every morsel of information possible is extracted from that Memorite crystal. We must pay close attention to any data regarding a possible presence in my room, and not just tonight, previous nights too. Jychanumun, you must listen first-hand to every single word of Nigh-kutu that I spoke. There has to be something to indicate what, and from whom, this is coming. If my senses are not giving answers, then we'll use everything else. You know your technologies, please use them."

"It will be done," Chia replied. He had a look of approval on his face.

"Thank you," I nodded, feeling relieved. "We have to go to the welcome for new attendees now, but perhaps we can keep it brief. Then we can discuss this strange occurrence with the rest of the team and all give it our attention. I, we, must discover what it is. It must be stopped."

FOUR

"It is alright, he is coming round." Shursa heard the words, but they sounded distant, dislocated from his jumbled mind.

Not yet. Go away! Shursa tried to shout, mustering all the strength that he could. He had to banish that insidious voice, but the words would not leave his mouth.

"You are alright. Shursa, open your eyes."

It was as if a light suddenly switched on in Shursa's head. Suddenly he realised that the voice was real, heard with his ears, not his mind. This was not the dark, velvety voice that he imagined in his head. This, he now recognised, was the voice of Gabriel.

More than a little relieved, Shursa slowly opened his eyes and tried to focus. Gabriel was holding him in a sitting position, while several faces peered over his shoulder, watching him intensely. The kutu analyst who had been sitting beside Shursa, taking notes, scrutinized him for a moment before returning to his notepad, scribbling furiously.

"It seems you had a slight reaction to retuning," Gabriel stated matter-of-factly. "It happens sometimes."

"Yes, yes, of course," Shursa murmured. "My humble apologies for the inconvenience. I am fine. Sorry, sorry, sorry." He bowed to those around him. He really did feel alright now. He wasn't sure what had just happened to him. Gabriel must be right. He must have had a bad reaction to the retuning. Now he felt fine.

He wiped at a tickle under his nose. On pulling his hand back, Shursa noticed that it was now streaked with blood. A hand appeared over Gabriel's shoulder. It was one of the pilots offering him a small cleansing rod.

Gabriel looked at Shursa carefully. "Are you sure you are alright?" He tipped Shursa's head up a little, observing his eyes.

"I am fine," Shursa said firmly, pulling his head back. "Was I out for long?"

"No, only for a brief moment. But it was the strangest thing. For a moment I thought that your eyes changed colour."

"I am sure that blacking out in a physical state would make any kutu's eyes darken," Shursa shrugged. He opened his eyes wide to Gabriel, "Am I alright now?"

"Yes, fine," Gabriel forced a smile.

I did not tell Shursa that his eyes had momentarily darkened, Gabriel thought to himself. *I just said that they had changed. How did he know?*

Gabriel watched Shursa as he removed the retuner from his forehead and carefully packed it back into his satchel. Suddenly the ship's interior felt claustrophobic. Gabriel sat, focussed on his breathing, thinking fast. *What if I have made a mistake about Shursa? What if everyone, including the Supreme, including me, has been fooled by him? What if I have indirectly accomplished everything he wanted: to be here, on Earth, with easy access to Iastha Tachra?*

Suddenly, Gabriel was full of doubt.

No, he argued with himself. *I have studied this kutu and monitored his progress for five years. He has striven to be a good being. He is a good being. This is just your own insecurities about your own competence surfacing. Broach the issue. Do not let it fester.*

"Shursa," Gabriel spoke aloud. "You will continue to strive to keep balanced, won't you? To be here at the temple is such a wonderful opportunity for any kutu."

Shursa cocked his head to one side and smiled. It seemed to be a genuine smile.

"I will not let you down. I will try hard," Shursa replied. "I will keep all my promises."

Gabriel stood, feeling as though the blood no longer flowed to his legs, but he certainly wasn't able to find fault with Shursa's reply, or find any hidden intention behind it. Shursa had already proved that he had changed for the better. He had passed every subtle test to date. Gabriel would be stupid to set back Shursa's improvement by calling off the temple visit for what appeared to be no more than a bad reaction to flesh retuning. No, Gabriel must not let his own fears taint the occasion. His role now was to be a good influence on Shursa. He had to remain positive.

One of the pilots, a tall, slim kutu under Nirrious' command, announced to all on board that they were approaching the last section of the Earth descent. They had five minutes to complete their retuning before the pod readjusted its energy.

"This will make you feel better," Gabriel decided, refocusing his thoughts and eliminating his doubts. He beckoned to Shursa. "You should move to the front of the pod and watch this. It is nothing spectacular visually, but teamed with the new sensations of the flesh, it is quite a marvel."

As if on cue, the entire front section of the pod became transparent, allowing passengers as well as pilots a full view of their final descent. There was not yet much to see through the portals, only an expanse of white, and Shursa stood, bracing himself for the energy judders that he'd heard all pods were sensitive to when approaching the blue planet.

The ship did not judder as it passed through the clouds, as Shursa had expected, but flowed smoothly, revealing a bird's-eye view of the subtle colours of the planet's surface. In the distance the horizon glowed, as if casting a protective halo over the distant, deep-blue sea. The land's surface rolled past with muted colours of green and gold, and in the distance the surface threw up jagged mounds with white tips that made the land look as if it reached for the stars.

Gabriel was right; the colours and forms of this place were not so much a visual spectacle, but when combined with the sensations that the planet emitted, the experience was astonishing.

The ship made a steep descent. Rolling expanses of green, nestled together like a patchwork of life, drifted past their view. The land became scattered with more patches of gold. And then coming closer, there it was amidst a patch of green: the Temple of Learning.

"It is beautiful," breathed Shursa.

Gabriel sensed his genuine wonder.

"It is," Gabriel agreed. "And I understand that all new attendees have a human-style feasting to look forward to. Apparently it has become quite the ceremony to welcome new kutu to the temple."

"Would you like to attend with me?" Shursa asked in earnest. "I would welcome the company."

"I will happily do so. I look forward to it." Gabriel replied.

The pod lowered and steadied, settling onto the ground. There was a scraping sensation, which sounded as if they had brushed a boulder. The pod readjusted itself.

Shursa stood in the cramped space, ensuring his robe was smooth and that his hair was neatly coiled at his neck as the exit opened. The small space instantly became filled with the smell of air, earth and water, with the delicate essence of grasses and blooms sweetening the sensation. Those closest to the hatch immediately began filtering out of the ship, their eyes too full of curiosity and wonder to speak. Shursa politely let those around him leave first, and then walked out to a bright Earth morning.

The first thing that struck Shursa about this planet was how gentle it felt. Although the sky was blue, the light had warmth to its colour. The clouds rolled together with calm purpose. And the green foliage, of every tone within the spectrum, seemed to invite tranquil wonderment and exploration. Even the ground beneath him seemed to have a pliable nature, the thick luscious grass giving comfort to his step. For a brief moment Shursa felt a strange sensation. It was almost inner peace.

"It is truly amazing how such subtlety can encapsulate beauty," Gabriel spoke aloud. "I see no colours like the scenes from Gemini Rock, and no feats of artistic achievement as on Eden1, but this does have a unique beauty. I could travel here a thousand times, and each time it would surprise me."

Shursa didn't reply. He was too busy focussing on the sight behind him.

The small pod had nestled on the lip of a valley, *the* valley. Behind them, the valley sloped down to a large glistening lake at its centre, *the* lake. Beyond the lake, situated against the edge of a long, narrow forest, was his destination, the Temple of Learning. And, standing in front of the doorway, a huge double entrance framed either side by statues of the Anumi, was a party of several kutu and one human. Shursa instantly recognised the colours of the kutu in that doorway, and that meant that the human could only be Iastha Tachra.

Shursa had practiced a thousand bows and short speeches for when his time finally came to meet this group of teachers.

All those speeches were fluent, short and polite, and rehearsed to perfection. But suddenly he found himself running; running towards the Temple of Learning and that group of teachers as fast as his legs could carry him.

Shursa had run at least half the distance between the pod and the temple before anyone noticed. As he approached the lake at the centre of Elysium, he could hear shouts behind him. At first it was just Gabriel, and then several others from the landing pod joined in, requesting that he stop and wait for them all.

But Shursa didn't want to wait. He wanted to run. He was compelled to run. And as he ran, he was sure that Gabriel was in hot pursuit. But it didn't matter. Shursa could run, and he *would* run, and he would get there first, and right now his legs were moving at a pace faster than he thought possible in the flesh.

Although the group of teachers were in deep discussion among themselves, Iastha Tachra obviously sensed his approach. The pale-skinned young female, clad in a long, flowing silken gown that shimmered with myriad colours, turned her head, her mouth falling open as she saw his approach. The two kutu flanking her stepped in front of her in unison, but she pushed through as if protecting them. But then the one he recognised as Stanze, the great, hulking warrior kutu, drew out the long, golden sonar rod from between his wings, and with two strides stood in front of them all.

It didn't matter. As Shursa approached the temple steps he thrust himself forward, aiming towards the group.

FIVE

It was the day to welcome the new kutu attendees to the temple. Normally, I'd be excited and eager to see who'd be arriving. But this time I was more anxious than excited. I couldn't take my mind from the strange anomalies I'd experienced in my sleep the night before, or the fact that Shursa would be among those arriving.

By the time the new attendees' ship had landed, Orion, Stanze and Kraniel had already been told about my unsettling sleep-talking. The kutu discussed the incident as we waited at the entrance of the temple. I couldn't hear their silent conversation with my ears, because my kutu friends conversed via their HOTS: High Organic Transmission Screeners. They had the tiny devices embedded inside their heads, allowing them to converse by mind whenever they wished. I merely eavesdropped on their silent conversation via my connection with Jychanumun. If I needed to say anything, I could speak via my natural link with him, but I chose to stay quiet. I was relieved that they considered the anomaly with the same gravity that I felt.

We waited at the temple entrance as the new attendees disembarked from their unusually small pod on the far side of the valley. I watched the last of the kutu leave the pod and the pods exit close. I couldn't see Shursa. In fact, there wasn't a single kutu wearing his customary bright-yellow attire, or a single kutu with over-adorned, over-glossy, long, yellow hair. None who had exited the little craft looked gregarious enough to be him. I wondered if Shursa had decided not to come here after all.

Chia stretched restlessly. We still had several minutes before the new party collected themselves and traversed the valley, and he clearly wanted to be doing other things. The microscopic little nanos in his body-suit rippled in response to his agitation, catching my eye.

"Chia," I pondered aloud. "Your uniform is only worn by those who must block out excess energy. Does that suit actually help to control the flow of energy?"

"It does," Chia replied. "This one is particularly efficient. It blocks out most of what I call background noise. Before this was designed for me, I was bombarded with unknown influences. It was very difficult to focus. This helps." He laughed to himself. "It helps to keep me sane."

"Would something similar help me?" I asked.

Chia considered this for a moment. "It might. I will have one made so you can try it."

As Chia spoke, I don't know what made me turn my head. Instinct perhaps. Or perhaps I sensed the movement of intent through the valley. I turned. Running towards us at a phenomenal speed was a lone kutu dressed in a plain, grey robe.

Chia and Jychanumun must have sensed my stare. Chia held up his arm in front of me. I thought he was stretching, but he wasn't. His arm pushed me back a little as Jychanumun moved closer to me, also lifting an arm in front of me. As I was pushed back, both Jychanumun and Chia took a step forward.

The kutu was still running. He'd already reached the lake. I didn't recognise his sallow complexion, his grey colours or his drawn-back hair, although his eyes were firmly fixed on me.

Those eyes! I could not forget those! I may not have recognised him at first, but I could not forget those pale yellow eyes.

It was Shursa.

Shursa had a wild look on his face as he headed directly for us, running with speed. I would not have Jychanumun or Chia hurt while protecting me.

I pushed through the two kutu, standing in front of them and summoning the strength of the Old One to aid me in whatever was coming next.

In an instant, Stanze, the kutu of the Anumi warrior clan, took two strides forward, standing in front of all of us. With a speed and agility surprising for one so large, he reached behind him, drawing out the long, golden rod that he wore down the armour on his back and poised it in front of him, clasping it with both hands as it glowed bright gold with his energy.

Shursa was almost upon us.

Stanze crouched and moved to block Shursa's leap.

Shursa leapt forward.

But Shursa didn't aim for us. He landed on the steps of the temple, prostrate, his arms outstretched and his face flat on the stone of the step.

"I beg forgiveness. I beg forgiveness. See me! I am a changed kutu. Forgive me for my past deeds!" Shursa's muffled voice cried out. "I beg forgiveness. I beg forgiveness."

I didn't know quite what to do. None of us did.

I did not sense any malice in Shursa. None at all. All I sensed was an overwhelming burden of shame. He was full of remorse for broken promises and lost honour. He was full of regret. Orion had said that he wanted me to look into Shursa's heart. I thought I would have to do this concealed, from a distance, once Shursa was settled into the temple. But standing here, I could see this was a changed kutu. All he wanted was acceptance and forgiveness. This kutu had no desire to control others any more. All I sensed was one who wanted to be compliant, even obedient. He was like an empty shell, hoping that someone would see fit to give him guidance and help him find purpose again.

Shursa was no longer damaged. He was completely broken.

"I beg forgiveness. I beg forgiveness," Shursa kept repeating.

I walked forward, lowering Stanze's weapon as I passed, and bent towards this ruined kutu.

"It's alright," I said softly. "Everyone can forgive you. You only need to learn to forgive yourself."

Shursa laid there, his face buried in the step and his shoulders shaking as if he were sobbing. His outstretched hand found the hem of my gown and he grasped it, as if I was his lifeline.

I had never seen a being in this state. I had seen physically injured animals and had helped, or tried to help, to heal them. I had seen animals, humans and kutu in states of mental stress, and had learnt that stress was often an indication of the unconsciousness fighting back when something was not right, or a way of heightening the senses to overcome difficulties. I had seen a kutu that had lost so much of his mind through projection disconnection that he couldn't function properly, and wouldn't function properly again until he'd been reunited with his lost part. I had seen and sensed many things, but nothing like this.

I do not know what to do, I silently said to Jychanumun with my mind. *He is truly broken. Speak to Orion through your HOTS, because I have no idea how to deal with this.*

Almost instantly, Orion walked forward. He and Stanze took an elbow each and gently encouraged Shursa to stand.

Shursa stood, albeit hesitantly, and Orion kindly brushed the dirt from his robe while quietly speaking to him.

By now, the remainder of the new attendees were standing at the base of the temple steps, watching, unsure as to what to do or the appropriate protocol to adopt in such an extraordinary situation.

Orion looked up, smiled, and, with all the noble proprieties of a kutu leader, introduced Shursa to the team.

"Team, you all know Shursa. Shursa, you remember Iastha Tachra, Jychanumun, Chia, Kraniel, Stanze and I. We welcome you. Please enter, you will be directed to the welcome feasting."

Gabriel moved forward and adeptly escorted Shursa into the temple before he could say anything, while Orion seamlessly continued with his introductions to the other kutu.

Following Shursa came a more sedate and astute looking kutu named Gattal. It transpired that Chia already knew him. His eyes were the brightest blue I had ever seen, and his skin was bronzed and glowing. A long, crystal tattoo ran down one side of his face; it was a mark that distinguished him as the head of his department on Eden1. The crystal tattoo glowed the same blue as his eyes. I could immediately tell that this kutu was very clever, with a mind that was not used to being wrong about anything. I knew instantly that he and Kraniel would either become the greatest of friends or avoid each other like a bad case of Gummi-leaf.

Over twenty introductions later, I'd already forgotten most of the names and wished I'd been able to concentrate better. Orion watched the last attendee walking down the corridor, escorted to the feasting by a kutu who was soon to graduate, as was customary, and then ushered us all back into the temple and into the closest empty room, shutting the door behind us.

"We have all already been given the outline of the recent

anomalies by Chia," Orion whispered hurriedly. "My instincts smell trouble, especially as the Nigh-kutu have been mentioned as possible originators of the anomaly more than once. By Eskah! I've learnt enough to know that minor incongruities usually precede greater ones. Solving this is our first priority. We all start work on it immediately. But at least one of us must attend the welcome feasting."

Orion looked around at the team expectantly.

Chia was the first to speak. "I cannot, I must extract data from the Memorite. That must be done first. Until we have that, we can do nothing."

"Jychanumun must translate it straight away," I added.

"And Stanze, I need you to personally check every room and chamber in the temple and outer grounds for anything suspicious or unusual," Orion instructed.

Orion looked at me.

"You want me to go to the kutu feasting?" I asked, rather surprised.

"Well, do you have anything more urgent?" Orion raised his eyebrows.

I suddenly felt very annoyed.

"Yes, I have something more urgent! I must examine the data of everything that's happened in my room and been spoken through my lips while I slept, because if anyone will make sense of it, I will. Why can't you go? This is a kutu tradition, and, as you well know, I am not kutu. But my main objection is that I would feel uncomfortable around Shursa at this moment, especially considering his obvious unpredictability. I do not want to go, especially not alone!"

"You are angry," Orion stated, rather taken aback.

I gritted my teeth, stopping the frustration that was churning in my belly. I didn't reply. I knew something I didn't mean might leave my lips.

"So would you be," Jychanumun intervened. "Tachra shapes her choices because she loves you all, but she is not a kutu tool. You request her to do many things, daily."

Jychanumun's cool interception quelled my annoyance.

"Alright, I'll go," I sighed in defeat. I always did give in, in the end. Wearing the clothes they deemed appropriate, teaching the classes they wished me to, staying here, eating their vitamin-enhanced diet to keep me healthy so that I did not miss classes – I always ended up doing my duty. Yes, I chose to, but many decisions were borderline ones, swayed by my love for my kutu friends.

"I will go too," Kraniel volunteered. He looked at me and shrugged. "Well, if you give Tachra the job of kutu babysitter, when her skills are clearly needed elsewhere, you may as well send the genius too. We must both have nothing better to do."

His irony made me smile. "Thank you, Kraniel," I nodded my appreciation.

With no time to waste, the team departed. Kraniel and I headed to the feasting while the remainder of the team left to attend to their tasks. The feasting was being held in the central chamber, as usual, and I could hear the kutu chatter over enchanting music as I approached.

In the centre of the chamber, around sixty kutu now sat around a large table, shaped like the outer ring of a circle. The table was filled with an abundance of food and drinks arranged on huge, golden platters. Every taste had been accounted for, from kutu-made delicacies to valley-grown earth fruits, and from simple apple wines to colourful kutu drinks that gave off smoky hazes. The water-well in the centre was now surrounded by small fires, all raised up on podiums. Between the flames, suspended in the air, music crystals hovered, projecting a colourful array of images that moved with the music, in time with the gently flickering flames, and enhanced by the earth water far below them. The effect was simple yet breathtaking, and created an atmosphere that would relax even the tensest of beings. It was the perfect way to mark the arrival of the temple's new attendees.

I smiled to myself as I entered the feasting. Orion was probably right to ask me to attend. To see and experience this relaxed unity was exactly what I needed to ease my own spirits.

It transpired that Kraniel was the perfect host at the feasting. For a kutu who enjoyed his isolated pursuits in his laboratory above anything else, he certainly knew how to captivate the others with his stories. This took a great deal of strain from me. My mind was not on socializing. I wanted to review the data as Chia extracted it. Nevertheless, I made sure that I smiled, greeted and talked to every kutu at that feasting as if I had all the time in the world.

Shursa sat with Gabriel and was not the over-enthusiastic kutu he had been earlier. Now he was very reserved. He would talk, yes, but it always felt as though his replies were what he knew was appropriate to say, rather than what he wanted to say. I considered that perhaps I was being more critical of him than I would be with any other kutu. I disciplined myself with the reminder that I must treat Shursa just like every other.

Although I did not stay at the kutu feasting for long, by the time I left I was exhausted. I sensed Soul's location, intending to see her, but picked up that she was talking to Stanze. I decided I would speak with her later.

Jychanumun informed me that it would still be some time before any data was ready to view, but I headed for the lecture room at the very back of the temple anyway. It was the room that was seldom used and I guessed that he and Chia would be working there. I liked that lecture room. It always felt calm, and was usually Chia's favourite place to study.

I knew I'd picked the correct room, as Kraniel caught up with me just as I reached it. It transpired that he too had endured enough social merriment.

"I'm glad you are both here," Chia bowed as Kraniel and I entered the room. "Tachra, I would like your consent to extract the data from the Memorite extending further back than last night, but I do not wish to view your personal data. Knowing there is no way to separate the two is causing me concern."

"Thank you for being so considerate," I smiled. How grateful I was that a kutu thought to ask me such a thing. "Please view it all. I've nothing to hide."

"Very good," Chia replied. He pointed to an anatomy mannequin in one corner. "I also took the liberty of having this constructed while the imaging reproducer was busy processing."

The mannequin looked approximately the same size as me, and it was wearing a matt-black body-suit, very similar to Chia's.

"It's accurate to your size. The fabric will sense your skin and conform to it. Do you require gloves?"

"I don't think so," I replied, walking over to the protective suit. "You do much of your sensing through your hands, but I do not think it is the same with me."

"Where would you like reinforcement?"

"Do you mean, to prevent my feeling the energy of others?"

"Yes," Chia nodded.

"I'm not sure." I moved the mannequin around, looking at the body. I had not considered that certain parts of my body might be more vulnerable to sensing than others, but now Chia mentioned it, I knew he was right. I pointed to the top of the neck and down the spine.

"Down here," I requested, "and also on the front, between the ribs. The head is affected too, probably the worst of all, but I do not wish to wear a head covering."

"Hmm," Chia considered this. "I will research an alternative. Meanwhile, I would suggest practicing your own skills. I know about your ability to mind-connect to others, so would imagine you could do the same with kutu. Take the concept of that process and practice reversing it." He paused and glanced at me. "None of this may work for you, Tachra. You know that this suit is based on kutu energy and yours is very different."

"I know," I agreed, "but it's still worth a try. I'll practice the mind-barring as you suggest, and I'm hoping the suit will stop the background noise from the kutu around here. The energy of the Old One is peaceful and complete. I wouldn't want that blocked."

As we spoke, Orion entered the room, clasping a small, silver case. He placed the case down in front of Jychanumun, and then, without talking, strode around the room, locking all the doors except one, which he left wide open. He then delved in his gown pocket, pulling out what looked like four small, metal rods.

"Kraniel?" Orion indicated towards the doorway.

Without saying a word, Kraniel took the metal rods from Orion. He observed the doorway for a moment, and then placed the rods onto the wall, one at a time, a hand's-width away from each corner of the opening.

Once all four pieces of metal were in position around the door, Kraniel knelt and placed his palm against the left-hand, bottom rod. He then pulled his arm back, thrusting it forward as if he were about to jam the metal into the stone wall with his bare hand. I winced, imagining the pain such an impact could make, but Kraniel's hand stopped short and a bolt of bright green energy shot forward, embedding the little shaft deep into the wall.

Once all four rods were securely embedded around the door, Kraniel walked over to the back of the room, behind the podium, where the walls were clad in an opaque white substance. The white wall was a kutu imager, and the kutu had devices to make the entire wall fill with three-dimensional pictures. Kraniel didn't activate the imager. Instead, he ran his hands down two parallel areas of the wall.

Immediately, the white wall began folding down on itself, as if the flat smoothness were made of a thousand panels. As the panels moved in sequence, the wall behind revealed compartments, and each compartment housed a kutu device: thousands of devices, in every shape, size and colour possible. There were so many that they filled the entire expanse of the wall. I was amazed. I had never known they were there.

Kraniel selected a small, flat cube from the wall and started moving his fingers over each surface, as if tapping a sequence. He walked to Orion and tapped some more, then to Chia, and then Jychanumun, each time doing the same tapping motion.

"Stanze too," Kraniel murmured, and then tapped a bit more. He looked at me and raised an eyebrow, but he did not tap anything onto that little cube.

Kraniel placed the small cube on the floor, in the centre of the doorway. Instantly, a bright flash illuminated the opening and then began shimmering like a wall of pale silver-blue. Where there had simply been an opening, there was now an energy barrier sealing the open doorway. The energy barrier was strong. I could feel the power emitting from it, even though I stood in the centre of the room.

"Would you all try it, please?" Kraniel requested, he then looked at me. "But not you Tachra, not yet."

One by one Orion, Chia, Jychanumun and then Kraniel himself walked through that doorway and back. The shimmering energy gave way to them as they walked through, as if nothing was there.

Kraniel guided me to stand in front of the barrier.

"We have no way of calibrating kutu technology for your energy. Your link to the Old One renders it too complex," he explained. "So, you must discover a way of passing through this force-field yourself."

I nodded, although I had no idea how it could be done. I had encountered a similar energy barrier before, when I first met the kutu, and that barrier had been like a solid wall to me. But I understood now that such things were only made of energy, so passing through it should be possible.

I held out my hand, touching the transparent wall. The shimmering energy felt unyielding to my touch. I pushed, and it seemed to push back at me. I thought of the desire to be on the other side of that invisible wall and pushed harder, but still it did not give way.

Need, I concentrated. *Your abilities arise only from need.*

I kept my hand pressed against the invisible barrier, closed my eyes and though of the kutu around me. I thought of their need to protect and be protected. I thought of my future need to speak with them in a place that they deemed safe. I needed to be able to help them; that much was real, and that need meant that I must be able to pass through this doorway.

"Tachra," I heard a gasp.

I opened my eyes. My arm was now fully extended through the shimmering barrier.

Holding on to the knowledge of my need for such a thing, I slowly walked through the doorway, paused, and then, still holding tightly onto that notion, quickly walked back again.

Orion was staring at me. "You did it!" He sounded surprised. "Never have I seen such a thing."

"It takes a great deal of focus," I stated, matter-of-factly. "But now I'm aware of the thought process it requires, I can learn to speed it up."

"I knew you could do it," Kraniel said, satisfied. "In one of your own lectures you say, 'Do not let your ideas on limits, limit your ideas.' It has made me realise that with you, discovery is the key."

"There was a need," I explained. "It is my link to the Old One that makes it possible. I couldn't walk through solid walls; my flesh would not permit it. But this force field is energy. The Old One's energy is everywhere; that energy my flesh can traverse at all times. But if something is an intentional barrier, I must draw upon the need to pass through."

Orion nodded, accepting my reasoning, and moved around to the windows, ensuring each was closed and secured.

"From now on, this room is our work room," Orion explained. "I have learnt caution, and so when the temple was built I had this room made into a protected room. These windows are Mazium crystal. The walls, ceiling and floor are lined with both Mazium and then Memorite. Every panel is embedded with sensors. Any conversations in here will stay in here. And, as you see," he indicated towards the panels in the wall, "we have enough equipment for a dozen kutu laboratories."

"What is this?" Jychanumun asked, indicating to the small silver case next to him.

"A great deal of data," Orion replied. "Ancient texts. Everything from theories behind curses to mental transportation. I am hoping to find better understanding and at least a few pointers as to how to proceed, as we have so little to work with."

"Should we also peruse kutu personal data?" I asked. It was a delicate question. The kutu had strict rules about privacy.

"For what purpose?" Orion enquired.

"To discover if any kutu is doing experimental work, particularly with projection or unusual languages," I suggested.

"Although it is a good idea, it is also highly speculative. The quantity of work involved would be immense. It would take months," Orion considered. "There are other options first. But if they do not bear fruit and the anomaly continues, we can consider it."

"Then, could we just check Shursa's background?" I asked. Although I didn't want to treat Shursa differently, surely his records should be examined. He was the one who had contact with the Nigh-kutu the first time around.

"Unnecessary," Orion replied. "His progress has been monitored constantly for the past five years. I have seen his records myself. Although he is over-zealous and insular, and does have the tendency to talk to himself, he shows only commitment to rebalancing and study. Anyway, I understand that the words you spoke were fluent Nigh-kutu. No Shaa-kutu has ever mastered the language."

I had to concede his point. I couldn't see any reason to argue.

"We must concentrate on what we know of the Nigh-kutu," Orion continued. "We know they are our counterparts, living on the other side of existence. We know they exist within shadow, as we do in light. We know they will constantly search for Jychanumun's whereabouts, but we also know that they will never find him. They cannot. He is safe in the light. But how it is that you, Tachra, are sensing anything that is Nigh-kutu is a quandary. We must understand why and how, and it must be stopped."

"Are you confident that the forgetfulness you put in the Nigh-kutu's minds worked?" I asked.

"Yes," Orion confirmed. "It is an effective method of removing memory. The Nigh-kutu could not possibly remember anything about us."

I pondered for a moment. "And you're sure that when you sent them back to their home-world, they reached it? They're not drifting around somewhere closer, this side of the light?"

"Impossible," Orion shook his head. "We used every morsel of a rare essence called Psia. They would have had no choice but to go directly home."

"But something must have changed. There must be a reason why I'm involuntarily speaking Nigh-kutu in the middle of the night." I was frustrated, and I had run out of suggestions.

"That, my dear Tachra, is exactly what we will find out, so we can stop it." Orion looked at me matter-of-factly. "You cannot be the potential point of contact for this terrible race. That would put us all in danger."

"I know," I said quietly. Orion was only saying what everyone else was thinking. If that was the case, and I was to become the one thing that drew the Nigh-kutu back to this place, there was only one solution.

"I would not put any of you in danger. If it transpires that I am the problem, then I will leave this mortal flesh and take my place with the Old One. That would stop any potential contact and keep you all safe."

Orion walked over to me. He took my hand and kissed it tenderly. "You are a brave being for one so young. Tachra, Iastha Tachra, part human, part kutu, part Old One, I value you. Your life brings us joy. I will do everything in my power to stop this. You have my word."

Orion's display of sincerity brought a lump to my throat, and I remembered why I loved the kutu so much.

"Thank you," I whispered.

Orion looked over my shoulder at the mannequin and smiled.

"Good," Orion nodded his approval. "Tachra, wear the body suit. You have to take every precaution to sever the link that is being made. Put up your own barriers, or whatever it is that you do. I will arrange for protective shields within your chambers. Between us, we will find a way to stop this connection."

I was relieved. Orion and his kutu team were taking this matter seriously. Anything to do with the Nigh-kutu should be treated seriously. As much as Jychanumun was originally from the Nigh-kutu, he was different: he was a good being, with a good heart and good intentions. The Nigh-kutu as a whole were not. The thought of them filled me with dread. My Shaa-kutu friends and I had only ever met the Nigh-kutu once, for one brief day, but that once had been terrible enough to make even their name give cause for concern.

It was fortunate that today was the one day in the month that there were no classes. This was the day when temple attendees either settled into their new habitat or readied themselves for their return home. Those leaving would spend most of the day with those newly arrived at the feasting. As a result, we could work uninterrupted. And work we did. By the time darkness began to fall outside, we were all mentally exhausted.

Jychanumun had scrutinized every section of the recording from my room, repeating it back word-for-word. It was a Nigh-kutu curse, yet it also summoned his help. None of it made any sense. He came to the conclusion that the first section was missing. It certainly did sound like I was repeating a conversation that I'd picked up mid-way. It seemed more like the words were intended for Jychanumun, not me, and it seemed that my bond to Jychanumun was creating a barrier for this contact attempt.

Orion had begun the laborious task of examining the kutu data. Kraniel just sat, arms crossed, wearing a frown. Orion offered him work to do several times, but Kraniel just held up his hand. "I am thinking," he would say.

Stanze went out briefly and returned, bringing news of his reconnaissance, although there was nothing abnormal to report. I asked Stanze if he was well, trying to ascertain if Soul had spoken with him without asking the direct question. Stanze gave a rather a shy smile and told me that he was particularly well today. Whatever he and Soul had discussed, I knew it had turned out fine.

Chia had gone further back into the Memorite data, extracting more anomalies from earlier nights in my room. There were noises and clatters, me shouting "go away" several times, but no more of the Nigh-kutu language. All these things could easily be explained away as nothing more than a restless night's sleep, or Meah's comings and goings in my room. Chia had also tried everything he knew to clarify the dark image I had seen in my room, but nothing he did gave a better image than what my own eyes had perceived. We all agreed that something was there. We all agreed that it was kutu-shaped. But that was as much as anyone could see.

By the end of the evening, although we were all exhausted, the mood around us had improved considerably. We had found nothing untoward, nothing to create suspicion, or nothing that would indicate a deeper, sinister plan. And although the entire team remained alert and cautious, I knew they were starting to hope that the anomaly was no more than another of my extraordinary nightmares. Orion even made the passing comment that, with all my unusual capabilities, was it not possible that I could just 'pick up' the Nigh-kutu language?

Gradually, the lightened atmosphere rubbed off on me. Stanze brought in food and drink, suggesting that we all needed to maintain our strength, and everyone did pause for refreshments. I put on the new body-suit, and although it felt strange, I did manage to laugh at the joking remark Kraniel made about my new attire. Only Jychanumun's frown did not ease as he played and replayed the fragmented Nigh-kutu words. I could sense that something was on his mind, like an itch that he couldn't scratch, but even he did not know what it was.

Chia had just finished accessing yet another section of Memorite when a slender, fair-haired kutu requested entry to the room to speak to him. I recognized the visitor as one of the pilots who had arrived earlier that day. I struggled to recall his name – Adriel I thought. He was one of the new pilots, training to fly the new design of pod, and a past comrade of Chia.

The team paused in their work while Chia went to the doorway, deactivating the barrier to speak to the kutu. Our room had been tagged as 'no interruptions unless vital,' so everyone was curious as to what could be so important.

"Excuse my disturbance," Adriel addressed Chia with a deep bow. "I was not sure if this matter was important enough to warrant your interruption. My superior assures me that it is."

Chia lifted his eye-ware, rubbing his eyes. I could see that he was tired.

"That is fine, Adriel, please speak," Chia bowed back.

"Cain reports that the pod has taken some minor damage in landing. It appears superficial and nothing more than indents from the uneven landing site, and he says it should operate fine when returning to Eden1 tomorrow. Nevertheless, he would like to exercise prudence. As you are the senior sensitive, and a pilot well-versed with the specifications of all ships, he asks if you could double check the mechanics and chi levels of the craft before departure tomorrow."

"Where is Cain now?" Chia enquired.

"Examining the pod," Adriel replied.

Chia turned to the rest of us, "I am about finished here for the day, anyway. I'll continue with this tomorrow, and attend to the pod now. I know these crafts like the back of my hand so it should not take long."

I smiled at Chia. I knew his passion was flying, and he had a unique bond with many kutu biomechanical crafts. He always enjoyed spending time working with them, even if it was nothing more than repairs.

"I thought you were supposed to be at the feasting?" Chia asked Adriel.

"Yes, I should be," Adriel replied.

"Go on then," Chia nodded, smiling. "Make the most of it. Hard work and lessons begin tomorrow."

As Adriel strode away in the direction of the kutu feasting, Chia turned, shrugged and, with a small laugh, headed out to inspect the new pod.

Orion agreed that enough had been done for one day. We all needed to approach the task with fresh minds. He arranged an early start for us all, meeting well before classes began, and then began packing away the crystal rods, carefully marking which had already been perused. After placing the silver box in a safe-guard, Orion stretched, saying he was going to exercise his skills in social etiquette with the new attendees at the feasting. With the room secured, we all departed, heading in our separate directions.

I wandered back to my room with Jychanumun. In the distance, I could hear drunken laughs and shouts coming from the kutu feasting. It would probably continue until high-moon. Those new attendees, with their heightened physicality, would sleep well this night, but they surely would have aching flesh in the morning.

"I hear the kutu at the feasting," I said to Jychanumun.

I stopped in my tracks, touching his arm and breaking into a wide smile.

"I hear them, Jychanumun. I hear with my ears, yet my head is almost quiet."

I looked down at my body, now clad in its new, matt-black body suit, and rubbed it with my hands, sending the little nanos into a state of frenzied, multi-coloured activity.

"Oh, by the skies! This suit works. I will never take it off!" I exclaimed.

I opened my true vision. The colours of all things instantly sprang into life. The corridor was a haze of energy, with a bold, multi-coloured line running down its centre, showing the paths left by the many who had passed this way. The carvings on the wall became three-dimensional, displaying the meaning of the stories they depicted. And Jychanumun? He became a fusion of black and white, his energy close to his body, moving in perfect swirls, but as clear and defined as he always was. My true vision was not at all affected. This body suit was a miracle.

Can you still hear me? I asked silently, with my mind.

Always, Jychanumun replied. *It would take more than a protective suit to break our link.*

I smiled. *Oh come, let us both traverse the forest again tonight. Let's both go exploring with Meah. And fly. Let's fly all night. I am so happy.*

And I was. Perhaps this suit could really work! Perhaps it could keep me safe!

I laughed with sheer relief. My laughter made the corridor fill with sprinkles of multi-coloured light. Perhaps I had found the answer. Perhaps something as simple as a nano-embedded body suit could stop any involuntary kutu links, Nigh-kutu included. Perhaps it really could be that simple.

SIX

On Immorah . . .

Aeons away, on the far side of infinity, where the shadow was darkest and laughter now rare, Mardoch, senior warrior of Nigh-kutu warrior clan, paced a darkened room in agitation.

"You cannot try again; you are not strong enough!"

On the far side of the room, motionless on the resting bay, lay a Nigh-kutu. His black wings, tinged with darkest cyan, were tendrils of energy hanging limply to the floor, as if frayed by a thousand battles. The remnant of a tattered healing sheet lay across him. It was an antique, something Mardoch had been lucky to find. The healing sheet was almost depleted now, scantly charged with what little energy Mardoch dared take from supplies.

"I am strong enough!" the bed-ridden Nigh-kutu replied with surprising vehemence. "Do not let my crippled appearance deceive you."

He closed his eyes, as if the energy to speak so strongly was a thing he could only sustain for a moment.

Mardoch walked to the doorway of the room, checking once again that the long, dark corridors were empty, and then strode to the side of the resting bay. The coarse dust on the bare floor crunched under his heavy boots. He knelt down to the injured Nigh-kutu, his black dreadlocks hanging forward, making the little emerald green crystals embedded in his hair chime out.

"Let us swap places so you can heal yourself. It is my turn to try. You can teach me what to do," he implored the injured kutu.

"No, we agreed: one to burn, one to turn. You must keep your strength to stay safe, to see this through. The future of our clan, even all Nigh-kutu, will rest on you."

"But you are too weak to succeed. This requires new strength. Cranun, my brother, you must let me try."

Cranun the brave, one of the last of the clan, a senior warrior now spent with weariness, mustered a smile.

"I will not fail. The strength at the end is the strongest, my brother."

"No! This will not be your end. I will not lose you too!" Mardoch protested under his breath.

"Mardoch," Cranun sighed. "We are too few. We have lost too many. You know what I must do. Using my life energy is the only way. I must do everything I can to warn and protect our brother. Rejoice that *he* lives. Rejoice that we now have hope."

The injured Nigh-kutu strained to lift his hand. He brushed the hair from his brother's concerned face, holding onto one tendril that glimmered with several of the small, green crystals.

"These," Cranun closed his eyes, "each one of these crystals is all that is left of the spirit of one of our old clan. You are their keeper. You keep them safe now. You will know how to save my spirit. If it comes to that, to my end, keep my spirit with you too. Hide my consciousness deep in another crystal. Then you must find Jychanumun. Save my spirit, save them all."

Mardoch wanted to fight against the old kutu's words. Cranun was precious to him. He was the head of the Walker clan, his true original clan. Now they were the last of the Walker clan. Their kind, those who could move between realms, had been slaughtered and hunted by Arrunn's armies until only the two of them remained. They had survived by deception, keeping their true identities secret, adopting the lives of warriors instead of the Walkers that they truly were.

Seeing his clan-brother prepared to sacrifice himself in such a terrible way for the chance of life for others angered Mardoch. It angered him enough to want to rip out his own heart. But he was a warrior now, warrior as well as the keeper of the Walker clan. He knew what must be done. He must honour Cranun, honour his action as the fearless chief that he was.

Mardoch straightened his shoulders, fighting back his own turbulent emotions.

"Do you still have it?" Mardoch asked.

"Of course," Cranun lifted his chin, pulling down the top of his armour, which covered his throat. Embedded in the base of his throat was a small, glowing, green crystal.

"Very good," Mardoch smiled.

He covered his brother once again, ensuring that Cranun was as comfortable as he could be in such a dire situation, and then moved to the old metal table at the side of the bay. There, he began silently mixing a healing potion. He had not been able to get any of the Psia to add to the potion. That potent, living liquid was too heavily guarded. What he had would have to do.

Mardoch carefully ground the substance, adding oils to make a soothing poultice, hoping it would help ease Cranun's pain.

"I do not know why you bother," a voice suddenly came from the doorway.

Mardoch's mind spun, but he disciplined himself not to move. He must not act suspiciously. He managed to shrug dispassionately, as if he didn't care.

"If he heals, then he is another worthy warrior to add to your army," Mardoch stated flatly. "Surely you wish every strong kutu possible. If he does not heal, so be it."

"He is not worthy," the voice in the doorway said with scorn. "Any warrior who loses a leg during nothing more than arena combat is not worthy. Let him go. He is stripped of his rank. He is no longer High-Warrior: you are. I do not wish you to have further contact with one so weak. Understood?"

Mardoch paused. "Understood," he nodded. He casually put down the healing potion, now properly mixed, within arm's reach of Cranun, and then turned to the voice in the doorway.

"Arrunn," Mardoch bowed.

"Come with me," Arrunn commanded, and then turned and walked away.

Mardoch shot a glance towards Cranun; such a brave kutu. A kutu so skilled as a warrior that he could direct full arena combat precisely enough to make a turn, a dodge, two thrusts, and then another turn, all in such a way as to ensure that his leg would be removed clean at the thigh by one of his opponents. It was purposeful. It had to be done, and done in a way that did not cause questions. Nothing less would give Cranun the solitude he required in his rooms; the solitude needed for him to take more acts, not just as a brave warrior, but as the head of the outlawed Walker clan. Cranun would fight to the end. He just wouldn't fight in the same way.

Cranun, his clan-brother, was not unworthy. Cranun was the most worthy of them all.

Before he followed Arrunn, Mardoch nodded to his brother. A thousand unsaid words were in that nod.

They both knew they would not see each other again.

Once Mardoch had left, Cranun did not reach out for the poultice left for him. There was no need. What he intended to do did not require that leg. It only required his skills and sheer will. There was no point wasting valuable energy and time trying to heal the open wound. And he did not want to dull the pain, because the pain helped him to stay focussed. He had to stay focussed to remember. He would need to summon every memory of his old skills to do what he was about to do. For Cranun had not always been a warrior. Cranun had once been much more.

In times long ago, forgotten by most, when the Nigh-kutu were beings of good intent, honour and beauty, Cranun had lived peacefully on a small planet, Assendia, close to their home-world, with over two hundred other Nigh-kutu. Back then, the Nigh-kutu often lived in groups that had similar skills. Those groups were called clans.

Cranun was from the clan known as the Walkers. They could walk between realms, between shadow and light, between death and life, between dream and consciousness, and between the physical and the unseen. Each skill was different, yet all derived from a similar make-up in their energy. Cranun had the gift of balance, and he taught the Walker clan how to enhance their skills and how to work together. The Walker clan had lived on a breathtaking planet with three moons and energy winds brisk enough to make the wings soar without movement. It had been a beautiful world.

The peaceful existence of the Walker clan had all changed when Arrunn, leader of the Nigh-kutu warrior clan, had decided that their skills could be utilised to his own ends. The Walker clan had not complied. As a result, Arrunn had sent in his warriors to take those he could use. The Walker clan had defended themselves as best they could. They wanted the right to live in peace. But their defence was no match for Arrunn's growing army.

Jychanumun, Death-Path-Walker of the Walker clan, had been captured during the first attack from Arrunn's army. He had been taken to Immorah, the huge planet that was the Nigh-kutu home-world, and kept deep in one of their underground cities. Arrunn wanted to use his skills to manipulate fate, but Cranun knew that Jychanumun would never do such a thing. Cranun had tried bargaining for his brother's release, but in return, only lost more of the clan to murder. Meanwhile, Jychanumun had kept contact with Cranun, passing messages via their mind link as often as he could.

Over time, Jychanumun's messages became increasingly fragmented, rambling about a world beyond worlds, death and the light. One day, his mind had simply fallen silent.

Meanwhile, although Jychanumun had been captured, Cranun and Mardoch had not. They had defended their clan-planet, Assendia, until one by one, the clan had seen its demise and only the two of them were left.

Cranun and Mardoch had managed to find refuge on a distant desert planet. They stayed in hiding, driven near mad by their depleted energy, until the opportunity arose to stow away in a Nigh-kutu reconnaissance ship. They had killed two isolated Nigh-kutu warriors, stealing their identities, and had journeyed to Immorah to join the masses in the great underground cities. They could never say they were from the Walker clan. The Walker clan were considered dead. So, they had started new lives. They were now the lowest rank of Nigh-kutu warriors.

At first, Cranun and Mardoch searched for Jychanumun, but all whispers in the great underground cities implied that he was dead. It explained his silence. It also explained the emptiness that Cranun felt in his heart. Without Jychanumun's unique skills, those of the Walker clan who had died could never return from the spirit world. Mardoch and Cranun felt hopeless. So, with nowhere else to go, and no one to turn to for refuge, they had stayed in Immorah, surrounded by fellow Nigh-kutu, yet more alone than ever.

Time passed. Cranun and Mardoch made covert plans to liberate the Nigh-kutu from Arrunn's hold, only to learn that most Nigh-kutu followed Arrunn by choice.

More time passed and they began looking for a weakness in Arrunn to overthrow his leadership. But Arrunn was strong in mind, energy and body. Without the entirety of their clan, the two remaining Walkers had no chance of success.

And yet more time passed. More Nigh-kutu came to live willingly under Arrunn's command and to train as warriors. Libraries full of memories and gentle arts were destroyed. Arenas designed for joy were converted for battle practice. All robes were replaced with armour. The Nigh-kutu became a race of warriors. This was how their kind now chose to live. Cranun and Mardoch pushed aside their old memories of the Walker clan. They stopped acting as warriors. They *became* warriors too. Only by sharing hushed stories in stolen moments of solitude did they retain any recollection of who they had ever been.

Over the millennia, Cranun rose in rank until he became one of only three High Warriors, the highest rank possible. He even learnt to enjoy his work, leading one third of Arrunn's armies. It was his task to train the soldiers. Training was rigorous: the weak would fall, the strong would grow stronger. And for each fallen comrade he knew to embrace the rage and cut free all else that he felt. It was the warrior code: better to have a thousand who could not lose than a million who might not win.

Most of the outer branches of Nigh-kutu, the original clans, had been extinguished whilst Arrunn's armies grew stronger. At first Arrunn extinguished or converted only certain clans. The Walker clan had been among the first; the Weaver clan and the Seeker clan had soon followed, all dead. Now, to kill any who did not follow Arrunn's way was every warrior's aim, and the precious life energy taken from the dead became the spoils of war. Each lost life was a life that ended too soon, and the time left unspent became a precious jewel, a crystal full of the most potent of energies: time itself.

Life was time.

Killing stole this time.

And Arrunn collected it all.

But then, five years ago, with only a few, scattered outer branches of the Nigh-kutu left to extinguish, Arrunn commanded that his warriors' training should change. He spoke boldly of a world full of priceless bounties, far greater than their current spoils. That world was beyond theirs, far into the light. They were to train to cross into that light.

As High-Warrior, Cranun was privy to more information than most. Arrunn began to speak to his High-Warriors of what he knew, preparing them to train their divisions for what was in store.

It transpired that Arrunn had made an agreement with a kutu. But not a kutu like them, one from another world, from a world made of light: a Shaa-kutu. That bonded agreement had not been fulfilled, and all Nigh-kutu knew that such a bond could never be broken until complete. From the mind of that Shaa-kutu, Arrunn had learnt many things. What he learnt, he spoke of, and what he said fired the hearts of every Nigh-kutu for war, no matter what they were to face.

Arrunn revealed that the fogginess some of them felt in their minds had been created intentionally. An entire division had been forced to forget about a world they had discovered when scouting. That world was full of bounties, guarded by a small creature. That small creature had a name: Iastha Tachra. This being protected creatures much like them, but made of light: the Shaa-kutu. It was the Shaa-kutu who had affected their memories.

Arrunn declared that these Shaa-kutu had life energy in abundance. They had more food, minerals and energies than they could ever use. These light-loving kutu were now the enemy. Their treasures would become Nigh-kutu spoils. Arrunn would give all these spoils to his warriors. All he wanted was a few select Shaa-kutu, the creature Iastha Tachra, and one small, insignificant planet.

For five years, the Nigh-kutu warriors trained. They learnt how to fight in the brightest of lights. They learnt how to fight with their bodies tuned to the flesh. They learnt strategies and manoeuvres that could conquer a world fifty times their size. All the warriors would train, but only one division would be selected to join Arrunn in this new war. Arrunn would select the most proficient division and as this war offered the greatest spoils, they all wanted to be chosen.

Finally, six weeks ago, their last stage of training was to begin. Arrunn had called his three High Warriors in for one more briefing. It was in that briefing that Cranun learnt something. That something had changed his course entirely.

The last section of training, Arrunn revealed, was to involve the procedures to capture and contain one of their own kind: a Nigh-kutu. This one had been lost to them many millennia ago, and now lived with the light-loving Shaa-kutu. Arrunn wanted this one captured. He was to be taken alive. This one was one that Arrunn claimed for himself. His name was Jychanumun.

As soon as Cranun had heard the name, he had nearly faltered. Jychanumun?

Jychanumun!

His clan-brother. He was alive!

Cranun had managed to remain self-contained. He said nothing in that briefing. He listened to Arrunn's words with the same stony silence that he always adopted. He treated with gruffness anyone deemed inferior, offering savage remarks when asked for. And he exuded nothing but the resolute might expected of a High Warrior. From the outside, everything seemed as usual. But what he had heard had changed him. Every old memory of who he used to be had resurfaced, leaping into the front of his mind, making his thoughts race.

Cranun had thought Jychanumun was dead. Now, many millennia since his brother's silence, it transpired that he had not died. Somehow, he had escaped this place. Somehow, Jychanumun had found the world he had seen in his mind.

With the news that Jychanumun was alive, with all his skills in death-walking, and seeing the inevitability of fate, there was now a chance for all the Walker clan again. Cranun and Mardoch, two of the last of the Walker clan, now had the one thing they thought they had lost forever: hope.

Jychanumun was the one kutu who could see fates. The Nigh-kutu world was doomed to die. He alone knew of the things that could change that. Jychanumun could traverse the death paths. He alone could bring back the spirits of their clan, who were stuck between life and death. But all these things would only be possible if Jychanumun remained alive and uncaptured. He had to be warned of Arrunn's plans. He had to be kept safe. Somehow, Cranun and Mardoch had to warn him and help him. And then they had to get the crystals of their dead brothers' spirits into his hands. It seemed an impossible task.

For six weeks now, since that last briefing from Arrunn, Cranun had been trying to send Jychanumun warning. It was not an easy task, sending a message to one now residing in the light. It would be impossible without old Walker skills such as Cranun's. But, as much as his arm was strong, his warrior instincts finely tuned, and his reactions swift, Cranun's skills in the old ways had grown rusty. And, as if this depletion were not hindrance enough, Cranun had discovered that the small creature, Iastha Tachra, was like a barrier to Jychanumun, a barrier that protected him, making Cranun's limited skills barely functional. The only energy potent enough to breach such walls was time. That potent energy, as all kutu knew, was stored and guarded by Arrunn.

There was only one solution. One of the remaining brothers, Cranun or Mardoch, had to sacrifice his own life and use his own time energy to try to contact Jychanumun.

Cranun and Mardoch had argued deep into the night. Each valued the other too much to let them willingly choose death. The argument had not been resolved.

Eventually, the two Nigh-kutu had agreed that a game of chance should resolve the issue. A mere spin of a perfectly balanced kutu blade would decide who would use his own life energy to warn Jychanumun, and who was to traverse through the light and find him, taking the life crystals of their clan with them.

Cranun knew that his brother would spin that blade in his, Cranun's, favour, but he also knew that Mardoch had to survive. Mardoch was the protector, the keeper. Only he had the capacity to protect and many had died shielding that knowledge from Arrunn. So, Cranun had used some of his skills to push that blade a little more, until it pointed at him.

It was decided; Cranun was to sacrifice himself. His own life's time energy would be used to contact Jychanumun. But it had to be done in such a way that suspicion was not aroused. It was also to be done in such a way that his death would be drawn out, to give him the opportunity to make contact. The perfect solution was to sustain an injury during battle training.

So here he was, wounded, defeated and crippled in the arena, yet not defeated in his heart. He was no longer Arrunn's High Warrior; Cranun's place was now to die. But he would die in his own way. He would use his life-time energy to good effect. Arrunn would never have it.

Cranun made his essence relax, quelling his instinctive defence against the pain that was to come. Almost immediately the agony shot though him, saturating his every nerve.

Good, he thought. *Use it. Take all that pain, and focus.*

He had enough life energy for one more attempt to contact Jychanumun. He had to make it count. If cutting off his other leg would have helped, he would have done it. With the shadows of fortune falling over him, he hoped he could hold onto consciousness for long enough to make this a smooth ride.

Cranun conjured an image in his mind, an image of his long-gone brother, Jychanumun. And, knowing that Jychanumun was beyond the light, Cranun gathered the last of his life energy and aimed it beyond the end of their world. The last breath left his body, but his mind was sharp. Cranun closed his eyes, concentrating with all his will, and thrust his life's energy in front of him, through the light.

This is it, Cranun thought, *Goodbye, my brother Mardoch. Goodbye, my sweet glories. Goodbye, my loyal comrades. Goodbye, my life; take me on my final journey. Goodbye . . .*

As he left his body for the final time, a smile touched his lips. *There you are, darkness, my friend.*

SEVEN

The night was brighter than usual, as a near-full moon shone down on the ground below us. Jychanumun and I had been flying all night. It was breathtaking.

I wanted to watch dawn rising from the skies, to feel the freedom of body as well as mind when the darkness of night began to give way to day. The protective body-suit from Chia seemed to be working. My mind felt clear. The clarity of my senses was wondrous.

The wind rushed past my face, chilling my skin, but the warmth of Jychanumun holding me as he flew meant that I didn't feel cold. I could hear the wind against his wings as he slowly drew them to a point and pushed down, letting us both glide up high on the currents of the night.

Suddenly, Jychanumun's arm tensed so fiercely that my ribs felt as if they would break.

Jychanumun let out a muffled cry.

Something was wrong.

What's the matter? I hurriedly asked, connecting to his mind.

But all I could hear in return was a deafeningly high-pitched noise in Jychanumun's head.

Jychanumun let out another cry. It sounded as if he was in pain. His whole body tensed, and he nearly let me go. He struggled to keep control, grasping at my clothing to better his hold of me, but this new body-suit offered nothing extra to grasp. He found my wrist instead, forcing my arm around his waist, as if silently warning me to hold on. He couldn't control his flying. His body twitched in frightening spasms. He started spiralling. I clung to him, as he could no longer hold my weight.

"Land! Descend! Go to the ground!" I shouted at the top of my voice.

But Jychanumun didn't seem to be able to hear me. He now gripped either side of his head, his face contorted into an expression of agony, as I clasped his waist for sheer life. His legs kicked, as if trying to push something away, and his back arched. He was spiralling faster, his body rigidly tensing with violent spasms. I could not hold on for much longer. Something terrible was happening. If I didn't get us to solid ground the result would be calamitous for the both of us.

The pit of my stomach knew alarm. Instinctively, the Voice of the Old One, the Voice of command, rose from my stomach and burst forth from my lips.

" LAND! LAND NOW, LEST YOU DAMAGE US BOTH!"

Still spiralling, and writhing in agony, Jychanumun descended, falling the last short distance and landing on the ground with awkward heaviness.

I fell quite a way away from Jychanumun, landing hard on barren, grass-free land. My leg was damaged, but I felt no pain as I focussed, stumbling towards Jychanumun.

"What is it? Please? What is it?" I asked, as I reached his side.

But still the writing did not stop. Jychanumun was in pain. He hit the side of his head with his hand. He hit it again. He was trying to tell me something.

I quickly sat, putting his head on my lap. I thought of the peace in the forest, the healing of my beautiful lake, the solitude of the flatlands, and the harmony of everything. I put my hands on his head, over his hands.

Feel peace. Put the pain into my palms. Let it go. I will carry it away, I pushed my soothing thoughts out to him.

My hands started to grow cold, ice cold. At the same time, I felt Jychanumun's tenseness recede. Jychanumun opened his eyes. I pulled my hands away, noticing that my palms glowed a deep cyan.

I expected Jychanumun to remain still for a moment, to recover himself. But, as if in slow motion, he stood, his eyes never leaving an area just in front of him.

We had landed in a sparse area, rather like the flatlands, but littered with tufts of rangy grasses. The smell of salt was heavy in the air and the ground beneath me was damp. We were on the edge of a sea. So near that the sand was still damp from the tides.

Suddenly Jychanumun turned to me.

"Tachra, take off the body suit."

I hesitated.

"Now. I have no time to explain."

I could see something was wrong. I pushed aside my modesty and hastily stripped the matt-black suit from my flesh as fast as I could.

As I peeled the last of the suit from my skin, standing naked in the cold air, my mind became full of noise once again. I looked in the direction of Jychanumun's stare and took a step forward to stand behind him. There, a mere arm's length away from him, I could now see the same patch of darkness I had seen in my room.

Jychanumun grabbed my hand. The connection between us immediately magnified. Slowly, the patch of darkness in front of us grew in clarity, and the shape of a kutu started to form where the darkness had once existed. But this apparition looked more like the opposite of a kutu, made of shadow, his edges outlined in light. His lips were moving but he did not make a sound.

"Cranun, brother," I heard Jychanumun whisper.

I slowly slid my consciousness into the back of Jychanumun's mind, taking an invisible, passive role, watching through his eyes. Jychanumun did not block me out.

Jychanumun could see this apparition clearly, as if a kutu stood, in the flesh, right in front of us. Jychanumun knew this one. He was his friend. And more than that, Jychanumun could hear the words this shadow kutu was saying, even though they were but barely a whisper. Although I could hear them through Jychanumun, I did not know their exact meaning. They were speaking Nigh-kutu. I could only feel Jychanumun's reactions.

I stood transfixed, holding my breath. I did not need to understand the words to recognise a kutu with good intent. This one meant neither me nor Jychanumun harm.

The silent conversation did not last long, but a great deal seemed to be said. The shadow kutu finally stopped, paused, and then said something, indicating towards my body, towards my hands. I looked down at my hands, their palms still tinged with cyan energy. The energy was moving. When I looked back up the shadow was fading. The Nigh-kutu seemed to smile. He saluted, putting his fist to his chest.

As soon as the shadow disappeared, Jychanumun turned, lifted my hands and quickly pushed the cyan energy that saturated them into a small, compact ball. He held the ball in the palm of his hand and it seemed to grow smaller, until it was nothing more than a tiny, glowing crystal. The crystal seemed to move around within its form, as if it was alive. Jychanumun took the small object and threw it with such a force that I barely saw it shoot from his hands.

"*Home!*" he shouted, directing his words towards the glowing pebble.

I felt the ground beneath me tremor.

Jychanumun stood for a brief moment, watching the speck of cyan energy rapidly disappear into the distance, and then put his hand to his ear.

"*Team!*" Jychanumun shouted. He was talking through his HOTS. "Orion, Chia, Kraniel, Stanze, *listen!*"

He paused a moment, obviously waiting for them to reply.

"Team, I have no time for details. This is urgent. Secure the temple immediately. Secure all kutu within the temple. None are to leave. We are in danger!"

There was another moment's pause.

"Immediately! I am on my way. And someone have a robe ready for Tachra."

Jychanumun dropped his hand from his ear. His usually expressionless face now showed a mixture of grief and alarm.

"Who, *what* was that shadow you were talking to? Was that the one I've been trying to block out?" I asked.

"Yes. He is ... he was," Jychanumun paused, correcting himself. "He was a good kutu. He was my brother. I will explain, but I must think first. We must return to the temple in haste."

Jychanumun strode towards me, put his arm around my naked waist, raised me from the ground, and, without a further word, began flying at a ferocious speed.

The wind rushed past me as I held onto him. Never had we flown so fast. I sensed the urgency, I felt the adrenaline, but when I tried to link to Jychanumun, the sadness was almost overwhelming. It felt like his heart was breaking.

EIGHT

Mardoch waited patiently in Arrunn's main chamber. Arrunn seemed to be purposely delaying speaking to him. Was he testing his patience? Perhaps. It didn't matter; Mardoch had enough fortitude to wait silently for millennia.

The smooth black walls and floor in Arrunn's chamber were tinged with colour. All around the outside of the room were jewel-flowers, hundreds of them. The tiny crystals at the centre of each flower glowed, lighting up the gloom with unnatural brightness. Mardoch had heard of this place, but it was the first time he had seen it with his own eyes and it had an eerie beauty. Here Arrunn kept his favoured lives. Each small crystal was the remnant of one life's last energy, taken from a victorious slaughter that Arrunn had wreaked. If in death a kutu's remaining lifetime was placed here, then Arrunn considered it worthy.

Ten guards were placed in the chamber and two more outside. The guards stood silently around the room, their backs to the walls, their hands behind their backs, their black attire and wrappings around their faces concealing everything but their cool, watching eyes. Each guard looked exactly the same as the other. They were the same height, the same build, the same clothes, and had the same dark eyes that revealed nothing.

Arrunn stood with his back to the room and his hands behind his back too. He appeared to be staring at a blank wall.

"Do you see this?" Arrunn spoke aloud.

Mardoch was not sure if he was talking to him.

"No, of course you do not," Arrunn continued. "You do not have the expanse of vision like I do."

He turned to look at Mardoch. "Do you?"

"I do not," Mardoch stated. He had to discipline himself not say 'sir.' Arrunn did not like being referred to as 'sir,' 'master,' 'king,' 'lord,' or anything that implied importance. Arrunn believed that leadership was earned by actions, and obedience to that leadership stemmed from actions, not words: words alone were merely a display of weakness.

Arrunn lightly touched the wall in front of him with his hand. Immediately, a section in the wall became a transparent, rippling field.

"Come, see," Arrunn motioned to Mardoch.

Mardoch walked forward. Through the transparent section in the wall, he now saw a part of their underground citadel that was rarely seen. Below them, spanning the distance of a hundred warships, was what used to be the huge arena for the calling, an old Nigh-kutu custom that had long died out. Now it was a city within a city.

Within the city within a city, small creatures moved among randomly scattered, metallic, cubic dwellings. Their misshapen, pink flesh seemed cumbersome and awkward as they moved. But for all their unsightliness, these were clearly not senseless creatures. They seemed to move with purpose. They even seemed to communicate with each other.

Mardoch spotted a group of three of the creatures sitting around a table, their wrinkling flesh bulging over the sides of their small stools. Each had a plate of perfectly prepared food in front of them. They were eating with meticulous care, their stubby little fingers carefully choosing and then picking up a piece of food to smell it, before placing it in the small holes that Mardoch assumed must be their mouths. The process appeared slow, not because they were awkward, but because they seemed to display joy at what they were doing and were savouring the motions.

Mardoch stifled a thousand questions. It was not his place to question.

"My little children," Arrunn said fondly.

He turned to one of the guards, "Bring me one." He paused, looking through the portal again, considering the creatures below him. "That one."

Arrunn had indicated towards an average-sized creature that ambled between the small metal dwellings. The creature was not alone; beside it was another of similar size. They walked closely together, as if partially leaning on each other, rubbing their flesh against each other as they moved. If the creatures had not been so misshapen, their actions could almost be considered endearing.

The guard left without saying a word.

"I have made you High Warrior now," Arrunn stated, without looking at Mardoch, "It is the highest rank. As you know, I have three High Warriors at any one time. I am now trusting you with one third of my army. Those fourteen thousand warriors are now your warriors. They are in your charge. You must train them well. I therefore deem it necessary to convey certain facts to you. Do you deserve all this trust?"

"Of course I do," Mardoch almost spat the words. He must only show strength. He must never show nerves or hesitation.

"Good," Arrunn approved. He indicated towards the city below them. "These are my little children, my creations; three years of genetic manipulation. These children of mine are ugly, are they not?"

"Very."

"Indeed they are," Arrunn nodded. "Do you think that they are mindless?

"I do not."

"Very good," Arrunn stated coolly. "Look at them. See how they have only the very best foods to eat. They grow fat from the joy of eating. Does it bother you that these creatures feast on plentiful foods when you and your armies almost starve?"

"Yes," Mardoch said flatly, "It does."

Arrunn considered Mardoch's response for a moment.

"I like your strength, Mardoch," he decided. "You are worthy of High Warrior."

Mardoch did not reply.

"I did not make these creatures for their beauty," Arrunn said matter-of-factly. "I made them to love life. See how they move quicker when they see another that they wish to communicate with? They have formed family units. They take pleasure in company. They take pleasure in food, rest, play. These things are created to enjoy many things. They enjoy because they love life."

Arrunn moved his hand over the portal, making the transparent section black once again, and then turned around to face Mardoch.

"The more a creature enjoys life, the more it values that life. The more a creature values life, the more it will want to stay alive."

The guard who had left earlier returned, carrying one of the creatures under one arm. It had a hood covering its head. The guard put the creature down: it was smaller than Mardoch had expected, standing no taller than Mardoch's thigh, and the hood almost reached the floor. Underneath the hood, the creature seemed to be shaking.

The guard pulled the hood from the creature. The little thing looked around at them, clearly bewildered and scared. It did not seem to be familiar with kutu, or this place. A stream of urine pooled on the floor around it.

"It is necessary to let it feel fear," Arrunn said coldly. "I do not enjoy it."

Arrunn selected an area in the seemingly smooth wall and pulled out a small panel, turning it around to reveal a complex instrument. He tapped in some codes, showing Mardoch the result.

"Ninety-two point four. That is the life value of this creature just before we brought it up here," Arrunn stated.

He held the instrument towards the small creature. The instrument appeared to be scanning it. Arrunn held the results for Mardoch to see without glancing at them himself. The read-out display had risen to over one hundred and twenty.

"By allowing it to fear for its life, the creature realises that its life is valuable to it, and so its life value increases," Arrunn explained.

He gave the instrument to Mardoch.

"Keep it pointed towards the creature," he instructed.

Arrunn walked closer to the small, shaking thing, careful not to step on the wetness on the floor, and then he crouched down so he could be face-to-face with it.

"You are going to die," Arrunn stated to the creature. "You will never see your family again. Your family will pine for you forever. They will beat themselves because they miss you so much. They will feel pain because you are not there, and that pain will cause them to die, slowly, terribly. You will never see your friends again. They will weep that you are gone. They will never feel joy again.

You will never feel joy again. You will be dead. Gone. Your life will be no more," Arrunn paused for a moment. "Now, how much do you want to live and go back home?"

The small creature began squealing. The pathetic sounds seemed to be pleading. It seemed as though the creature had understood Arrunn's words, and now it begged for its life.

Mardoch struggled to remain impassive. The creature's squeals resonated through his energy. He wanted to take that poor creature and return it to its home. But this was a test, and he knew it. He had to remain staunch. For the sake of Cranun, Jychanumun and all his clan-brothers, he had to win Arrunn's trust.

Arrunn stood, putting his hands on his hips.

"What is the reading?" he asked Mardoch.

Mardoch glanced at the read-out display in his hands. "Two hundred and seventeen," he replied, keeping his voice calm.

"Very good," Arrunn seemed satisfied. He reached down to his boot, pulled out a long, thin blade and swiftly stepped forward. With one precise move, he planted the blade deep into the top of the creature's head.

The creature fell down, dead.

Mardoch did not move. He felt strangely relieved that its suffering had ended.

Arrunn took the instrument from Mardoch, opening a section in the back and removing a small, grey crystal. He slowly pulled his knife out of the creature's head, wiping away the excess blood on its own dead skin, and then placed the crystal on top of its flesh. Slowly the crystal started changing colour. The dull grey took on an orange hue, the colour intensifying until it became bright scarlet.

Arrunn picked up the scarlet crystal, examining it. "There are two hundred and seventeen units of time energy in this. It is a satisfactory amount. Anything over two hundred is acceptable for one of these creatures."

He threw the crystal towards Mardoch. Mardoch caught it with a mere flick of his hand.

"Activate it," Arrunn commanded.

Mardoch looked at the little crystal. He didn't know how to activate such a thing. He thought that Nigh-kutu could only use their own life energy. Nevertheless, he tried crushing the crystal with his hand. Nothing. He tried biting it. Nothing. He examined it, but nothing in the little stone looked accessible by either strength or energy.

"I cannot," Mardoch finally replied, frustrated to admit such a thing. "I do not know how."

Arrunn walked forward and took the little crystal, holding it in his palm. For an instant, his eyes seemed to darken. Suddenly, the little crystal raised from his palm, suspended in the air.

"Of course you cannot," Arrunn smiled, handing the stone back to Mardoch. "Such a skill is mine alone. The crystal is now activated; it can now be used at will by anyone. It is yours," Arrunn said airily, as if such a precious thing meant nothing to him. "I am giving one to each of my three High Warriors. Use it effectively during battle."

Mardoch said nothing, unceremoniously tucking the activated time crystal into one of the pockets in his armour. Thanks were not protocol. Gratitude was weak. But he could not stop his mind racing. He had a time crystal! With it now activated, Cranun's life could be saved.

Arrunn's attentions were already elsewhere. "Why is this still here?" he questioned the guard, indicating toward the small, dead creature on the floor. "Take away this stinking flesh. Serve it as food to them."

Arrunn watched the guard collect the corpse and exit the room. He waited until the echo of the guard's footsteps had faded away and his room was silent once again, and then turned back to Mardoch.

"With the deaths of all my little creations, I will accumulate enough time crystals to create a gateway through the light. I will select which of my High Warriors and his legion to take with me. We will pass through that gateway. We will triumph over the light and all things in it. This will be my best conquest yet, Mardoch, High Warrior. Do you consider your division of warriors the most worthy to join me?"

"Yes. My warriors are the most competent. They would be the obvious choice," Mardoch replied. He made sure it sounded as if he didn't care. Another battle? So what? It was easy for him, easy for his warriors, easier than sleeping or eating. Fighting and winning was who and what they were. He had to sound as if he didn't care, but he did care. He knew too well that he *had* to be chosen for his own plans to succeed. If he or Cranun had been selected for the last war that took place on the other side of the light, their entire clan would be free by now.

"Your warriors are indeed well trained," Arrunn considered, "but what about you, Mardoch? My other two High Warriors are far more experienced in their duties, and their warriors are also well trained. Would *you* be the most competent choice?"

"Of course!" Mardoch replied angrily. "Test my warriors. Test me! You will see."

"Maybe I will," Arrunn considered. "If I do select you, Mardoch, under my command, you will lead one third of my army: over fourteen-thousand Nigh-kutu. From these, you will have selected one hundred Warrior-Firsts. You will follow my command and direct those who answer to you. When we are ready to strike, we will strike with speed. You must learn, before the two-moon eclipse, all that my other High Warriors have spent five years learning, if you wish to compete with them for the honour," Arrunn paused, looking at Mardoch analytically. "Because of this, you are permitted to ask questions."

Mardoch did not need to ask many questions. For five years now they had all trained for a place in this war, and he'd paid close attention to all of the relevant procedures: new weaponry, formations, communications, strategies and objectives. They were all clear in his mind. The only difference was that he had now risen in rank, due to Cranun's injury, but although the chain of command had been altered, the principles remained the same.

Mardoch did not allow his thoughts to linger on Cranun, even though his heart was desperate to be gone from this place and to be at Cranun's side, giving him the precious time crystal that now sat in his pocket. He had to stay focussed.

"I have only one question; when do we leave?" Mardoch simply asked.

"Before the two-moon eclipse. There will be a seven-day advance warning. The specifics have variables."

Variables? That was an uncharacteristic situation. Was Arrunn testing him? Probably. It required questioning.

"Am I to be made aware of the variables?" Mardoch asked.

"Not necessary," Arrunn replied. "The variables merely relate to timing. We will have a guide to our destination, a Shaa-kutu. He journeys here soon. It is his journey time that is out of my hands, at least until he passes over to this side of the light. These Shaa-kutu have not yet fully harnessed the use of time energy. In the long run it is to our advantage."

Mardoch's insides churned. The Shaa-kutu had not even harnessed the use of time energy? How could they protect themselves? And this Shaa-kutu traitor? How could any kutu from the light believe he was coming to a better place? How wrong he was!

"I understand our Shaa-kutu guide may bring specimens of their finest warriors," Arrunn smiled to himself, seeming to take satisfaction from the thought. "I think you will enjoy testing how far their skills go."

Mardoch quelled his anger at such treachery, placing his anger into words that would suit the situation. "Any light-lover would not be a match for even our Nadir Warriors," he sneered.

"Agreed," a smile touched Arrunn's lips as he glanced around his room, admiring the crystal flowers on display. "Although, I will enjoy the show before adding them to my rose garden. They will be the first of many of their kind to add to my collection."

Leaning forward, Arrunn touched a section of Mardoch's hair, sliding a small, green crystal from one of the dreadlocks. He held it in his hand, rolling it around on his palm with his thumb.

"And what is this that you collect, Mardoch High Warrior?"

"Memories," Mardoch replied.

"Of what?"

"Victories that give me pleasure. The final moments of a defeated enemy."

Arrunn's eyes glazed over. Mardoch knew that he was accessing the memories in that little green crystal.

This is it, Mardoch thought. This is the test that he had hoped would never come. He had hidden the last life essence of each clan-brother deep within each crystal. He had then concealed their essence, covering each one with his genuine memories of battles and slaughter. Had his skills as protector been strong enough? Had he concealed the essence of his dead brothers deep enough? Cranun had taught him that the best place to hide something was clearly within sight. So, Mardoch had chosen to wear those crystals in his hair, pretending they were no more than tokens of victories, like tattoos or necklaces made from spoils. Had he been right? Had he remembered his own skills well enough? The test was now.

Mardoch had to make sure his pulse never changed and that his breathing stayed constant. He made himself smile, as if relishing the idea that Arrunn would be watching one of his victories.

The milky haze that covered Arrunn's dark grey eyes cleared.

"So it was you who finished off the leader of the Sanshin Society. Done with elegance too. Such memories are worthy to collect."

With the green crystal still in his hand, Arrunn walked to the wall, plucking out one of the crystal flowers on display around the room. He held the flower up, turning it slowly, admiring its form.

"That is all," Arrunn indicated to Mardoch, while still appreciating the bloom. "You may leave."

Mardoch desperately wanted to request the return of the green crystal. He could not. Nor could he show any hesitation, in case he aroused suspicion. Instead, he made a small bow and strode from the room.

"And Mardoch . . ." Arrunn called out, just before Mardoch passed the threshold of the door. Mardoch turned just as Arrunn threw something. Mardoch caught it. It was his green crystal.

"All memories are sacred," Arrunn said, simply.

Mardoch gave a curt nod and walked away.

As soon as Mardoch left Arrunn's chambers, he wanted to run, but he couldn't. He wanted to sprint and fly as fast as he could to get back to Cranun. He had a time crystal. He could prevent Cranun's death if he could get back soon enough. But Mardoch could not run. He could not attract attention doing anything untoward for a High-Warrior. Such things would have him stopped and questioned.

The dark passageway to Arrunn's various chambers was heavily guarded. Two warriors stood either side of every locked door that Mardoch passed. He kept his eyes straight and his stride constant, ignoring the inferior warriors that he passed, even the ones that he recognised; it was not appropriate to acknowledge them. The air smelt musty, the confined space offering no ventilation, and the only sounds were his heavy boots on the well-worn floor.

Mardoch tried to hurry his pace without it seeming obvious. Now he had only one thing on his mind. He had to get to Cranun and give him the crystal before it was too late.

Once beyond the passages that led from Arrunn's rooms and the restricted storage sectors, the way became quieter. Mardoch quickened his pace as much as he could without drawing attention to himself. He strode through the halls that used to house ancient sculptures: now only empty, square patches of rough stone, not covered by the usual dark grey slabs, now indicated that anything had ever stood there. It was a sad sight, but Mardoch did not dwell on it this time: he was in too much of a hurry. He made his way through three sets of gated zones without faltering, into the upwards shaft, the empty space that once housed the magnificent golden travel portals. Wings out, push upwards, up one floor, and he was stepping onto the stone floor without slowing his pace. He was nearly there.

The last passageway to both his and Cranun's rooms was long, showing a line of open doors. The doors all belonged to the rooms of warriors currently out practicing their weapon skills. Mardoch sensed the emptiness of all the rooms and began running. He ran past his own room, pulling out the life-energy crystal as he approached Cranun's quarters. He half sprinted, half flew the last section, desperate to get to his destination.

Hold tight, my brother, Mardoch thoughts raced as he approached the final door. *Do not leave yet. I have something that will save you.*

He rushed past the threshold, bursting into Cranun's room.

No . . .

No.

No!

Mardoch was too late.

Lying on the resting bay was his clan-brother, or the form that used to be him. His colours were gone, his wings were gone, and every morsel of energy was now drained from his body. Cranun's form was now as dull as the spent healing sheet draped across his lower half. The two were now fused together into pure matter, compounded into a stone as hard as Jinan diamonds, yet matt grey. This was no longer Cranun, this was now a lifeless statue of the great being that once felt, thought and acted so honourably. He was energy-less, lifeless, without spirit, will or thought. He was now pure matter.

The poultice still sat on the table, unused. Cranun's face expressed peace, and a smile even touched his lips, but Mardoch knew that the end that he had sacrificed himself for would mean the pain of eternity. Cranun was dead, suspended in that in-between place, feeling neither the peace of eternal rest, nor the purpose of life.

Mardoch glanced at the crystal in his hands. He felt as if his rage at this injustice would burst from his chest.

Take the rage, channel it, let go of everything else, he quickly disciplined himself.

Taking a deep breath, Mardoch walked towards his motionless brother. After taking a moment to bow his head to his last remains, he leaned down, feeling along the ridge of the grey stone that used to be Cranun's chest armour.

There, he had it.

Mardoch snapped off the top protruding section of stone, at the base of Cranun's throat. There, embedded in the stone that use to be Cranun's flesh, a small green crystal with a dot of cyan at its core, shone brighter than the South Star.

Whispering a final prayer of praise to one so brave, Mardoch ceremoniously threaded the crystal into his hair.

Cranun, my brother, you are with friends once again, Mardoch thought. *I will keep you safe. I will keep you all safe until you can come back. I will be chosen to travel through the light. I will not let you down.*

NINE

Jychanumun landed in front of the temple. He hadn't said a word during our swift journey. I sensed sorrow from him, but his need for urgency made him push his own emotions from his mind.

All the windows and doors to the temple were closed, including the access to my own room. Tarrian and Brave, two of the Anumi warriors, stood either side of the sealed main gates, their eyes watchful and their weapons at the ready. Stanze stood between them, clearly waiting for us.

Stanze indicated to a folded robe on the ground, his eyes never ceasing to scan the surroundings. The gates opened enough for us to enter. I grabbed the robe, wrapping it around me as we walked. I had to run to keep up with Stanze and Jychanumun's pace as they strode the long corridor towards the meeting room at the end.

"All Anumi must be at the ready," Jychanumun spoke gravely. "Both here and on Eden1. I hope we are not too late."

"The temple is sealed," Stanze replied. "All kutu here on Earth have been summoned to return. I have put Anumi everywhere on high-alert. We await your briefing before taking further action."

Suddenly, from the far end of the corridor, Kraniel shot from the meeting room and began running towards us. He wasn't looking at us. He clasped a read-out panel in front of him, intensely watching the screen with a look of concern on his face.

"Chia . . ." Kraniel gasped, as he passed us, moving down the corridor with speed. "Outside . . ."

"Stay here," Stanze directed, and then turned and ran to catch up with Kraniel.

Jychanumun's eyes glazed over.

"I cannot connect to Chia via our HOTS," he said. "He is injured."

Chia injured? Without a second thought I dropped down to the ground, lying on my side with my head flat on the cold stone. I would go to Chia. Perhaps I could sense him.

I could feel the stone under my skin. Its coolness was peaceful and protective. I understood it. I pushed out my senses, threading through the building and out to the land beyond, as fast as I could. As soon as I knew that my consciousness was beyond the walls of the temple, I let my senses plummet deep into the welcoming earth, where clarity and strength were pure, and then threaded my awareness out to sense anything that felt like Chia.

There, I had him. He was not far away.

I forced my energy forward and up with speed, rising from the ground to encompass Chia's body. I let my energy seep into him, saturating his cool flesh. Something was definitely wrong. He was barely alive.

I gathered strength from the land around Chia's body, pushing it into him, trying to heal him. I felt Chia become aware of me. He began thrashing. The thrashing gave him great pain.

You must keep still. Help is coming, I tried to tell him with my mind.

Tachra?

His thoughts were not clear, but they were clear enough: he could sense me. He stopped moving. Then everything went black. Chia's mind was dark. He was unconscious.

"Get every tool you have for healing kutu." I spoke urgently to Jychanumun as I remained lying on the stone floor. "And a retuner. Chia is hurt, badly. He must be retuned away from the flesh and healed, quickly. I must stay here and keep my connection to him. I must keep him alive."

I didn't notice Jychanumun move silently away. I knew he would do what needed to be done. I had to stay focussed. Chia needed me. I had to feed him strength. His body willed him to walk the death path, because it was so damaged. I would breathe for him. I could keep him alive until he had retuned.

Chia's flesh became my flesh. I made his chest rise and fall in slow, deep breaths. I felt the blood in his body and pushed it, urging his heart not to stop, but I had to keep it slow; it seemed he had lost so much of the vital fluid.

I felt Chia being moved, slowly, but he was not doing it himself. Kraniel and Stanze must have found him.

I felt a searing pain as something was removed from my side, Chia's side. I gasped with agony as I took his pain. And then another in my chest. That was even worse. I had to focus on Chia's need to stop my own mind going black. I felt a strong hand push down on the pain, but more pain followed, on my legs, Chia's legs, the shoulder, and the head, right at the base. Something was being wrapped around Chia's numb, damp head and neck.

Chia was being moved, carried. His weak presence was growing closer. My own mind was dulling from the pain. I had to stay focussed. I had to ensure that I held onto the connection until I knew him safe. But, I also knew that I had to let go as soon as the retuner was placed on his head. If he retuned while I was still connected it could damage us both. But I couldn't let go until I knew it was done. Chia could not hold on by himself.

And then I felt it. A small cool disc was being placed on Chia's forehead.

Leave now, I heard Jychanumun instruct me. The words felt distant from me. I couldn't tell if they were real. What if they weren't real? What if I just imagined them because I wanted them to be? I had to be sure. I couldn't leave if I wasn't sure.

Suddenly, a blinding flash filled my mind. The power hit me with such a force that it disconnected my energy from Chia's flesh and flung my body back from the floor. I hit the wall behind me and crumpled into a heap on the floor. I couldn't move. I was winded. I couldn't breathe.

It'll pass, my foggy mind told me. *Think of nothing. It'll pass.*

I must have lain there for several moments. The next thing I knew, a pair of hands was lifting me.

"Take as deep a breath as you can," Stanze instructed. "It's only pain."

The irony made me laugh, or try to. I coughed instead.

"Where's Chia?" I gasped.

"He is here," came a reply.

I looked up. At the end of the corridor was Kraniel, walking towards me. He was supporting Chia.

Chia was conscious, barely, and walking, albeit with Kraniel's aid. His body-suit was in tatters, ripped to shreds with several stab holes and long gashes. The rips in Chia's body-suit revealed angry scars that pulsated as they strained to heal while his body rebalanced from the retuning. He had retuned to be of higher energy and less physical now, his exposed skin radiating violet that rippled as he walked. The wound now healing on Chia's right side went straight through his body, where his suit was now gaping open, still saturated with the remnants of his blood. His long eyes, now uncovered, were clouded with the pain that he was obviously suffering, but there was life in them and I knew that his mind was not hurt.

Chia held onto Kraniel's shoulder with one hand and clasped a healing rod in the other, tending to his own wounds as he walked. Behind them walked Jychanumun. He was clearly communicating with someone via his HOTS. He carried several long blades. All the blades were stained red, covered in blood. Chia's blood.

"Chia, you must not walk. You have to rest," I protested, still unable to catch my breath properly.

Chia held up a hand.

"Fine . . . safe-room . . . get in . . ." he rasped.

"Who else is missing?" Jychanumun asked Kraniel. His face was indeed grave. "Orion is not responding."

Kraniel looked at his read-out panel as we entered the safe-room.

"There are nine kutu and one pod unaccounted for. Cain, the pilot, is missing. I assume he is flying the missing pod. Two groups of three kutu are missing, but I'm not concerned about them. One lot went to the mountains to meditate yesterday, so I suspect they'll be back shortly, and the others were planting trees beyond the valley. Orion isn't responding. I'm hoping he's out rallying the tree-planting stragglers to return to the temple. But there is also Shursa. He must have left the feasting. That does concern me."

As we got into the safe room, Stanze wrapped another healing sheet around Chia.

"I am fine," Chia nodded, heading to the communication port. "The pod has launched . . . must contact Una to intercept immediately. Urgent."

"It is already done," Kraniel said, indicating that Chia should sit down. "I realised the ship was missing before you were."

"Did you mark it as urgent?" Chia asked. "It must be stopped without delay."

"Urgent and critical. I spoke to the Supreme himself," Kraniel replied. "Pilots to intercept the pod, in our fastest ships, were launched as I spoke."

Chia nodded, although not looking relieved. Even though his body was healing, he looked terrible.

"Orion is in the pod, unconscious," Chia bowed his head. "I could not get him out. Shursa is also in the pod; very much conscious, although he is now bearing a few hefty cuts of his own."

"Orion? Unconscious? In Eskah's name, what's happened?" Kraniel exclaimed, rather aghast.

Stanze offered Chia a drink of something. Chia took a long draught.

"I was in the pod with Cain, checking the ship was not damaged from landing. Someone attacked me from behind. I was knocked out straight away," Chia began to explain. He took another long draught from the goblet, catching his breath.

"I started to regain consciousness, aware that the pod had been activated," Chia continued. "Orion was next to me, unconscious. I have no recollection of him being placed there. I tried to rouse him, to no avail, so got to the front of the pod and asked Cain what he was doing. His reply was to attempt to knock me out again. I used my vapour daggers to fend him off, but Shursa appeared from behind me and thrust a blade through my side, and Cain took the opportunity to plunge a spike into the back of my neck. I was fighting them both. I should have been fast enough, but I was disorientated. They pinned me against the wall. I took several more cuts, but did start to rally. The next thing I knew, Cain had released the exit hatch and I fell. The pod was hovering about forty cubits up. That is the last I remember."

There was a short moment of silence. The kutu were stunned. I could sense their anger and distress.

"Eskah's damnation. This is an outrage," Stanze fumed. "What was Orion's condition?"

"Unconscious," Chia replied. "With a head injury. I think he had been given sleep inducers too."

"I am furious," Kraniel's eyes flashed green. "I should never have agreed to Shursa coming here! I would like to get my hands on him . . ."

"All the Anumi will not be pleased," Stanze growled. "Once he has been detained, I will request that the Supreme send Shursa to rebalance with my warriors. They will know how to straighten his mind."

"I know we are angry," Chia intercepted. "But, we must focus. What can we do?"

"Do you know where he is going?" Kraniel asked.

"I have no idea," Chia shook his head. "It does not make sense."

"Wherever he is going, he will be apprehended in no time," Stanze remarked.

I said nothing as the others talked, I only listened. I was shocked, I was horrified, but I was not surprised. I did not trust Shursa. In truth, I did not like him. He had done terrible things in the past and those things could never be erased. He could have been a great kutu, but the balance of greatness can be tipped either way. And he had made appalling choices in the past. It seemed that his decisions had not improved.

While the others talked, I had been watching Jychanumun. I knew that he had something to say. I sensed the speed at which his mind was working as he gathered the information he had gleaned into a complete whole before he spoke. I also sensed that he was straining to compose himself. I had never seen Jychanumun hurting before. He concealed it well, but I still sensed it.

Stanze, Kraniel and Chia talked together, discussing how long, and with what strategy and how many ships, the flight team would take to track and capture the missing pod. Stanze was about to leave the room in order to locate and question Gabriel about Shursa's activity before the event, when Jychanumun slowly stood up. His energy bristled around him in small jagged bursts, as if he was trying to contain it. The others fell silent and looked at him.

"Shursa will not be apprehended," Jychanumun shook his head. "You will not see Cain alive again. We will be fortunate to see Orion alive again. Shursa has not lost his mind. He has gone to find the Nigh-kutu."

For a moment nobody spoke. The gravity of Jychanumun's words sunk in.

"Is that possible?" Chia finally asked. "Could Shursa reach the Nigh-kutu before he is intercepted?"

"He could," Jychanumun nodded. "I understand that this newly designed pod can jump instantly in time. What are its capabilities? How much time energy does it have?"

"Time energy?" Chia queried. "We do not have such a thing."

"You do," Jychanumun nodded. "It is what creates the jumps, as you call them."

"No, no," Chia disagreed. "We use excess kutu energy for the jumps. We collect all the residue energy that kutu produce when they move. It is gathered up and compounded until it inverts. It is very potent, but there is not very much of it."

"I am aware of that," Jychanumun replied. "Within that kutu residue is time energy. It is time energy that makes the distance jumps effective. It is not that the pod is moving fast, it is moving ahead in time to a physical point that it would not have reached until that quantity of time had elapsed."

"And you have always known this?"

"I have," Jychanumun replied, "but it is not knowledge anyone would have benefited from."

Chia rubbed his brow. "As much as I would like to argue, my friend, I know you well enough not to. So, tell me, what do we need to know and do now?"

"How much time energy does the pod have?" Jychanumun asked.

"I've no idea," Chia replied. "I know that as the prototype of its kind it had every spare morsel of compressed kutu residue. I know there was enough to make eleven more journeys from Eden1 to Earth and back. Plus it has the standard pod power source, which is self-renewing."

"Then we may have a little time," Jychanumun considered. "The pod will not have enough time energy to get to Immorah, the Nigh-kutu home-world, in one single instant. But it can make a jump sufficiently far to render intercepting it impossible."

"But we must still try."

"Yes, you must," Jychanumun nodded. "It is imperative."

"Then we must send, not only our fastest ships, but ones with the widest tracking capabilities to search for it," Chia decided, getting up and moving, still limping, towards the communication port. "I will contact Nirrious, my old captain, all the head pilots and the Supreme, and notify them all at once."

"Tell them that if they locate the pod but cannot catch it, they must destroy it," Jychanumun stated flatly.

Chia faltered.

"But Orion . . ."

"If they cannot catch it, they *must* destroy it," Jychanumun repeated. "To prevent the death of thousands more. I assure you that it would be a better end for Orion than reaching the Nigh-kutu."

I sensed that Chia flinched inwardly at Jychanumun's words, and rightly so. Orion was his friend, his closest friend. I knew that Chia would not be able to give a command to destroy any kutu, yet alone one that he cherished.

But for me, the true horror of Jychanumun's words sunk in. I knew of some of the Nigh-kutu's capabilities. Jychanumun had shared some of his past with me – not much, but enough to understand the atrocities they could and would enact. Jychanumun was right; the Nigh-kutu would take what they wanted from Orion, by any means, and then, when they had no more use for him, they would give him death.

Chia activated the communication port. The flat panel lit up with the images of several kutu. Some I recognised, some I did not. I heard him talking in hurried, urgent tones, obviously passing on information. After a moment, several kutu images disappeared from the screen at once, leaving only the face of Una, the Supreme. His face looked grave, yet composed.

Una was a good kutu, a good leader. He was balanced and wise. I had always liked him.

Chia moved his palm above the screen and the image faded. A moment later, the entire wall along one side of the room lit up. The life-size image of Una stood in the middle of a white room, empty but for two large, pale statues. The image was so clear that it looked as if he was standing in front of us, in the flesh.

"Jychanumun," the image of the Supreme bowed. "The instructions that you wish me to give cannot be given without careful consideration. But I understand you have information in areas that we do not. I do not doubt you, but if I am to consider destroying a ship with three kutu on board, one of whom is completely innocent in this insurgence, then you must give me reason to believe it is the only solution."

"Supreme," Jychanumun bowed in return. "I have been informed that Shursa goes to join the Nigh-kutu, and that he will lead them to Earth and Eden1. You must stop that pod, by any means, if you wish to prevent this."

"And how can you be sure of the accuracy of this information?"

"Because my clan-brother gave his life to guarantee that the information reached me," Jychanumun bowed his head. "I would have trusted him with my life. I personally guarantee the information."

It was those words that made me understand Jychanumun's sorrow. The kutu he had seen earlier was his brother. Not a brother as I might have, as a human, one bonded by the same flesh parents, but a brother of energy. Jychanumun had mentioned once that the Nigh-kutu used to exist in brotherhoods, that he himself was part of a clan and that most of his clan had been killed. There had been a few of them left. They were the last of all that were good in the land of shadows. Jychanumun had been prepared to sacrifice himself to protect them. Now, it seemed, they were prepared to do the same for him. I could not even imagine such a loss.

"Summarise," the image of the Supreme nodded.

"The Nigh-kutu have plans to attack the Shaa-kutu," Jychanumun stated. "The forgetfulness that we put in their minds did work, but it transpires that Arrunn, leader of the Nigh-kutu, made a bonded promise with Shursa. A bonded promise cannot be erased and is an open link between those who swear such an oath."

"A bonded promise?" Una asked.

"It is not known among the Shaa-kutu," Jychanumun replied. "It is a promise made in a mind share. The mind share cannot be broken until fulfilled, and until it is fulfilled, the bonded mind can be persuaded and besieged by the sharer at will."

"I did not sense this mind share in Shursa," the Supreme remarked. "And I have ensured he was closely monitored."

Jychanumun shook his head. "Shursa would be himself and uninfluenced most of the time. Arrunn is a powerful kutu; he would know how best to manipulate his mind. He would ensure that he only entered Shursa's mind at moments of solitude. It would be impossible to detect."

"Do you have proof of this bonded promise? Could you not have warned us such things were possible?" the Supreme asked. His face looked unusually stern. "We could have learned this art. We could have learnt it, to at least be wary of it."

Jychanumun closed his eyes, as if the Supreme's words pained him.

"I did not know such a thing was still practiced among Nigh-kutu," he paused. "If I were to warn you of every possibility, I would not have stopped talking for this last five years." He paused again. "Much Nigh-kutu information is better unspoken; it corrupts. The Nigh-kutu world is no longer my world. It is no longer my choice. I wish to have no part in it. Nevertheless, I choose to open my heart and mind to warn you now. Yet you still require proof. If my word is not enough by now, it never will be."

He looked at directly at the Supreme, his black, pit-like eyes flashing within their shadow.

"I will ask *you* a question Una, Supreme of Shaa-kutu. What more do you want of **me**?"

The Supreme did not reply immediately. He held Jychanumun's gaze, silver white eyes observing unfathomable black orbs, the black orbs returning the stare.

The Supreme performed a deep bow.

"I understand," the Supreme nodded. "Yours is not an easy path. I want nothing from you that you do not choose to give. Jychanumun, your choices are honourable."

Jychanumun returned the bow. "My love and respect for the Shaa-kutu ensures that I will help. I will transcribe the message I received from my brother and send it to you directly."

"Thank you," Una responded. "I will be in contact shortly with news and strategy. Meanwhile, I need you all to control the situation there."

Jychanumun nodded and the Supreme went to close their communication.

"And Supreme," Jychanumun added, before the port was closed. "If the pod is not stopped I recommend that you prepare all Shaa-kutu for Tumultus. If the Nigh-kutu come into this world, war will be inevitable. It is their way."

The wall went blank. The communication had finished.

War? I thought, my insides overwhelmed with dread. *If they do not stop the pod, war is inevitable?*

While my mind raced, Jychanumun had walked to the sample cabinet and was now examining the crystal specimens. He eventually picked out a small piece of Memorite.

"May I use this?" he asked Chia.

"Use anything you can find." Chia nodded.

Jychanumun knelt on the floor and set the small piece of stone down in front of him. He placed one hand just above the Memorite and closed his eyes. Almost instantly, energy began pouring from his hand, enveloping the stone with a bright, reflective light.

Only a moment later, Jychanumun handed Chia the small piece of Memorite.

"I have infused this with my memory of Cranun's message," Jychanumun stated, "along with a translation from Nigh-kutu to Shaa-kutu. It is an accurate conversion."

Chia took the piece of Memorite, seemingly doubtful of its properties, and then placed it flat on one palm while holding a data crystal in the other. It seemed that he was now transferring the information into a standard format, a transmission crystal, using his own body as the medium and the flow of energy as the portal. His face looked grave and grey. It was clearly exhausting him still further, but he knew that time was now of the essence. He was working to save his friend's life, and perhaps even to prevent a war.

As Chia worked, Stanze left the room to perform another sweep of the temple. Jychanumun tried contacting Orion via the HOTS, but it seemed that Orion was still unconscious. Meanwhile, Kraniel paced up and down the width of the room, his fists clenched; frustrated that he had not been able to reach the pod in time to prevent this.

When Kraniel paced, it meant that he was thinking. I knew that we all now needed Kraniel's genius to come up with something outstanding.

The thought of the Nigh-kutu coming here was a frightening thing. It was more than frightening. It terrified me and almost wiped the thoughts from my head. And a possible war? I felt useless. I did not have ships to move about in, wings to fly with, or powerful weapons to use. My mortal flesh was too feeble to stand up against any kutu. Yet if there was to be a war, help I must, somehow, and in order to help I knew that I must not feel fear. Fear was what rendered any being helpless. Fear could kill the mind. No matter what, I had to be strong.

"This war, if it happens, will affect all kutu and humans," I said to Kraniel. "We must know how to defend ourselves."

"I am coming to the same conclusion," Kraniel nodded as he paced. He glanced around the room. "We must also prepare a defendable area. This temple is not suitable. Eskah! I must know how much time we have!"

Suddenly Kraniel stopped pacing and began rushing around the room, pulling out pieces of equipment from drawers and from compartments in the wall, arranging them in lines on one of the tables. "I have all sorts of relevant data. I can put them together. It won't be precise, but I am sure I can discover whether it is days or millennia."

Kraniel talked to himself while he worked, looking through data on various storage cubes, muttering numbers and names. He would stop, tap some numbers into one of the panels, and then continue. Eventually he had over a dozen devices linked together, and he worked on them furiously.

Suddenly, Kraniel stopped working. He stood completely still, his mouth ajar.

"Eskah! Three to five Earth months," he stated.

"Three to five Earth months what?" Chia asked.

"Until the Nigh-kutu could get here. It could be as little as three to five months; that is all," Kraniel replied, looking up, his eyes wide.

"What calculations have you used?" Jychanumun asked. I guessed he was trying to ascertain what lee-way we might have.

"Many kinds," Kraniel replied. "I have assumed that the pod is not intercepted, that all the new jump energy is used, that the Nigh-kutu depart as soon as Shursa arrives with them, and that they have the capacity to create a jump the entire distance from them to us. Plus more, many more. This is the minimum figure." Kraniel walked towards the communication port. "I must inform the Supreme."

I listened as Kraniel relayed the message.

"No, you did not hear incorrectly," I overheard Kraniel telling the Supreme. "Possible Nigh-kutu contact could be in as little as three to five Earth months – less than eighteen kutu legions, if we do not stop that pod first."

A thousand images flashed through my mind. My heart felt as if it had sunk to the pit of my stomach. If the pod were not intercepted, there may be war in as little as a few moons. How could we possibly ready in such a short time? And what of my friends and family? How could my fellow humans, my loved ones, cope with such a thing? But all this possible horror was dependant on many things. The first was that Shursa did reach the Nigh-kutu. Stopping Shursa had to be the first aim. What if I could rouse Orion from his slumbers? Orion might be able to take control of the pod and simply return to Earth. He was a strong kutu.

Yes, I decided, I must first try contacting Orion using my mind. If I could rouse him, he could take command of the pod.

For such a difficult task, I needed a space where I could ensure there was no possible distraction. I left the others to their work and quietly moved to the back of the room, where the tables had been pushed to one side. After squeezing into the gap in the corner, surrounded and concealed, I huddled down onto the floor to work. Once again, I pushed my energy out through the building and into the land.

Threading my consciousness through the soil was easy. I set a direction and found my awareness stopping at the point where they had found Chia only moments before. I pushed up through the soil, launching into the air, tracing the remaining essence that I could still sense of Orion. My mind went high above the clouds, high above the places where I felt comfortable, and into territory that my mind rarely traversed. I passed beyond the place that smelt like metal and out into the dark expanse. I kept moving, as fast as I could, not allowing myself to think about the ever-growing distance.

Suddenly I faltered. The trace of Orion ceased. It didn't fade away. It was just no longer there.

I kept still, my mind now in a place far beyond the familiar boundaries of Earth and its skies. It did not feel as if Orion had died. I was sure I could still sense him, but just not here. Maybe I had been mistaken in my chosen direction. Maybe my senses had pushed me slightly off course. I knew that I was far from home, far from my flesh. Perhaps I had gone too far.

I decided that I really should turn back. Experiencing such a great distance between my mind and body made me nervous. Surely this could be dangerous.

Do not let your ideas on limits, limit your ideas, the thought entered my head.

The realisation washed over me; I was setting my own limitations. I believed I was too far away from my body. I believed that the distance could be dangerous to me. But distance shouldn't matter. The Old One's energy was everywhere. I must not fear such great expanses. They are only great to my flesh, not my mind, and my mind is far greater than my flesh.

Be brave! I disciplined myself. A crisis has no room for fear.

Holding onto that thought, and without allowing myself a moment's more doubt, I leapt forward, blindly heading in the direction where I thought I still sensed Orion. I travelled faster than any kutu wings could ever move, faster than the strongest winds, faster than light itself. I moved through the consciousness of the Old One, driven forward by nothing more than my will to help Orion and prevent a war.

Suddenly, my sense of Orion returned with a vengeance. It was as if he simply reappeared, as if from nowhere. I homed in on my strongest sense of him, the space and substance around his essence meaning nothing. *There!* I had him. I had found him. It was definitely Orion. He was alive!

I eased my essence into the place where I sensed Orion's body, moving through his motionless flesh until I found his mind.

Orion's thoughts were almost stationary, just a few strange

images merging into nonsensical pictures. It was as if he were hallucinating, in a state far deeper than sleep.

I tried talking to Orion's mind, but fragments of my words just moved around his thoughts, becoming part of the illogical imagery floating aimlessly around in his dreams. I couldn't make him hear me. It seemed that his sleeping state was too deep. Chia had said that he had been given a sleep inducer, so I tried harder, attempting to make him listen. But I couldn't. Eventually I knew I had to stop. Orion's sleep was too deep, too forced, and I didn't want to cause any damage. I put an imprint of warning in Orion's mind, hoping that what I had told him would still be there when he woke.

Unable to do any more to rouse Orion's mind, I spread my awareness beyond his body. I sensed the containment of organic metal and the presence of two other beings in close proximity to him. I brushed against the essence of one and instantly recognised him as Shursa. The other, I knew, had to be the pilot.

Having a sudden moment of inspiration, I flung my consciousness into the pilot's mind.

Turn around. Return to Earth, I told the pilot with my mind. *You must not do this. Turn around.*

I felt the pilot's mind spasm in response to my intrusion. He heard me. He was shocked.

I buried my thoughts deeper into his, so that when he heard me again the words would feel like his own.

Return to Earth, I told him again, making him feel my urgency. *This is not right.*

I pushed the need, my need, into him, ensuring that he felt that it was vital. I tried to make him feel as if he must bring the pod back to Earth, making him believe that the desire was his own desire. I made him realise that he had done a bad thing and the best solution was to return to Earth.

Turn around! I commanded.

I felt his mind comply. He wanted to bring the pod back to Earth!

I felt his mind switch, as if he were talking. He must be talking to Shursa.

I felt an argument break out. I felt the pilot trying to manoeuvre the ship while the argument continued. The argument made the pilot's mind fluctuate, and it was difficult to hold on. It felt as though I was a bird perched on a very tall tree on a very windy day, but I would not let go of my hold. Suddenly, his mind became focussed, not on my words, but on a physical pain. He was injured, badly. Shursa must have injured him.

I began feeding the pilot strength so he could rally. He could get up. He would get up!

Get up, I urged.

Suddenly my thoughts, his thoughts, felt cold. Something was numbing him.

Get up! I commanded.

But it was useless. The pilot's mind was now as stationary as his body. Only a few insignificant images remained in his thoughts. They began drifting together into nonsensical pictures. It seemed that he too had been given a sleep inducer.

Enraged, I pushed my mind towards Shursa.

Turn around! You must not do this. You must return to Earth, I shouted into Shursa's thoughts.

I felt Shursa falter. He was aware of my presence in his mind.

"Get out. Whoever you are, get out, get out, get out!" Shursa screamed inside his mind and aloud.

Shursa's thoughts were strong, trying to repel me, or at least create a wall to block me out.

I went deeper and gripped tightly. He would not be rid of me that easily!

Shursa, you must return Orion and Cain safely to Earth. Now!

I could sense that Shursa was battling with himself. I pushed him harder, urging him again.

"Return the pod to Earth! Now! I commanded.

Maintain direction, I heard a voice calmly state. It was very clear, as if the speaker were standing next to me. It was not Shursa.

What was this? Someone else in Shursa's mind? How could that be?

Suddenly I could see someone. A figure stood in front of me, its arms crossed. It was watching me. It wasn't Shursa. It was a kutu that I'd never seen before. His long, dark hair and dark grey eyes reminded me of Jychanumun, but this certainly didn't feel like Jychanumun. I could sense his presence, but I felt no emotion from him at all. He was in Shursa's mind too!

And you are?

The figure was talking to me. He could see me too.

Shursa must return to Earth, I repeated. I think it came out as a mental stutter, such was my surprise.

No, he must not, the dark-haired one coolly disagreed.

GET OUT OF HIS MIND! I commanded him.

No, he calmly replied, with a nonchalant shake of his head.

It didn't work. The mental command didn't work! How could that be? I sensed jeopardy from this new figure. He had a dangerous, calm power. I felt myself mentally back away a step. The stranger seemed to be evaluating me.

What are you? he asked, moving closer.

No-one, I replied. I would not let him sense that I was unsure.

Shursa, banish this one from your mind and return to Earth! I commanded again, backing away another step.

Where do you think you are going? the figure asked.

I turned around, but the stranger suddenly appeared behind me, blocking my retreat.

I think I will keep you, he said. He seemed to smile, but it wasn't a nice smile. ***Do not worry. I will keep you safe here. And when we have arrived, you can use Shursa's body***.

I felt the strength emanating from him. His words sounded almost persuasive. I had to get out. I realised I could not get to Shursa, but now the danger was to myself.

The dark-haired one moved forward. His energy uncoiled from him like a seething mass of a thousand snakes. The tendrils wove through the air towards me, curling around my body.

Move! I thought to myself. *I must leave now.*

I tried backing away, but the tendrils held me firm. Every moment that passed bound me more tightly to the spot. He had me trapped. I could not pull my mind back to my body.

My mind spun with possibilities and solutions. I was trapped, and each moment that passed was a moment closer to being unable to get away.

Think! Think quickly.

I wracked my mind, trying desperately to remain calm.

'Containment of form' – the words sprang into my thoughts. The Old One had once told me that my form was my own illusion, something I imposed on myself, and that my true form had no shape or substance. I could try to disperse my mind so there was nothing for this stranger to hold on to. If this stranger would not let me go, I must let go of myself.

I had never tried such a thing as letting go of my awareness of form. I had no idea how it could be done. And if I did manage it, I knew that I might not be able to find my body again and that my body might die. But it would only be death of the flesh. Death of the flesh would be far better than having my mind entrapped. I didn't like the idea of trying to disperse myself, but I could not think of any other option.

I quickly focussed on the image of energy fizzing above the lake in my valley. I thought of spilt water evaporating from desert sand. I thought of the warmth radiating out from a hot coal and the smoke from a fire disappearing into the air. To be released from this hold I must become that smoke. I had to let go of myself.

I pushed my consciousness out to everywhere and every time until my mind dislocated, my thoughts fragmented into millions of pieces. Each one held only the same imprint: *go home.*

Then I could no longer think. I felt too dispersed.

Everything went black.

Nothing.

Go home.

Home.

Home?

. . .

. .

.

"Tachra?"

"Tachra?"

I think I recognised that name.

"Tachra, come back. Hear me. Let my voice guide you."

I could hear a velvety voice. I liked the voice. It felt like a warm blanket on a cold night. I wanted to follow it.

"Come back. All of you. Come back," the voice coaxed.

My tumbling thoughts started to regroup. It was Jychanumun's voice that I could hear. I recognised it now. But I couldn't speak. I couldn't move.

Body, I thought, *Get back to your body. That is the part of you that has eyes to open.*

I slowly opened my eyes.

"If you can hear me, draw all of yourself back," Jychanumun instructed. He was leaning over me, his black eyes watching me intently. "You can do it."

I tried to speak, but although my lips now moved, no sound left my mouth.

"Tachra, draw yourself back!" Jychanumun instructed, fiercely this time. "All of you! Do it now!"

I mustered my strength and concentrated, focusing on the centre of my torso, drawing myself in, although I wasn't quite sure how or what I pulled. My mind slowly cleared.

I pushed myself to sit. My body gradually responded and Jychanumun helped me.

"I found Orion," I managed to croak. "He's alive. I couldn't make him hear me."

The look of relief in Jychanumun's face at hearing me speak only lasted a moment.

"You tried doing mind travel as *well* as undertaking a mind probe? Alone? Without anyone to bind you and to keep you grounded? You should know better! You should have asked to be bound. Tachra you must never . . ." He stopped mid-sentence. He closed his eyes and took a deep breath, his face softening. "It is Eskah's fortune that you survived," he whispered.

"I was not entirely sure what I was doing," I admitted as my senses regained clarity. "I was trying to help. I tried to rouse Orion, but could not."

I looked at Jychanumun. "That bonded promise you spoke of; the one Shursa made. I think I met the one whom the bond is with. He came in to Shursa's mind and tried to bind me there. He nearly succeeded. He's frighteningly strong."

"You must avoid him and any form or presence of him," Jychanumun stated. "He is very dangerous."

"You think he's dangerous too?" I asked, surprised that Jychanumun would use such a word.

"Yes," Jychanumun nodded gravely. "He is the most dangerous kutu of them all. He is my nemesis. He is Arrunn."

TEN

The three High Warriors stood side-by-side in Arrunn's main chamber, waiting. This was the first time Mardoch had stood with Dragun and Deimom as their equal. They had not said a word to him. They'd merely glanced in his direction as they all entered the room, although Mardoch knew they had both appraised him with that one fleeting look.

"Eighteen legions?" Arrunn considered. "We have eighteen legions to wait until we can even consider an attack? That is the best you can do? And you have taken *all* the figures I have extracted?"

"Yes," Amaddon, senior forecaster of the Nigh-kutu, replied. He tried not to flinch at the inevitable reprisal. But Arrunn did not reach for his blade, he just stood, thinking.

"Of course we do not know the expertise of the pilot," Amaddon added, trying to give himself some leeway. "I doubt he would be as skilful as one of ours. Allowances should be made for his incompetence."

"It matters not. It tallies well with my plans," Arrunn replied, seeming deep in his own thoughts.

After a moment's silence, Arrunn glanced at the forecaster with condescension. "Why are you still here? Leave."

Amaddon backed away with a bow, averting his eyes from the guards' cold observations and exiting the room as fast as he could without making it look as if he was afraid. He was senior forecaster now, so he would know that his life expectancy was short at best. The last senior forecaster did not survive beyond the length of his first meeting with Arrunn. At least this one had surpassed that.

Mardoch stood with the other two High Warriors, Deimom and Dragun. He stood straight, wearing a look of distaste suitable for one of his status. It was his duty to hold contempt for any kutu below his rank, and the lowly Amaddon was not even a full warrior.

Arrunn turned to his three High Warriors and smiled.

"You think me too lenient, Mardoch?" Arrunn asked.

"Yes," Mardoch snarled the appropriate reply.

"Good," Arrunn nodded.

He walked before the three warriors, observing them.

"I require no such leniency from you," he instructed, "Any of you or your warriors. Any of your warriors performing below par will be arena fodder. For you it will be worse. Understood?" He glanced towards Mardoch.

"My warriors do not fail," Mardoch replied.

"I am sure they do not," Arrunn remarked. He considered Mardoch for a moment, his cold eyes giving no clue as to his thoughts.

Mardoch stood straight, hands behind his back, wings inverted, effortlessly attentive yet relaxed within his strength.

"Today," Arrunn considered, "I wish to choose which division of my warriors to take through the light. If any of you do not wish your division to be considered, speak now."

None of the High Warriors said a word.

"Good," Arrunn decided. "Then I will choose by contest, to see which division demonstrates the most proficient combat skills. A division is only as skilled as their High Warrior's capacity to direct them. I will be watching all of you closely. Arrange for full combat display. All of you. Immediately."

"Mode requested?" High Warrior Dragun enquired.

"Hand combat in flesh for your warriors," Arrunn decided.

Arrunn turned his back, indicating that the three High Warriors should leave.

As one, Dragun, Deimom and Mardoch strode from the room, activating calls to their divisions to gather in the combat arena. None of them made eye contact with each other as they walked. For the next short while, they would not be fighting together, they would be rivals.

Mardoch headed straight to the arena. He knew that his skills were to be tested more than anything else in this contest. He knew his division well. All fourteen-thousand of the warriors under his command were well trained. Cranun had seen to that. But Mardoch had only been High Warrior since Cranun's demise. Arrunn would be watching him. He could not fail this task. His clan needed him to survive and needed him to succeed. He had to win this contest. But this would be a difficult task; the two other High Warriors would fight to the death for the honour of being chosen.

Mardoch thought about the time-energy crystal, now threaded into his hair alongside the remnants of his brothers. In a crisis, he could still put the power to good use, but he did not intend to use the precious gem unless there was no alternative. And he couldn't use it now anyway. Arrunn had requested this contest to be a flesh combat. Any tool that utilized energy was not permitted.

The Nigh-kutu warriors were already gathered in the arena by the time their three chiefs had arrived. They looked a remarkable sight. Over forty-thousand finely tuned, huge kutu stood in perfect alignment. Their skin rippled with the power of their energy and strength of their flesh, their black uniforms immaculate and their matt-black armour dulled to flawlessness. Their weapons were almost invisible, clad around their bodies like extensions of their flesh, ready to be drawn and used at will. Each and every one stood tall and proud, confident in their skill, arranged in three faultlessly proportioned divisions. Each stood ready for whatever was requested of them. And each and every one waited self-contained: not a drop of energy escaping their bodies. The arena bristled with their intent.

Mardoch descended the steps to the arena floor, observing the division under his command. His one hundred Warrior-Firsts stood along the front of the bulk of his warriors, their black wings fully extended to create a wall of shadow behind them. Only senior warriors could exhibit their wings at such a time.

As Mardoch walked the first line, he inspected each of his Warrior-Firsts, nodding his approval. As he went, he made tiny, imperceptible movements of his eyes or eyebrows, or slight changes of expression. These were his silent commands, a close-kept secret among his division, the wordless language that Cranun had taught him and had used a thousand times before. It ensured that his warriors were as well-informed as possible. Most warriors were cruel and heartless, yes, but inside they were still kutu.

Each Warrior-First understood his silent command, his wings folding back as Mardoch passed. Another soldier was ready to fight.

Having inspected them all, Mardoch took his place at the very front of his division, at the centre, exactly six strides ahead. Only he and the other two High Warriors now still displayed their wings.

This was the first time Mardoch had commanded his entire division within the arena since being promoted to High Warrior, but he knew the drill.

The three High Warriors now stood facing each other, their weapon-clad fighters calm and poised behind them. They bowed, and then saluted each other. And then, in unison, they let out a cry. It was a shout so loud that energy spewed from their mouths, filling the arena.

Instantly, the three High Warriors leapt into the air. The entire force of kutu warriors behind them surged forward. Their speed was phenomenal. They drew their weapons with swiftness and stealth, meeting in the middle, clashing with a force so great that the ground trembled. Knife against knife, sword against blade, double blades, throwing discs, looping filaments to ensnare and take down, knuckle spikes, forearm batons, and anything else that required nothing but sheer physical strength. These were the tools of the flesh. In this mode of battle they trained with might, without assistance from any of their superior weapons. No sonars, no lasers, no magnetic blasts, no mind-heat, no ionic charges or energy diffusers were used. Hand to hand they fought. And they didn't utter a word or a cry. Only the sound of combat, weapon on weapon and flesh on flesh, now filled the air.

Mardoch didn't move. He hovered above his kutu, sending silent commands to their minds. *Group four, move forward and lunge. Group three, move back two steps. Group nine, watch your flank. Warrior four-three-seven, make a stab behind you. Warrior one-nine-zero, blade forward with your left and pick up with your right.*

This was what Cranun had taught him: spread your mind, command the overall movement as if it were a whole and, if you can, direct individual warrior's tactics as their eyes. By doing this,

Mardoch could protect their vulnerable areas and guide individuals to pick up those who were wounded but could still fight. If an injured warrior had the strength to get to his feet, he would always continue to fight, no matter what damage he had sustained.

The skirmish continued. Mardoch's warriors took a superior position when Dragun's division faltered. It was only a split second advantage, but it was enough. Dragun had been temporarily distracted by the sight of Arrunn walking down the arena steps. Mardoch had felt Arrunn's presence and had stayed focussed, utilizing the split-second lapse from Dragun to push his own warriors ahead.

Arrunn walked into the fray, giving any warrior several good cuts if he backed away from fighting him. Both his hands seemed motionless most of the time, only occasionally flicking out with almost invisible speed, a double-ended curved blade held in each fist. He would lash out, marking any kutu with a double cut whom he considered did not fight well enough. Several warriors now wore his brand, the inverted V, somewhere on their flesh.

Arrunn manoeuvred into the centre of the fighting, looked up and nodded.

"Stop!" Mardoch instructed, as the other High-Warriors did the same.

Instantly, the warring kutu paused their fighting. Thrusts stopped mid-lunge, defensive forearms poised mid-air. Silence fell over the arena. For a fraction of a moment, all was still.

Simultaneously, the warriors returned their weapons to their holds, and stood straight.

"Reform," Mardoch commanded.

The warriors moved, realigning to their original positions. Several wounded kutu managed to arise from the ground and stumble into position, but several more did not arise. Mardoch noted that one of his own warriors had his head almost severed from his body. Number seven-eight-eight-two would not heal. It had been necessary for Mardoch to do this, to win this fight. Still, he could not help feeling it was a waste of a brave kutu.

Having resumed his position on the ground at the front of his division, Mardoch stood awaiting the verdict. He had done well. He knew he had. His warriors had taken the central ground and driven both other divisions back. He was proud of them, proud of himself. But he didn't let it show. His dispassionate expression revealed nothing.

"Very good," Arrunn nodded to Dragun. "Perfect formation. Disappointment about the lapse, but it was only momentary."

Arrunn began walking towards Mardoch, but stopped, considering something. He turned back to Dragun, tilting his head to one side.

"Of your one hundred Warrior-Firsts, which three are the most proficient?" he asked.

Dragun nodded to three of his warriors. They strode forward and bowed.

Arrunn considered Dragun's choice of kutu for a moment. He didn't inspect their armour or their weapons, but just looked each one in the eye, unmoving, his facial expression never changing.

"Fight me," Arrunn suddenly ordered the three Warrior-Firsts.

Without a pause, the three warriors lunged forward, drawing their weapons. Arrunn fought back with apparent ease, gracefully slashing and pushing the three warriors back. Suddenly, one of the warriors sidestepped and rolled, thrust forward and up with one hand as Arrunn blocked him, but giving Arrunn's calf a deep slash with the other. Arrunn instantly drew his long blades from either side of his hip and thrust in both directions with both hands. All three warriors were held back, with some part of Arrunn's two long-blades now touching their necks.

"You may stop," Arrunn stated calmly, poised with all three kutu at arm's length.

The kutu relaxed, repositioning their weapons.

"And you are?" Arrunn asked the warrior who had given him a good cut.

"Valic," the warrior replied. His tone was fearless.

"Valic, you will be a High Warrior if Dragun under-performs again," Arrunn stated matter-of-factly.

"And Dragun," Arrunn turned to the High Warrior, took his double ended blade and slashed his cheek.

A deep cut now welled with blood that dripped down Dragun's face, but he did not flinch. Instead, he pulled out his own blade, slashing the other side of his face himself. Arrunn merely raised his eyebrows.

"If you falter again . . ." Arrunn chided, "you will sacrifice your life. It is only because it was my presence that made you falter that I spare you. You will not do it twice."

Dragun said nothing.

Arrunn walked to Mardoch, his dark eyes narrowing as if figuring Mardoch out.

"You are new to this, yet already you surpass the others. You have executed your role adequately."

Mardoch did not reply. A reply was not required.

"And I see you have the loyalty of your division," Arrunn commented, glancing down the line of Mardoch's Warrior-Firsts.

All one hundred Warrior-Firsts in Mardoch's division had survived. None had fallen. All stood strong, ready to fight again.

"All my warriors are resilient," Mardoch replied.

"Yes. Your warriors are also well directed," Arrunn nodded. "Of your Warrior-Firsts, which three do you trust the most?"

Mardoch shouted out the names of three of his most trustworthy, experienced Warrior-Firsts. He trusted Shemya the most, but Shemya had only just risen to the rank of Warrior-First, taking the position that Mardoch had left behind following his own rise in rank. Shemya still had much to learn. Mardoch knew that he could not risk such an inexperienced kutu if Arrunn required direct combat.

The three warriors Mardoch had selected walked forward to stand directly behind him. They were not of Mardoch's clan, but all three of them he could trust to fight well in any battle. And they had a great deal of experience. Mardoch knew that all three would perform well against their leader if required.

Arrunn walked around Mardoch's three Warrior-Firsts, considering them. The warriors stood poised, ready for the inevitable command to fight.

Suddenly, Arrunn drew the long black blade from its hold down his back and in one swift move slit the throats of all three.

Mardoch had to stifle a gasp.

The three warriors looked in disbelief as their life's blood flowed from them, running down their armour and trickling onto the ground around their feet. Their eyes widened with surprise, but none tried to cry out. One put his hand to his throat, holding his bloodied fingers up in front of his eyes as if in disbelief. In turn, all three slumped to the floor, two falling to their knees and one remaining standing until he, too, crumpled.

Mardoch was horrified, but he did not let it show. He set his jaw and forced himself to stay focussed.

"I do not need warriors that are loyal to you," Arrunn said, his cool demeanour unflinching, as he wiped his blade and returned it to its scabbard. "Warriors are loyal to me, not you. You are merely the instrument of my voice. Understood?"

"Yes," Mardoch replied, through gritted teeth. This time it took no effort to scowl. He was furious with himself. This was his test: not the test of his warriors, a test of him. He had done too well and Arrunn wished to give him a reminder of who held the true power. He should have neither won nor lost the skirmish. He should have stayed firmly in the middle. Now he'd caused the deaths of three good kutu. He may have even jeopardised being chosen to accompany Arrunn through the light.

Leaving Dragun with his bloodied face and Mardoch with the ground around him stained red with the life of his most trusted kutu, Arrunn walked towards the third High-Warrior, Deimom.

Deimom stood ready, seemingly calm. Mardoch noticed that he did not look Arrunn in the eye, but kept his gaze in his general direction, yet unfocussed. It seemed a good tactic to adopt.

Arrunn walked up to Deimom, glanced at him and his division, but said nothing. He simply turned and walked away.

"You have eighteen legions until we leave. Train wisely," Arrunn stated, as he left the arena floor. "This war will be the greatest war. This war, I will take *all* my armies. You have *all* been chosen."

All? Mardoch thought, as he remained standing to attention until Arrunn had let the arena. Yes, he was relieved that he was going. It was crucial to his and Cranun's plan that he was chosen. But all three divisions? That he had not anticipated.

Mardoch's thoughts raced with the new information. His plan had been to be chosen, with his division, to accompany Arrunn to this war. He had planned to create chaos among his warriors just before the attack, giving the light-walking Shaa-kutu a chance to mount their own successful attack and himself the opportunity to find Jychanumun. But with all of them going? The divisions under Deimom's and Dragun's command would not be affected by his orders. This changed everything. The Shaa-kutu would not stand a chance.

By Eskah! This time we all go, Mardoch considered. *What devastations are intended for these light walkers?*

As soon as Arrunn had left the arena, Mardoch turned back to his division. After instructing them to rest and tend to the injured before they continued practising, he looked down at his three dead Warrior-Firsts. It was a waste of three good lives. It was his fault. His role of protector had not helped these three souls. They had not been given time to prepare for death, and so they would not even leave their matter in solid form as a mark of their passing. No, there would be no death statues of these three to place in the warriors' death-hall, for all to honour their memory. These three had died when tuned to be in the flesh, Arrunn had used the black sword of time to take their life energy, so all that was left of them would merely decompose to nothing in an unceremonious burial hole.

Mardoch bent down to the three dead kutu, closing their open, staring eyes.

I will remember you names, Mardoch thought. *If nothing more, I will honour you in my thoughts.*

He took the first golden tag from around the neck of one of the dead, a well-built warrior named Myat, known for the scar shaped like a face on his shoulder. He placed the small disc on Myat's tongue and closed his mouth. The disc was a token made from Uana, the potent golden ore. Many warriors believed they could use such a precious token in death. They thought they could use it to plead with Eskah to allow them entry into eternity. Mardoch knew that no such thing existed. If Eskah was the being who governed all things, then Uana would have no weight to persuade him. But the warriors took solace in their beliefs, and Mardoch was glad of any hope they found to hold on to.

A kutu bent down beside Mardoch, taking another of the dead Warrior-First's golden discs and placing it into his mouth. Mardoch glanced to his side. It was High Warrior Dragun.

High-Warriors did not usually help any kutu, dead or alive, who was not from their own division.

Dragun had not tended to his own cuts yet and the blood still dripped down. Some splashed onto the dead kutu's face as Dragun leant over him. Dragun carefully wiped the blood away.

"I'm sorry," Dragun muttered under his breath as he worked.

Mardoch was surprised, but he didn't let it show. No warrior was ever supposed to show remorse, sorrow, or any form of pity for anyone.

Mardoch quickly scanned the area without pausing in his work as Dragun moved onto preparing the third fallen warrior. No one else was around them. No one else could hear.

"They were good kutu," Mardoch replied quietly. He purposely did not refer to them as warriors as he was supposed to. He was testing Dragun's reaction.

"Many are," Dragun replied. He glanced at Mardoch. "We did not all start life as warriors."

Mardoch caught his breath, quickly continuing with his task so as not to be noticed. What was Dragun inferring? Did he know of Mardoch's Weaver clan origins? No, that was impossible; the Weaver clan were now long-forgotten among Nigh-kutu. Could this be a test? Had Arrunn set up the situation to test him? High Warrior to High Warrior was surely a potent situation that could be used to draw out any dormant weaknesses.

Mardoch knew that he had to be careful. There was something about Dragun that sat in the back of his mind, like a shadow memory that would not form. Every morsel of his training told him not to trust this kutu, but his instincts said otherwise.

Dragun finished preparing the dead kutu, and then got up. He glanced again at Mardoch before walking into the midst of his own division to tend to his own fallen and wounded.

Perhaps we have not all lost our way, Mardoch thought as he worked. He immediately banished the notion from his head. He could not even permit such thoughts in such a public place. His facial expression or body language could give him away. He must be nothing but strong. He must banish his own thoughts, embrace the rage from the death of three worthy Warrior-Firsts and move on.

Mardoch took a deep breath, letting the anger of all injustices fill his soul, and then stood up. After ordering the dead to be removed from the arena, ensuring that his commands were as harsh and emotionless as always, he made his kutu train again, and then again. He made sure he pushed them beyond fatigue, practising their strategies, their co-ordination and his skills to lead them, until not a fault could be detected.

But all the time that Mardoch commanded and led his warriors, training them to bring death to their opponents, in the back of his mind was a new light. It was faint, yes, but it was there, even when he did not dwell on it. The small light of hope glimmered in Mardoch's sub-consciousness: perhaps not all remaining Nigh-kutu had truly lost their way.

Exhausted and spent, Mardoch finally allowed his warriors to take time out. They all headed off to eat whatever meagre nourishment had been allocated to them, seeming in high spirits, even relaxed, as they marched from the arena. Perhaps they were just glad to be allocated rest time at last. Perhaps it was because they knew they would soon be going into combat to a world deemed full of spoils. After all, Mardoch considered, this is what they trained every day for: war.

With all his warriors departed, Mardoch stood in the middle of the empty arena and looked around. Soon this place would not be part of his everyday life. All the bloodshed, battles, and contests that had been fought here would be in his past. Mardoch would be going to the war of the light and he did not intend on coming back. He would be leading his division. That part of his plan, Cranun's plan, had fortunately succeeded. But there was now a new predicament to overcome. Arrunn no longer wished to take just one division; this time he was taking them all. This was something neither he nor Cranun had made any contingency plans for.

Mardoch considered the possible implications of the new arrangement. Now there would be two more divisions, with thousands of additional warriors, that Mardoch had absolutely no control over. He had not been entirely sure if he could manoeuvre all his own fighters to create chaos at the point of attack. Now, knowing that there would be the full army, which had never been deployed in its entirety before, Mardoch had to face the fact that he had no chance of manipulating them all. It would be impossible, even with all his hidden skills.

Mardoch knew that this was down to him now. All his brothers to whom he could have turned for advice were now merely gems in his hair. This would be Mardoch's true test as both a warrior and a Walker. He alone had to form a plan that could work.

ELEVEN

"You must go home," I told Soul. "You must go back to Iris and stay with my parents. And you must tell them everything."

"But you have to come too," Soul pleaded.

"I will, but I can't yet. Tell my father all I have told you. Make sure all the villagers know to make hiding places and to start storing provisions of food and water. Tell father to warn the villagers in Longplain and Whitehill too. Tell them all to spread the word. And Soul, please, make every safety preparation. Promise me."

"I promise," Soul nodded. "I'm scared."

I nearly told her that I was scared too. But Soul's expression stopped the words coming out of my mouth.

"Don't be scared," I managed a smile. "If war comes to Earth, which it probably won't, the Shaa-kutu will protect us all."

Stanze and Brave were now walking down the corridor to join us. Brave was taking Soul home. Stanze wanted to, but his allocated warriors from Eden1 were about to arrive. Stanze nodded at me, indicating it was time for me to attend the welcoming.

"I have to go," I said to Soul. I hugged her. "I will see you soon."

Soul put up one hand as I walked away. In the other, she clasped a small bag. I had given her a communication device so we could stay in touch. It wasn't much, but it made us both feel better.

Stanze walked with me to the main temple doors, where his warriors would now be waiting outside. The thought of having more brave Anumi here gladdened my heart.

The doors swung open.

My heart sank. I tried to conceal my dismay.

In front of me stood fifty Anumi warriors. Only fifty!

How these few could fend off the Nigh-kutu armies, if they came, was beyond me.

Stanze stood in front of me, only inches away, and turned to face me, leaning down and talking to me in quiet tones. His bulky body obscured my shocked expression from the warriors waiting behind him, standing to attention on the grass in front of the temple gates. The afternoon brightness reflected off Stanze's golden armour, dazzling my eyes, so I shut them, listening as he spoke.

The perils of the situation consumed me, but as Stanze spoke my dismay quickly turned to gratitude, and then to heartache. These were Stanze's fifty best warriors. His most trusted. His strongest. They were his friends. They would be stationed here, with him, as the last stand against the Nigh-kutu, if it came to that. We were lucky to have them.

I now understood the kutu Supreme's reasons for sending so few of their warriors to Earth. He believed that the Nigh-kutu would strike Eden1 first. The vast majority of their Anumi army was now gathered around their home-world, headed up by the chief Anumi, Peniva, busy fortifying their own planet and its surrounding space. Strategically it did make sense. They knew that their best approach was to stop the Nigh-kutu at Eden1, where their own energy was strongest and their knowledge of resources best. There they could prevent the Nigh-kutu from advancing to the smaller Shaa-kutu colonies, including Earth. They assumed that Earth wouldn't see any fighting. It was a hope that I decided to hold onto as tightly as I could.

The Anumi had always held a special place in my heart. They were mighty in mind and body, yet their spirits were kind and just. When many Shaa-kutu had wavered in the past, led by the belief that Shursa could offer them greater glories, the Anumi had remained staunch. Stanze and Peniva, two of the head Anumi, had made a stand for justice with their warriors. Their inner goodness had prevailed, inspiring them to save all Shaa-kutu. Now, it seemed, they were going to risk their lives to do the same again, and in front of me stood fifty of their bravest.

Knowing the facts, I quietly urged Stanze to take himself and his warriors to Eden1. He should join Peniva; Peniva would need as many good warriors as could be. If Eden1 was where they believed the fighting would be, then they should all be there to protect their own kind. As much as the selfish part of me wanted my family and friends protected, we could hide. It was the kutu whose lives were precious.

Stanze calmly pointed out that Peniva would not accept his or his warriors' return to Eden1; the chief Anumi had clearly outlined several defences just for Earth. Peniva loved this little planet, even humans, even me, too much to leave it defenceless. He personally wanted us protected. Stanze also said that it was a strategic necessity to have Anumi presence on all planets that were potential first-attack points for the Nigh-kutu. Most colonies had now been evacuated to Eden1 and most Anumi warriors, several thousand of them, were now stationed there too. But although they had calculated that their home-world had a ninety-eight percent chance of being the primary target, Earth could not be ruled out. The warriors here were a necessity, and fifty was the right number to allocate.

I saw the sense of Stanze's logic. As he finished speaking I composed myself, blinked back my tears, gave him my heartfelt thanks, took a step to one side, smiled, and bowed deeply in honour of the waiting Anumi.

The normal entourage of greeters that used to welcome newcomers to the temple was now whittled down to just me. Everyone else was too occupied with vital matters. I, on the other hand, felt that it was the least that I could do. So, as Stanze directed the warriors into the central chamber, I gave them each my thanks and my respect, and, most of all, I let them know how much I treasured their presence. The warriors responded with nods and few words, but their eyes showed their appreciation.

There were no pleasantries such as feastings laid on for these brave kutu. Instead, Stanze marched them straight into the central chamber for a briefing before allocating them their duties. I left the Anumi at that point and headed back to my own room.

The corridors were unusually quiet, and my footsteps echoed as I walked. The temple was virtually empty now, and the energy inside had changed. It felt less serene, and even a little eerie.

All teachings in the temple had been temporarily suspended, and the humans had returned to their homes. Soul had been the last to leave.

Most of the kutu who had been here on Earth had since returned to Eden1, but about twenty remained. Those kutu now worked night and day. They spent their time helping with the construction of the new buildings, honing their own weapon skills, and making safe areas for people. They didn't stop. They only came back to the temple for supplies. Even for the newly arrived Anumi warriors, the temple was only to be their temporary home. Work had already started on their concealed barracks some distance from the valley. It was near these barracks that, as from tomorrow, the Anumi would start training.

It had been twenty-seven days since Shursa had absconded in the pod with Orion as his prisoner. I know, because I kept careful count. Despite the kutu dispatching dozens of their fastest tracking crafts, none had yet detected the missing ship. They all said that it was too early to lose all hope of finding it, and that there was still a chance that the pod could be detained. They reasoned that the journey from Earth to the Nigh-kutu home-world was far, so they still scoured the universe, but as yet had found nothing. Every day that passed, I felt their hope fade a little more.

I headed back to my room with the intention of trying to contact Orion again. Every day it was becoming more difficult to locate his presence out there, far beyond the skies. I could sense him, which was good as it meant he was alive. But as much as I tried, I still had not succeeded in waking him. It seemed that whatever Shursa was using to keep him unconscious was very effective.

It concerned me that each time I tried linking with Orion the connection was increasingly difficult, as his presence moved further away. I knew that I couldn't keep trying forever. Orion had almost reached the maximum distance that I could go to. I'd learnt that as much as my mind could travel anywhere, if I wished to return to my flesh, there were definite limits.

My room was a mess. The floor was littered with books, crystals, partially drunk glasses of water, and crumpled blankets that I'd pulled off my recliner so that I could work throughout the night while sitting on the floor. I scolded myself for leaving it in such disarray.

Looking at the items strewn over my floor gave me a pang of guilt for treating such treasures as if they were nothing. I decided

I would tidy as soon as I'd tried contacting Orion again. I think I used that justification quite often.

I sat on the floor, amidst the disarray, and relaxed my mind, concentrating on reaching Orion.

I assumed that I'd locate Orion's presence relatively quickly, as I'd learnt to follow on from the points where I'd previously sensed him, but this time was not so quick. When I did eventually locate him, he felt very faint. His location was further out than expected. I guessed that the ship he was travelling in had performed its second distance jump. This was not good.

I realised that this was probably the last time I would be able to connect to Orion. I suppressed my anxiety and focussed my adrenaline on the task. This time, I had to make it work.

I mustered all my strength and pushed my energy out as strongly as I could, leaping into Orion's mind. I tried talking to him. I tried stimulating his brain. I tried looping into the strange images that wafted through his thoughts and connecting them to try to make sense of them. I attempted every measure that I knew of to rouse him, but nothing would make him wake. I couldn't even make him acknowledge or understand me at the most basic level. Even an unconscious mind should stir to some degree, but Orion's did nothing. There had to be something preventing this.

I couldn't detect any damage in Orion's mind, so I left his head and searched through his body for any sign of injury that could be the cause of his state. I was shocked at how low his energy felt. And although I could find no severe wounds, I was drawn towards the centre of his spine.

Dotted down the length of Orion's spine, no larger than bites from an insect, were several small holes. At first, I thought nothing of it, and then I felt myself being drawn towards the holes, as if something were pulling my energy towards them, trying to expel me from Orion's body. The pull felt compelling, like the current of a rushing river. Orion's energy, as he made it, was not moving around his body like blood in the flesh, it was rushing out of these puncture marks, and beyond the puncture marks were slim tubes, filtering his energy into something.

The pod! Orion's energy was helping to feed the pod!

I moved forward, towards the puncture marks, hoping I could seal them. But, I had to stop when it took all my energy just to resist the pull. The force was great. I couldn't move any closer or the strength of the pull would force my own energy through those openings too, and my energy would also just be used. Orion was not just being injected with something to keep him subdued, he was having his energy drained away and used via these filtering points!

I searched for any way to stop the process. But, it seemed that whatever I could do, the outcome would be my demise too. What could I do? I couldn't feed any energy to Orion. Any energy that I gave him would just end up being filtered out; it wouldn't stay in him to revive him. I couldn't mend his mind; I'd tried every means possible already. And I couldn't get any closer to the points where the pull was happening or I would simply be drained away too. I could do nothing!

Sensing I had stayed away from my body for as long as I could, I flung my consciousness back into my body. I came to, feeling disorientated, but forcing myself to focus. They knew of a way to drain energy from kutu. That was how Shursa or Arrunn were keeping Orion unconscious, yet barely alive. They could probably do that to him forever, using his energy for whatever means they deemed appropriate. This was terrible.

I got up and immediately activated the little communication port in my room, sending a message to Chia, Jychanumun, Kraniel and Stanze. How this new information could help, I had no idea. But, I had learnt from my own travels that the more information one had, the better able one was to deal with difficulties. The only positive thing I could find to say to the kutu was that if Orion's energy was useful in anyway, then he most likely would not be killed. It did not seem to make them feel any better.

Having relayed my message, I should have hurried from my rooms to oversee my next task. But I needed to let my mind settle first, lest I cause more problems than I solve. So, I wandered around my unkempt room, picking up items from the floor, while Meah watched in approval.

I neatly stacked the writing instruments and data crystals back into their make-shift box. I had collected every piece of information I could find about the Nigh-kutu language and was attempting to learn their tongue. The best resource I had was the transcript Jychanumun had made of the final message from his clan-brother, Cranun. Using this, along with his word-for-word translation into Shaa-kutu, had already provided some markers as to the way they spoke. The Nigh-kutu language was complex and I was struggling to learn it. If I had thought that the Shaa-kutu language was difficult, Nigh-kutu was a hundred times worse.

Although Nigh-kutu and Shaa-kutu sounded similar to my ears, the effects and meaning of the words were nothing alike. Shaa-kutu spoke with words generated from honest meaning and true intent. I had understood them with relative ease once I'd used my true vision to understand the meaning behind the sounds. But the Nigh-kutu language felt corrupt. Although they also spoke in three-dimensional sounds, the intent behind many of the words had changed so that now their meaning was a lie. This, coupled with the deep guttural noises they used in conjunction with a word, which my own throat could barely imitate, made learning it almost impossible.

In truth, I did not know how learning the Nigh-kutu language could help, if at all. But I guessed that it might come in useful. In truth, when it was late and I could not sleep, it gave me the small comfort that I was doing something constructive.

While I tidied my room, Jychanumun sent a message stating that he would be calling on me. I'd not seen Jychanumun much over recent days. He had thrown his energies into overseeing fortifications and worked day and night.

I opened the door to my room as Jychanumun walked down the corridor. He looked troubled. He was tense and his energy chaotic, rather than its usual self-contained state.

"Come in," I smiled as he approached.

Jychanumun remained silent, walking into my room, closing the door and then taking a seat at the table.

"I have made a difficult choice, but I am still uncertain," Jychanumun stated, looking at me.

It was unusual to hear Jychanumun say he was uncertain about something, about anything.

Do you wish to share it with me? I asked silently with my mind, giving our conversation complete privacy.

Yes, Jychanumun silently replied. *I wish to teach the Shaa-kutu how to fight the Nigh-kutu way. But I avowed many millennia ago never to fight again.*

You were a warrior?

I do not class myself a warrior, Jychanumun replied, *but I have trained as such in the past. My skills were proficient.*

My surprise quickly passed. I understood enough about the Nigh-kutu to know that most trained as warriors at some point. Why would Jychanumun be an exception? I contemplated his dilemma. Was to train fighters to condone fighting or merely to prepare for defence? Did it matter?

"I can sense that you've already made your choice," I spoke aloud. "Not all choices are clear like water. Some are murky and require greater consideration. But as you have already made the choice to teach your skills, let go of your remorse; it serves no purpose."

"It was not a choice I wished to make."

"Of course not," I affirmed. "But one cannot say what choices life will present. Some have only good outcomes, whichever option is selected. Some have only bad. Not all choices are easily weighed."

"You do not judge me?"

"Never!" I replied with vehemence. "I do not judge. And if I did, I would find you worthy. Never doubt my respect and love for you."

Jychanumun looked relieved that I understood, even if he was not relieved about the choice he had made.

"I will inform the Anumi," Jychanumun decided. "It will mean I travel to Eden1."

"Eden1?" I asked, trying to conceal my dismay.

"Yes, it would be necessary."

My stomach churned. I didn't want him to go. But it was a selfish thought, and I knew I was wrong to have it.

"It was a difficult choice," Jychanumun said quietly.

I didn't say anything. I couldn't. I just nodded.

"I will teach the Anumi here first. They in turn can teach the remaining kutu here, as well as the humans. And then I will travel to Eden1 and teach the Anumi there. Tachra . . ." Jychanumun looked at me, "You may choose to find any humans who would want to learn the art of defence. Humans may wish to protect themselves too. We do not fight just for kutu lives."

Humans fighting kutu? Just the thought of it made me almost laugh aloud with shock. Yes, my head told me that I too should learn the art of defence. But I could not imagine how my jellified legs could even function in front of the sight of a warring Nigh-kutu, yet alone do any specific moves. Running away would be the first option. But nobody could run forever. Maybe one day we would have no choice but to defend ourselves.

"I will find those who wish to learn," I eventually nodded. "I will travel to every village if need be."

"It will not be an easy task," Jychanumun considered. He stood and bowed and, as he did, he caught my hand. He put my hand to his forehead, his mouth, and then his chest. Without a further word, he turned and left the room.

The rest of the day was a blur. Within moments of Jychanumun's departure I was informed by Stanze of the strategy to assemble any humans who wanted to learn defence. I was allocated the new, rather awkward, task of travelling to each village, finding the village representative, informing him or her of what could be in store, and discussing defensive and protective options. I was to start straight away. Tarrian was en route to escort me.

Before Tarrian arrived, I just about had time to contact Soul and my parents. I made sure they were making their own arrangements to stay safe. Father had already spoken to every villager in Threetops. Tomorrow he would be travelling to the neighbouring village, while mother and Soul dug into the under-floor to make cool areas for storing food and water. When I spoke to father, I was glad the communication between us was the sort without pictures. I did not want him to know I was crying. With my family I allowed myself to feel the reality of my fear. And I missed them. A part of me wanted to be a girl again, with tending the crops my only concern, and with hot stew and a comfortable bunk to look forward to.

Tarrian, one of Stanze's kutu warriors, soon arrived. We were heading for the closest village first, Meadsins. It was not far from the valley by air, being just over the mountain range, but there was no luxury of a pod, as every craft was now put to better use. So Tarrian simply carried me.

Meadsins was on the border of the dry lands, a pocket of neatly cultivated, fruitful land surrounded by sparseness. Tarrian informed me that Ren, who had attended the temple twice, would be a good person to approach first in this village.

Hearing Ren's name made me smile. I had met him on my travels before I had discovered the kutu. He had been a boy then, a talkative, cheeky, delightful child. He had spent two full summers at the temple, learning at an incredible speed, where he had also had charmed a girl who helped Nana in the kitchens. Now Ren was a young man of fifteen, paired to that same girl, and with his first child already nearly due.

I couldn't see Ren working in the fields, so Tarrian directed me towards the hut that was listed as his abode. People watched as we approached. Some waved, some smiled, some bowed, and some backed away, still unfamiliar with the sight of a kutu. We approached Ren's hut, and Tarrian respectfully stood back as I knocked on the door.

Almost instantly, the door was flung open. Ren stood before me with his hair awry, freckled face mucky from the fields, a swaddled new baby in one arm and large piece of flat-bread in the other. He was chewing hurriedly, with an overfull mouth.

"Tachra, green-eyes," Ren smiled a huge smile, showing me his half-chewed bread.

"I see that fatherhood has not tempered your cheek!" I laughed. "Congratulations, young Ren. I assume mother and babe are both well."

"Two babies!" Ren exclaimed happily. "She likes me so much that she gives me two at once. Now I can't so much as eat in peace. The skies see fit to punish me! But yes, we are all well. Come in, Tachra; my hut is yours."

"I wish I could, Ren," I bowed. "I would enjoy spending time with you and yours, but I have tasks I must attend to. I merely wish to ask if the village has an allocated elder or speaker I could hold council with."

"Yes," Ren smiled. "I'll take you to him. Just a moment . . ."

Ren dashed back into his hut. "Don't you look at me with those loving eyes," I overheard him saying to his mate. "Take this one too. I'll be back in a short moment."

Ren re-emerged moments later, minus the baby, but still clutching the flat-bread. He beckoned us to follow and promptly led us to a hut in the centre of the village. This, it transpired, was the hut of Temar, one of the originals, the first humans to be placed on Earth. He was now allocated as carer for the village. Carer – I liked that title.

Temar welcomed all three of us into his humble abode. He was lean and tanned and his face was well-lined, yet kindly. His hut was clean and neatly kept – sparse, yet with the necessities. There was no eating table or benches, just a solitary wooden chair and small table by the hearth. It was very humble and I saw no sign of a mate.

"Please," Temar indicated to a mat on the well-scrubbed floor. "The young ones of the village have made better use of my spare chairs."

I joined Temar, kneeling on the floor. Tarrian did the same. Ren asked if he could stay; I thought it a good idea, so he joined us too. I'd never met Temar before, but it turned out that he had spent time at the temple one winter, when I had been visiting my parents. Temar was familiar with the kutu, and I was relieved that Tarrian's presence did not intimidate him.

I informed Temar, as spokesperson for the village, that the Nigh-kutu could come to Earth and that there could be fighting. I tried to convey the potential gravity of the situation without causing fear, but I couldn't temper the possibility of how bad it could be either. It was a delicate task. For five years now, the rumours of the Nigh-kutu had spread among humans. They were already feared. Some depicted the Nigh-kutu as many-headed monsters. Some as shadows that came to life. And some did not believe they were real at all. Temar, thankfully, had heard of the Nigh-kutu during his studies.

"So the kutu gods may war," Temar considered. "Tell me, why do they bring this war here at all? We are undemanding creatures. We do not cause trouble. Could they not simply war on their own worlds and leave us in peace?"

"The Nigh-kutu could still end up here," I replied. "They may leave us alone, or they may wish to harm us. Either way, we should be prepared."

"But this is no more than maybe after maybe," Temar objected. "If the chance is a small one, surely it is not worth worrying the people of my village. Let them live in peace. We are simple farmers."

"Some may also wish to be defenders," I insisted.

"Defenders?" Temar laughed wryly. "Look at us. Look at the size of them," Temar indicated towards Tarrian. "How could any of us stand up against even just one as strong as him? And that's not even taking into account their abilities or their powerful machines. No, we could not stand up to them. It makes no sense."

I continued pressing, approaching my point from various angles, but Temar would not change his mind. I understood why. In many respects, I agreed. But I remembered the Nigh-kutu. I had an inkling of their ways. The least we could do was be prepared to defend ourselves.

Temar finally held up his hand.

"No," he stated. "That is my decision. I will not worry my people about something that is only a possibility, and, even if it did occur, something that they could do nothing about."

I felt deflated.

"I'm offering the opportunity to learn the art of defence. Will you not even give them the choice?"

"My lady," Temar bowed his head. "The villagers have already made their choice. They nominated me as their spokesperson. I already speak for them."

There was nothing more I could think to say.

"I understand," I returned the bow and stood up. "Thank you for taking the time to listen."

I turned to leave, but could not. "Please, Temar," I begged. "Even if none will learn defence, please prepare to stay safe. Prepare hiding places, food and water, mending ointments. Please tell everyone in your village. Promise me that. It is the least you can do for them. "

Temar got up, his old bones clicking as he slowly rose, refusing Tarrian's offered hand to assist him.

"I will not tell them," Temar said. "For that is also nothing but a worry for them. But I will prepare those things for all my villagers myself."

"I'll help him," Ren interjected. He looked at Temar and shrugged. "Well, I know now. It's already my worry too."

Temar hesitantly nodded his consent as Tarrian and I went to leave.

"Tachra," Temar said, touching my arm. "You are one of us. Do not take the cares of all things upon yourself. You are still young. Live your life."

"Some things are not that simple," I smiled. "But, thank you Temar. You are a good man."

Temar's departing words made me feel sad. He had made me realise that there was a part of my life, as a girl, that I probably would never fully enjoy. I left the hut, silently walking with Tarrian to the nearest clearing so we could take to the skies and move on to the next village. This meeting had not gone well. I hoped the visit to the next village would be rather more fruitful. Would none choose to defend themselves or their loved ones? Would they all rather chance falling into Nigh-kutu hands, facing death or, worse still, life under Nigh-kutu cruelty? By the skies! Did they not see that there were worse possibilities than death?

Ren silently walked with us, rather more subdued than his usual self.

"We should all have the choice," Ren said quietly. He turned to me, looking quite perplexed. "You must let me learn to defend myself. You must!"

"But your elder speaks for all of Meadsins. Would you go against his advice?" I asked. I wanted Ren to learn defence. I wanted them all to. But I did not want to upset the balance of a good village.

"It's my choice," Ren implored. "I would choose to defend my mate and children. I would defend them with my life. They *are* my life. You *must* let me learn."

I could feel Ren's angst. "Then yes, of course you must learn," I assured him. "If you are sure that's what you want."

"It is," Ren replied, his eyes set with determination. "And I'll spread the word among the other villagers. Temar is a good man, but it is only fair that in this matter we all have the choice. If I can find more, when and where would you want us?"

I was not sure on that point. I looked to Tarrian.

"In ten days, kutu will come to the centre of the village to collect any who wish to be trained," Tarrian instructed. "You will be given weapons and shown how to use them for three days. If time permits we will arrange further training sessions after this."

"Ten days," Ren affirmed to himself. "Thank you. Thank you both."

188

Tarrian nodded, caught a hold of my waist and, without further ado, launched us into the sky.

We headed straight for the next village. Tarrian and I followed the same procedure, locating the person who spoke for the village, and holding a discussion with them. The conversation with this village elder did not go well either. I understood the reluctance. The thought of war scared me too. But Ren's courage had inspired me. So this time, at the end of the conversation, I changed my words. I told him that it was his duty to ensure every villager had choice in such a grave matter. I told him that he had no right to claim this choice for himself. Reluctantly, he had to agree.

I left the village exhausted. My heart heavy at being the bearer of such dismal news. The village elder couldn't get me out of the village quick enough. I felt decidedly unpopular. Nevertheless, I valued their lives; I would tolerate it.

It was already growing dark, but I still had many villages to work through. Tarrian moved us on and I tackled another village, and then another. I excused the late hour, and my intrusion to their rest, each time we entered the abode of another spokesperson. I grew so tired that sometimes I fell asleep as I talked. It did not do the meetings any harm. In fact, the lateness of the hour and my exhausted state seemed to better impress upon them the gravity of the situation. Eventually, dawn was breaking and I was spending more time trying to wake myself than actually staying awake. Tarrian made the decision that I must rest.

The next thing I knew, I was awakening to a bright mid-morning. I was still fully dressed, in my room, on my recliner, with a blanket carefully wrapped around me. I must have slept the entire journey home and the entry into the temple.

As much as my body did not want to move, I made myself rise from my bed and checked for messages on my communication port. Tarrian had left a message stating that we would commence with the next batch of villages again that day, from mid-afternoon. There was nothing from Jychanumun.

The anxious knot in my stomach seemed to awaken along with my flesh. That horrible feeling had become a constant companion. Needing to keep busy, I picked up some food and went outside to see Meah.

Meah came to meet me at the forest's edge. I ruffled her fur as soon as I saw her and we played for a short while. From the forest's edge, I noticed muddied and tired kutu returning to the temple. They were changing shifts. I left the remainder of my breakfast to Meah and hurried to catch up with the kutu who were about to leave.

In front of the temple gates the fifty Anumi were preparing to leave for battle training, even though they had all already done a full day's work on the fortifications. Most kutu journeyed by their own wings, but some were allocated to carry items in pods. I noticed an assortment of bladed weapons and unusual armour neatly stacked in the back of each craft.

I caught my breath. For a moment, by the pods, I thought I was seeing Nigh-kutu warrior. It was Jychanumun.

Jychanumun looked very different. His hair was slicked back from his face, which was painted with black marks down one side. The marks appeared to be symbols, although they were none I recognised. His torso was bare except the wide bands of strapping crossing his body, each interwoven with multitudes of narrow metal throwing blades. His usual sarong had been replaced by sturdy black trousers, each leg concealing a knife with only the haft showing, its polished metal glinting in the sunlight. His habitually bare feet were now clad in heavy boots, and his lower arms were encased in matt-black armour. Although he still wore his upper armlets, his arms and shoulders were striped with what looked like liquid metal, a type of fine kutu shielding. With his black wings, weapons and armour, Jychanumun looked more like a Nigh-kutu than ever.

Jychanumun finished talking to Stanze, and then walked towards me.

"If you have time, you should watch and learn. Soon you will train too."

I agreed with Jychanumun that observing the training was a good idea. In truth, I had hoped to be asked. So, having made one last check of the weaponry in the crafts, Jychanumun took us both, by wing, to an area of green flats beyond the valley.

Stanze and several Anumi were already waiting in the area designated for battle training. The remainder of the Anumi soon arrived, taking positions in a circular formation according to Stanze's wordless directions. Once all were present, Jychanumun took over, walking into the centre of the circle.

"Invert your wings," Jychanumun instructed. "Contain your energy for maximum efficiency during training."

The Anumi immediately complied.

Jychanumun continued, talking in short but effective terms about what he was going to do and how he was going to train them. The speech did not last long. He decided that a demonstration was the best explanation. He picked two kutu at random, summoning them to stand in front of him.

"Attack me," Jychanumun instructed.

Neither of the Anumi moved. They just looked at him, unsure.

"Fight me, attack me," Jychanumun repeated, beckoning them towards him.

The two Anumi moved forward, bracing their double swords. They went in for a tackle, but even I could see it was half-hearted. Jychanumun matched them both, driving them backwards with several swift knife thrusts.

"Stop," he instructed them, lowering his weapons. He shook his head. "Do you think the Nigh-kutu will be so feeble in their attack? If you do not fight me, and fight me properly, next time, I will cut you both."

The Anumi looked surprised at Jychanumun's words.

"But we are Anumi warriors. What if we harm you?" one of the kutu asked.

"You will not harm me," Jychanumun growled. It was definitely a growl. "Look," he pointed to a section of warriors: each was holding a healing rod at the ready. "They are all waiting with healing rods. I do not think it is I who will need their use. Now attack me. I will not ask again. Fight now!"

The two Anumi launched forward, with more vigour this time. Jychanumun moved at a speed that almost made me dizzy. Clasping a short blade in each hand, not only did he fend the two Anumi off, but he attacked with such great force that the two had little choice but to concentrate on defence. The Anumi increased their momentum and, as they did, Jychanumun counter-balanced their actions, always keeping ahead of their moves and in the superior position. Jychanumun alone was a more dextrous fighter than these two strong and skilled warriors together. It was a side of him that I never knew existed.

I watched and absorbed the way Jychanumun worked. The remarkable thing was that he did not fight with his body. He fought with his mind. As Jychanumun fought, his body simply manoeuvred in response, skilfully weaving around his opponents as if he were a blade of grass in the wind. His feet and arms moved like a dancer's, gliding smoothly into place, allowing his hands to strike with sudden shifts that would be impossible to mimic in a human body.

I opened my true vision to watch Jychanumun's moves. His energy wove around him, gliding around the two warriors, sensing their intent so that he could avoid their thrusts and attack their vulnerable points. It was as if Jychanumun knew their next move before they made it.

The two Anumi fought well. Although they were constantly overpowered, they gave it their all. Jychanumun did not cut either of them and I was glad of it. When the first demonstration was finished, Jychanumun bowed to them both and I saw a look of respect on every Anumi's face.

Jychanumun did not rest, nor did he let any of the warriors rest.

"War does not schedule for Kiyala breaks," he told them, when they suggested he take a moment to catch his breath.

After several more rounds of demonstrations, Jychanumun divided the Anumi into groups of three, each taking turns to fight in pairs while the remaining kutu attended to any cuts or bruises with a healing rod. And then he grouped them into fours, two against one and one to heal, each time rotating their roles.

The Anumi were fast learners. In a short space of time I saw them alter the way they used their minds and their energy, tuning to a higher sense so that they fought with their minds first and their strength second. It was an amazing transformation. I had seen the Anumi practice before now, and they were a fearful sight: well-trained warriors possessing great skill, strength and dexterity. But now, now they were something more. Now when they fought, they *were* the fight.

The afternoon passed quickly and although the Anumi were exhausted, they decided to continue training into the night. Only three would not continue. Tarrian was one, as he was appointed to escort me to the next batch of villages. I felt bad about this. It was clear that he didn't want to leave.

"Show me how to fly a pod," I suggested.

"It uses kutu energy. It will not work for a human," Tarrian replied. "Iastha Tachra, I am honoured to escort you."

"Yes of course. You would rather be carrying me around half the continent than learning valuable new skills," I replied. "Tomorrow, please choose another for the chore. It's only fair."

Tarrian went to object, but I would not hear of it.

After hesitantly agreeing, Tarrian and I wasted no time beginning the task of approaching villages again. We worked through the hot afternoon, past sunset, and deep into the night. One village blurred into the next, and then the next, my speech becoming more concise each time I made it. I talked until exhausted and even uttering a whisper made my throat feel as if I had swallowed sand. Tarrian was also faltering, although he denied his fatigue. I knew he'd not slept for several nights. Eventually, I made the decision that we should stop for the night. Tarrian needed rest. And me? There was something I wanted to do before morning. I wanted to see Chia. I was worried about him.

Tarrian left me at the place where the new buildings were being built. It was still dark and the area was dotted with light crystals. The glow effectively lit the entire vicinity, revealing trees, hillocks, and odd-looking rock formations. I thought the kutu would have selected flatter land. This looked like the most difficult place to build anything.

Part-formed buildings in various stages of completion already stood erected. I had expected the structures to be angular. Instead, they had irregular, rounded perimeters. They looked strong and solid, created from great boulders of stone and saturated with protective energy. On top of this, earth was shaped around them. Even trees and greenery had been placed on the mounds to make them look natural. I saw the objective. With the entrances concealed, these constructions would merely look like part of the landscape.

I found Chia working with a small group of kutu. He stood muddied, eye-ware pushed up above his eyes, guiding stones and technology into place. The kutu around him worked at a phenomenal speed. I had seen them work fast before, but they were now exceeding even that pace. They were tuned to be part energy and part physicality, their movements so fast that my eyes only saw a blur. Their strength was immense. They moved great stones, twice my height, with their bare hands, using their weapons to precisely dig and excavate as they distributed boulders into place.

Chia noticed me observing him and approached, rubbing his eyes. He was frowning. The expression had not left his face since Shursa had taken Orion.

Although tuned to high energy, Chia's usually vibrant eyes were lack-lustre and his wings barely there. He was beyond exhaustion and still not fully recovered from his wounds. If he did not rest soon, I knew he would surely collapse.

Chia stood beside me, looking around at the site.

"It is a sore choice when the greatness of our kind must be put to such a use," he remarked.

"That greatness clearly needs protection," I nodded. "Can I do anything to help?"

"I hear you are already doing more than anyone could ask for."

"It does not feel enough," I sighed. "Chia, are you well?"

"I am busy. We are building deep," Chia stated, avoiding the question. "We are creating tunnels and safe areas below the surface, at specific points all across the continent as well as here. They are for humans as well as kutu if the necessity arises. I hope not, but I must account for any eventuality." He pointed out an area of yet un-built upon landscape. "We still have a great deal to do. Over there will be another concealed barracks, all linked in to a central hub. Eskah! It should be closer to the trees."

He shouted some co-ordinates to a group of kutu, instructing them to redirect the excavation, and then turned back to me. "It will look natural. From the sky, no one will ever guess these are here . . ."

Chia stopped mid sentence, dropping his arm and looking at me.

"Why is this happening?" he sighed, shaking his head. "Why do these Nigh-kutu want to fight? What if they kill us all, what do they do then? What is their objective? Are they not the same as us? This all seems so illogical."

"I've thought the same," I agreed. "You Shaa-kutu travel to new worlds for new resources. Perhaps the Nigh-kutu are similar, but they see each other, and now Shaa-kutu, as potential resources too. Or perhaps fighting is just the way they've come to live."

"I feel so useless," Chia shook his head.

"Useless? Look at all this," I waved my hand across the huge expanse of buildings. "You do so much!"

"I do so much because I feel useless!" Chia exclaimed. "My powerlessness makes me angry. I must focus that anger, so I do this: shift dirt and rocks. But all my best efforts still may not be enough. Enough? Enough! Eskah knows I try, but it never seems enough! My enough did not help Orion. I doubt that my enough will help now, either!"

"It will," I assured. "You'll see. Orion is alive. If he is alive then he can be rescued. And we've fended off these Nigh-kutu once, so we can do it again."

"And then what?" Chia scowled. "They return in another five years? Or do we exist with the constant threat of the possibility? Is this defining the future course of our existence? Because I choose it not!"

Little jagged shafts of violet energy spat from Chia's mouth, embedding into the ground like daggers before dissipating. Chia's body shook with rage, his body bleeding out the little energy he still had. It trickled from his ears and his nose and dripped from his fingers onto the ground, like blood made of light.

Chia paused, gritting his teeth. "I am sorry, Tachra. I am not angry at you."

"Let it out. Be angry!" I replied. "I can cope. Holding in your feelings is not helping you; it's eating you away."

"I must contain it," Chia frowned. "But my mind is so fragmented I can barely concentrate."

"When did you last rest or sleep?" I asked. "You are exhausted. You need rest. You need a clear mind. We all need your clear mind."

Chia tried to interrupt, but I was not having any of it. "Chia, at this rate you will exhaust yourself to mindlessness before the next moon is due. What good will that be, for you, for anyone, for Orion? You must preserve your energy to focus your skills."

"I know," Chia nodded. He rubbed his brow, smearing the dirt even more with streaks of escaping energy. "But I cannot find rest. Eskah knows I have tried."

"Right," I decided. "Whom do you hand over to when you do try to find rest?"

Chia indicated towards another, equally muddied kutu.

I called that muddied kutu over and insisted, despite Chia's protests, that he must assume responsibility until Chia's return. I then marched Chia to the small area that had been assigned for kutu rest. I made him lay down on a dusty, make-shift recliner and put his eye-ware back over his eyes, before covering him with both a healing sheet and a blanket.

Chia continued to insist that he could not possibly find any rest, but I gathered energy from the heart of the earth and sent him the peace of the Old One's energy. I watched as his tenseness loosened, and it took only moments for his protests to quieten. Within seconds, Chia was in a deep, natural sleep.

I quietly left the area, giving strict instructions that he was not to be roused unless the matter was urgent.

I walked to a nearby small hillock to find some rest myself. The elevated view gave a good view of the building work being done. I watched the kutu work with great momentum. From within the blur of movement, a kutu would occasionally stop, calculate his next move, and then fulfil that task at a ferocious speed, weaving around the others with tools or rocks, moving items into position. When several worked in one area, it looked like a mass of movement upon movement. In many ways, it looked similar to their battle training. They were all tired and weary, but still they moved with precision, focus and strength.

When I opened my senses to the true vision, the weariness of all the kutu alarmed me. It was not just Chia who was beyond exhaustion.

Maybe I can help, I thought. I might never be able to wield a weapon like a kutu, or move boulders with my bare hands, but I had one or two of my own skills. Perhaps they could be of use.

I lay down on my belly so that I could be close to the earth, while my eyes never left the activity below me. Using my true vision I watched the energy of those working. At first, the extent of rapid movement made me feel sick, so I stopped trying to touch them all individually and just observed the blur of movement as a whole. Once accustomed to the rhythm of the flow, I picked out a particularly exhausted kutu who was repositioning a large boulder. I sent energy through the soil, pushing out and giving him strength. I felt his pace quicken as he rallied, suddenly able to push the heavy mass the last few inches into place.

I concentrated again on the blur of activity, preparing to select the most exhausted kutu to help. But all the kutu were exhausted. It wasn't just one or two needing immediate help, they all did. But I could only help one at a time. It would take all night. And what if this was a battle? Such a delay could mean life or death. I suddenly realised what it was that I now had to learn. I had to discover how to help several kutu at once.

I kept my energy linked to that first kutu, still giving him more much-needed strength, while my attention was drawn to another. A slim, fair-haired kutu was struggling to cover the buildings with earth and rocks. It was Gabriel. His energy was very low and his arm was hurt. There was at least one fractured bone, yet he still used that arm and clearly wasn't putting time into healing it. I had to try linking with Gabriel to heal his arm and give him strength, but I also wanted to keep my link open to the first kutu.

I tried creating two connections at once, but my concentration kept jumping from one kutu to the other. I could increase the speed, but I was still only helping one at a time. I was obviously not doing something right. The more I tried, the more frustrated I became. I had to learn to do this. If this were a battle, it could well save a life.

There was only one being that I could ask to help me in such a way. I severed all the links and closed my eyes. I would ask *him*, the Old One.

A warm breeze brushed through me. It felt as if my body was sinking into the soil. The Old One had felt my connection to him straight away. He must be sleeping lightly.

Again, little one? was all he said.

I disturb you, I am sorry. For a moment, I thought about retreating from his presence. But the need to learn this skill, if it were possible, held me firm.

I know you can touch all things, everywhere, I told him. *But why can my energy only touch one thing at a time?*

Little one, he responded straight away, *either come to me with real questions, or join me in eternal slumber where you will have all answers.*

But that was a real question, I replied. *It could save lives. If you always hear my thoughts, you'll already know that I hold this mortal life precious. I've eternity to spend with you. Be glad for me that I still have the choice of something else.*

You choose a lesser existence?

For now, yes, I replied. *You once told me that I made you remember the value of all life. Without this lesser existence, there would be no such thing.*

By the skies, I should shut myself up! Who was I to tell this great being such obvious things, and tell him as if it were my right to correct him? I stifled myself to silence.

But the Old One sensed these thoughts, too. I was grateful that he was not angry. He could snuff out my existence in an instant.

I'll find peace with you one day, I tried explaining to him. *I know that once I've joined you and felt that harmony, I'll never want a mortal life again. I know I'll wonder why I didn't join you sooner. But for now, I choose this mortal life, because the things that make this a lesser existence also make it precious.*

I understand, he replied simply. I could feel that he did. At that moment, I truly felt connected to him.

I sensed the conversation was over. His presence gradually pulled back from me.

You are like a river in your mortal life, I heard him say, his voice tailing off as it grew further away. *The forks in the river are your choices; they are also your thoughts, your energy, your direction. Little one, you already have the answers to your questions.*

And then he was gone. I could still feel his presence through the land. He had merely withdrawn from my mind, dormant once more in his dreaming.

I thought about his words. "You are like a river," he had said. "The forks are your choices."

The image of my beloved river was now fixed in my mind. I had walked along that course of water for months until it had led me to the lake in the valley. Along my travels, that river had forked many times, each time creating a choice as to my path. I had made a choice, only to be presented with another fork, another choice, and then another. It was the way of the land: each time the river created a new additional direction for the water, but without stopping any one path. And yet, although the river had many paths, it only had one source.

The realisation suddenly hit me. *The river is like my energy. I am the source!* It was a revelation to me. Suddenly, it all made sense and I was surprised I hadn't realised such an obvious thing before now.

I looked down at the working kutu once again, making a connection with one. I followed the flow of my energy, observing it like a line of iridescent light, as if it were a river spanning between us. I concentrated on creating a fork in that river of energy. It took a great deal of focus, but slowly, from the centre of that line, a new trail opened up. I retained my focus, directing the second line towards another kutu. I fed that kutu energy, pushing healing into his damaged hands, all the time retaining the first link I had made.

I can do this! I thought. It was just about repositioning my energy.

I created a third fork, directing strength to another who busied himself with heavy tasks. I kept that line open, too, creating yet another fork, pushing soothing thoughts, healing and strength into one who sat, exhausted, drinking water, yet refusing to take much-needed sleep. I felt him recover, stand up and brush himself down to get to work again. And then I created another fork, and then another and another. It made my mind spin, trying to keep so many connections open, but I knew I could learn to encompass more if I stayed focussed.

I was about to stop trying out my new-found skill, deciding that I would resume practice the following day, but then Jychanumun's words sprung to mind. "War does not schedule for Kiyala breaks," he had said. So, I pushed myself on and kept pushing, creating new links and sustaining them until my thoughts could barely hold themselves together.

I stayed there for the rest of the night, forcing myself to sustain the connections that I had made. I managed fourteen at once. It was the most exhausting thing I had ever done. By the time light started to fill the sky, I felt as though I had climbed a mountain and back.

Exhausted, and with a new day starting, I withdrew my connections from the kutu below me and rolled onto my back. I was too tired to sit and too tired to find somewhere more comfortable. I was so spent that I didn't even hear Chia's approach. Or perhaps I did hear his approach. Perhaps I was too mind-sore to care.

"That was remarkable," Chia stated, standing over me.

"You slept well?" I asked, not bothering to open my eyes.

"No. Well, yes, but not that," Chia replied. "Tachra, I sensed what you were doing. It was remarkable. It was like a cobweb of light, filled with good intent, each part touching one of the kutu."

"You saw it?" I asked, opening my eyes.

Chia was looking down at me, smiling. He certainly looked much better. His eye-ware was pushed up onto the top of his head and his eyes were almost back to their usual vibrant self.

"I sensed it," he stated. "I do not see as you do. I sense things."

"You look much better," I smiled, closing my eyes again.

"You don't," Chia laughed. "Come."

"I'm alright. It's comfy here," I sighed.

Nevertheless, Chia scooped me up with one arm, telling me he would return me to the temple to rest. I tried to protest. I really was quite happy just lying out on the ground on that hillock. I was so tired, I think I would have been quite happy lying anywhere.

The following day, after a brief patch of sporadic sleep, saw more villages to travel to, more people to speak to, more battle training to learn from, more energy training for me, more buildings being constructed, more language lessons and very little rest. I kept in regular contact with Soul and my family. I treasured stolen moments of solitude with Meah. The days started to roll together. No one seemed to have time for anything other than the necessities. There was no respite from the work or the worry.

The days crept by and turned into weeks.

The kutu knew it was time to accept they would not find Shursa's pod, yet still they searched. Jychanumun left for Eden1 and I worried for his safety. The humans began battle training and trained well. The new buildings became inhabited by most of the kutu and some of the humans in training. Meetings were held, strategies were formed and more and more weapons were made. My father came to train. Soul came too. Many women came. In fact, there were many more people wishing to learn how to defend themselves than I had ever expected. The buildings were complete and even I could barely distinguish them from their natural surroundings.

The weeks turned into months.

There had been no news of Shursa, Cain or Orion. There had been no declaration of war. Nothing changed, except that restlessness began to manifest itself. Humans started to return to their homes, taking their newly honed weapon skills and weapons with them. They returned to try to live their lives with their farms, their crops and their mates. Kutu threw themselves into training every minute that they were not resting, in order to quell the anxious anticipation. They too started to speak of the day when they hoped to return to Eden1.

As the days, weeks and months passed, the strain of the

constant threat of war started to take its toll. I could barely eat or sleep. It took much of my energy to remain focussed. I began to dislike everything that we had to do. I became insular to stop my tension affecting others, but saw this restlessness growing in everyone. I saw that waiting for war could be as destructive as war itself.

I did not welcome war. The thought of unnecessary suffering appalled me. But if war was going to come, a part of me wished it over and done with. Our anxiety was eating away at our spirit. But, I had made the choice to continue with this mortal life. And this mortal life was indeed precious to me. It was the beings that I loved that made it precious. No one had the right to take away their lives or their freedom. So, for the beings that I loved and all the wonders of this world, I would defend the Earth with my own life. For them, I was ready for this war.

TWELVE

Arrunn had called his three High Warriors to him. Mardoch, Dragun and Deimom now stood in his rooms, waiting.

"We leave at last light. Are your warriors ready?" Arrunn asked.

"Yes," the High Warriors replied in unison.

"As I would expect," Arrunn nodded.

Arrunn faced them with a box in his hands. Behind him, the wall of his room was transparent. The citadel beyond was now visible, emptied of the small, plump inhabitants that Arrunn had called his children. The scene of the empty citadel looked like a ghost town, with part-lived lives still evident in the half-eaten food and open doorways. Mardoch was relieved that his skills had not been called upon to help kill the creatures for their time energy.

Next to Arrunn stood a kutu the likes of which Mardoch had never seen before. It had taken all his discipline not to stare. This unusual kutu shone, illuminating the area around him. He was a kutu made of light. He was a Shaa-kutu.

Mardoch guessed that this Shaa-kutu must be the one that Arrunn had made a bonded promise with. Mardoch wanted to like him, simply because this one was from the race that his brother had chosen to exist among, but Mardoch had taken an instant dislike to him. Something about the demeanour of this yellow-haired Shaa-kutu made his skin crawl. This was not one to be trusted.

"This is Shursa of the Shaa-kutu. You are all to show him respect," Arrunn announced, as if sensing Mardoch's distaste. "He will be journeying with us. He is our guide through the light."

Shursa, Mardoch mulled the name over in his mind. The distasteful Shaa-kutu stood next to Arrunn, as if it was his right, and they, as the most superior of warriors were expected to respect him? It would be a difficult task.

"I expect all of you to protect this Shaa-kutu with your lives," Arrunn added. "This is the one who has made this possible. I have made a promise to him that will be fulfilled . . ."

"I'm going to be king," Shursa suddenly interjected, with a triumphant smile.

Arrunn paused, clearly displeased.

"Shursa, never interrupt me," Arrunn said coldly. "Yes, I have promised that you will be king of Eden1, but that does not make you my equal. Remember that."

Shursa very nearly said something, but managed to stay quiet, shuffling, looking around and then examining his fingernails disinterestedly. It was an offensive gesture and Mardoch could feel the bristling anger of the other High Warriors.

"We have here, in this box," Arrunn eventually continued, glancing down at the small box in his hands, "half our store of time energy. It has been compounded. You may wish to avert your eyes for this."

Arrunn opened the lid of the box. Suddenly the room was lit with a blinding light. Mardoch had to shield his eyes.

The room grew dull once again as Arrunn closed the lid once more.

"I require more time energy," Arrunn stated. "It would be illogical to spend years creating more creatures when we are ready to leave now. Therefore, I require kutu to offer their lives. Kutu time energy is potent, so I do not require many. I only require four."

Mardoch's heart quickened. He concentrated on controlling the speed of his breathing so it did not show. Other than Arrunn and Arrunn's guards, there were four kutu present, including him. Were they to be expected to sacrifice their lives?

"Dragun?" Arrunn paused. He moved forward, offering out a small empty crystal to Dragun. "Choose four of your warriors and sacrifice their life-energy. Bring me the crystal once it is full."

Dragun hesitated. "Now?" he asked.

Arrunn glanced at him. "We leave at last light. When else would I mean?"

Dragun took the crystal and immediately left the room.

"Deimom," Arrunn directed his stare to the High-Warrior next to Mardoch, "you will be personally responsible for Shursa's protection. I had no use for the pilot, other than to add his life energy to this," he glanced at the box in his hands. "But our guest, Shursa here, does require looking after."

Arrunn performed a bow to Shursa. It was clearly a derisory gesture, but the Shaa-kutu seemed to delight in it.

"You will be king of Eden1, won't you, Shursa?" Arrunn asked.

"Shursa1," Shursa corrected him, smiling broadly. "King of Shursa1. I shall change the name."

For a second, Mardoch thought Arrunn would rip the Shaa-kutu's head off. Shursa had just corrected Arrunn. No kutu was permitted to do that. It was the second grave misdemeanour in a short span of time and Arrunn was clearly not pleased.

Arrunn had stopped his reflexes. Mardoch noticed him relaxing his hand from the haft of his sword.

"Also, I have another Shaa-kutu," Arrunn continued, ignoring Shursa. "Mardoch, this one is for you to monitor. I want this one constantly accessible to me. I will not be leaving him here."

Arrunn gestured to one of the guards. The guard promptly left the room.

A few moments later, the guard's footsteps returned, accompanied by slow, soft shuffles. The guard reappeared. He was shouldering the strangest kutu Mardoch had ever seen. If his bright, scarlet red hair was not extraordinary enough, his red eyes and flickering red energy were unlike any kutu he had ever seen. He was a pure red. Kutu were not thought to be able to be of pure red energy.

This red-haired kutu was a mess. His pallid skin was slick with sweat and his long, raggedy hair matted and clung to his damp, bare chest. He could barely lift his head; it rolled around on his shoulders, unable to support itself. Drool trickled from his mouth as he opened and closed it, as if trying to speak. In the centre of his forehead was an embedded crystal. It was one of Arrunn's crystals, the flesh around it still raw and weeping from its deep incision.

The guard let the red-haired kutu go, reassuming his position on one side of the main door. The red kutu slumped down to the floor. He clearly did not have enough energy to stand of his own accord. The yellow-haired one, Shursa, seemed to enjoy the broken state of his fellow kutu. And, as the red kutu slumped onto his side, Mardoch noticed half a dozen crystals and black tubes looping in and out of his spine.

"This one, the Shaa-kutu call Orion. Our legends call him the Dhasmiel. He is, as you see, composed of red energy. He is useful to me," Arrunn stated.

Orion? Dhasmiel? Mardoch's mind spun. Hadn't he heard the name Dhasmiel in their legends, before they were confiscated from the libraries? Cranun had told him stories about it. Was Dhasmiel not the one prophesised to create something of significance in the future? The one to create a word, or a name, or a song to awaken all things? Mardoch made a mental note to revisit and rejuvenate these memories in private.

"Mardoch," Arrunn glanced towards him, "this red kutu will be in your charge. He will be accompanying us through to the light. Make arrangements for his protected transportation. He must be protected, at any cost. Understood?"

"Understood," Mardoch nodded. "I will guard him with my own and my warriors' lives."

Arrunn nodded towards on of his guards. The guard left his position and unfolded a section from the wall. A kutu-sized, sturdy matt-black box, slid from its hold, gliding into place, suspended horizontally above the floor.

Arrunn picked a silver band of metal from the centre of the kutu-box and handed it to Mardoch. Mardoch had no idea what it was, but could not ask. Ignorance was not acceptable in any circumstance. The band appeared the appropriate size for a wrist, so Mardoch quickly slipped it over his hand. It fitted perfectly. Arrunn's expression did not change. Mardoch had done the right thing.

"The band connects you to the transport box; for Orion. He is in your charge now," Arrunn stated flatly. "You have control of the box. It is your duty to bring the red kutu to me whenever summoned."

Mardoch nodded in affirmation.

"And to Shursa . . ." Arrunn stated, turning around to look at the yellow-haired one.

Shursa looked back at Arrunn attentively. He had a strange look in his eye, a mixture of obedience, worship and submission.

Mardoch despised this kutu, but something about him invoked a strange pity.

Arrunn lifted his hand, as if to gently wipe something from Shursa's face. And then, in one swift move, Arrunn clasped the back of Shursa's head and drove his thumb hard against his forehead.

Shursa shrieked in pain, staggering back, holding his head in his hands.

Arrunn let Shursa go, giving him a slight shove away.

Shursa fell backwards.

Shursa, still shrieking, sprawled on the floor. He let go of his head, putting his hands in front of his face, staring at his own bloodied palms in disbelief. He looked up at Arrunn, back at his bloodied hands, and then tentatively touched his forehead. Now, in the centre of his forehead, was an embedded crystal. It was set in deep and already glowing, the connections already made to his flesh and energy. The crystal could not be removed without death. Shursa shrieked again when he felt the foreign object in his head.

"Shut up," Arrunn commanded. His voice and face were calm, yet filled with power.

Shursa's shrieks immediately lessened to a whimper.

"When you are king," Arrunn stated coolly to Shursa. "It will still be called Eden1. Never interrupt me and never correct me, because I am never wrong."

Arrunn turned his back to them all. The meeting was over.

"Leave," he stated. "Take your wards. I will see you all in the arena at last light."

Mardoch took two strides forward and lifted the red-haired kutu, Orion, placing his cold body into the transport box. Orion did not put up any resistance. The Shaa-kutu was clearly no longer capable of doing so. Having sealed the box and ensured maintenance systems were activated, Mardoch marched from the room. The box glided along beside him. As Mardoch walked, he knew he now had someone important in his keep. He just wasn't sure if this new possession was something to save or destroy.

Mardoch decided to return to his room for some brief solitude, to think, before they all had to leave. He needed to decide what to do with this new cumbersome object. He also still needed to come up with a plan that might work now that all three divisions of warriors would be heading into this war. He had but a quarter of a day left to come up with that new plan. So far he had racked his mind and thought of nothing that could work. Time was running out.

The tunnels on route back to Mardoch's quarters were quiet, the rooms that he passed even quieter. Most of the warriors were already congregated in the arena. Mardoch could imagine their highly charged, bristling energy as they methodically checked their weapons and dulled their armour while they waited in anticipation. This is what they existed for. This is what they loved. For a while Mardoch had believed that he loved it too. But now, remembering his origins, having a greater cause to fight for, war for the sake of power seemed so pointless.

Having manoeuvred the transport box containing Orion into his room, Mardoch sat in darkness on the one solitary chair. The chair's broken legs and back had been mended a hundred times. Its seat was almost worn through. It was unrecognisable as the beautifully carved and painted wooden throne it once had been, yet it still held firm. Mardoch felt just like that chair.

"I have my suspicions about you," a voice came from the darkness.

Mardoch froze. He could hear breathing. It was coming from the far corner of his room. Mardoch quietly stood, put one hand on the hilt of his sword and with the other reached out and partially illuminated the room.

Standing in the corner was Dragun. He had his arms crossed and his eyes narrowed. He was alone.

"Suspicions? How dare you?" Mardoch growled, placing his other hand on the second hilt, ready to draw both swords.

"You fight too well. You sense too much. Who are you really?" Dragun asked.

"Do not misdirect your own incompetence in battle into questions about me. You wish to challenge me?" Mardoch moved forward a step. "I accept your challenge."

"As would I," Dragun laughed scornfully. His eyes looked wild.

Mardoch kept close attention on Dragun's hands, knowing the warrior could move and lunge with the speed of darkness.

Dragun slowly unfolded his arms, putting both his hands on the hilts of his own short swords, and moved forward a step.

"I ask again; who are you really, Mardoch?" Dragun paused. "Are you High Warrior to Arrunn-kin. Or are you really what my eyes truly see, the protector from the Walker clan? Tell me Mardoch, where does your allegiance lay?"

Mardoch caught his breath. Dragun knew! He knew who Mardoch really was!

Instinctively, Mardoch pulled out his sword, lunging forward, holding the blade against Dragun's throat. Should he just kill Dragun now?

Dragun let out a short laugh. "You think me scared of death? Your actions speak greater than any answer you could give. You could have ordered me executed for slander, if I were wrong. Mardoch, who is obviously of the Walker clan, I suggest you look down."

Mardoch quickly glanced down without relaxing his hold. There, pointed towards his central core, ready to pierce the very heart of his life energy, was a short jagged blade. But this was no normal blade, and not standard Nigh-kutu weaponry: it was made of Axiona. Mardoch had not seen a blade like that in many millennia. Blades such as that had been confiscated long ago. Blades such as that could pierce his armour and go straight through him.

What the High Warrior Dragun held was a traditional blade of the Weaver clan. Each blade was made by a Weaver at his point of ascendance in learning his art. Each Weaver would only ever make one, and only a Weaver could wield his own blade. The Weaver clan had been a good, honest clan. They were a clan that could blend energy and substance using just their hands. They could weave time with scents, memory with water, energy with stone, emotions with the inanimate; they could weave many things that would not normally exist together. They had been a peaceful clan. They had been considered allies of the Walker clan. But Arrunn had killed every living Weaver, displaying their severed hands for all to see. So surely Dragun wielding a Weaver blade was not possible; the Weaver clan were considered dead.

"So who are you really?" Dragun asked again, pressing the dagger a little harder against Mardoch's armour.

It was in that instance that Mardoch took a risk. He trusted his instinct. He trusted that shadow memory in the back of his mind that would not form, and then uttered a word that had not left his lips since arriving in Immorah.

"Walker," Mardoch whispered in Dragun's ear.

"And I am Weaver," Dragun whispered back.

For a moment, all the two Nigh-kutu could do was stare at each other in astonishment. Two remnants from the oldest allied clans still lived.

Dragun took a step backwards, showing his blade and then placing it inside an invisible tuck in his amour. Mardoch reholsterd his swords. He did not know if he was smiling. He was still too shocked to smile, or at least too shocked to be aware of his facial expressions, but Dragun started laughing to himself.

"Eskah smiles upon us. A Walker and a Weaver still live," Dragun smiled.

"How did you know?" Mardoch asked.

"I've had my suspicions for a few weeks," Dragun replied. "I was a Weaver; a Rock Weaver. I can still feel the changes of things from the stone all around us." He placed his hand lovingly on the solid stone wall. "I felt Cranun's death. The stone told me the truth of who he really was, and that made me pay more attention to you." He indicated to the crystals in Mardoch's hair. "They are not just stones. Now I look, they also tell me many things."

"You hear them?"

"No," Dragun shrugged. "I merely sense them. As a Rock Weaver, I can separate energy from matter."

Mardoch was relieved. Only a Rock Weaver could do such a thing. It was not something any other Nigh-kutu could do. The spirits of his brothers remained safe.

Mardoch checked the corridor outside his room. Like all the other rooms, it was still empty. "Very well, Dragun of the Weaver clan," Mardoch nodded. "So I know who you are, and you know who I am. What do you want, and what do we do now?"

"The red-haired kutu must be protected," Dragun indicated towards the containment box containing Orion. "He cannot go back to Arrunn's hold. His own kind may call him Orion, but he is undoubtedly the Dhasmiel. Legends say that the Dhasmiel can summon the heart of all things. That, I believe, is Arrunn's intent."

"Why, in Eskah's name, would Arrunn want to do that?" Mardoch asked.

"Are you blind, Walker?" Dragun look incredulously. "Arrunn has spent millennia looking for the heart of all things, to be conscious within it, because only then can he end all life and retain his link to the heart; he would be whole, perfect. I have heard Arrunn refer to all living beings as imperfect and flawed. Do you not see how much Arrunn dislikes imperfection, how much he dislikes life, us, any living thing? Is that not why you became High Warrior too, to be of use to Arrunn for as long as possible and to avoid death for as long as you can? He only keeps us alive now because we are still of use to him."

Mardoch stood in shock for a moment. "I know our world is fated to die unless something changes," he eventually replied. "I know because my brother, the Death-Walker, told me. But I did not know how or why that fate was to occur. I just know Jychanumun intended on trying to change that fate."

"No wonder Arrunn wants Jychanumun captured so badly," Dragun frowned. "Well, if death continues to be our fate, by Eskah I will do my best to delay it. I like life," he added. "Which means keeping this red kutu away from Arrunn."

"And Jychanumun."

"Yes, and Jychanumun. Although that one is currently out of my hands. This one however," Dragun nodded towards Orion in the transport box, "I could do something about."

"You would be discovered."

"I won't be around to be discovered."

"You are going to leave?"

"Eskah yes!" Dragun exclaimed. "I shall take the opportunity when we are through the light to escape. I will not fight these Shaa-kutu. I can stomach our Nigh-kutu to Nigh-kutu warring now, because that is the code that we all live by. But I will not wage war on those who would otherwise live in peace. It is not right. But if fate says we are to die as a whole anyway, then I'll do what I can to delay it and then try to live whatever time is left in some sort of peace. Perhaps I will find a nice deserted rock planet and just live out my remaining time there."

"But fate *can* change," Mardoch protested. "Jychanumun *is* the Death Walker. He can change that fate. Let us both find my brother and help him. He has found the world he always spoke about, where kutu do exist in peace for life. I agree that we cannot let Arrunn destroy them all too. Join me, Dragun. Let the Weaver clan and the Walker clan work together once again. We could help to make a difference."

Mardoch halted his speech. Every word he had just uttered was treacherous towards Arrunn-kin, punishable by death, and he knew it.

Dragun walked forward a step, his face grave. He suddenly broke out in a wide smile and slapped Mardoch on the back.

"Walker, I had hoped that you would say that," Dragun smiled. "I have an idea. It is not a perfect idea, but it is a start."

So Mardoch and Dragun talked. They talked for as long as they could and covered as much as they could in the short space of time that they had. Dragun was right; his idea was not a perfect idea. They could not stop the war entirely and undoubtedly there would still be bloodshed. But it *was* a plan, which, with Dragun's help, was more than Mardoch could have concocted.

Dragun knew how to conceal the red kutu and how to remove the traceable crystal in his forehead using his skill with stones. Mardoch would be able to connect with Jychanumun, once they had passed through the gateway into the light. And Dragun had something else, something he had carefully stolen many millennia ago midst the chaos of battle, over two-dozen whole time crystals. Arrunn was now not the only kutu who knew how to activate time crystals. Now there was also Dragun.

Dragun's plan was not flawless. Neither was any part of this plan a certainty. But at least it was a plan, and one that was, at last, about making a stand for the right reasons. Mardoch and Dragun, a Walker and a Weaver, would stand side-by-side once again. They would stand for peace, justice, choice and life. And if they had to make the choice, they would fight with those who chose life. They would join the Shaa-kutu.

THIRTEEN

It was at exactly high moon when the terrible news came. That moment will be etched in my mind forever.

I had chosen to stay in the temple so I could stay close to Meah. She had grown fat and lethargic of late, and refused to leave either the temple or its grounds. I had spent the evening learning more of the Nigh-kutu language with Meah asleep on the table, hogging the entire space while I sat with my books on my lap. I had eventually found sleep, early in the evening of the fourth day of no rest – it was a relief.

I awoke abruptly, to a loud pounding on my door. The pounding had become part of the dream I was having, yet another dream of shadows and fear. I shot up, suddenly aware that the pounding was real. I could hear shouting too. I knew instantly that something had happened. For a brief, naïve moment, I hoped that it was news saying that they'd found the pod with Orion safely onboard.

I ran to the doorway, feeling nothing even as I stubbed my foot hard on a chair.

"They have hit Eden1," Chia gasped, catching his breath as if he had been flying frantically.

"Nigh-kutu?"

Chia nodded, his eyes wide.

"Jychanumun?" I asked.

"Alive," Chia replied. "Fighting. Passing news via the HOTS. Most communications from Eden1 have collapsed."

"Collapsed?" I asked, my heart beating so hard it could have burst from my chest.

"Yes, it is bad. There are thousands of Nigh-kutu fighters. More than expected. They just appeared from nowhere. The surprise attack meant we lost half our warriors almost immediately. It is mayhem."

Thousands of them? Mayhem? I felt the blood drain from my head. My vision narrowed and the world seemed to be falling away from me. I put my hand up to touch something, to steady myself, grabbing hold of the door's edge.

Damn body, don't you give in on me now! I cursed my feeble flesh.

"What's to be done?" I asked.

Chia had already marched into my room.

"Where is your bag of spare clothing? I asked you to prepare items for leaving here," Chia's tone was anxious.

"Here," I pulled out a small bag, pre-packed with a few of my necessary possessions.

"It is time to come with me to the fortified buildings," Chia stated.

"I'm staying here. I'll be safest here," I replied. "I know this area better than anywhere."

"No," Chia stood, shaking his head. "You must be with us. Tachra, we may need your earthly ways. You may certainly need us to protect that human body of yours. You must come with me."

"No, no," I protested. "I will not leave Meah."

"Meah will be fine," Chia insisted.

No, I thought. Meah is the one thing I cannot chance to lose.

"I'll not leave her," I repeated. "I cannot. She's not been well of late."

"She is not sick," Chia hurried, raising his hands in disbelief. "She is with cub."

With cub? My thoughts faltered. I should have known. It seemed so obvious now. But right now, to me, it was even more reason why I should not leave her.

"I don't want to leave her. I can't," was all I could say.

"Tachra," Chia said gravely. "You can and you will. Believe me, Meah will be safer without human or kutu close to her, including you. It is only temporary. You will always have that connection to her; you can still go to her in mind. She knows the forest. It is her home. A wildcat and cub will need their forest, not a building. If you want to keep her safe, then you *must* leave her for a short time."

It felt terrible. I knew Chia was right. Meah could and would be safer without me close to her if the Nigh-kutu came here. I loved Meah. I didn't want to leave her, but I loved her so much that I knew I had to. It was in her best interest. I took solace that it would only be for a short while.

Meah seemed to understand what was being said. She had leapt from the table and now prowled anxiously by the exit to the forest, wanting to leave the room.

I went and knelt beside her.

"It's that time again," I told her. "I must leave for a while. You understand; you must not follow. Stay safe in the forest. Stay safe. I'll be back very soon."

Meah pushed her head against my face. We had been here before, Meah and I. She knew I would return.

I opened the door from my room and Meah strolled away, into the depths of the forest. A large wildcat, a male, was already out there waiting for her. She didn't stroll past him this time. She walked directly to him. Together, they disappeared into the darkness.

With Meah in the safest place, I picked up my bag, grabbed the portable communication panel that was linked to Soul and my family, and ran from the temple with Chia.

A pod waited directly outside. It was merely two strides from door to craft. Stanze was behind the controls and I leapt into the small available space behind him, jamming myself between stacks of metal boxes. Stanze wasted no time launching the pod, with Chia following close behind.

I tried connecting to Jychanumun's mind during that short flight. Jychanumun sensed me. I briefly felt his focus amidst great turbulence, but it was for a mere fraction of a moment before he blocked me from his thoughts. I sent my family and Soul, via the stolen kutu communicator, the single prearranged symbol so that they knew to be extra vigilant.

The pod flew directly to the fortified buildings and straight into a concealed entrance. The entrance closed behind us, leaving us encompassed in pitch black. Automatically, several guide lights switched on, illuminating a large craft-hold containing several pods and two small dispatch crafts.

Chia caught up with the pod as I climbed out. Stanze left immediately, returning to the darkness and his warriors outside. He and his warriors had trained for this. They would now be in place, pocketed together in small concealed groups, in positions of strategic necessity, watching and waiting.

Chia directed me from the craft-hold, pointing to one of the sealed doors. Without a word he opened the door, showing me the simple yet heavy locking system and energy barrier.

"How is Eden1 faring?" I asked, as Chia led me down a dimly lit tunnel.

"Not good. They are holding, but only just. They cannot cope with any more."

"Will the Nigh-kutu attack Earth too?" I asked

"I do not know," Chia replied. "Every kutu here has his energy and body concealed. If it is kutu they are after, this planet will appear empty of us."

"They will attack Earth," I thought aloud. "Shursa will direct them here."

"Which is why you needed to leave the temple," Chia said simply.

I followed Chia down a long, steeply sloping passageway that led underground. After several twists and turns, he turned into a shadowy alcove, disappearing from sight. I followed him, the darkness opening up into a huge, low-ceilinged chamber.

On each wall of the octagonal chamber were many huge screens. There were hundreds of them. On every screen was a picture, and each picture constantly changed: stars, hills, forests, grassland, deserts, villages. It seemed that from here I could watch the world and its skies.

"I am a sensitive, but a little equipment can be of great help too," Chia remarked.

"Can you see Eden1?" I asked.

"Yes," Chia stated. "It is not something that I recommend you see. I will show you to a room where you can sleep."

I sensed Chia's anxiety. I sensed that he had already seen terrible things on those screens. I sensed that he did not want to put me through that. I did not want to see the kutu warring, but I needed to. I needed to see so I could learn how to help.

"I must see too," I insisted. "I can cope. I have seen a man's flesh fall from his skin, as he burnt alive. I have seen inside warped minds and the evil that they think. If I am to know how I can help if the Nigh-kutu arrive here, then I must see."

"It will hurt to watch, knowing that you can do nothing," Chia sounded as if he knew too well how that felt.

"I will cope," I whispered. "I have to."

Chia pointed to a screen. The image of scrubland littered with sparse trees suddenly changed. At first, I could not tell what I was looking at. Flashes of bright light against a pitch black sky raged like the greatest storm. Something flew towards the screen and an energy bolt exploded. I winced as if expecting the screen to explode, but the picture remained.

Chia changed two and then three more screens on one wall, all showing different views. These images were closer to the battle and each scene was different. I could tell straight away that the Anumi warriors were vastly outnumbered. Their armies were fragmented into groups that needed to work together if there was to be any hope of success. Most of the Shaa-kutu were not warriors, although I saw many fighting.

I looked at the first screen. There, the bulk of the Anumi warriors still held together. Great crowds of black-winged Nigh-kutu, thousands of them, surged back and forth, trying to break the line. In front of them was a double line of Anumi, holding off their attack. Energy flashed through the dark sky above them as they propelled bolts of might. With each attack, the line of Anumi deflected and quickly reformed. I saw the line curve, some of the Anumi throwing bolts of energy in a second direction. Another advancing mass of black-winged was drawing closer.

"That," Chia pointed to a dark area of sky without any stars, "is where the Nigh-kutu arrived from. It was suddenly just there, and they marched through. And then another lot, twenty-five or thirty thousand of them, all warriors."

There was a tiny glimmer within the dark spot. I was about to ask Chia what it was, but Chia was already ahead of me.

"Eskah, no! There are more of them. More come! We cannot cope with more!"

The tiny spot within the dark gateway flashed. From within the light I could see forms. The forms grew larger and more distinct. It was more Nigh-kutu! Thousands more of them.

Chia put his hand to his ear, speaking aloud through his HOTS so that I could hear too.

"Yes, more. Quantity; I am not sure . . ." Chia touched the screen on the wall, trying to estimate the numbers. "It is another formation. Similar size as before. Yes, between ten and twenty thousand. What do you mean? There may be more after this? Eskah's oblivion! Jychanumun, if you can, tell Una to make defence priority. Safeguard the inner core!" He nodded animatedly. "Yes, she is here. No, I won't. Yes, I will, yes . . . Jychanumun . . . Jychanumun?"

Chia stopped communicating and moved in towards the screen. "Eskah's damnation," he muttered. "What is he about to do?"

Chia activated all the screens, turning around, scanning the image on each one. He stopped on one image. Suddenly, a Nigh-kutu flew past at a tremendous speed, black wings fully expanded, leaving a trail of white and black light. He was wearing black and gold armour. I recognised that kutu. It was Jychanumun!

Over a dozen Nigh-kutu were close behind Jychanumun, flying after him with ferocious force, throwing jagged shafts of energy towards him. Jychanumun twisted and turned as he flew, dodging the hits and redirecting several of the shafts back at his pursuers. Suddenly he twisted, lunging towards the Nigh-kutu. There was a flurry of movement as Jychanumun wove around them. He wove so fast he was merely a blur. As he spun, the Nigh-kutu kept throwing shafts at him, but the shafts bounced off the spinning light, flinging the bolts back at them. Jychanumun suddenly stopped, and then moved around the Nigh-kutu in one swift loop. As he moved, he cut the throats of them all.

Jychanumun wasted no time watching the Nigh-kutu crumple. He had already set his sights on the formation that was now passing through that dark doorway.

Suddenly pausing, mid-air, I saw Jychanumun gather his strength, drawing in the energy around him, as if breathing in air. He rose higher as he did so, until he looked down at the opening in the cosmos and the legion of Nigh-kutu now passing through. He directed his gaze at one Nigh-kutu whose armour was different to the rest. He seemed to be leading this new formation of warriors.

Suddenly, Jychanumun beat his chest hard, let out a roar powerful enough to make the screen tremor, and then plummeted down towards the entire formation.

A blinding flash lit up the screen. For a moment I could see nothing.

"Turn it back on!" I shouted to Chia.

Chia ran to the central hub, working the invisible controls. "It is not off. There is nothing wrong with it," he panicked.

I glanced at the other screens. Nothing.

I waited. The hum of equipment and my own fast heartbeat sounded abnormally loud to my ears. The empty moment seemed to span forever.

Suddenly, one of the screens behind me started to flicker. Then another. And then another. I kept my eyes fixed on the one I had been watching. It shuddered. Finally, the image returned.

I did not know what had happened in that brief moment of darkness. Whatever it was must have been immense. The image now showed utter chaos.

Pieces of body floated through the air. Nigh-kutu were scattered, crumpled and unmoving. At least a half of the new regiment of Nigh-kutu had been destroyed. The remaining half seemed in turmoil. One uninjured Nigh-kutu started shouting something, opening his wings and rising above the remainder of this new group of warriors, shouting at them as if to reorganize them. Any Nigh-kutu who could rally, rallied. They regrouped and began marching forward again, pushing through the debris of their dead as they moved.

"Jychanumun? Jychanumun?" Chia repeatedly tried contacting him through the HOTS.

He turned to me, "Nothing. He is not responding."

For a moment the world froze. I opened my mind to him.

Are you alive? I tentatively searched for any sign of Jychanumun.

Yes. Silence, he replied. That was all he said – no more – but it was enough.

"He's alive," I told Chia. But I could not look at Chia. My eyes were drawn to the image on another screen.

A small circle of about twenty Shaa-kutu stood grouped together atop a high structure. Half were Anumi warriors, half were not. Light flickered around them in layers, multiple protective barriers designed to defend them within a multi-layered dome of light. They had a good position, able to see much and attack out at all angles. Above and around them were Nigh-kutu, hundreds of them. The Nigh-kutu swooped in unison, landing astride the outer dome of energy, striking at it with their fists. The energy shattered and the Nigh-kutu rose back into the sky, swooping down and breaking the next layer, and then the next.

The Shaa-kutu inside the dome threw energy at the dome of protection, adding more layers, but each time the layers were broken a little quicker than they were repaired. And each time the Nigh-kutu inched closer. The Anumi fired attacks from inside the dome. One hurled bolts of vibrant blue. A bolt hit a black-winged one and thrust him backwards, spinning through the air, his own

energy depleted, and a hole now through his side. Two Nigh-kutu
appeared from outside the screen and took his place, joining the
group for the next onslaught. Three Anumi crouched around the
outside of the small group with long, golden sonar rods balanced
on their shoulders. Huge pulses of colourless energy exploded
forth, launching into the Nigh-kutu. The Nigh-kutu crumpled,
only to slowly straighten, and then advance again.

A mutilated body drifted past the scene. It was without limbs
or head. Only the perfectly untouched chest plate told me it was
a Shaa-kutu.

"How long can they hold their position?" I asked Chia.

"This group has a strong combination of energy weavers and
defenders. They will hold for some time," Chia replied.

"Will the Nigh-kutu eventually break through?"

Chia said nothing. His silence was dreadful confirmation
enough.

"Some have breached the city defence," Chia gasped.

I glanced at the screen Chia was watching. Six black-winged
Nigh-kutu strode down a wide, white corridor. I gasped, noticing
that one carried the head of an Anumi in one of his hands. The
head still wore its golden helmet, the matted hair hanging down
in bloodied clumps.

From a doorway further down the corridor, three Shaa-kutu
emerged, all Anumi. They ran directly towards the Nigh-kutu, and
then suddenly stopped, completely still. The Nigh-kutu stopped
too. One of the black-winged ones, carrying a long sword, moved
forward a step. He lifted his sword, thrusting the tip hard into
the floor. A wave of pitch-black energy rolled forward like a
dark cloud. Just before the cloud hit the Anumi, however, it hit
something else. An invisible shield shuddered from the attack.
The three Anumi kneeled, working some boxes as they placed
them on the floor, moving back a step, placing more boxes, and

then another step, and more boxes. Each time they would activate something and another invisible shield would rise into place.

Once several boxes had been put in place and additional shields created, the Anumi stood and nodded to each other. They moved back a few steps and then launched forward at phenomenal speed, the shields allowing them to pass through.

The three charging Anumi hit the black-winged ones with force, flinging them back. The Nigh-kutu started to rise, drawing their weapons, but the Anumi leapt forward, blades in hand, attacking with terrible agility. Their hands were merely a blur and their feet danced, weaving around the counter attacks, using their wings to keep them balanced. I recognised this; this was the fighting method Jychanumun had taught them. The skills of the Nigh-kutu and the Anumi appeared equally matched, but this was three Anumi against six Nigh-kutu.

I wanted to keep watching, willing the Anumi to win, but my eyes were drawn to the horrors occurring on a different screen.

Four heavily armoured Nigh-kutu had cornered what first appeared to be a single Anumi warrior. I noticed that behind the Anumi was another badly wounded Shaa-kutu; he was unconscious. The Anumi was shielding him. I could just about see the face of the one being protected. I recognised him as Adreniel, an honourable councillor, a fair-haired, gentle spirited philosopher whom had spent several months at the temple.

The Anumi shielding Adreniel had lost a hand, the stump of his arm now oozing with blood and energy. Two broken-off serrated spears protruded from his side. Both had gone straight through him, and his armour was pierced and bent. More blood and energy seeped from under his chest-plate, staining his legs. He was no longer wearing his helmet, but a partial fragment of the golden metal was embedded into the side of his face, the gaping wound pulsating as it tried to heal itself and repel the metal.

The horrific situation made my heart stop, but it was the expression on the Anumi's face that made tears involuntarily stream from my eyes. He was trying so hard. He would fight to the death to protect his kind. His eyes shone with courage, honour and pain, while his jaw flexed with determination.

I recognised those eyes! My hand went to my mouth in horror. Although the injuries had initially made the face unrecognisable, I knew those eyes well. That Anumi was Peniva, wonderful Peniva, chief of all Anumi. Peniva had spent a great deal of time at the temple and was good friends with all the teachers, myself included.

The one-handed Peniva was drawing short blades from a holder on his thigh, flicking the blades with force and speed towards the Nigh-kutu, holding the black-winged ones back. As the blades moved, shafts of golden light flashed, propelling them towards their target. One Nigh-kutu was already peppered with blades, yet still stood, refusing to die. The Nigh-kutu standing next to him used his comrade's wounded body to shield himself as he approached Peniva, while using his other arm to deflect any curving blades. The two remaining Nigh-kutu followed him, slowly moving forward, quickly removing any shafts that struck them, and hitting away the remaining shafts with their forearms.

The lone chief Anumi battled on. His body should have collapsed by now, but his will and courage kept him going. His energy was almost spent.

I felt desperate to do something. *I must help Peniva! He needs healing. He needs strength!*

I pushed out my energy, soaring high above the Earth. I stopped momentarily, to sense my direction, and felt a ripple in all the universes as the battle raged its chaos far away. I thrust my consciousness towards the chaos. I had to help.

My concentration suddenly snapped. Chia was shaking me violently.

"NO!" Chia shouted. "You cannot do this. I have read your reports on your energy travels. Eden1 is too far. You would not be able to return to your body. You would be lost forever and unable to help any kutu. Stop this!"

"Peniva needs help," I protested.

"You will be of no help if you are dead and sleeping with the Old One," Chia scowled. "I warned that watching this would hurt."

I knew he was right. I didn't want him to be right. I hated him being right. I had to help. I could be of no help. I hated myself for my incapacity to do something. I shook myself free from his hold.

Chia went to turn off the images on the wall.

"No," I said, pushing his hand down. "I must see."

The four black-winged Nigh-kutu were now very close to Peniva. One of the Nigh-kutu was now peppered with shafts and unmoving as his cohort held him up as a shield. The brave Anumi had run out of short blades and now wielded a double ended sword, weaving it around in front of him to keep his attackers at bay. Suddenly, the three active black-winged ones leapt forward, thrusting shafts of black into his already badly wounded body. Peniva, head of the Anumi, injured beyond anything I had ever seen, grabbed hold of the unconscious councillor and tried to run, shaking himself free of the three Nigh-kutu who now clung to him and repeatedly hammered blades into his flesh. I saw Peniva stagger amidst splattering flesh and energy, yet still he tried to fight them off. He fell to his knees, shielding his wounded friend from the onslaught.

My heart felt as if it was breaking. I drifted towards the screen, reaching up and touching his image as if I could bring him to safety. The tears streaming down my face made the image blur.

"No, no, no. Help him," the words involuntarily escaped my lips. "Please help him. Somebody, anybody, please. Help him, just help him. Please. Please . . ."

The image went blank.

Chia had turned it off.

He sat with his back to me and hung his head, covering his face with his hands. His energy had darkened. It looked as if he was weeping.

I walked to Chia and wrapped my arms around him, sending all that I could muster from the earth around us to try to calm his pain, my pain, our pain.

"Peniva is my friend," Chia dried his eyes. Luminous violet liquid had streamed down his face. "So many have fallen. With each one, it feels as if a part of me dies. The Nigh-kutu have breached the city defences. We cannot win."

Chia looked at his hands, now stained with the luminous violet energy of his tears.

"What is this?" he asked, dismayed. The way he said it, he seemed to think that he was bleeding.

"You are crying," I explained.

"Crying?"

"Yes," I nodded. "It is when the heart has something important to say, but there are no words big enough. When words cannot cry out, the body does."

Chia shook his head, gritting his jaw. "Eskah! Focus, focus, focus, Chia!" he exclaimed. "We need a miracle. We are losing this war."

"The Earth's energy must be able to do something. Anything. Is it not worth trying to wake Him?" I fretted. I paced up and down. I could not keep still.

"You know it is not," Chia shook his head. "Risk ending all existence? Tachra, you know better!"

"Then could I not go to Eden1 to try and help?"

"Humans cannot exist beyond this world. You body would not survive."

"If I could save twenty, ten, even just one Shaa-kutu, it would be worth it."

"If we cannot win now, we never will. Your death would be in vain."

"That's not true! Even one saved would be worth it. Chia, they must live to fight another day! If we're losing, any that are left now will die out there if we don't do something different. We must think of something. Get them here. Any who are still alive, get them here so they can hide and heal in the tunnels you've constructed. Make them live and we can figure something out. Live to fight another day! Please Chia, please. Find a way to get them to a safe place."

Chia considered this for a fraction of a moment, and then spun in his chair, working screens and controls at a ferocious pace. "Eskah," Chia cursed. "I cannot do this quick enough!"

"Damn it Chia; tell me what to do!" I exclaimed.

"Tachra, you have kept me focussed. You are already doing more than you know."

Chia worked frantically. I paced. He worked more. I paced more. I could not stand still. My mind tried to focus but it didn't want to. I did not look at the terrible images that still filled the screens. They just numbed my mind and filled my spirit with pain. I had seen all that I needed to see in order to learn from the black-winged beasts. The slaughter and mayhem sickened my soul. The bravery and courage of the Anumi was so intense that my heart felt like it was bleeding. The Shaa-kutu were losing this war. Now it was about getting anyone out who could be saved.

The moments turned to minutes, and outside, the solitary screen that still showed Earth's skies above the temple indicated that dawn had broken.

"Eden1 has tunnels through its Memorite core," Chia eventually spoke as he worked. "Some Shaa-kutu will know of them. They will be adequate temporary safety points for those trapped and injured in the cities. I also have a good knowledge of many uninhabited planets that offer other safety bolts. Any too injured to fight outside the planet can make their way to, or be taken to, those safe places. I have sent messages and signals on every frequency. You are right, Tachra, if we cannot win now, we must live to fight another day. At the very least the injured must be provided with safe places to heal."

"A cat, no matter how hungry, does not attack an entire herd. It picks one off at a time. Even one kutu, working with precision, can gradually pick off many opponents."

Chia did not reply. He was too busy concentrating. Instead, he nodded. He knew what I meant.

Suddenly there was a loud pounding on the door to the hub.

Chia froze. I noticed the wary look on his face and sensed his unease. I automatically ran to my bag, pulling out my trusty knife.

"Every kutu here knows how to enter. They would not need to knock," Chia whispered under his breath.

He quickly changed the image on several of the screens.

The screens showed the corridors around the room we were in, plus the surrounding exterior of the building. Nothing seemed amiss outside the building, but by the door to this room, several shadowy figures now crouched.

One of the shadowy figures banged on the door again.

The image directly outside the door was too dark to ascertain exactly who and what was trying to get in. But one thing was certain. These were black-winged ones.

"Nigh-kutu!" I gasped quietly, as if they could hear me through the walls.

"I must be rid of them before they alarm their entire armies that we are here. Hide," Chia hissed.

I scanned the room for somewhere to hide, but the area offered nowhere for concealment. The chairs hovered above the ground, the screens were embedded in the wall, and the central controls rested on a stand that not even a mouse could find refuge behind. The only place I could think to hide was right behind the door when it opened.

I ran into position next to the door, feeling frighteningly exposed, with my knife at the ready. Chia drew out a pair of fine vapour daggers from their concealment in his boots and crept towards the door, putting his finger to his lips, indicating that I must be silent.

I looked at Chia, silently mouthing the word 'light' and then 'more light', indicating with my hand that he should make the room brighter. I had an inkling that the Nigh-kutu did not tolerate brightness as well as the Shaa-kutu did.

Chia understood. He immediately directed some energy towards the lighting until the room was flooded with a white brightness. He crept quietly towards the doorway, standing flat against the wall on the opposite side to me.

Quietly, Chia touched the handle of the door. The door glided open.

Three Nigh-kutu tumbled in together.

Chia leapt upon them, wielding his daggers in a torrent of energy.

Suddenly Chia stopped. He was poised mid-attack, astride all three, his blade touching the throat of one of the unknown Nigh-kutu. This Nigh-kutu, his black hair embedded with green gems, was carrying two others. Both were unconscious. One was a badly wounded Jychanumun!

"Heal him!" the Nigh-kutu gasped in his own language. "I am not enemy. Heal him. Heal them!"

I understood him! My lessons in Nigh-kutu had worked. I quickly translated for Chia and then, perhaps foolishly, I ran straight towards them, towards Jychanumun.

"Stay away!" Chia barked at me, stopping me in my tracks. "We cannot trust him! We can only trust Jychanumun."

"Move back there," Chia commanded to the conscious, gem-haired Nigh-kutu, his blade still at his throat. "Tachra, translate for this beast, and then fetch me one of the boxes from over there. Tell him to slowly move back against the wall."

I translated and then ran to get one of the boxes. The Nigh-kutu slowly moved backwards, pushing back with his feet without getting up. Chia kept his grip on the blade with one hand, holding it against the Nigh-kutu's throat, directing him backwards. Jychanumun and the unconscious stranger were left crumpled, motionless and bleeding, on the floor.

I took the metal box to Chia, holding it to him as he worked the catch and fumbled with the contents of the box with one hand. With his eyes never leaving the Nigh-kutu, Chia placed four small cubes from the box on to the wall, two by his feet and two above his head, driving them into place with his one free hand. An energy barrier immediately sprung into place, holding the Nigh-kutu against the wall like a shimmering second skin.

Chia beckoned me over, directing me to stand in front of him. He gave me his spare vapour dagger and positioned my hand so that I was holding it against the Nigh-kutu's throat too. I could feel the edge of the blade pushing against the skin. Only the invisible barrier stopped the dagger from drawing blood.

"Just to be safe, as I do not know how far their skills go, keep the dagger there. Do not let him move," Chia instructed, as he relaxed his own hand.

I held the knife in place, my arm stretched upwards, observing from the corner of my eye.

Chia moved Jychanumun and the unconscious Nigh-kutu from their crumpled state so that they could both lie flat. It was clear that Jychanumun's wounds were severe. Chia bent to him, wiping the blood from his face. I heard him gasp as more blood trickled from Jychanumun's closed eyes, as if the eyes themselves were bleeding. Chia wrapped healing sheets around him and placed repair discs over his eyes, moving on to inspect his gaping wounds, tending to the worst cuts with a healing rod. All the time the unknown, unconscious Nigh-kutu lay outstretched on the floor, bleeding profusely.

I could hear Chia talking quietly via his HOTS while he tended to Jychanumun. He was talking to Stanze. At first, he seemed relieved to hear Stanze's voice. It seemed he'd expected the worst, fearing that the lack of Stanze's intervention meant that he and his warriors had been killed or incapacitated. But Stanze was well. His warriors were well. None of them had detected any intruders.

With the skies so well monitored, Chia asked Stanze, how had this Nigh-kutu entered the building unseen, carrying Jychanumun and another wounded Nigh-kutu? From the half of the conversation that I could hear, it was clear that they both thought it was impossible. Stanze and his Anumi had good watch points. So, however this had happened, it was not something either of them was pleased about.

Chia informed Stanze of the full situation, telling him that he did not require assistance – all was now in hand. He would be in contact with an update shortly. With the conversation closed, and satisfied that Jychanumun was well tended to, Chia moved to the unconscious Nigh-kutu.

The unconscious Nigh-kutu was severely wounded. Blood and energy now pooled on the floor around him. Chia dragged him against another wall, on the opposite side of the room, and set up another barrier around him. Once satisfied that he could not move if he woke, Chia put partial fragments of healing sheets on to his wounds. They would be just enough to prevent the damage worsening and to stop the bleeding, but not enough to heal him. It was a wise solution until we knew who these kutu were, and what they had to do with Jychanumun.

"I know of you," the gem-haired Nigh-kutu in front of me spoke in his native tongue.

"Be quiet!" I told him.

He fell silent for a moment. "Iastha Tachra? The protector?" he quietly asked.

I was shocked. I tried not to let it show.

"How do you know my name?" I asked.

"Do not converse with them," Chia instructed me. "We know not what trickery they can do. We must heal Jychanumun before anything else."

I stared up at the Nigh-kutu, my arm already aching from holding my knife so tensely up to the neck of one so tall. I narrowed my eyes, indicating that he should not try to mess with me.

"Don't try to fool me, Nigh-kutu," I said, mustering a snarl. "I do not know you, or trust you."

The Nigh-kutu looked down at me. Suddenly he smiled. It was a broad, genuine smile. It made his eyes shine as brightly green as the strange beads in his hair. He looked relieved, even happy. It took me by surprise.

"I am Mardoch," the Nigh-kutu stated. "I am Jychanumun's clan-brother."

FOURTEEN

Eden1 was conquered. The skies around the bright planet were now littered with the debris of war. The few remaining Shaa-kutu had fled or been captured and Nigh-kutu now roamed the great white cities in droves, taking anything that they wanted.

Arrunn had set up his twelve personal guards around a large, white room placed at the top of a tall, domed building and had duly summoned Amaddon, senior forecaster of the Nigh-kutu. Amaddon had expected their chief to be happy with their victory, but Arrunn was clearly far from satisfied.

"What do you mean, you cannot find Orion's body?" Arrunn asked. His cool, penetrating stare made a bead of sweat form on Amaddon's forehead.

"There are body parts scattered everywhere," Amaddon explained. "We will find it, but it will take some days to gather everything that is left of the dead, and many more days to find out who is who."

Arrunn sat back heavily in his chair. The movement was

deceiving. He did not look relaxed. He was visibly not pleased at the reply. The yellow-haired Shaa-kutu, Shursa, sat on the floor by Arrunn's side. He seemed highly delighted at the unfolding events, smiling to himself as he shuffled through a large pile of data crystals.

"I do not care about the others," Arrunn scolded. "Surely, finding the only red-haired, red-eyed, kutu, firmly housed in a transport box, should not be too difficult."

"No, it should not," Amaddon nodded, trying to appease his superior.

"Then I am glad we agree on something," Arrunn frowned. "He has a life crystal embedded in him; track it. I am putting you in personal charge of this, Amaddon. I want him found. Every hour that passes and he is not found, you will lose a finger. Once I have run out of fingers, I will move on to toes, and then your eyes, and I will keep going until only your nerves remain, so that you can still sense the entirety of your losses. Do you understand?"

Amaddon quickly nodded.

"Then leave," Arrunn commanded. "Send in my High Warriors."

Amaddon bowed and hurried from the room. He was not going to be the one to tell Arrunn that two of his three High Warriors, both Mardoch and Dragun, were missing. He was not going to be the one to explain why no remnants of their bodies had been found either. No, he would let Deimom do that. Deimom could explain why he was the only High Warrior who had survived the attack on the light-lovers home-world. Let him bear the brunt of Arrunn's dissatisfaction for a change. Amaddon decided that he needed to start looking after his own interests. He already had his body parts in jeopardy.

The long corridors on this strange Shaa-kutu world were too

bright, and they had a softness underfoot that would unwisely mask any approaching footsteps. The black-clad guards, with their cold, unnerving stares, situated at each corner were of little comfort to Amaddon. If a hiding Shaa-kutu did lunge at him from some concealed doorway, the guards would probably do nothing to protect him. Yes, of course they would eventually kill that light-loving kutu, but they would almost certainly let Amaddon act as bait. They wouldn't put any effort into saving him. He was just a low-life to them. They were only bothered to protect Arrunn.

Amaddon knew there was no point asking a guard if he knew of Deimom's whereabouts. The guards would just ignore him. And so he nervously searched alone, peering into all the areas where he thought Deimom might be resting or celebrating their victory. Amaddon had memorised the layout of the current floor. It was a hideous place to negotiate, with twists and turns and mind-spinning travel points that left you not knowing what direction you had come from, or what direction you were heading in.

Eventually Amaddon did find Deimom. He was at the far end of a huge, high-ceilinged room. The vast space was as big as the main battle arena on Immorah, while filled with rows of luxuriously soft seats that looked down on a wide, semi-circular stage. Amaddon guessed the stage was for fighting contests, but it didn't look very sturdy. It was now filled with Nigh-kutu warriors, some victoriously practising with the strange new weapons they had plundered, others sitting in groups, examining strange looking devices and drinking pale, smoking drinks. They all appeared in high spirits.

Having cautiously wound his way through the bawdy warriors, Amaddon finally got to Deimom. Deimom was sitting astride a high-backed chair while one of his Firsts added the marks to his arm denoting his latest conquests. The fine black dots now wound over his shoulder in compact, intricate detail.

"Done. You are now the most marked warrior of us all," the First said as he admired his finished work.

Deimom glanced at his new marks approvingly and stood up, purposely not replacing his shoulder armour so that all could notice his achievements.

Amaddon cleared his throat loudly, waiting for the opportunity to speak. Deimom just raised an eyebrow at him.

"Arrunn requests seeing all his High Warriors," Amaddon duly announced.

"Does he know that Mardoch and Dragun are dead?" Deimom asked.

"It would not be my place to mention such a thing," Amaddon hurriedly excused himself. "Especially as I have no proof that they are dead."

Deimom looked disapprovingly at the forecaster. "When and where does Arrunn wish to see me?"

"Immediately. In the top room of the tall white building."

"All these light-lovers' buildings are tall and white, you fool," Deimom laughed derisively. "You can lead the way, and do not dawdle."

Amaddon knew better than to hesitate. He headed back out from the midst of the congregated warriors as fast as he could, only glancing back to ensure that Deimom was following. Amaddon wanted to hurry. He had really wanted to start searching for Orion's body straightaway. But he could not refuse a request from a High Warrior. Almost an hour had passed already; that was one digit he would most certainly be forfeiting.

Once Deimom had been directed to Arrunn's chosen room, he dismissed the inferior Amaddon and entered.

Arrunn was standing at one of the large windows, looking out over the vast white citadel that was the heart of Eden1. It was strange to see architecture above the land, rising towards the light. It did not seem natural. It made Deimom feel surprisingly uncomfortable to be on solid floor yet so high above the ground. The yellow-haired kutu was in the room too, sitting in a chair, reorganizing data crystals on a large white table in front of him.

"What happened out there?" Arrunn asked without turning.

Deimom started to recount the manoeuvres of their earlier attack, starting from the moment he and his warriors had passed through the gateway: Surround, send in his Firsts, attack, curve the line, launch a second attack . . .

"Stop," Arrunn interrupted, turning to face Deimom. "Do you think I do not already know this? I am asking you why the event took all night when we were supposed to control the situation straight away. Why was my plan not adhered to?"

"It did not help that Mardoch's legion was attacked and Mardoch killed . . ." Deimom began defensively.

"But you did not see Mardoch killed," Arrunn interrupted. "No one did. Can you personally guarantee or provide evidence that Mardoch is dead?"

"No, but . . ."

"Then start again," Arrunn growled, clearly dissatisfied, "And ensure accuracy this time. Why did our advantage take so long to achieve?"

Deimom cleared his throat, rehearsing the words in his head before speaking them aloud. "Mardoch's division was without a leader almost immediately upon clearing the gate. Many of that division were destroyed, and the remainder hesitated in fulfilling their manoeuvres without their chief to guide them. My own division had to abandon its strategy to compensate for this, delaying overall victory."

Arrunn nodded, seemingly satisfied at the answer. "Do not concern yourself; I do not hold you responsible. You fought well.

Your warriors fought well. Nevertheless, my plan was not adhered to, which meant that victory was disordered. I do not tolerate a messy victory. I should be asking all three of my High Warriors why, but as you are the only one here, it is you that I ask."

Deimom did not reply.

"Did you see what became of High Warriors Mardoch or Dragun?"

"I did not."

"And the red-haired kutu that I put in Mardoch's charge, do you know what became of him?"

"I do not." Deimom considered his reply carefully. "The last I saw of the transport box was mere moments before the flash of light, which coincided with Mardoch's . . . um . . . disappearance."

"And you yourself reported spotting the deserter, Jychanumun. Did you see what became of him?"

"No," Deimom replied. Again he hesitated a moment. "May I vocalise an assumption?" he asked.

"Speak," Arrunn waved his hand dismissively.

"It seemed, although I cannot be sure, that the flash of destructive light was caused by Jychanumun."

"Agreed. And his body has also mysteriously evaporated," Arrunn nodded. "There are too many coincidences. A bolt of light energy, if powerful enough, could indeed vaporise these missing kutu, but I do not think this is the case. Why would Jychanumun wait to strike at the last division, when attacking the first would have been strategically more advantageous? And if Mardoch and Orion were vaporised, they must have been at the heart of the attack. Why them? Perhaps Jychanumun did not like this Orion."

Arrunn seemed deep in thought. Calculating. Putting together the discrepancies. The room fell silent. Even the weakling, Shursa, tentatively stopped what he was doing, frozen mid-movement,

242

his eyes wide. Though Arrunn was deep in thought, the change in Shursa's stance did not escape his notice.

"Shursa," Arrunn walked towards the yellow-haired one. "You have something to say?"

Shursa suddenly looked worried. "Maybe," he considered, his eyes widening even more with trepidation.

Arrunn stood waiting.

"Then speak, my little king friend," Arrunn stated, folding his arms and smiling, as if he had all the time in the world.

"Orion and Jychanumun were friends," Shursa eventually stammered. "Good friends. Jychanumun wouldn't harm him; he'd save him."

"And how much do you know of Jychanumun?"

"Not very much," Shursa cautiously answered. "I did not like him. He was strange. He and Orion were always having secretive meetings. They were on the same team."

"Team?"

"Yes, a group of them. They always did things together. They even took over the Earth project. That was *my* project."

Arrunn's interest immediately picked up. "Earth project?"

"Yes," Shursa nodded. "They lived there. Can I have it as part of my kingdom?"

Arrunn leaned towards Shursa, patting him on the shoulder. "But you have Eden1, Shursa. How could you rule more than one empire?"

Shursa frowned, looking at the palms of his hands and rubbing them as if they were dirty. "But Eden1 is broken now," he mumbled disconsolately.

Arrunn laughed. "A broken kingdom for a broken king – how fitting. No, my little friend. You will look after this place, once I have taken what I want, and you will have some of my kutu to help you. That was our arrangement. With that, my side of our bonded promise will be complete."

Shursa went to say something else, but seemed to think better of it, returning to moving items around on the table instead.

"It seems that my friend here, Shursa, has a great deal of information that could be useful. I want this information extracted from his mind and categorized," Arrunn said to Deimom. "Have Amaddon see to it immediately. I want what is in his mind."

Shursa stiffened. "No, no," he began to stammer, "you are not taking anything from my mind. What are you going to do to me?" His voice had risen to a high shriek. Clearly scared, he moved away from the table.

Deimom stepped forward with a single stride and hit Shursa with the back of his hand. The Shaa-kutu went flying.

Arrunn walked up to Shursa, lifting him to his feet and gently dusting down his robe.

"Do not take my mind," Shursa beseeched him. "I can tell you anything you want. You can just ask."

"Shursa," Arrunn soothed him. "That would take far too long. And we will not take anything that you would not willingly give. Your past is pain. I will take that pain away from you. Let us say it is my gift to you."

Shursa still didn't seem to like the sound of it. He backed away from Arrunn, shaking his head.

Arrunn just looked at Shursa coolly. "You made the choice when you assented to the bonded agreement. So here you are and I have made you king of Eden1, as I promised that I would. All I asked for my part of the bargain was to take what I wanted. You agreed to that. That was our bonded promise. Now, I want your memories," he said matter-of-factly. "So choose again: keep your promise or don't. Either give me your memories and live as king on Eden1, or do not and live in death as a little glowing crystal, another bloom in my rose garden."

Shursa's eyes darted back and forth, as if searching through his mind for any argument he could use that might work. Suddenly he looked deflated. He could clearly find no argument.

Arrunn disinterestedly turned his back on Shursa, turning his attention to Deimom once again.

"I know the red-haired kutu did not die. I want him found," Arrunn instructed. "I want every available resource put on it. Understood?"

"Understood," Deimom confirmed.

"And I want any Shaa-kutu stragglers gathered up. If I cannot use them, I will have their time energy. What losses did we sustain?"

"The live Nigh-kutu head count stands at three-two-two-nine-four, of which approximately a tenth require healing. We lost almost ten thousand."

Arrunn shook his head, frowning. It was clearly a higher loss than he had calculated for. "Their time crystals?" he asked.

"Being put in your portable vault as they are collected."

Arrunn's seemed somewhat mollified by this. "I'll leave the wounded here to heal," Arrunn decided. "Select three of your Warrior-Firsts to oversee matters here with half the army. They are to clean out any remaining light-lovers and search for the red-haired one. You will come with me with the rest of the warriors to Earth. I have overpowered the mind of this universe of light, now I shall conquer the heart."

Deimom seemed to consider this. He had thought Eden1 was the primary target. "Permission to question?" he asked.

Arrunn nodded, indicating that a question, just one, was acceptable.

"Is there a bigger target than Eden1 in these universes?" Deimom tentatively asked.

"Bigger, no," Arrunn replied. "More significant, yes. But you would not see that. You do not have my vision, Deimom. A different type of strength, my strength, will be needed to conquer the heart. I see the heart of all things. The heart goes beyond the dark and the light. It is the only perfect thing left."

Deimom did not understand, but he was not going to show his ignorance by questioning the matter further.

"A tiny planet and a great deal of time is all that I require," Arrunn smiled to himself. "Deimom, do as I have asked and gather one half of my warriors. Have them ready above this city. We leave for the heart. We leave for Earth. Inform me when they are ready."

He turned his back to view the great, white citadel once again.

"Go," Arrunn commanded. "Take Shursa with you. I want his memories. And when you find Amaddon, remove one of his fingers before you hand Shursa over."

Deimom glanced at the yellow-haired one, waiting for the inevitable protests, ready to use a quick swipe of the back of his hand again. But Shursa just rose and took two steps towards Deimom, his head bowed in obedience. Thankfully, it seemed that even this light-lover was a quick learner.

With the stark white room empty once again, Arrunn nodded to the two exterior guards and sealed the doors. Once satisfied that the room was secure, he moved to the centre of the space, bending down to outline a circle on the floor around him with his finger. As his finger touched the cool stone, he released energy. Once complete, a perfectly circular pool of darkest matt brown rippled under his feet. He stood straight, closed his eyes and concentrated.

The pool of energy around Arrunn expanded upwards, growing in height until it consumed his body. He pushed it further, the energy raising higher until it passed his head. Arrunn stood, barely visible, encased in a column of deepest brown energy. He flexed his shoulders and rolled his head, comfortable in the saturation of his own essence. Suddenly, he pushed out. The energy expanded, flowing along the floor and rising higher until it encompassed the entire room. The pale space was now cast in shadow, Arrunn's shadow.

Arrunn let out a comfortable sigh. The space was clean now. At last he could work.

As Arrunn concentrated, the shadow in the room slowly started to reveal specks of light, each one a tiny flicker of life essence. The little specks intensified until the entire space looked like a miniature version of the night sky. Arrunn held onto his focus, keeping the scene in place, and examined the miniature universe around him.

Yes, here, directly in front of him, were grouped together thousands of these specks of light: this must be Eden1 and all the life forces on it. The taste of so much life-energy in the air was foul to Arrunn. Each speck of light was a life, each one tainted with a hint of colour according to that life, and each one was flawed. They all tasted bad. Some tasted worse than others. More tiny specks of life dotted around the entire room: fourteen there, six here, several dozen there. Arrunn knew that these must be either small kutu colonies, or Shaa-kutu that had fled from the battle. It would be so easy to gather them up, but they were not important enough for his personal attention. His warriors could see to them.

To Arrunn's right-hand side was a dark spot. This was the gateway back into the shadow. It would remain open for a while longer. The energy used to create it would take time to dissipate. Arrunn put his hand out, as if caressing the dark space. The darkness took the bad taste from his mouth even as he gazed at the brightness in front of him.

Directly in front of Arrunn was the light emitting from a small planet. Its surreal, iridescent glow touched everything around him, extending far beyond the boundaries of its little galaxy. This was Earth. No planet, star or sun should shine like that. It had to be the correct place. It was alive with an energy unlike any other. It touched everything. It had to be the heart.

Arrunn ignored the discomfort of the life energy that assailed him, and walked around the representation of the small planet, looking for signs of Shaa-kutu inhabitants. He hoped their life energy would shine bright against the planet's glow, but the entire planet radiated light and masked any other possible life forms that might exist there. He would have to act with caution, as always. He could not see if the planet was deserted, or whether legions of Shaa-kutu armies lay in waiting.

Arrunn finally walked around the room, now searching for any sign of a red speck of light. He had to find and maintain control over the red kutu. Did Orion know that he was the Dhasmiel? Probably not. But Jychanumun would. After all, Jychanumun had written that prophesy in the first place.

Arrunn had long ago ensured that all copies of Jychanumun's prophesy had been destroyed. He still had his own personal copy of course. But he did not need to look at it. He knew it word for word.

It had been prophesised that in a time to come, still several thousand years from now, a kutu made purely of red energy would write a song of enlightenment and summoning. That song would awaken and summon the heart of all things – the last remaining universal consciousness, the one, whole, perfect consciousness. The heart of all things would awaken from eternal dreaming. And when it did, it would connect to one being: Arrunn. And once Arrunn had established that link he would give it all his memories of being fragmented, being imperfect, being broken, and then he would use the power of the One to end all imperfect life. Because in doing so, Arrunn would understand perfection.

But did the Shaa-kutu have knowledge of such prophesies, or of the capabilities of the red kutu? Surely not. Surely those light-loving kutu would have made better use of such powers, if they had known of them. No other pure red existed among the kutu. Now he had found the source, and it had been snatched from him. He would find it again; it was only a matter of time. And when he did, he would put that red kutu to great use.

Arrunn searched twice for any sign of the red kutu's life force. There was nothing. The red kutu had not died in the battle. Arrunn would have sensed if he had. No, it was not death that had removed Orion from his grasp. There were only two primary possibilities: either Orion had passed back through the gateway to the shadow, or he was on the little blue planet, concealed by the greater light.

There was a third possibility. But Arrunn knew that possibility had long been rendered impossible. He himself had spent millennia ensuring it remained impossible.

Nevertheless, Arrunn considered this implausible option for a moment. Could someone else know how to use life's time energy? If they could, Orion could now be beyond this galaxy. No, there had not been any evidence of even a shred of the necessary skill to use time crystals for thousands of millennia. Every book, text, statue and memory with any reference to the subject had been destroyed in a time so long ago that it was out of memory's reach. Anyone who knew any details of Arrunn's skill had been destroyed, by his own hand, many millennia ago. Any clan that showed natural abilities with energies or stones was quickly wiped out. Not one kutu from the Weaver, the Caster, or the Gatherer clans had survived the first annihilations. Even their names were now forgotten. Arrunn had personally seen to that, too. With them gone, the only kutu who had any capacity for manipulating life's time energy was him. No one else could even see what he could see. They did not have his skills. They did not have his memories.

Arrunn perused the scene around him one last time, ensuring the image was etched in his mind, and then took a deep breath, withdrawing his own energy back into himself. He inverted his energy until it was nothing more than a tiny potent spark in the centre of his torso. And then he cut off his memories. After all, the best way to keep something secret was never to tell anyone at all. Even better if you can make yourself forget too.

Only the single primary objective remained in Arrunn's mind, the one thing that he could never forget: perfection. And if perfection became impossible, annihilation. In Arrunn's world, the two options were exactly the same.

FIFTEEN

The images of Eden1, shown on the screens that encircled me, had calmed. But the calm wasn't a good calm, the serenity that came from peace. It was the calm following death and defeat.

The Shaa-kutu planet was ravaged. Many of its beautiful sculptured buildings were forever scarred, and many were fallen, just like the Shaa-kutu themselves. The skies were now empty of life and full of broken weapons, body parts and indistinguishable debris. It was awful beyond words.

But not all hope was lost. Some Shaa-kutu had survived and had gone into hiding. Chia was sending messages, directing them to even more places where they could hide a little longer. Jychanumun had also survived, so far, although his condition was not looking good. He now lay behind me, unconscious. And me? I had been instructed to guard one of the unknown, black-winged Nigh-kutu who had found his way to our own bolt-hole, the one who called himself Mardoch.

"But, he doesn't want to kill us. He's not bad," I insisted to Chia. "Let me help you instead."

"No, hold your position," Chia muttered through gritted teeth. He was clearly busy and trying to concentrate. His fingers moved so fast that I could barely see them. He worked feverishly, sending more and more messages via the central console. I knew that he was forwarding the co-ordinates of additional safe places and bolt holes on any frequency that might be heard by their kind. It was a crucial task. It could save kutu lives. Amidst all this, he contacted Kraniel, requiring immediate assistance.

"But . . ." I tried protesting again.

"Hold!" Chia snapped. "By Eskah, Tachra, do not argue. This is critical."

The tone of Chia's voice made me feel like a badly behaved child. So, I did what I was told and kept Chia's vapour dagger poised against the throat of our captive.

It wasn't just that I didn't want to guard this Nigh-kutu, I didn't think that he needed guarding. I found myself liking him. His openness shone inside him, illuminating his shadow. He was a good being, and, no matter how deep I looked, I sensed only good intentions from him. And if all that was not enough, I couldn't see the point of holding a vapour dagger to this throat when there were kutu barriers already holding him firmly trapped against the wall. But I knew Chia was just acting with caution. There were no assurances that this was a good Nigh-kutu, and no confirmation that he didn't have the skills to break an energy barrier such as the one that held him.

From the corner of my eye, I watched Jychanumun. He was still lying motionless on the floor, and there hadn't yet been any signs of recovery. I felt like I should be tending to him. I felt like I should be helping Chia. I felt like I should be doing something of more use in this terrible time. Nevertheless, with the images of the desolation of Eden1 still illuminating the screens around me, and feeling frightened about everything that was going on, I knew Chia was right. It was better to act with caution. After all, Shaa-kutu lives were at stake, the Nigh-kutu had attacked their home-world, and this one in front of me was still a Nigh-kutu.

Without warning, Kraniel stormed into the room, making me jump.

Kraniel launched into the centre of the space like a whirlwind and suddenly stopped. He was holding a strange-looking weapon in each hand, had ill-fitting Anumi chest armour slung hurriedly over his torso, and was poised, partly crouched, ready to attack at any sign of trouble. Kraniel glanced around the room, assessing the situation, and then without a word checked the barriers against both of the confined Nigh-kutu.

Satisfied that the barriers were secure enough, Kraniel tucked his weapons into a concealed pocket and moved to stand beside Chia, joining him in forwarding co-ordinates. He and Chia conversed hurriedly with each other, glancing regularly to check that the Nigh-kutu could not and had not moved, while my up-stretched arm became more and more numb.

I noticed that Jychanumun was starting to stir. His hands started clenching and unclenching, as if he were trying to wake himself. His mouth moved, as if trying to talk.

"Jychanumun?" I called out, hoping he could hear me.

I wanted to run to him, but I dared not leave my position. I tried connecting to him with my mind, to tell him that he was safe, but I couldn't reach him. His mind felt too fast and fragmented, as if he were still amidst battle, fighting off multitudes of attacks from every angle. Jychanumun's energy felt dispersed and weakened, pulsing feebly. And the sight of his body was even worse. His armour was in tatters, and his exposed, partially tuned flesh was a mass of cuts, scrapes, gashes, bruises and angry, pulsating holes that still oozed liquid, trying to repel the remnants of energy bolts that had struck him.

"Done!" Chia suddenly exclaimed, punching the last send message hard. He turned around and rushed to Jychanumun's side, adding another translucent, shimmering healing sheet, gently instructing him to keep still, reassuring him that he was safe and that he was back on Earth.

Suddenly, Jychanumun sat bolt upright.

"Mardoch?" he called out, although he was still barely conscious.

"I am here, brother," the green-eyed Nigh-kutu that I was guarding said quietly in his own tongue. "That was a great feat that you achieved."

Jychanumun pulled the healing sheet from him, even though the wounds were still raw. He awkwardly tried to stand. Chia tried to help. Jychanumun pulled away from the touch, but Chia told him that it would be alright.

Jychanumun let Chia help him to his feet. He swayed a little on the spot, and then patted his face, feeling the obstruction against his eyes. Without a word, he ripped off the healing discs.

Suddenly, Jychanumun froze. He dropped the two healing discs on the floor. They clattered.

"What is it?" Chia asked.

"I cannot see," Jychanumun said flatly.

Jychanumun lifted his head. The bleeding from his eyes had stopped. Dried blood and dead black energy now stained his cheeks, blending in with the smudged remains of the fighting marks that he'd painted onto his skin. His normally black eyes, which radiated darkness like a shadow that attracted light, were now lifeless and empty, just gaping holes in his face, stained with dried blood and energy. It looked gruesome. I felt my stomach retch. Jychanumun had no eyes.

"Eskah!" Chia exclaimed.

I could feel tears running down my cheeks. What had they done to him? This heroic, beautiful kutu was disfigured. This was so wrong. I had no words for the terrible wrongness that I felt. I wanted to say something, but no words would form in my mouth. I was too distressed to say anything.

Chia glanced at me, and then Kraniel, uncertainly, as if not sure what to do. And then I saw him collect himself, his body suit rippled with his energy, like a wash of violet light moving over him. He leaned in towards Jychanumun, inspecting his empty sockets.

"It is alright. It will be alright," he said, although I wasn't sure if he was speaking to Jychanumun or reassuring himself. "I am going to replace the healing discs. You must keep them there for as long as you can. They may still do some good."

Chia hurriedly placed fresh discs over Jychanumun's wounded sockets.

"Damn, what did they do to you?" he asked.

"They did nothing," Jychanumun replied. "It is a consequence of my actions. Perhaps a small price to pay. Will they heal?"

"I do not know. I have never encountered this before," Chia replied, ensuring the discs were secure. "You have no eyes at all; energy or substance. I will speculate that yes, they will rebuild, but it could take months, or even years."

Jychanumun visibly stiffened at hearing this. How would he survive without his eyes if the Nigh-kutu came here? This was terrible.

"Can you still use your energy for sensing?" Chia asked.

"Yes," Jychanumun nodded, not allowing his anguish to show. "Although sight would be useful, too."

I felt Jychanumun pushing out his senses, feeling his surroundings. "Tachra?" he said, his face inclined in my direction.

"I'm here," I answered. "I'm guarding the Nigh-kutu, Mardoch."

"Mardoch does not require guarding," Jychanumun replied.

I glanced at Chia. Chia nodded. I relaxed my knife from Mardoch's throat.

"Tachra, link to me," Jychanumun requested. "I must use your sight for the moment."

Without a second thought, I opened my mind to create a stronger link with Jychanumun. Normally this meant that I could share what he was seeing, but this time his vision was empty, a barren blackness like a starless night. He could see nothing at all with his own sight. Nevertheless, Jychanumun could now see through my eyes and hear my thoughts. He now saw my vision of his own wounded, battered body and depleted energy, and sensed my horror and anxiety at what had befallen us.

Do not fret, Jychanumun silently told me.

There is much to fret about, I replied.

You must be strong.

I know. Inwardly I grimaced. At this moment, the only strength I had was nothing more than a fragile façade over my quivering insides.

Jychanumun moved towards me, assessing his step and direction though my own eyesight. I moved forward to assist him.

"Where are the others?" Jychanumun hurriedly asked Mardoch in his native Nigh-kutu tongue. My own basic knowledge of the Nigh-kutu language was no longer needed; I could now feel the meaning of every word through my link with Jychanumun.

"Others?" Mardoch enquired. "I came with you and Dragun. Dragun too is injured."

"Where are our brothers?"

"Jychanumun," Mardoch said quietly. "I thought I was the last. You were considered long dead. But now we are the last. The others . . ."

"But I saw them," Jychanumun interrupted. "When you came

through the gateway, they stood behind you. They saw me. They gave me their strength."

Jychanumun had moved forward enough to touch Mardoch. He felt the barrier, immediately tracing its edges with his fingers and removing the corner stones from the wall that held the barrier in place. The barrier collapsed.

Mardoch flung his arms out and clasped Jychanumun, rejoicing to see him. Tears of green shadow-light streamed down his face as he patted Jychanumun's arms, back, and then face, as if barely able to believe that he was there. He caught a hold of one of Jychanumun's hands, bringing it up to his head, guiding Jychanumun's fingers to feel the crystals embedded in his dreadlocks. "This is what is left of our brothers."

Jychanumun fell silent, his fingers tracing each one of the crystals. I felt his sadness.

"I am their keeper now," Mardoch confirmed. "I will guard their spirits until life finds them again. They have taken the death of the flesh, yet they have not walked the final path."

Chia walked forward. "I assume that this Nigh-kutu can be trusted," he stated matter-of-factly.

"Yes," Jychanumun replied, speaking in Shaa-kutu once again. "This is Mardoch, my clan-brother. He has made many sacrifices to help us."

"And him?" Chia indicated to the still injured Nigh-kutu in the corner.

I glanced at the slumped, black-winged one. Jychanumun followed my stare.

"His name is Dragun," Mardoch intervened, speaking to Jychanumun in Nigh-kutu again, noticing our stares. "He is not one of our clan. He is the last survivor of the Weaver clan. The Weaver clan can weave energy and substance. They were an honourable clan. Dragun is a Rock Weaver."

"I thought they were long dead," Jychanumun said.

"As did I," Mardoch nodded. "He is the last. Arrunn thought he had annihilated them all. Dragun has been hiding amidst Arrunn's armies for millennia. His clan was linked to our clan a long time ago. It seems that he has not forgotten. He is a fine warrior and a fine kutu."

Jychanumun turned his head to where Dragun was still laying slumped, held in place by an energy barrier. I felt him push out his energy towards the Nigh-kutu. His energy moved around Dragun as if assessing him, and then suddenly propelled into the centre of his forehead.

Through my link with Jychanumun, a thousand images began flashing into my mind.

Do not look at this, I heard Jychanumun tell me. *This is not something I like to do, but times are grave.*

But I couldn't help looking. My link to Jychanumun was too strong not to see. The images just flooded into my mind and I couldn't stop them. It was as if Jychanumun was examining this kutu's life, but not just his past; Jychanumun was looking into this kutu's possible future. It was something that I knew Jychanumun could do, but he had never done since I had known him. And although I saw the images in my mind, I was glad that they were too fast for me to make sense of.

Jychanumun withdrew his energy from the wounded Dragun and turned to Chia.

"His name is Dragun. We can trust him," Jychanumun simply said.

Behind us, I could hear clattering. To my mind it was a simple noise, and my ears traced its direction, but my link to Jychanumun enhanced the noise so that I saw it as he did. Jychanumun not only heard the physical noise, he also saw it as flashes of blue light with defined edges and a multilayered scent unlike anything on Earth. Jychanumun's senses were not at all intrusive to my mind; I was so used to the true vision of the Old One. I turned around to see Kraniel delving through a pile of metal boxes, looking for something.

Kraniel seemed to find what he was looking for.

"We can implant translators into these two Nigh-kutu," he suggested, holding up two long, transparent tubes in his hands. "We do not have codes for the Nigh-kutu language, but these are self-adjusting. They will assimilate and adapt accordingly."

Jychanumun nodded, explaining the devices to his brother. Mardoch nodded his agreement. I was surprised that Mardoch agreed; the thought of having a tube as big as that stuck into me sent a shiver down my back.

Kraniel took one of long tubes and touched one end of it against the side of Mardoch's head. For a horrible moment, I thought the entire tube was going to be pushed into the Nigh-kutu's ear. But Kraniel pulled the tube away, confirming that the translator implant was complete.

As Mardoch spoke to himself, listening to the sounds of the Shaa-kutu language spill from his own mouth, I guided Jychanumun towards Dragun, the Rock Weaver.

Dragun was still unconscious and slumped in the far corner. He was a huge Nigh-kutu, easily as big as the Anumi, with wide shoulders and defined muscles that were barely contained by his tattered black armour. His ragged, light-brown hair half-covered his face, sticking to the blood that had not yet been cleaned from his sealed wounds. His large black wings, tipped with brown, hung down around him in frayed shreds, the energy barely able to hold them together. He was too weak to draw them in and too weak for them to heal. Even still, he was a mighty kutu to behold.

Jychanumun bent to the unconscious Rock Weaver, releasing him from the barrier, while Chia brought a full healing sheet and covered his still wounded flesh. Kraniel brought in the second translator and implanted the invisible device, while Jychanumun placed his hand on the Nigh-kutu's chest, giving him a small amount of his own sparse energy in order to keep him calm as he woke.

The Rock Weaver known as Dragun immediately began to stir. He was trying to rouse himself. His head shook back and forth as if trying to wake from a bad dream. He suddenly opened his eyes, staring at Jychanumun.

"Death-Walker?" he asked hoarsely. "Am I dead?"

"You are alive and safe," Jychanumun replied, removing his hand. "A translator has been implanted so we can understand you."

Dragun didn't reply. From his slumped position, his eyes glanced around the room. His expression never changed, but I could tell that this Rock Weaver had evaluated and noticed everything in that one fleeting look.

"We are on Earth. Our escape was successful," Mardoch told him. He helped Dragun to his feet, despite the fact that he was clearly still too badly injured to stand. Mardoch bowed towards Chia. The Rock Weaver cleared his throat and bowed too.

"I am Dragun. I have come to help."

"Why?" Chia asked. He was hesitant, understandably, and clearly unconvinced. He turned to Jychanumun. "I do not doubt you, my friend, so please do not take offence at my suspicion."

"We wish to live the Shaa-kutu way: to live for ascendance, for peace, not for war. We request sanctuary," Mardoch stated simply.

"Sanctuary?" Chia stated in disbelief. "We are amidst a Tumultus. We are at war and our warriors are out-numbered. Our chances are slim and likely to get worse. You will find little sanctuary with us at this critical time."

"Yes, this is a critical time," Mardoch replied, "but I cannot ignore the chance to live an honest life, even if it is a short one. It would be better to live a brief life but true than forever and falsely."

"And you are absolutely sure we can trust them?" Chia asked Jychanumun.

"I would stake my life upon it," Jychanumun nodded. "Mardoch is my clan-brother. I trust him and his judgement about Dragun."

Jychanumun drew out two long blades from concealed pockets on each of his thighs. He handed Mardoch and Dragun a blade each and turned his back to them.

"These Nigh-kutu have enough energy to kill us all in an instant," Jychanumun told Chia. "And they could now also use the blades in their hands to kill me and use my body as a shield to escape. Mardoch, Dragun," Jychanumun instructed, "if you are our enemy, kill me now."

I caught my breath. There was a pause filled with terrible possibilities, a moment that seemed to go on forever. I considered leaping forward and grabbing the blades from the Nigh-kutu, but I could feel Jychanumun's sureness. His conviction that all was well calmed my racing heart. I stood watching, not wanting to move or make a sound.

I heard the clatter of metal on the floor. The Nigh-kutu had dropped the knives.

"We are not your enemy," Dragun declared, frowning, thumping his chest with his fist. "If we must fight, we fight *with* you, not against you. I have waited millennia to find more kutu with integrity. If this is my last breath, then I breathe it gladly, knowing I have found others who remember the love of life. My own clan was slaughtered. I am a Weaver. I will always be a Weaver. Fighting is not in my chi, but I am a good warrior. I do not desire to fight. But I can fight and I will: for peace, for life, for the right to choose, with all my might if need be. Give me the chance to make a stand with other good kutu, for life. Even if it is my last fight, let it be for the right reasons. I have . . ."

Chia held up his hand, halting the kutu's passionate speech.

"I sense the truth of it," he simply stated.

"I too am a good warrior," Mardoch added. "No speeches. Just tell me what you would like me to do first. I will fight. Or I can negotiate. I have secured a bargaining tool that may be of use to you. It could be used to persuade Arrunn to release many of your captured comrades."

"A bargaining tool?" Chia asked.

"I have charge of the one for whom Arrunn has been searching for so long. He will want him back, at any cost. I know where the red kutu is."

"Orion?" Jychanumun quickly asked. "You have the red kutu? Explain."

Mardoch began speaking quickly, his hands making unusual gestures as he spoke. He was telling of places and people that I had never heard of, briefly explaining many things. When the kutu talked fast, it was with so many layers of sounds that it was almost impossible to keep up with him. My mind reeled.

". . . the prophesy foretold of a red kutu." Mardoch explained. "He was known as the Dhasmiel. The Dhasmiel is of importance to Arrunn. Arrunn would want him back to use his power to summon the sleeping one in the future . . ."

Summon the sleeping one? This sounded familiar. But the future? Hadn't this already happened? Were they not talking of the Old One and the Summoning Song? I went to ask Jychanumun, but he had already heard my thoughts.

I will speak with you about this, Jychanumun told me with his mind. *There are things that you should know.*

It sounds like it, I replied tentatively. I didn't know why, but for some reason my stomach was churning. *I think you should tell me now.*

Soon, Jychanumun replied, and I felt that he was tentative too. *As soon as we have a moment without crisis.*

I strained to pull my concentration back to the here and now, trying to push the new anxiety to the back of my mind. *Focus,* I disciplined myself. *Jychanumun is right. This is not about you. There are kutu lives at stake.*

"Orion . . . is he well?" Chia was anxiously asking.

"He is weak, but stable," Mardoch answered.

"Where is he?"

"I have hidden him. He is safe."

"Where? I must go to him."

"He is very, very far away," Dragun intervened. "Without lifetime energy, it would take thousands of millennia to reach the correct planet."

Mardoch put a hand on Dragun's shoulder. "If your energy is not too weak, show them," he requested.

Dragun nodded, took a step back, drew a deep breath, and shut his eyes. His energy resonated around him, a deep golden brown, translucent and shimmering. Slowly, his energy then drifted to one side of his body, holding its form, a perfect copy of Dragun, while his body remained still. It was as if I was seeing two versions of Dragun, one solid and one energy. One arm of the energy form reached into the torso of Dragun's solid body, and then pulled out its hand. The hand was holding something. The energy then took a step sideways so it was back around the solid body, drawing inwards until Dragun was one – energy and matter – once again.

Dragun opened his eyes, held out his hands, and unfurled his fingers.

On Dragun's palm were over a dozen small, radiant stones. The little stones lit the area with a brightness like the moon. It made the kutu's faces glow with the reflection of an energy that seemed so potent, yet fragile, that it made me gasp.

"It has been necessary to conceal them," Dragun told us. "Only Arrunn is allowed to posses them and only he can activate them, at least, so he thinks. As a Weaver, I too can activate them. Each one of these holds the most potent energy of all, time. These are time crystals." He held them out so that Chia could examine them. "I used some to put Orion further away than a kutu would travel, beyond this galaxy. It was safest."

Dragun mentioned a measurement of distance that wasn't familiar to me, but I ascertained from Jychanumun's thoughts that it was too far for a kutu to travel without the aid of time energy.

Dragun had used some of these energy crystals and jumped so far away, in an instant, to a desert planet far away from Earth's galaxy. Once there, he had then used the energy from another crystal to propel Orion deep into the planet's core. Orion had been buried so deep that he would not be found unless by someone who knew where to search.

Chia was horrified. "Orion is buried inside a planet? He won't survive!"

"He will," Mardoch explained. "Orion is confined to a transport box, with its own protective and life-enhancing mechanisms, accessed through implants in his back. His position will not damage him any more than he already is."

This horrified Chia even more. He wanted the Nigh-kutu give him full directions to the place and details of Orion's injuries so that he could plan his rescue.

"It would be too far for you to travel in a standard Shaa-kutu craft. You would need time crystals to get there, retrieve him and get back," Dragun replied. "About nine time crystals."

"How many do you have?"

"Just these. I originally had twenty eight, but I have used fourteen already," Dragun looked at the little stones. "I had activated some and given them to Mardoch. He used them to enhance Jychanumun's attack as the warriors came through the portal. Jychanumun's light-blast and the proceeding chaos gave us the opportunity to get away unseen. I then used more to move and hide Orion, and then more were used again to bring the three of us to this place. They are also the reason that we three got here unseen," he added.

I saw the relief on Chia's face. At least that explained why the Anumi did not detect them arriving.

"If those things are so useful, how do we get more?" I asked.

"By killing a kutu and removing his remaining life-time energy," Dragun replied. "Or Arrunn has thousands of them. We could steal them if we could get close enough."

My mouth had dropped open. Each one of those little stones held the condensed life-time energy stolen from a being? Stolen by slaughter, execution, or murder? Each one represented a murdered life of a kutu. It was atrocious.

I was suddenly repelled by the strange beauty of the stones, as if I were looking at a decaying corpse. The image of the first dead body I had ever seen gruesomely entered my head like an unwelcome guest. The very nature of these stones tainted their potent beauty.

"Stanze, are you getting all this?" Chia spoke though his HOTS. He had been keeping an open connection to the Anumi warrior at all times. He nodded in response to something Stanze said. "Yes, that is now primary."

Chia looked to Mardoch and Dragun. "I will want all details on Orion's position and knowledge on how to get him back so we can formulate a plan to retrieve him. Do you know of Arrunn's plans now?"

"Has he conquered your home-world yet?" Mardoch answered with a question.

Chia shot the Nigh-kutu a sharp look. "So it seems," he spat the words. "Although all are not lost."

"My heart grieves for every kutu death," Mardoch bowed to Chia, noticing that the frankness of his words had caused offense. "But I am only used to talking straight. If Arrunn has control of your home-world he will strip it of its resources, take the Shaa-kutu who are useful to him and end the lives of those who are not."

Chia closed his eyes, clearly trying to stay focussed. "Then will he leave?" he asked.

"I do not know," Mardoch considered. "Our brief was to contain the Shaa-kutu home-world, nothing more. How many kutu are here?"

"Seventy nine. Fifty warriors, twenty nine others."

"A mere handful," Mardoch considered. "Hopefully, not enough to interest Arrunn, although I would advise you to get them all into these underground rooms."

Chia looked unsure.

"Listen to me," Mardoch gritted his teeth. "I know enough to tell you that Arrunn wants none of you alive unless you are of significant use to him. He has given this mission greater planning and more resources than any I have ever known. He wants you all dead or enslaved. You must get underground so you are better protected," Mardoch waved his hands in exasperation. "You said yourself you are grossly outnumbered here. If you are concealed, you may be overlooked. If not, you may fortunate enough to sit it out until he leaves."

"You think he will come here?"

"Of course he will," Mardoch replied. "Won't he, Jychanumun?"

"I have tried everything I could to prevent this," Jychanumun shook his head. "Yes, he will come here, although I do not know when."

Chia nodded, and then touched his ear. "Yes, agreed, very well," he spoke to Stanze through his HOTS.

"Stanze agrees that they should regroup here," Chia announced. "He and the Anumi are en route. They will convene here to revise strategy."

Within moments, the first of the Anumi began to arrive. Chia handed out large goblets of Ochrah to each one, to sustain their energy, as they hurried into the central hub. They all looked cold and sombre, yet resolute and strong. I felt better knowing that they were close and safe rather than exposed outside.

I must speak with you now, Jychanumun silently told me. *I do not think it can wait.*

I felt the urgency in his words. My stomach churned again. I suddenly wondered if I actually wanted to know what Jychanumun needed to say.

Jychanumun must have sensed this. He caught my hand, leading me through a doorway on the opposite side of the room.

The doorway opened onto a dim corridor. The light sensors illuminated, having detected our presence, showing a long passageway that sloped down further than the eye could see. Jychanumun closed the door behind us. The corridor fell silent. I felt his consternation as if it were my own.

I have tried to protect them all, Jychanumun told me. *For thousands of years I have tried to stop Arrunn coming into this universe of light.*

This is not your fault, I touched Jychanumun's arm consolingly.

You do not understand, Jychanumun shook his head. *Because I have not told you what I have done.*

Then tell me, I said, pushing aside my growing anxiety. *Show me.*

Jychanumun hesitated for a moment, and then nodded. I saw his stark black and white energy start to move around his body, moving further away from his skin. This time it seemed to be pulsing, as if reacting to my own heartbeat. I pushed out my own energy, tentatively brushing against his. And then he pushed forward until our energies became as one.

My skills mean that I can see the inevitability of life, Jychanumun began to explain. *I do not see all futures, just significant things. Long ago, I saw the future for all kutu: their total demise. It came about because Orion summoned the Old One and Arrunn used my skills to force a link with the Old One. With that link established Arrunn would end all life. This future was not set to happen for a long time – about fourteen thousand years from now.*

But if this is not due to happen yet, why are we hiding now? I asked.

Because I changed that future, Jychanumun replied. *I got far away from Arrunn so he could not find me. I found Orion. I put hints of the codes that he would use to write the Summoning Song into texts that I knew he would read. As a result, Orion composed the Summoning Song earlier than originally fated. I changed everything that would be effective, without harming any other.*

But Arrunn still comes here, I said. It didn't seem as if Jychanumun's actions had changed that fate at all.

Yes, Jychanumun agreed. *All my actions have done is rearrange that same outcome with a different story leading up to it. All I have succeeded in doing is moving things forward. Arrunn still comes here, even though that Summoning Song has already been played and can only be effective once.*

I knew that was true; the Summoning Song would have little effect on the Old One now. I remembered how angry he had become when the Summoning Song had been played, back when I was a girl. I remembered feeling his wrath. I also remembered how, when he had heard it again, he was less affected, until my memories of it meant nothing to him.

There is one aspect to this fate that is changed, Jychanumun added. *One thing that could make a difference. You. The Old One hears your choices. Your choices change things.*

Only for me! I objected. *My choices cannot change something so great as thousands of warring kutu. I'm a mere grain of sand in a very large desert in all of this.*

Jychanumun was silent for a moment. *Your choices will be true,* he simply said.

What? That does not help me at all! I exclaimed. *How would I ever know if I was making the right choice? Have I already missed things? Jychanumun, please: if what you say is true, you must guide me. I trust you. If anything I can do is imperative. Please, you must tell me.*

I felt Jychanumun pull his energy away from mine. I was left looking at him, feeling very disorientated. Jychanumun picked up both my hands in his.

"We will tackle such necessities if and when they arrive," he said aloud.

I nodded, but I didn't feel any better. The gravity of what Jychanumun knew resonated in my mind. The end of all life? That was a terrible thing to be aware of. I was not surprised that Jychanumun had tried everything in his power to change that fate.

"We need to be back in the hub," Jychanumun's voice suddenly interrupted my thoughts. He opened the door back into the large underground room.

By now, Stanze and over half the kutu that had been stationed around the land here on Earth had returned, and were now congregated. Stanze stood talking to Chia, Dragun and Mardoch, and several gathered around them, listening for news, watching the two new Nigh-kutu in their midst with wary eyes. Kraniel was busy at the central console, deeply engrossed. I walked over towards the console with Jychanumun to watch the screens on the wall.

Suddenly, Jychanumun stopped.

"They come," he whispered.

Everyone stopped and looked at him.

"I feel them! They come!" Jychanumun now shouted, his blind, covered eyes directed up to the ceiling. "Get the rest of the kutu into hiding. Now!"

Chia needed no further instruction. He had already run to the console and was shouting messages, as was Kraniel. The kutu who were still en route to the hub were to get to a safe place, *any* safe place. Noise broke out all around me. Stanze was shouting messages. Mardoch and Dragun were shouting advice. It was chaos.

A chill ran through me. I looked up to the screens around the room, several of which now showed the skies, far above Earth, above the clouds, beyond the atmosphere. One screen seemed to have what looked like a large black storm cloud. The cloud moved, rolling, as if alive with its own wind, breathing within its darkness. Edges of the cloud broke away, forming another cloud. The mass grew, like a heaving ball of shadow, growing larger, growing closer.

As the cloud grew closer to the screen, I could make out the distant forms of Nigh-kutu, flying in perfect symmetry, branching out and taking new directions as they approached the planet's surface. There were thousands of them, too many to count, all in ordered formation. High above them all flew a lone Nigh-kutu, his huge, dark, outstretched wings rippling with shadow energy. His size was no greater than any of the others, yet his power looked immense, with rays of shadows wrapping around him and then casting down on the entire formation of approaching warriors.

I could not take my eyes from this lone Nigh-kutu. A fear entered my body, rooting me to the spot. I felt paralyzed, my body refusing to respond, my heart beating hard, my breathing shallow.

"Arrunn," Jychanumun suddenly growled, seeing the screens through my eyes. His words were guttural, as if he were speaking the Nigh-kutu tongue. "The beast comes here himself."

Jychanumun's voice sounded different. It felt different. *He* felt different. I could sense that he was feeling something very odd, very horrible and intensely strong. It was like anger, yet far more severe. It overpowered me, making me feel destructive to the point that it froze my mind. It was as if all my thoughts became focussed into one thing, a dark thing that I did not like, and I could see nothing else. It made me feel destructive to the point that I would enjoy destruction. It made me feel taller and bigger, yet furious and focussed, as if I wanted to leap on something and rip it apart with my bare hands.

Jychanumun severed the connection between us. I could no longer feel what he was feeling.

"What was that?" I gasped, catching my breath.

Jychanumun turned his face from me. "That," he replied, "is something you should never understand."

I sensed his resolve. I was glad he would say no more. Even feeling it for a brief moment seemed wrong.

As the noisy chaos continued around us, Jychanumun quickly composed himself, reconnecting to me, allowing him to see through my eyes once again. He returned his focus to the movement around us. He spoke aloud, recounting what Arrunn would do, which direction he would take, and where he would send his warriors. Chia listened intently, redirecting the Shaa-kutu who had not reached the central tunnels according to Jychanumun's instructions, finding them appropriate hiding places.

Through my connection to Jychanumun, I was aware of a darkness in his thoughts, but it was well shielded from me. I stood amidst the noise and movement, a still point, watching the screens so that Jychanumun could see through my eyes. As the black-winged ones grew closer, I could feel their dark intent, and what I saw made me too scared to move. Nigh-kutu, thousands upon thousands of them, raged through the skies directly above the planet.

I felt as though I was in one of my own nightmares. My mind raced and would not focus. The kutu around me seemed to move in slow motion. I had been witnessing the horrors of death and chaos all day on Eden1; I had seen things that would scar my thoughts forever. Now they were here, coming towards this vulnerable and gentle place, tainting the air with their malicious intent, growing closer to the defenceless planet that I loved so much, and all the people and creatures that felt like part of my soul. My fear for them grasped my heart. I could now think of only one thing: my own loved ones.

As if in a dream I walked, I floated, towards Stanze, touching his arm as he shouted commands. In the chaos, Stanze looked down at me: a small girl, a woman now, barely as tall as his chest. I didn't want to disturb him, but my body seemed to be acting of its own will.

"My family, Soul, Meah, my fellow humans . . ." the words fell from my lips. I could not stop myself. Love was love, no matter what species or part in this war.

And then Stanze did the one thing that I did not expect, but the one thing that was truly Anumi. He listened. He stopped shouting, he looked down at me, his eyes shining with compassion, and then he bent to my height.

"Do not worry little sister," his words soothing. "I have made sure that people have somewhere to go. Do not think that I would count their lives less valuable than our own."

As Stanze returned to shouting orders, I retrieved my bag and backed into a corner, so as not to be in the way. I tried not to fret, but I couldn't stop it. I rummaged through my bag, finding the communication device that Stanze had given me to keep contact with Soul and my family. I held the screen up, shakily telling Soul that the Nigh-kutu were here, telling my family that they should hide and keep safe, and that I loved them. It didn't feel enough. It felt as if I should be with them. If this was our end, I should have taken Meah to Threetops to be with my family.

I must help, I disciplined myself. I must not let this fear paralyze me. I must do something.

I thrust out my energy and sent my senses soaring through the earth, my panic over-ridden by the need to help, to warn. I felt people – hundreds, nay thousands of them. *Be safe*, I repeated, hoping they would sense my intentions.

As I soared through the land, I felt the energy of the Earth shudder. I could feel the Nigh-kutu presence. I could feel their aggressive intent and pent-up desire to fight. It made my insides hurt. The Nigh-kutu were here.

If I could stop this Arrunn, paralyse his mind and body or cast him far away, surely his armies would be less without their leader. I could stop him. I could use my skills and my link to the Old One to stop this atrocious being. I could even kill him. Surely destroying such a terrible being would not be wrong.

I started to push out my energy to find this dark soul. As my essence soared through the land, it was not difficult to find him. Everywhere pointed to him. I fixed my sights and flung my consciousness upwards, to intercept his flight.

"No!" I suddenly heard Jychanumun shout. He had shouted with his mouth as well as his mind. His cry broke my concentration.

You must not do that, Jychanumun silently told me with his mind.

But I may be able to stop him, I replied, frustrated that my attempt had been blocked.

No, you must trust me, Jychanumun said. *If you trust me only once in your life, then trust me now. You must not use your power, your link to the Old One, for destruction. Ever.*

My body involuntarily shuddered, my empty stomach violently retching bile that splashed through my fingers. I did not know why Jychanumun was right. I just knew that he was right. I had almost done a terrible thing.

So I did nothing except feel fear and dread and horror. From my position in the corner of the room, I found myself struggling to remain coherent. I took solace in counting the Anumi and their fellow Shaa-kutu as they found their way through the tunnels and into the control room. Seventy nine, Chia had said was their number. So far, I had counted sixty safe.

Several kutu were deep in the connecting tunnels, en route to safety. One I could feel was not far, but was stuck in a partly constructed area without any through-tunnel. It was an Anumi, the one known as Brave; he was trapped with nowhere to go. Nigh-kutu now swarmed the skies above us, and his position was perilous.

I was worried. Brave would be discovered if he stayed there, and spotted if he left. My mind raced, trying to think of a way to save him. I couldn't think of anything. I could barely think at all.

All my thoughts were now laced with fear and trepidation. My fear was clouding my thoughts, but even worse, it was paralyzing my mind and my body. I was terrified for everyone and everything, and my body seemed unable to cope.

Suddenly, the air around me seemed to tremor.

I automatically put my hand out to steady myself. I half-expected to hear the crashing sound of Nigh-kutu landing directly above us, or the sound of energy bolts being flung into the ground where we hid, or the rage of pounding against the door as Nigh-kutu tried to enter the room. But the screens showed that the Nigh-kutu still traversed the skies directly above the land, their ominous presence casting darker shadows within the evening gloom. The shuddering around me continued. This was not coming from the Nigh-kutu. Nevertheless, something did feel wrong, very wrong. Even the air around me felt disturbed.

Do you feel that? I silently asked Jychanumun.

What is it? Jychanumun asked.

I slowly stood up, leaning against the wall to maintain my balance.

I cast my eyes around the room. My fear made everything seem ominous, but nothing physical was moving. I expected to see signs of an earthquake or a fight erupting, but I did not. This was not physical. This was deeper, more intense. It made me dizzy. It made my insides hurt, and the pain was increasing. Matter everywhere, my body, the ground, the objects around me, the air and space in between, all oscillated as if trying to rebalance themselves.

It was the movement of energy and it was in everything.

Suddenly, I could not avoid the truth of what I felt. That extent of movement could only have one source: the Old One.

From his eternal slumbers, the Old One had sensed wrongness.

The Old One had awoken.

The Old One was angry.

War or not, I was now truly scared.

"The Old One has awoken," I said aloud, not knowing if anyone listened. "His dreaming has been disturbed by the presence of so much ill intent."

I looked around me. The movement of energy was increasing. It looked as though everything around me was undoing. Within the blur, I could see that the kutu felt it too. They had stopped what they were doing. They were looking at me.

The kutu looked afraid.

"The Nigh-kutu must be stopped," I spoke aloud. "The Old

One could snuff out all life in an instant. We will all be nothing. They must be stopped."

"The Nigh-kutu outnumber us. We cannot stop them."

I think it was Stanze who spoke. His words were unclear, drifting around the room, breaking apart as they were spoken.

"Too many, too much," I managed to say.

This was from the Old One. Nothing, no one, had the power to stop this. Even my most primal skill, my Voice, *the* Voice, could not be used, for that voice stemmed from the Old One himself. I had no power against this.

The Old One was disturbed. He wanted this disturbance stopped. He would stop it in the only way he knew how. I knew what he was doing. I could feel the truth of it. The Old One was undoing life itself.

Is this our end? Jychanumun silently asked with his mind, walking towards me.

It was. I knew it was. But I couldn't answer. My lungs would not take in breath. My body felt like it was melting into the air. By now, the pain of energy moving so violently around me, *through* me, was almost too much to bear. I sank down to the floor, the pain overwhelming my flesh. I could see that even the kutu were feeling it too. They looked helplessly at their own energy moving and dissipating around them.

I gritted my teeth, trying to keep conscious through the agony. I think Jychanumun was trying to tell me something. He knelt to me, holding me. I couldn't hear him.

Jychanumun, I tried to shout with my mind, but then I could say no more. The pain now overwhelmed my thoughts. I think I was screaming. It was as if my body was turning to liquid, undoing itself, and I could feel every change with agony.

Suddenly, I could feel the Old One pulling me to him.

I had no power over such a force.

Little One! **COME!** The Old One's voice boomed through my head.

I felt a shift in my consciousness. For a brief moment, I felt nothing. The absence of pain was euphoric. I was between worlds, but conscious of both. In one world I lay motionless, with Jychanumun holding me, and in the other I saw the rawness of the Old One's existence, angered that his peace was disturbed, pulling me to him.

I had to go to him. I had no choice.

And then I was gone, pulled away from the body that lay motionless on the stone floor, devoid of breath. I was with him. The Old One had drawn me to him.

Chia had reset the protection of his bodysuit to maximum, but still the surges of energy overwhelmed him. His body seemed to be losing substance. His energy could barely be contained. The pain was intense.

He removed a glove, looking at his hand. The violet energy bled from his fingers, dissipating into the air as if his very substance was undoing. He looked around. Tachra had collapsed. She looked dead.

Chia managed to get a healing sheet, falling the last few steps towards Tachra's body, roughly covering her motionless flesh before he could no longer feel his feet.

"What is happening?" Chia asked, stumbling towards Jychanumun. The words came out jumbled, fragmenting into the air as they were spoken.

"This . . . is the end," Jychanumun replied, the words also fragmenting, bleeding into the air as he spoke them. He spoke as clearly as he could. "Not just her end or our end: the end of all things."

Jychanumun pulled the healing sheet off Tachra's head,

stroking her face. His fingers were numb; the energy had already left them. He ignored the strange pains that wracked his body. He was used to pain. He could block it. If this was his end, he would not let pain mar it.

Chia knew what Jychanumun meant, they all did. They could see their energy bleeding away from their bodies. It was as if the foundation of everything was becoming undone. They knew that this might be the last few moments of existence.

Jychanumun began singing. It was an old song. A song to honour life and death. A song long forgotten. Sitting cross-legged on the floor, his head bowed, his eyeless sight remembering all that he had seen and loved, he gave that song life.

Chia found himself knowing that song. He knelt, joining in. Mardoch began humming, as did Dragun. Stanze and the Anumi knew that song too. From the depths of their awareness, knowing that their lives, all lives, were coming to an end, their oldest memories surfaced. They all joined in. They all remembered that song.

The kutu drew together, their energy bleeding from their bodies and drifting into the air as if it was smoke, using the last of their life to create one last thing: a song of honour.

The song united them. If this were the end, they would die united.

I was encompassed in wrath itself.

Please, I begged the Old One, *Do not do this. Let this not be the end of all things.*

You ask too much! he boomed furiously. The words exploded around me, feeling like a thousand deafening blows in my mind.

Please, I begged.

The pressure in my head made me think it was about to explode. The Old One was angry: more than angry, he was enraged. I had known him capable of anger, but the extent of this new emotion was all-consuming, beyond anything I could have imagined and anything I had words for. His fury whipped around me, through me, consuming my every nerve, every morsel of awareness with a burning sting.

The rage of the Old One was too much for me to fight against. I was like a leaf being flung around by a great storm. I closed both my eyes and my true vision, allowing the nothingness to take me away. I felt as though I was rising, or was it falling? I was falling with a speed so fast that it felt motionless.

And then I stopped. Everything around me felt still.

I opened my eyes. The scene was a blur of angry energy whirling violently all around me. I was in the middle, untouched, giddy at the vastness of such might. The noise had lessened. I could still hear the distant roar of his might all around me, but it was muffled now, as if I was walled from it.

I should be scared. I knew that I should. Never had I witnessed something so all-consuming. But the sheer overwhelming power that I now witnessed did not scare me, as I knew it should; somehow I felt blocked from this, as if my fear had been removed. I was numb. He had brought me into the eye of his storm, and I was safe there, walled off from his terrible fury.

Within the movement of everything around me, a thousand pictures flashed before my eyes, each one a fragment that was part of his storm. Within the mass of movement I saw many things, all part of the world beyond me now. A woman crouched, holding two frightened young children to her chest. A wolf backed fearfully into the corner of his cave, its eyes wide and nostrils flared. An elderly couple sank to the floor, speechlessly holding each other. A young man crawled anxiously through dirt to reach his hut. A Nigh-kutu flung himself backwards, beating his head with his fists. Birds flew frantically, shouting to each other in warning, seeking a safer place. A mass of ants rushed to the shelter of their nest. A Shaa-kutu in a darkened tunnel collapsed, his eyes seeing only defeat. A lone child sat on a wooden floor, crying.

Everything everywhere was being touched by this storm, his storm. The Old One was restoring peace in the only way he knew how. He was removing the source of the disturbance - life.

But this was the end of everything that I cared for. My loved ones, my friends, they would soon be no more. The thought of that wrenched at my heart.

You would end everything, but not me? But all life is precious, I beseeched him.

He paid no attention to me, his storm only gathering even more momentum, undoing the life everywhere that disturbed his peace. My mind raced, trying to find something, anything to reason with him.

The kutu, look at them, you remember them, I implored. *You did not destroy them back then, when time began. Show mercy now. Let them learn to love you as they are.*

Mercy? he roared. I had his attention, but he seemed even angrier from my words. *Love? These are names for incomplete beings. They are not my way, yet you bring such things to me. Through my connection to you, you give me awareness of mercy, of pain, of fear. I will not tolerate these things. They are not true!*

Please, I begged. *Please let them live.*

No! he roared. His energy moved inwards, whipping around me like a storm with a thousand stings, touching my essence.

I tried to back away, but had nowhere to go. It was as if he wanted to hurt me.

The Old One sensed my fear of him.

You will understand. His voice had calmed a little, but the anger was still there. *When you have dreamt eternity, you will understand. With me, you will not know fear or mercy or such imperfect things. Your peace will give me peace.*

My peace? My fear. Is it me causing this? I asked.

*It **is** me,* I suddenly realised, with utter certainty.

I was horrified. It was *my* connection to him, the Old One, and *my* feelings of fear and terror that had disturbed his slumbers. My link had given him awareness of terrible things. Without my link to him, he would have kept sleeping his eternal slumbers. I was the cause of his anger against everything that was not right. It was my fault.

I make you aware of these things. I bring these disturbances to you. I whispered. This was terrible, beyond terrible. I could not be responsible for this. I gathered my strength. *Please, no!* I beseeched. *Kill me; let them live. Or can I release you from our bond? I do not wish to, you are my soul. But I will. I do. If that is what I must do to save them, I release you. I release you!*

I felt the tempest around me lessen. He had stopped, frozen in time, timeless.

You release me? he asked.

Yes, I replied, and I knew that I was crying. The thought of breaking my link to him hurt greater than any sufferings that my body could ever endure. The thought of being without him made my heart feel as if it had fallen from me. I didn't want to break our link. But if it was the only way to save life itself, save so many others, what choice did I have?

You are my soul, I wept. *I know no life without you. But I will choose to sever our link to save life itself. I see them. I love them too. So, if I must choose, then please, let them live; I relinquish our link. If that means killing me, then so be it. Please choose: kill me, sever our link, but let life go on. Please.*

The wind around me died down. The light dimmed so I stood in darkness and silence.

I cannot destroy you, his voice echoed though the quiet, *for you are part of me, and such things cannot be undone. But you release me? You choose to release me? Yes, little one. It is done,* his words drifted off into the distance.

Go, he said, the words now barely audible. *Do not call me. Do not talk to me. I will sleep deeply without you. You have made your choice. Take your life. It is not mine. We are no more.*

SIXTEEN

"Order!" Arrunn turned and faced his army.

On the final descent to the planet's surface, once they had passed the long, cooling clouds, fights had broken out among Arrunn's warriors. As they had scoured the skies, looking for signs of Shaa-kutu colonies, extraordinary waves of energy had begun rippling through their bodies. It was as if the entire energy of the planet oscillated through them, draining their very essence away.

The warriors could see what was happening to their dissolving energy. They felt the pain of their depletion. They became fearful. And, as their fear grew, madness had overtaken them. The warriors slashed and ripped at each other. Some even slashed at themselves.

"It is a cursed place," one warrior shouted.

"It is Eskah's oblivion," another yelled out.

The mention of Eskah's oblivion had sent all the Nigh-kutu warriors into a greater frenzy. It was one of the few things that they feared. Some tried to pull back from their descent, others tried to keep them in place. Some simply froze in mid-air, too fearful to do anything as they watched the energy bleeding from their bodies. Deimom struggled to overcome his own fear and control the warriors. Eventually, he too hovered unmoving, gazing in horror at the energy draining from his essence as the lines of his body and wings slowly dissolved into the air.

Arrunn felt no emotion, but he could see what was happening, even to his own essence. The energy of the planet had suddenly shifted and then fragmented, passing over them and through them, through everything, taking the life energy of the Nigh-kutu as it moved.

Arrunn too had felt his own life force draining from him, weakening him. He saw the dark swirls of his own essence bleeding from every part of his body, dispersing into the air as if it were nothing more than smoke on the wind. Yet he had striven to continue their descent. He had taken over from High Warrior, Deimom, issuing commands, fighting through the pain and ignoring his own growing weakness. His wings were depleting fast. He could barely feel the haft of his sword in his hands anymore.

Suddenly, as unexpectedly as it began, the energy shift stopped.

The air around the warriors stilled. Their essences stopped bleeding away. Their energy slowly moved back towards their bodies.

"Order!" Arrunn commanded again. He breathed deeply, pulling back his energy as quickly as he could, pushing it into his failing wings.

The Nigh-kutu warriors did not hear Arrunn's command. Although they were regaining strength, they still fought and slashed at each other and themselves. This was no longer the energy shift that was causing their madness. This was because they could not control their fear. Arrunn had to act quickly.

Fear, Arrunn considered, was something he knew very well how to control.

Arrunn knew that to extinguish uncontrollable fear, all he had to do was replace it with a greater, yet controllable fear.

"Stay here," Arrunn commanded his unmoving guards. They did not respond. They did not need to.

Arrunn slowly removed the black sword from the sheath on his back.

"Order!" he commanded again.

The warriors paid no notice, so entrenched within their own fear that they were. Arrunn moved towards the closest kutu, severing his head in one swift move, allowing the dark rays from the sword to fall on those around him. The warriors immediately around the beheaded kutu looked on in shock. The shock brought them to their senses. The sense of a greater fear, that of imminent death unless they stopped brawling, made them quickly fall in line.

Arrunn calmly moved further in to the mass of warriors, selecting a second kutu who was creating much disturbance, again removing his head with his sword. Again, the warriors closest to the fallen one stopped and came to their senses, while those further away still fought among themselves. Arrunn increased his momentum, soaring through the lines of his army, beheading any warrior who displayed uncontrollable weakness. Several warriors in their frenzy lashed out at Arrunn as he moved among them, but he wasted no time clearing them effortlessly from his path.

Several hundred dead warriors later and the Nigh-kutu army was at last silent. They had regained control of themselves: Arrunn had seen to that.

Arrunn sheathed his sword between his shoulders. The heat from its blade warmed his back and its structure bristled with so much life-energy from those slaughtered that the excess seeped through his skin, saturating his essence. Arrunn flew past Deimom towards the line of Warrior-Firsts. He knew that if he was to feel anything, it would be both anger and disappointment. All of them were weak.

The warriors still displayed signs of fear, their eyes shifting, checking their limbs for further signs of energy bleeding. But they contained themselves, standing in formation, their jaws set in grim determination, hovering above the planet's surface, wings motionless, tentatively awaiting orders.

"Are you Nigh-kutu?" Arrunn coolly asked the warriors. He did not raise his voice. He did not need to, because the clarity of his words reached even the furthest ears. He scanned the masses. "Cowards have permission to leave," he stated simply.

This was a carefully selected word; the greatest insult. Warriors were trained to believe that death would be a better choice than cowardice.

None of the kutu moved.

"Then be warriors," Arrunn commanded. "Search this place. Find the light-lovers. Bring them to me."

A roar erupted. The roar of battle. It filled the air with a resonance of its own, making it tremor.

The High Warrior Deimom swooped down, and the entire legion of warriors followed. Like a blanket of thickest black smoke, they covered the skies above the land.

SEVENTEEN

I came to, but did not open my eyes.

We are no more; his last words reverberated in my head. The loss felt overwhelming. I wished he had chosen to kill me. I would rather be dead.

Along with the echo of his last words, I could hear singing. My ears heard it as quite beautiful, yet I felt nothing. I knew I was back in the world of flesh and mortality. That I felt more than ever. Jychanumun was holding me. I knew I should feel joy that he was alive, yet I felt empty. I felt lost. I felt alone. Even with dozens around me, never had I felt so alone. I could no longer feel the Old One. I had relinquished the very soul of me.

The singing slowly petered out.

"It has stopped," I heard someone say. It sounded like Chia. "The Earth energy has stilled once again. It has stopped. We live!"

A murmur broke out around me. I didn't care. I felt someone trying to open one of my eyes. I sat up and pulled myself away from the touch, struggling to my feet.

Dozens of kutu faces all looked towards me. It was as if they were waiting for me to say something. Kraniel started to ask a question. Jychanumun held up his hand to him, silencing him.

I know what happened, Jychanumun silently told me with his mind. *You chose to sever you link with the Old One to save us all.*

Jychanumun's words sounded muffled in my head without the clarity of the Old One to enhance them. But the fact that I could hear them at all surprised me. I stood looking at the kutu around me, feeling very alien in my own flesh.

Our bond has not changed, my brave Tachra, Jychanumun told me.

I am not brave. I am empty, I distantly replied.

You still have me, us, your family, friends, Meah. You, he held out a hand towards me, *you have not changed.*

Yes, I have, I silently told Jychanumun, ignoring his hand. *I am different. I am less.*

But you still have your own skills. You will learn who you are without your link to him.

When I die, I will be dust. No more. I have no soul.

Jychanumun fell silent at that.

You will never be dead to me, he finally replied.

I looked around at the screens on the wall. Nigh-kutu flocked down in masses, too many to count. I no longer had the power of the Old One. I was now useless in this war. I looked around at the kutu in the room, all watching me. The compassion on their faces was almost unbearable.

"I love you all," I whispered. "I'm sorry."

And then I turned and walked away.

EIGHTEEN

Arrunn left his legions scouring the skies, and lowered to the planet's surface, accompanied by his twelve personal guards. He had been waiting for this moment for a long time. He had not known where it would happen, or when, but he had always known that he would find the heart of all things at the right time.

He chose an area of land without structures to mar his view. His feet touched the soil. A wave of cold ran through his energy, bombarding his senses. He inverted his wings, solidified, and took a deep breath. Air hit his lungs with layered scents and tones that made his reduced energy ripple in response. The luminous energy of the heart of things was everywhere. It centred here and its rays radiated out far beyond the skies, further than Arrunn's inner eye could perceive. This was a small planet, but its scope was unending, rippling past him, through him.

For the first time, Arrunn *felt* the earth. It was strong. It was alive. It was beautiful. Yes, this place was indeed beautiful. But when Arrunn felt beyond the awe of that beauty, he hated the life that saturated this place with a passion beyond anything. The heart of all things was perfect. It reminded him of everything that he, that all kutu, were not.

It was surprisingly quiet. Arrunn could not hear any fighting. Neither could he sense any. His warriors still roamed the skies looking for Shaa-kutu, but had found none. It seemed that the light-lovers had concentrated on protecting their home-world, ignorant as they were. Although it was clear that the Shaa-kutu had been here. Arrunn could taste them. The light-lovers bitter-sweet essence touched his senses with a taste and smell like none other. But it was faint, very faint, and probably nothing more than the residue of their past presence.

Disturbing his contemplation, High Warrior Deimom, along with one of his Warrior-Firsts, cautiously moved into view, obviously having something to say.

Deimom was not sure whether to interrupt his superior. Out here on this exposed land was no doorway to request entry or kutu to act as intermediary. Arrunn's twelve guards would never speak to him; they just watched him, unmoving, as he awkwardly approached.

"Go ahead," Arrunn instructed without looking at him.

Deimom made a small bow, immediately wishing that he had not made such an obvious display of subservience. Arrunn made a sideways glance, but did not comment.

"No Shaa-kutu have been found," Deimom reported. "However, signs of past Shaa-kutu presence are numerous, primarily in one deserted building and its miscellaneous objects. Furthermore, wide varieties of species display the foundation of Shaa-kutu genetics. One species is particularly advanced."

Arrunn looked mildly interested. "Are there many?" he asked.

"Thousands," Deimom replied.

"Bring me one."

Deimom nodded, turned to one of his Warrior-Firsts and issued instructions to return with a sample. He immediately took to the sky.

Arrunn stood with his hands behind his back, perfectly still, watching the lone flying warrior disappear from sight.

"Did you retrieve Shursa's memories, as requested?" Arrunn asked.

"Yes," Deimom nodded, immediately delving into the inner safety pocket of his chest armour. He had kept the information-liquid close to his chest, in a protected vial made of unbreakable Mazium. He handed the vial to Arrunn, glad to be rid of such a responsibility.

Arrunn took the vial, tucked it into a section of his sword strap, and then stood, observing the landscape in silence.

Deimom waited for the warrior to return with the specimen. He could hear the breeze from the planet all around him. It made strange sounds against his armour and through his hair. He didn't like it. He didn't like anything that he couldn't see. There seemed to be far too many things on this little planet that moved of their own accord.

"Does this place make you feel uncomfortable?" Arrunn suddenly asked.

Deimom grimaced.

"You control it well," Arrunn nodded. "You will remain here with me. Select five hundred of the best warriors to stay here under your command."

Arrunn turned, indicating to one of his guards.

The guard moved forward to stand directly behind Arrunn, saying nothing. Deimom made a conscious effort not to take a step further away. He did not like these guards. He never had. They were not like other Nigh-kutu.

"Once Deimom has selected his warriors, escort the others home," Arrunn instructed the impassive guard. "When you have returned the warriors home, let them find sanctuary in the inner shrine."

The guard nodded.

Arrunn seemed deep in thought. "And when that is done, return here. Bring my portable vault with all my collection of time crystals, including those from Immorah."

Deimom's thoughts were racing. Arrunn had mentioned the inner shrine! He had to ensure that his own face remained expressionless. Those warriors would be taken to the inner shrine? How blessed those warriors were!

Before now, Deimom had thought the rumour of the inner shrine to be mere hearsay. But if Arrunn was referring to it, it had to exist. Oh what wonders! The other warriors must have surpassed themselves to be deemed worthy of such a place. They must have performed so well in battle that they were ready to ascend to greatness. How Eskah's fortune smiled upon them. Deimom tried not to feel envious of those warriors who would be returning to such an honour. He too aspired to such greatness. He would have to ensure that he performed better next time. Perhaps then he would be considered worthy of the inner shrine.

Deimom knew that questions from one so obviously unworthy were inappropriate, but the words fell from his mouth nonetheless.

"Do you not wish for the inner shrine?"

Arrunn merely raised an eyebrow, his gaze never leaving the planet's surface.

"I choose not to have such selfish aspirations," Arrunn replied. "For the greatness of all Nigh-kutu, I remain. I see when their time is due."

"All Nigh-kutu are honoured."

Arrunn nodded. "You have done well this day. Once you have

chosen your warriors, let them rest. They will be in your charge. Disorder will not be acceptable."

Deimom did not reply. He knew what their leader was insinuating. He had failed to maintain order amongst the warriors earlier, yet here he was being given another chance. Even if he had not been granted the wonders of the inner shrine yet, he was indeed lucky. Eskah's might was still smiling upon him. Every Nigh-kutu would want to be High Warrior; such a position would produce even greater glories once he was admitted to the inner shrine.

He stood even straighter, his wings bristling. He would not let Arrunn down again.

Arrunn let the High Warrior talk, deeming it inappropriate to respond. Such trivia did not mar his concentration. The words and questions were mere surface thoughts. They did not disturb his focus.

The strategists had been wrong about the armies of Shaa-kutu on this planet. Earth had not been fortified by multitudes of light-lovers as they had projected. They had said to expect a battle here. They had thought such a precious place would be fiercely guarded by the light-lovers. And yet there were no armies, no guards and no defensive weapons at all. The Nigh-kutu had simply invaded without hindrance. The strategists had been wrong. Arrunn was right in his decision to remove them. He always was. They had outgrown their usefulness.

The mass of Nigh-kutu warriors still roamed the planet, searching again for any Shaa-kutu to satiate their want for war. But without the expected defence from the Shaa-kutu, there would be no great battle here. There were no great battles left for them to fight anywhere. The majority of both Nigh-kutu and Shaa-kutu had now been conquered. Arrunn would no longer need the strength of so many warriors. They would be a hindrance now. They had served their usefulness.

Now Arrunn could send most of his warriors back to their home-world. It would be their final flight. The time had come when their life energy would be more useful to Arrunn contained within a little crystal rather than expended through the wielding of their swords. They would go to the inner shrine believing they were to ascend. Arrunn had not lied. To him their death was ascendance. The time had come when the bulk of his army would be of more value to him dead.

Now, without the predicted battle, Arrunn's strategy could move on towards the next stage of his plan. This would be the final stage.

In this final stage, Arrunn would summon the heart of all things and force his own memories into that last universal consciousness. Once connected to the heart of all things, all imperfect life would be in his control, and he would know perfection. It was all quite simple really. Simple and inevitable. All Arrunn needed now were a few who were dedicated to him, the red kutu, Jychanumun, and a good quantity of time.

Arrunn smiled to himself, observing the land, casting his inner eye over the small, potent planet. With his inner eye he could see all life, and the energy all around him almost blinded that inner vision. He could not make out the life-light of his own warriors roaming the skies, because the brightness of the planet concealed their illumination with a more concentrated brilliance. His life-seeing skills were of little use to him here, but this was something he had foreseen, even if his strategists had not. He had found the correct place. Now, for the final part of his plan, he would utilize his own skills.

This was the heart of everything. Arrunn knew it. His warriors were blind to it, ignorant of its source, its past, *their* past. They could not remember that this heart of all things had split them, divided their purity and forced their incomplete, fragmented existence. But Arrunn did remember. Arrunn could never forget. He could see their imperfections. Arrunn alone had that memory.

With the twelve guards' cold eyes never leaving him, and with Arrunn clearly deep in thought, Deimom was relived to see his Warrior-First approaching with the requested specimen.

The Warrior-First landed. A limp, surprisingly kutu-like, small creature lay across his arms.

Arrunn turned around. The Warrior-First walked forward and dropped the creature at his feet.

The creature didn't move.

Arrunn leaned down, picking the specimen up by its hair. He held it up so he could inspect it, bringing its face close to his, its feet no longer able to touch the ground. He slowly turned it around. It made no response, but hung limply from his hand.

"What did you do to it?" Arrunn asked the Warrior-First.

"Nothing," the Warrior-First cautiously answered. "I just picked it up and flew it here."

"Obviously, flight does not agree with its structure," Arrunn mused. "Do you know what is it, or what function it has? Or why it was made to resemble kutu?"

"I could not get any information. They do not speak Nigh-kutu," the Warrior-First replied.

Arrunn waved the Warrior-First away, leaving him and Deimom to consider the small creature. It looked oddly like one of them, yet small, fragile and insignificant, with barely any energy. It was clearly alive, but it seemed to have shut down. It looked as though it was sleeping.

"Shall we kill the species, or is their life-energy worth salvaging?" Deimom asked.

"Do you have a reason to kill them yet?" Arrunn asked.

Deimom said nothing.

Arrunn held out his free hand. One of the guards stepped forward, handing him a small piece of equipment, which Arrunn activated, holding it towards the unconscious creature. A number flashed up on the screen. He looked at the results, mildly surprised.

"Less than one unit," he said to himself. "Their allocated life-span is very short. Their lifetime would be of little use. I would need thousands for one small crystal. They may be more useful alive. We do nothing until we know what their best use is."

Arrunn dropped the creature on the ground. It crumpled.

"Why make a complex species with such a short life span? I require further information. I will set up base at the deserted kutu building," Arrunn considered, looking towards Deimom. "Leave," he directed. "You have your five hundred warriors to select. Rest, replenish; I will call you when needed."

Arrunn then turned around, heading in the direction of the deserted golden building, leaving the specimen crumpled on the ground. Deimom watched the guards wait for Arrunn to pass them, and then, once Arrunn had overtaken their position, eleven of them turned around and followed him. The remaining guard took a step forward to stand beside Deimom.

Deimom waited a few moments, until Arrunn was gone from view.

"Do you have a name?" Deimom asked the guard.

The guard did not reply.

"I assume you are waiting for me to select my five hundred warriors so you can escort the others home."

Again, the guard said nothing. His eyes did not move from Deimom, but watched him coldly, waiting for him to complete his task.

Deimom pushed out his wings and launched into the sky before they had even finished forming. The sooner he did this task and rid himself of this silent guard the better. But as much as he did not like these guards, how he wished he could be flying home too. And as much as he liked nothing better than a good war, no war could surpass what he had heard of the inner shrine. How fortunate those warriors were to be welcomed there. Deimom focussed his resolve. He would complete his tasks, and complete them well; soon he too would be awarded such glories.

Arrunn stood at the entrance to the golden building. It stank of Shaa-kutu. The self-indulgent light-lovers had even put giant effigies of themselves either side of the doorway. Nevertheless, it was of sound construction. It had good-quality minerals in the build and a well-designed, multifaceted outer shell. It would offer adequate sanctuary while he worked. If it was not for the grotesquely decadent design, on Immorah he might even have considered it worthy of his personal occupation.

His guards had already checked the golden building for hiding light-lovers. It was deserted, and had been deserted in a hurry. There was a vast array of technology left behind, but all of it was relatively primitive and useless to him. He would give it all to Deimom's selected warriors, and they would consider the trinkets as gifts. Gifts given with a controlled harshness would enhance their subservience.

Arrunn followed the natural course of the wide corridor through the building and into a large central chamber. Apart from the dome, which let in far too much light, and despite the distraction of images on the walls and the pointless water-hole at the centre, this was a good place to work. His guards automatically took up position around the chamber, while one exited the building to darken the dome and take position at the main gates.

As the room darkened, Arrunn removed the vial of Shursa's memories from his belt. The small container shone a vibrant, bitter yellow. It was the substance of Shursa's memories, all of them. The essence was ill-matched to Arrunn's. Consuming them was not going to be pleasant.

Arrunn relaxed his energy, allowing it to flow around him like water. He put a barrier of energy around him, and then snapped off the vial's seal. The essence from the vial smoked upwards. With one deep breath, Arrunn breathed in the bitter fumes.

The yellow energy wreathed through Arrunn's essence like slime-weed from the ravages of the waste rivers. It tried to escape him, but Arrunn held it firm. With nowhere else to go, the memories that used to belong to Shursa needed to find a home, a consciousness to hold them. Slowly the energy submitted to Arrunn's will. It found its place, its new home, the only place that it had available to it. Shursa's memories settled into Arrunn's mind.

With these memories now firmly absorbed, Arrunn quickly partitioned them. He wanted access, yes, but he also wanted them restricted. He could not have them taint his own essence. Once Shursa's memories had been isolated, he closed his eyes, exploring his newly found knowledge.

Shursa's memories were filled with data and events. Obviously, Shursa had not always been the disjointed being that Arrunn had experienced. His memories showed him to have been meticulous in his information gathering in the past. Arrunn smiled to himself, absorbing the bounty of new facts as they settled into his mind. Arrunn now knew everything that Shursa had known.

Suddenly, Arrunn's mind froze on a piece of information: the Summoning Song. What was this? Had it already been played? No, it could not be true. What . . . ?

Arrunn searched for evidence to the contrary. But there was none. All evidence, and a great deal of it, said the same thing:

the red kutu had already written the Summoning Song, and the Summoning Song had already been played.

No.

No!

NO!

Arrunn's eyes opened, the darkness of his shadow flashing through the room. The rage. He would not suppress the rage. He would not suppress *this* rage!

His energy lashed out, flinging jagged shards all around him. The air smelt of burning. The ground seemed to tremor. Arrunn launched himself at a column at one side of the room, bringing the giant stone mass down with one hit. Dust and fragments flew up all around him, drawn towards his angry energy, spinning chaotically. With the speed of a raging beast he circled the room, bringing every portrait and statue crashing down to shatter as they hit the floor. He hurled energy bolts at the floor, so that great cracks opened up.

Amidst the rage of drawing in might to bring down the great crystal dome, Arrunn suddenly found himself surrounded. The guards had left their positions around the chamber and now blocked his assault, one absorbing the last energy bolt without wincing.

One of the guards stretched out a hand, touching Arrunn's forehead.

Arrunn looked at the guard coldly.

"Do not do that again. I wanted to show that rage," Arrunn said. "I had not lost control."

The guard said nothing. None of the guards said anything. They simply turned around, making their way through the debris to resume their positions around the room.

Arrunn drifted back down to the ground, his mind racing.

The Summoning Song had already been played? But that song was not destined to be written yet. How could it already exist? The red kutu, the Dhasmiel, could not even know what he needed to know in order to write it until the future. This should be impossible.

Arrunn had thousands of millennia of planning behind him, each moment carefully controlled so that his fate would not change. Everything until now had unfolded just as he had wanted. But this? How could something so fundamental change? The Summoning Song had already been written. And implemented? It should not be possible. And if that was not significant enough, Shursa's memories showed him even more that he had not planned: how could a mere human, a kutu-manufactured, unworthy, weak, part-life, now have that link to the heart of all things? That link was surely destined to be his. This would change everything.

Arrunn forced his mind to calm until coldness raced through him once again. The coldness gave him clarity. A new future started to map out in front of him. It was a future with exactly the same outcome, merely a different lead up to that outcome.

Yes, this might change the course of things, Arrunn considered, but the goal remained the same. So, the Summoning Song had already been performed and a link already made to the heart of all things? Then he would simply change his tactics accordingly. Perhaps his task had just been simplified. With the Summoning Song played and a creature already having the link, all he had to do was go back in time and take her place.

It would have to be a considered time jump, one to the exact time when the link was made. He could not risk creating a time fissure. So, all Arrunn needed to know was the precise moment when the link occurred.

Arrunn scanned through Shursa's memories on the subject of this human. Shursa had been detailed in his information-gathering, memorizing facts to the point of obsession. But nowhere in the vast array of data was a time or date mentioned when this link between the human and the heart of all things had been made.

Arrunn summoned one of his guards.

"Find if this information is present anywhere on Eden1, or within any of the captured Shaa-kutu," he instructed.

The guard nodded, turned around and left. He needed no further details.

And if none of the light-lovers had this information? There was always another source, the source itself: the human. He could find the human and extract her own memories, discovering the exact time and location of the event. And what good fortune that these creatures could not leave this planet. They had been designed for this place, existing in one solid form and able only to exist on land. Could it be any easier?

Arrunn scanned through the possible flaws in his logic. There were none.

Arrunn started laughing. Fate could never outwit him! No, fate had just made a change that would help him. What Arrunn thought he would have to wait millennia for, fate had now placed in his imminent grasp.

Arrunn glanced around the large, darkened chamber. The debris from his rage had already been heaped in one corner by one of his guards. He smiled to himself. He felt no joy, but he remembered what joy could feel like; smiling was appropriate. Today was a good day.

NINETEEN

I had severed my link to the Old One. I'd left the central hub, making my way through the tunnels, going deeper underground. I had no idea of where I was heading. I didn't actually care. But I'd decided that if I couldn't be in my forest, curled up with Meah, in the only place that had ever given me my own sense of peace, then I just wanted to be alone.

I knew the Nigh-kutu still raged above ground, but what could I do? Without my link to the Old One, I was useless to both kutu and humans. I felt horrible. I felt empty. I had severed the very soul of me to save my friends. Did I wish there had been another choice? Yes. Would I choose the same again, even if I knew how terrible it would make me feel? I knew that yes, I probably would.

I was like a walking corpse, empty and devoid of the peace and understanding that had always been part of my life. The tunnels grew darker and less finished as I walked. It seemed appropriate. I think I was looking for a nice dark corner to lie down in and just give up.

I passed several part-constructed rooms off the main tunnel. One had a large array of tools and instruments stacked neatly around the edges. What looked a bit like a large spade made from a sleek, silver substance, glinted in the distant light. I walked several steps past that room, stopped, turned around and went back. I picked up the spade and continued through the tunnels, dragging it behind me as I walked.

I took a turning where the tunnel became rougher and less finished, and the earth beneath my feet had not been smoothed or hardened. Rock protruded from the walls of the part-finished tunnel, their smooth surfaces glistening in the dim light. I walked to an area and began digging. I had a purpose. There was one last thing I could do to help.

I had been digging for some time when I felt someone was standing behind me. I didn't need any extra senses for that. Whoever it was, they were blocking out my light.

The presence of my silent observer made me feel annoyed. I wanted to tell them that I wanted to be on my own. Instead, I ignored their presence and continued digging.

"You are feeling sorry for yourself," the voice finally said from behind me.

I could have hit him with this nice, heavy spade. Sorry for myself? How dare he! And although I hadn't recognised the voice, I did recognise the guttural accent. It was one of the Nigh-kutu, his words coming out as Shaa-kutu from his newly embedded translator, yet the accent remained.

"Go away," I eventually manage to spit through gritted teeth. I replied in Nigh-kutu. *That will confuse his nano-translator*, I thought.

But he didn't go away. He continued to block out my light. He just stood there while I continued digging.

"What are you doing?" he finally asked.

"I'm digging."

"A little creature like you? That is going to take a long time," the Nigh-kutu remarked.

"I guess so," I replied. "But hey, I may have another fifty or sixty years of life left, if I survive your war. I should manage it by then. And my name is Tachra, thank you."

The Nigh kutu walked forward.

"Why are you digging, Tachra Thankyou?"

I turned around, giving my best glare. I wiped the hair from my damp forehead with the back of my hand. Dirt smudged into my eyes, making them water. I tried to get rid of the dirt, but only succeeded in making it worse.

Through my bleary vision, I could see Dragun standing in front of me in the gloomy tunnel. Maybe I should be scared at being alone with any Nigh-kutu other than Jychanumun. But right now, I didn't care.

"If my memory serves me correctly," I told Dragun, "somewhere in that direction is a Shaa-kutu named Brave who is trapped in an unfinished tunnel. While you stand there watching and doing nothing, I'm going to help him."

"I think the warrior leader, Stanze, is arranging over-ground rescues at dawn for those trapped."

"Dawn might be too late."

Dragun nodded and looked around.

"That is solid stone in front of you."

"How observant of you."

"And you will not dig through it," Dragun shrugged.

"I know," I retorted, irritated and grumpy. "That's why I'm digging down. I will go around the stone."

Dragun just raised his eyebrows and pursed his lips.

I frowned at him. *If he so much as rolls his eyes at me I shall most certainly hit him with this spade*, I thought. *Giant kutu or not.*

"There will be stone further down too. Probably why the tunnel was not completed."

"Wonderful insight," I snapped. "I shall try anyway."

"I am a Stone Weaver," Dragun stated.

"And I'm an idiot," I shrugged, turning my back and resuming my digging with even greater vigour. "So what?"

Dragun burst out laughing. He laughed and he laughed, and the sound was so wonderful that I found myself laughing too.

"You are an impudent little thing, aren't you?" Dragun said through his laughter, pointing at me. "I like you."

Dragun moved to my side, standing in front of the solid stone that I wanted to get through. The dense, glossy stone had fine cracks in it. He put his fingers against one of the cracks, felt around a little, and then pulled away a large chunk of rock the height of my thigh and as wide as it was tall. He lifted the rock to one side as I stood and watched in awe. And then he picked me up, turned me around and sat me on that rock as if I were nothing more than a little corn dolly.

"I am a Stone Weaver," Dragun said again.

"You already told me that," I replied. "What does a Stone Weaver do? Make stone baskets?"

"I used to," Dragun shrugged, "but I have not done any real stone weaving for millennia, including baskets."

He came in close to me, his face only half a hand's distance away. I could feel his breath on my cheek.

"I could not," he whispered. "I was supposed to be dead."

He leaned back, hands on hips, looked at me and nodded. "Dead," he repeated, drawing a line across his throat with his finger. "I've seen my own passing recorded in the Book of the Dead. My name. Dead. Tick."

I was about to ask what happened.

"It is a long story," Dragun anticipated the question, "And

a very long time hiding in rocks. A Rock Weaver has a lot of patience." He looked at me, tilting his head to one side, his face smiling yet sad. "I am the last of my kind," he told me. "My kind were bonded to each other. I feel each loss every moment that I still exist. I cannot comprehend your loss, but," he touched his chest with his fist, "I have empathy."

"You know what happened?" I asked, surprised.

"No," he shrugged, "but I see your face. I recognise the expression."

Before giving me a chance to reply, he smiled and flexed his fingers. They crunched noisily as he bent them. He seemed to get satisfaction from their crunching.

"Let us get to work then," he nodded. "You are physical, yet can manipulate and move energy, yes?" Dragun asked.

"That is what I used to be able to do," I nodded. "I'm not sure if I still can."

"True skills never leave us," Dragun murmured, more to himself than to me. "I am the opposite. To me, energy does not move or change, but physical substances, matter, can be manipulated."

I just looked at the Nigh-kutu uncertainly. I couldn't imagine how such a thing could be possible.

"What direction is this brave kutu in?" he asked.

"His *name* is Brave," I corrected him. "Are you getting the name wrong on purpose?"

"I might be," Dragun replied. He smiled a wide smile. It made his brown eyes sparkle. It was very difficult for me to stay annoyed with him.

I pointed. "I think that straight ahead, at about this level, this tunnel should join with another one. Brave should be situated on the other side."

Dragun nodded, stood in front of the rock mass and slowly

moved forward. After half a step, it looked as if his face and chest were buried in the rock.

I panicked, worried that the kutu could be stuck. I let out a gasp. Dragun reversed his step.

"No noise," Dragun put his finger to his lips. "I must concentrate. I have not done this in a long time."

I nodded, wide eyed. The area of solid stone that Dragun had just moved back from was now indented with a perfect imprint of his body.

Dragun resumed his position and slowly started moving forward again. As he moved into the rock, I could see the stone condensing, moving away from him. Three steps in and a perfect silhouette of Dragun was formed into the stone. It was as if he were walking through a soft, malleable substance instead of dense rock.

I sat quietly, not making a sound, even covering my mouth with my hand so that my breathing did not disturb Dragun as he worked.

"Tachra Thankyou," I heard Dragun call after a seeming eternity of waiting.

I slid off the stone and stood at the front of the Dragun-shaped tunnel.

"Yes?" I called.

"Come here."

"Is it safe?"

"Of course."

I walked into the tunnel with more than a little trepidation. It was surprisingly warm, despite being underground, and my movement seemed unusually loud. I found myself tip-toeing so as not to disturb any possible loose stone. My imagination played tricks on me as to what it would feel like to be buried here, should it collapse. I tried to banish such thoughts from my head.

The tunnel was perfectly straight, and I soon caught up with

Dragun. He moved in a slow, wide circle, allowing enough room for us both to stand in the same area. I had never seen a kutu able to do anything like this; it was amazing.

"It smells beautiful, this stone," Dragun said. "Tell me, where is this Brave now?"

"If my memory is correct, the tunnel should be directly in front of you," I replied.

"As I thought," Dragun nodded. He looked at me. "I do not think the Shaa-kutu will be happy to see this face. He should see you first."

"You are probably right," I smiled. Brave would not know that this Nigh-kutu was our friend. It would not be good to surprise him with such a sight.

Dragun felt an area of stone, nodded to himself, and then used his hand to make a hole. He withdrew his hand and a cool breeze drifted into the tunnel. Dragun stepped aside and indicated towards the hole.

I stood on my tiptoes, poking my face into the gap.

"Brave?" I whispered. "Brave?"

Suddenly a pair of bright-blue eyes were staring right in front of me.

"Iastha Tachra? By Eskah, what . . . ?"

"We're getting you out," I whispered. "A Nigh-kutu is helping. He's a friend, so don't fight him. Stand back."

Brave nodded and disappeared from sight. Dragun enlarged the hole, just enough for the kutu to climb through.

"Go back out," Dragun instructed me, as Brave squeezed stealthily through the hole. "I will close this up."

I hurriedly led the way back through the tunnel Dragun had formed. For Brave it was much more of a squeeze. He was around the same size as Dragun, so had to walk straight and smoothly to prevent getting stuck. We eventually emerged on the other side, followed shortly by Dragun, who effortlessly pushed the rock back into place.

"I heard them," Brave stated "Nigh-kutu were everywhere . . ." His words petered out, and he looked at Dragun suspiciously. "Are you sure about him?"

I nodded, briefly explaining that Dragun was an ally and that Brave should join the others for a full briefing. And Dragun? Dragun seemed very happy with himself. He was beaming.

I watched as the two kutu walked away, back up towards the central hub. A Shaa-kutu and a Nigh-kutu warrior side by side? It was a strange sight, but, even though Brave did keep his distance from Dragun, it looked right.

What to do now? I sighed, once the two kutu's footsteps had faded away beyond hearing. The tunnel was empty once again, empty and dark. Suddenly I too felt empty and dark. What to do? How stupid I was. I could do nothing. For a brief moment, I had given myself a task to occupy my mind, now that was done and there was nothing else in front of me to focus on.

The sense of loss returned, overwhelming me. The link, my link to the Old One was no more. I couldn't feel him. My soul felt empty. My soul was empty. His presence was gone from me and I would never know true peace again. I would never speak to him again. My skills were gone, and one day I would die and be dust. I would never join him. I was forsaken by my own choosing.

I fell down on the ground and wept, and I kept weeping until my eyes would weep no more. I didn't care to think whether it was my own self pity that made me weep, the sheer shock of feeling so alone, or the terrible atrocities that were occurring everywhere. I wept for my family and the disappointments I had caused. I wept for Meah, my love for her and the fact that I had left her in the forest. I wept for Soul and her child and the father that child would never know. I wept for Jychanumun's sightless eyes, Dragun's slaughtered clan, all the kutu, all the deaths, all the maiming and the ill intent everywhere. I wept for the loss of my own soul and the choices I had made. The tears needed to come and I did not fight them.

Eventually, devoid of any more tears, I sat. I didn't know where to go or what to do, so I just sat amidst the dirt, covered in dirt, looking at the dirt, feeling numb. I did not want to face my kutu friends, my family or my loved ones. To face them would mean explaining the choices that I had made. It hurt too much to think about. To say it aloud would surely be unbearable. I did not want to make a fool of myself by weeping in front of the kutu. They had all suffered losses through no choice of their own. Mine had been my choice.

But I knew I would have to explain things to the kutu at some point. I would have to tell them that I no longer had the skills of the Old One to help them. I knew that they all secretly harboured the hope that I could use the Voice of the Old One at a time of great need. I no longer had that ability. I had burnt that away with one single choice, the choice for all life. My choice had made me useless, empty and useless.

Pull yourself together, I scolded myself. *You stupid girl, you foolish, self-pitying lump of flesh. Practice what you preach. You made your choice; live with it.*

I was suddenly very annoyed with myself. I was alive. In the past I had fought for my life, now I sat and wept about it? If this life was now all that I had, I should embrace every day as if it were my last. After all, it could well be. There was surely still a multitude of things that I could do. If my life was now changed, then I could also change accordingly. That much I could do.

Despite the fact that a part of me still wanted to do nothing except feel empty in this empty place, I pulled myself up from the dirt, brushed the worst of the muck from my dress and made my way back through the lower tunnels and up towards the central control area.

I could hear the hubbub as I approached. The kutu were relieved to have Brave returned safe and sound, but the topic of discussion was something else. Most of Arrunn's armies had left. They had just turned around and gone.

"Do not be deceived," Mardoch was saying, "Five hundred Nigh-kutu still outnumber us greatly. Arrunn is still here. He remains for a reason. We must use strategy. A single strike would disable us all."

"Five hundred Nigh-kutu may well be the smallest number we will see here. The others may return. We should strike while we can," Stanze objected.

The thought of these few courageous kutu attacking against such odds shocked me. They would not even have the blinded Jychanumun's full skills. Over a dozen Anumi were still trapped. Only around sixty-five Shaa-kutu, with Mardoch, Dragun and the injured Jychanumun, were present here and now. To stand against five hundred Nigh-kutu, who had the benefit of millennia of training as warriors, and many experiences of war?

"It would be slaughter," I thought aloud.

Mardoch nodded to me, glad of the support. "And what would you suggest, little Tachra?" he asked.

"I know nothing of war," I shrugged, "but animals either increase their pack size or take out an opponent one at a time."

"You see," Mardoch gestured, "even these animals have a more efficient strategy. We can do both of those things. We can increase our numbers by undertaking as many rescue plans around Eden1 as possible; as many as Dragun's stock of time crystals allow for. You yourself have said there are Shaa-kutu in hiding in various places around your home-world. And here we will operate with stealth: hiding, attacking stragglers and reducing their numbers until we can make a single attack. And we will investigate obtaining more time crystals."

"Agreed," Stanze nodded his consent. "The rescue of the stranded Anumi from around this location has already started and will be completed by night fall. But for the others, I do not know how these time crystals work."

"I do," Mardoch replied. "I can show you, although Dragun will have to activate them first. I will accompany you." He looked at Stanze, frowning. "But you will need to ensure that your own rescued warriors do not finish me off before I get you all back."

"That is a good point," Stanze considered. "In the dark you Nigh-kutu look much alike." He took off the golden belt to his armour, handing it to Mardoch. "It is made from Uana, wear it. I will give one to Dragun too."

Mardoch fixed the belt around his waist, and although I no longer had the power of the Old One to enable me to see the entirety of Mardoch's energy, his wings still loomed large and dark. Flecks of gold started to blend through the darkness, settling onto the edges of his energy wings. It was quite breathtaking. His huge black wings were now tipped with gold.

Chia immediately said that he wanted to use over half of the current stock of time crystals to retrieve Orion. Everyone wanted to see Orion back, but Stanze brought up the valid point that Orion could remain safe where he was, concealed and invisible, and able to stay alive for a while longer; at least until they obtained more time crystals. There were, Stanze reasoned, many Shaa-kutu injured and in hiding around Eden1 who would not survive unless they were rescued imminently. Those nine crystals that Chia would use to rescue Orion, who could survive, could be used elsewhere to save kutu lives. Chia had to concede the point.

"Exactly how many time crystals do we have?" Stanze asked.

"Only sixteen," Mardoch frowned. "Each mission will take between two and six crystals. You will need to plan so they are used to the greatest effect."

Kraniel was being unusually still. He was standing at the central console, his bright green eyes scanning the images around him. The screens Kraniel was observing revealed that it was already day-break outside. Dragun, along with three of the Anumi had wasted no time in beginning the first mission, and were now manoeuvring through the land while Kraniel gave them directions.

Using natural formations for concealment, the team of four flew low from hiding place to hiding place. Their destination was two Anumi, both trapped in a narrow but deep natural cave formation. The cave was set high in the sheer mountains, overlooking the flat-lands. Although the screens indicated that were no Nigh-kutu immediately around their position, their own view of their exit was restricted, and their position dangerously exposed.

The four rescuers stealthily approached the stranded Anumi's location. They were not aiming for the exposed cave opening. They were utilizing the more concealed area at the rear of the mountain. Because there was no visible entrance that way, I guessed that Dragun's skill with rock weaving would be put to good use once again.

Kraniel constantly kept the roving rescuers updated regarding the areas beyond their view. The strategy seemed to be working. The rescuers disappeared from sight and for a short while there was silence, and then they re-emerged, their number now six instead of four. They flew low to the land at a fast rate as Kraniel guided their return journey. He took them on a route that passed no Nigh-kutu, letting out a long sigh of relief when they finally reached the tunnel to this central hub. Two more could now be classed as safe. They had done it. But Kraniel did not stop; as soon as they were inside the hub, another group was sent out on the next rescue mission.

It felt wrong to be standing underground, invisibly watching the world outside. For the kutu it was the right thing to do. But me? I was no different to any other human now. I should be out there helping them. But how? I felt useless.

I glanced around the screens. Several villages and encampments were on view, and all looked surprisingly peaceful. They were quiet, yes. It seemed that the inhabitants were mostly staying in the safety of their huts and bolt holes. But my fellow humans were clearly not being attacked by the black-winged ones.

I watched one particular screen as a pair of Nigh-kutu wandered through a village that I recognised. Its sandy ground and close-knit, dark-wood huts told me they were in Hollow.

Hollow was unusually quiet, too. More than quiet, it looked deserted. The areas where women usually congregated were empty. No one was out working the fields, and no one wandered the usually bustling tracks. For a moment I panicked, thinking that maybe everyone had been taken away or killed. But then I noticed the eyes of someone looking cautiously out of a window. And there, there was another. And then I saw two young women cautiously run from behind a small wall and into a hut. The people were hiding.

The two Nigh-kutu paused to watch the running women. I held my breath, waiting to see what they would do. They talked between themselves and laughed, before opening their energy wings and launching into the sky.

The two Nigh-kutu had not harmed the people. They almost seemed amused by them. That surprised me. Perhaps, I dared to hope, my fellow humans would be left in peace.

Several screens did show the main position of the Nigh-kutu. Some were gathered in groups, laughing, talking, drinking and seemingly doing normal things. If it were not for the array of weaponry and sturdy armour that each wore, I would not think that these were warriors bent on destruction. Some of them even looked happy. If I had not been aware of their capacity for killing, I would never have thought these to be bad creatures.

One group of around fifty Nigh-kutu did appear more aggressive than the others. A brawl had broken out and several of the black-winged ones were fighting among themselves.

I smiled to myself. The energy of this planet would always have a strange effect on any kutu. It enhanced the truer, rawer side of them, promoting aspects of their being that may have lain dormant for years. For the Shaa-kutu this had proved to be a good thing. But for the Nigh-kutu? It would surely make their usual discipline more difficult. Good, I thought.

Most of the groups of black-winged ones appeared to be localized. One or two points on the landscape looked very familiar. Then, to my horror, I realised that they were on a section of grassland within easy walking distance of my valley.

I quietly looked around the room at all the screens, looking for an image of my valley, the temple or Meah. Without asking, Kraniel changed several of the images. He must have read my mind, as one of the screens now showed the forest edge, one showed my room, and the other showed the central chamber in the temple.

To my relief, I could not see Meah anywhere. It meant that she was in the heart of the forest. She would be safest there. My old room appeared empty. Some items appeared to have been moved, but it looked much the same as I had left it. But the central chamber? That was now very changed.

The grand golden room in the centre of the temple had been darkened. In the gloom, I could just about make out a scene of ruin. Most of the huge columns were broken. The walls looked fractured. The chairs and pictures had been heaped in a corner in a broken mess. And there, standing alone, at the far end of the chamber, was a Nigh-kutu. I could not see his features, but a chill ran up my spine. There was something fundamentally wrong about that kutu. I don't know how I knew, but I knew it was Arrunn.

Jychanumun was busy mending the last of his wounds with a healing rod. He walked towards me, his eyes still blind and covered by healing discs. But he could see what I was seeing, through my eyes.

"We should be able to get audio too, but whatever energy is being used in this room creates a frequency that puts everything into white noise," Kraniel stated.

"What is he doing?" I asked.

"Waiting," Jychanumun replied. "Waiting to see what surfaces."

"What will surface?" I asked.

"Nothing, if we do this right. We will out-wait him until we can strike."

Kraniel nodded in agreement. "We will rescue as many as we can while we wait. And then, when there are enough of us, we will rid our world of these black-winged ones and work on devising a way to stop any Nigh-kutu passing through any gateways ever again."

"Is that possible?" I asked, a faint glimmer of hope in the back of my mind. "Could you stop them ever coming back?"

"I have seen their gateway made," Kraniel replied. "If something can be made, then it can be unmade. I do not know how yet, but I will find a way."

I heard the determination in Kraniel's voice. If anyone could do such a feat, I knew that he could.

By now, several kutu were now standing behind me, observing Arrunn. I could feel their deep breaths on the back of my neck. I sensed their tension and anger. Jychanumun moved away, uncomfortable with so many so close to him. He seemed deep in thought. I noticed him clench his fists. Something bothered him, but he would not let me detect what it was.

Caught in the image on the wall, in the gloom of the central chamber, the lone figure Arrunn, his hands behind his back and his head bowed, took a step forward. It was as if there were a light on him. His head slowly rose until his face was in full view. He seemed to be looking directly at us. His energy was visible around him, winding around his body, its tendrils snaking out ominously towards us. His eyes flashed with shadow, his stare unmoving. Slowly, his lips mouthed the beginning of unheard words.

"Kill the connection," Jychanumun suddenly growled.

The screen went blank.

"Was he just looking at us?" Kraniel asked what we were all thinking. "It looked like he was looking straight at us."

"No, he was not," Jychanumun replied. "It is Arrunn's way. He can project his thoughts so that you see what he wants you to see. He can manipulate the mind for his own cause. He was looking for me."

"He was going to say something," I said.

"I know," Jychanumun replied. "And you should not listen," he added coldly.

"Why? Surely we must find out what he wants."

"What he wants cannot be changed. He is entrenched with abhorrence for all life. Even his thoughts are destructive."

I asked Jychanumun to tell me more, but he would not. He said he had said too much already.

Perhaps it was the way Jychanumun had spoken, or perhaps it was some subtle emotion or inflection that I picked up. But all of a sudden, I realised that Jychanumun knew a great deal more about Arrunn than he was letting on.

TWENTY

Arrunn drew his energy back into himself and let his body relax. He had almost made the connection. Something, someone, had broken it. That something reeked of the Death-Walker. Arrunn was right; the Death-Walker Jychanumun was here.

Arrunn had spent the morning absorbing information. The trinkets of equipment that had been abandoned by the light-lovers, initially dismissed as worthless, had proved surprisingly useful. Although none of the records gave the date that he was searching for, he had made other discoveries that could only help his search.

Amongst the retrieved data was a detailed analysis of the crude human language. Arrunn had quickly assimilated the concepts of the human tongue, and, as a result, had deciphered another broad selection of data and records. These had been written by a human, the one called Iastha Tachra. The results were fascinating.

It transpired that this human had a strong direct link to the Death-Walker. Iastha Tachra had resided here, amongst a group of light-lovers, calling many of them friends. As well as Jychanumun, another of those so-called friends was the red kutu, Orion.

How perfectly appropriate, Arrunn reflected, that the three creatures he required; the Death-Walker, the red kutu, and the human, Iastha Tachra, had all chosen to exist together. This could not be a coincidence. Jychanumun must have had a hand in that. Still, the Death-Walker would not outwit him. Arrunn could use this to his advantage. The three would naturally regroup. Find one and he would inevitably find them all.

Further research into Iastha Tachra's personal data regularly brought up the terms 'family' and 'friends.' Both described a kinship with an emotional bond. Any emotional bond was a flaw that could be utilized. Arrunn may not have found details of where Iastha Tachra was situated, but he did have information on her clan. He knew the co-ordinates of their living spaces. They would most likely have all the information that he required.

Arrunn contemplated his next move. He would infiltrate Iastha Tachra's clan. From them, he would find the date when she gained the link to the heart of all things. If her clan did not have that information, they would at least know her whereabouts.

To infiltrate Iastha Tachra's clan, Arrunn would need to get inside their minds. Such a task would require stealthy manipulation. This would not require brute force. This required subtle power and charm. This one was down to him.

Seeing no point for any delay, Arrunn glanced at the closest guard and nodded.

Immediately, six of the guards walked forward to stand around Arrunn, their backs to him, in the centre of the darkened chamber. They would keep his empty flesh protected while he was away.

Arrunn knelt to the ground, took a selection of small life

crystals from his ready supplies, chose one and placed it on the floor in front of him.

The little life-time crystal glowed dark purple, an energy that was subtle, intelligent, aware and precise. It was the correct selection.

Arrunn crushed the crystal with his palm. The contained energy smoked out of its broken shell. Immediately, Arrunn released his own energy, letting it drift from the confines of his body. Arrunn's essence gathered around the broken crystal, around the newly released energy. The two energies swirled for a moment, and then Arrunn's predominant darkest brown easily overpowered the dark purple, enveloping it like a hungry beast.

The two essences resonated, and then disappeared.

The human Marl would be Arrunn's first target. Marl was one of Iastha Tachra's clan, one she called her brother, her favourite brother. To Arrunn he was useful and expendable.

With the precise co-ordinates and the additional power from the life-crystal, it took no time for Arrunn to locate Marl. Using the power of the time crystal to move in an instant, Arrunn's essence was suddenly in the centre of Marl's known living space.

Marl appeared to be in a small, wooden building, and active. Other humans were around him. Arrunn's essence invisibly moved around Marl, assessing the target. For a creature made so predominantly of matter, this was not a strong construction. Its machinations appeared both clumsy and limited. Its insipid life force would offer little or no resistance.

Using stealth, along with a numbing gentleness, Arrunn seeped invisibly though the human's skin and into its body. He was in.

Arrunn waited a moment for his energy to settle within the human flesh. The tactic had been good: there was no reaction. He carefully moved, his own essence roaming through the host, overpowering every organ, nerve and cell, settling carefully into the fragile, human mind. Overpowering his host's thoughts and actions took barely any effort at all. Marl's mind froze, his own paltry energy now disabled. The human was now a tool: Arrunn's tool.

Arrunn immediately searched for the information he required from Marl's mind. This creature had virtually no concept of time or date. It was clear almost immediately that he did not have knowledge of the date when Iastha Tachra's link was created. Neither did he have knowledge of her current whereabouts. The only relevant information was that he considered her safe, healthy, and safe. She was with Shaa-kutu.

Refusing to let the task be a waste of time, Arrunn searched deeper through Marl's frozen mind. He learned that if this human wanted to acquire information about Iastha Tachra, he must ask one of two people: Dannel, her father, or Soul, her friend.

In Threetops . . .

Ila looked at her father, Marl. He had suddenly stopped mid-stride and now stood motionless with a large pile of logs in his arms.

"Father," Ila laughed, "you'll have no stew tonight if you don't put some of those logs on the fire."

She took the top two logs from her father's arms, throwing them onto the embers of the hearth, sending little sparks flying. The stew was only half-cooked, it was growing late, and it was her turn to cook again tonight. Now that they only cooked once each day, everyone would already be hungry.

Her father just looked back at her with a strange expression on his face. He held out his arms, as if expecting her to take the rest of logs.

Ila tutted, and then laughed, taking the logs a few at a time and throwing them into the corner of the room. Her father had clearly had enough toiling for one day. She wasn't surprised; this was the tenth pile of logs he had chopped that evening.

"I will be back shortly," Marl suddenly declared. He then turned around and walked straight out of the room, towards the main door.

"But father, it's already dark and food will be ready soon," Ila called after him.

But Marl didn't reply. He had left the hut and hadn't even shut the door behind him.

In Threetops again . . .

Soul tucked the little communication device that Stanze had given her back under her pillow. There'd been no news from Tachra all day. It was the first time in five years that Tachra had not found time to send any message.

The soup was getting cold. Soul took a long draught from the mug so as to have some nourishment before trying to find sleep. How tired she was. Little Iris hadn't wanted to go to bed again tonight; she'd protested and cried for hours. Soul knew that she was scared of having nightmares. It had taken all of Soul's soothing and several happy stories to mollify her daughter. How she now wished she had someone to do the same for her.

It had been a strange few days. First, there was the news from Tachra that the black-winged kutu were here, but then nothing happened. Everyone got ready to hide, but then hadn't seen any Nigh-kutu to hide from. They were still all tense. And then yesterday, everyone in the village fell sick. Initially Soul had thought it was just her, and had put the sickness down to worry. But, then little Iris had spiked a fever and Soul's parents had both gone to their beds early, barely able to climb the stairs. Since then, news had filtered through that everyone had fallen ill that evening. It left concerns that the town's well had gone bad. But Soul didn't think it was the water. Soul suspected that it was something to do with the black-winged ones.

An icy chill ran over Soul's skin. She pulled up a blanket to cover her legs, but the cold breeze still got through. It smelt of the dampness of outside. Had the door blown open?

"Soul?" A voice calmly called from downstairs, below her room.

The voice sounded like Marl, Tachra's brother.

Soul hurried from the comfort of her bed, not wanting any further calls to wake Iris, and tip-toed down the stairs, trying to avoid the planks that squeaked.

Marl was already standing inside the hut, the door open, letting in the evening chill. Soul assumed that they must have run out of food or logs. Theirs was the closest hut, so they often shared items. Marl would not usually call after nightfall, though, so it must be a necessity.

"Have you run out of something?" Soul smiled, as she reached the bottom of the stairs and closed the door behind Marl.

"No," Marl replied. He didn't smile back. "Do you know where Tachra is?"

"With the kutu," Soul responded, surprised at the question. "Why?"

"I must speak to her," Marl stated, his face expressionless. "Where is she?"

Suddenly Soul was worried for her friend. "What's happened? Is she alright? What's the matter?" she asked.

"Nothing has happened. I must find her. It is important. I thought you would know where she was." Marl said, looking directly at Soul. "Where are Tachra and the Shaa-kutu?"

Soul paused, thinking. Something was not right. Marl's voice sounded very much the same, but the words he used were different. He never called the makers the Shaa-kutu. And he never asked where Tachra was; he usually just asked *how* she was. Soul had known Marl for over five years, but for some reason she now felt very uncomfortable. Her skin felt prickly, and not in a nice way. Perhaps it was just her own anxiety, the late hour, or the fact it had taken several hours to stop her daughter's tears, but she had met many bad men, men who could turn in an instant, and men who liked to use women, so she certainly knew better than to ignore such a feeling.

Soul smiled sweetly, her best smile. She moved towards the cleaning bowl, picking up a cloth and walking to the opposite side of the eating table. She did her best to make it look like the surface required wiping down while creating a barrier between her and Marl.

"Tachra will be at the Temple of Learning as usual," she lied. "You'll find her there."

"Tachra is not in the building," Marl replied. "She has left."

"Oh well, you know Tachra," Soul replied lightly. "She never tells anyone where she's going."

"She would tell you."

Soul's discomfort grew. She knew that she needed to change tactics. She put her hands on her hips, imagining that she was scolding a naughty child.

"Marl," Soul tutted, "I am only her friend. We only talk about girl things, like friends do. You are her family, her favourite brother. She would tell you first. If she has left the temple then I should be asking *you* where she is."

Marl seemed to accept that answer, watching Soul as she wiped a bit more of the table. She pretended she didn't notice his stare.

"I have another question," Marl stated. He took two steps forward.

"Can it wait?" Soul asked, trying to close the conversation. "It's late and I'm very tired."

"It could wait, but I do not wish it to wait," Marl stated. "So I will ask you the question. This link that Tachra has to the heart of all things; do you remember when it happened? I would," he paused and smiled, "be happy if you could answer."

That was when Soul knew that her initial uncomfortable feeling had not been wrong. Marl was not just behaving strangely, and she didn't just feel wrong in his presence – it was his smile. That was not Marl's normal smile. Nor was it any normal smile. It was as if his face had contorted into something very ugly. Soul had long decided that she was not going to be pushed around by any man, ever again. She took a deep breath.

"I think you should leave. It's late. We'll talk tomorrow," she told him firmly.

"I will leave when you answer me," Marl replied.

Just one question? Soul thought. She had better hurry up, answer him, and get him out of there. She wanted him gone.

"You'd better," Soul scowled. "When you say the heart of things, do you mean the link to the Old One?"

Marl nodded.

Soul's mind raced. She didn't know when Tachra had gained her link, and even if she did, should she tell him? And yet, she couldn't imagine how such a piece of information could harm her friend, or anybody. It was the sort of thing Tachra would openly answer herself. But Soul didn't like the way Marl was acting. Should she just make up a date? Should she say that she didn't know? How would she know what was the best response? So, deciding that the truth could not possibly harm anyone, Soul chose the honest reply. She shook her head.

"I don't know when Tachra got her link to the Old One. I'm sure that she already had it when I met her, so it must have been before then."

"Before you knew her? So, someone who was close to her at a younger age would know? Her father . . . my father," he corrected himself, "would know?"

"I guess so," Soul replied cautiously. "But he is asleep. You can't wake him. He hasn't been feeling well."

Marl seemed to consider this. He just stood looking at her with a blank expression on his face. It was unnerving.

Soul decided that she was not going to let Marl go upstairs and disturb Tachra's father, who really wasn't well. No, Marl was behaving oddly, this had to stop here. She cast her eyes around the kitchen. There was a long-knife by the sink. Tachra's father had sharpened it only yesterday. That would do.

Soul moved the wiping cloth around in her hand, making it an obvious movement for Marl to see, lifting it up and glancing at it. She walked towards the wash area, as if to wet the cloth again, while her eyes remained firmly fixed on the knife. As she approached the sink, she surreptitiously put her hand on the knife's handle, dipping the cloth into the water with the other.

Holding her breath, her heart racing, Soul slowly turned around, smiling, ensuring the knife was well concealed behind her back.

Marl was nowhere in sight.

The front door was wide open again.

Soul quickly cast her eyes around the room. The damp boot-prints on the floorboards went no further than the doorway. She let out her breath. Marl was gone. He had simply left.

Soul quickly shut the door, put the knife back down on the surface, leaned against the side and started laughing. Oh, what a fool she was. How stupid to be suspicious of Tachra's own brother. How stupidly tense she had become these last few days, so much so that it was affecting her thoughts. Yes, Soul thought to herself, still laughing, Tachra was right; she definitely needed to find herself a man-friend.

Arrunn directed Marl outside the small hut. The energy from the purple time crystal was almost extinguished now. It was time for Arrunn to leave his host.

Having led the cumbersome human body towards a darkened area without dwellings, Arrunn regrouped his own energy, releasing Marl's mind. With a familiar dexterity, he relinquished all control of Marl's cells, nerves and organs, seeping back out through his skin. This time he did not bother to be careful. There wasn't any point.

As Arrunn pulled away, Marl's body slowly solidified. Its own life energy was now unable to sustain its altered state. What was left of Marl's own meagre energy simply drifted downwards, dissolving into the soil. Marl's body was now drained of all colour: flat grey, like a kutu death statue. But this creature's matter was too weak to hold its form in death, and, as the last of Arrunn's essence left it, the dead matter slowly crumbled. Within moments, only a pile of dust remained, ready to be blown away by the first wind.

Arrunn returned to his own body, in the middle of the large room, in the centre of the golden building. He rolled his shoulders. How much more comfortable it was to have his own form once again. He may be imperfect, but these human creatures were pathetically ill-made.

Arrunn had absorbed all that he needed from the human. Marl had known little more than Arrunn already knew. The human Soul had said that she didn't know what date Tachra had acquired the link to the heart of all things, and he knew that to be true. But she had not been telling the truth about knowing Tachra's whereabouts. She had lied about that.

Perhaps, Arrunn considered, these humans had learnt some skills after all. Soul had lied well, but she clearly was not aware of the change in her energy colours when she didn't tell the truth. Arrunn might have felt a mild appreciation for the feeble species if one of them had truly understood the concept of lying, but she hadn't.

And Dannel, Tachra's father? Arrunn knew that this was the human most likely to have knowledge of the date that he sought. Which one would be his next choice of host: Soul or Dannel? Which one would have the most imminently useful information?

The guards around Arrunn did not move; they sensed that Arrunn had not finished working. Arrunn delved into his immediate supply of time crystals once again. He picked out another dark-purple one. He would utilize the same purple energy and follow the same procedure again.

Still kneeling, Arrunn placed the second crystal on the floor in front of him. Once again he crushed the crystal with his palm, letting his own energy drain from his body and envelop the dark purple vapour. Once again, in an instant, he was gone.

Arrunn's essence reappeared at the correct co-ordinates. He was in a small room, almost black with darkness. Its door was closed and its shutters locked. In front of Arrunn was a bed with two humans. Both were sleeping. The human to the left was Dannel, Tachra's father.

Arrunn moved his essence around Dannel's body, slowly seeping in to him, passing through his skin.

Energy, matter and mind overtaken, Dannel was now the host.

This particular human body was even weaker than the first. Its heart was already strained to thinness and its organs impaired through age. Arrunn would have to act quickly: such fragility could only withstand a few moments of his presence. Arrunn leapt into the human's mind.

Suddenly, Arrunn's host was collapsing from the inside. Already the cells were breaking down, too past their prime to retain his powerful essence. Arrunn did not want the discomfort of hosting a dead body, even if only for a brief moment. So, without time to choose, he stripped as much information as he could from the creatures mind with one hard push, and then tried to leap back out of Dannel's body.

But Arrunn seemed to be stuck. It was as if something was holding him.

You will not hurt my daughter, Arrunn heard. *Leave her alone.*

It was Dannel's will speaking. In his dying moments, his awareness had increased. He was aware of Arrunn's presence and was trying to protect Iastha Tachra, his daughter.

I have no desire to hurt your daughter, or you, although I can, Arrunn replied, as he searched for the best exit from this crumbling body. *I require only information.*

At what price? the old man said. *My daughter's life? I don't think so.*

You are dying already, old man. You have no choice.

Dannel tried to push back. But he was indeed dying. As much as his will was strong, his heart had now stopped and his own life's energy was slowly draining away.

The old man made one last valiant effort to hold on, fighting against himself so he could block Arrunn. It was a pointless undertaking. The exertion merely quickened his end.

The last of the air exhaled from Dannel's lungs. All mechanics had stopped. He was gone. Dead.

Arrunn pushed his way through the collapsing cells and out of the empty, lifeless flesh that was now slowly disintegrating to dust. His essence felt dirty, contaminated. Worse still, he could already tell that he did not have the information he required. This had been most unsatisfactory. And what a waste of a time crystal. He had used barely a fraction of it.

But it doesn't have to be a waste, Arrunn smiled to himself. After all, the human Soul was in exactly the same building. This one, he would savour.

TWENTY-ONE

Time had an odd way of dragging and then rushing in this surreal, underground place. There seemed to be no difference between day and night. Only by constantly checking the screens in the central hub did I know that I'd been here for two full days and three nights. It seemed like forever.

The hub was a constant mass of activity. The kutu were stretched to their limits. I'd become invisible in an invisible place. I kept my eyes open, to substitute for Jychanumun's blinded sight, I kept quiet, and I kept out of the kutu's way.

I wanted to go home. I wanted to go back to the forest and be with Meah. But with Arrunn now using the temple, I knew that was impossible. This had made me miserable until I'd caught a glimpse of Meah passing through the forest on one of the screens. Seeing her looking so healthy had confirmed that I'd done the right thing. I had to stay away to keep her safe.

I also wanted to see my family and Soul. I'd not heard from Soul since my first night here, despite sending several messages. My common sense told me that it was probably nothing more than her having broken the communication device, but still I fretted. I watched the images of Threetops for signs of my family. My old village appeared as subdued as every other. Kraniel spotted my mother at the water well, but when I looked I would not have recognised her if it was not for the hand-stitched slippers on her feet. She looked gaunt and ill, walking stooped over, barely able to carry the pail. Why weren't Soul or my father doing the more able-bodied chores? I had seen my mother, but seeing her had made me fret even more.

The distance from here to Threetops was walkable. I could do it, although it would be a difficult journey through the mountains. I guessed that it would take around four to six moons, providing I kept a good supply of water.

I mentioned the possibility of my returning to Threetops to Jychanumun, but he strongly objected, saying that it had not yet been proven safe. But, from everything I'd witnessed, this war was between kutu. Evidence showed that my fellow humans had been left alone. I'd even seen people venturing from their huts, carrying out necessities without any trouble.

But Jychanumun was adamant that I must not leave this place, not yet, and he would not tell me why. If I didn't trust him as much as I did, I would have left for Threetops anyway.

So I stayed in the kutu underground hub, refusing to allow myself to grow miserable, and it was the kutu around me who made that possible. They became my inspiration. The kutu around me displayed such resourcefulness and goodness. I witnessed great feats of courage, perseverance and honour every moment of every day.

Already, the Shaa-kutu, with their two new black-winged allies, had performed five well-planned, difficult rescues of kutu in hiding around Eden1. In each case, time crystals were used from

Dragun's meagre store to travel instantly to a place where they had confirmation of those in hiding, retrieving all those they could. Over one hundred had been rescued so far. Most of them were injured, some badly. They'd all been anxious to rescue Una, the Supreme, but Una was under constant guard somewhere in the centre of the Shaa-kutu main city. But he *was* alive, and if he remained so they would find a way to rescue him.

It was a particularly tense moment in the central hub. Two complex rescue missions had finished simultaneously. Chia rushed to the healing rooms to tend the wounded, whilst Kraniel started preparing for the next mission and I handed out much needed Ochrah to those who were uninjured. Stanze and Mardoch, who had performed the rescue, returned to the central hub. They were midway through a heated discussion.

"No, it is too risky," Stanze frowned. "I cannot agree with it."

"It is my life at risk, none other's," Mardoch argued. "The possible result would be worth the risk. We could rescue many more as a result. You cannot stop me."

"Your courage is reckless," Stanze growled at the Nigh-kutu.

"I can do this." Mardoch would not back down. "We need more time crystals. We could do so much with just another fifty, or even twenty."

"No," Stanze said firmly.

"Tachra," Mardoch smiled at me as he approached, his bright green eyes flashing. "You will see my point . . ."

I went to object, but Mardoch continued.

"We will soon run out of time crystals. Time crystals can save lives. We have information that Arrunn's portable vault is arriving here. It is full of nothing but time crystals, and travels with only one guard."

"And I'm guessing that you want to try to steal some?"

Mardoch nodded. "Your opinion?"

I thought about this for a moment. To me, it was not a clear-cut choice, but for many more reasons other than Mardoch's personal risk.

"If it were simply a question of risk, then of course it is viable," I considered. "I would happily risk my life to save many more. But I don't think that's what you should be asking. The question is: are we not following Arrunn's example by putting so much worth on these time crystals? They are made from a life, a murdered kutu, a kutu who has loved and lived. If it becomes the primary objective to gain them, where would it stop?" I looked at Mardoch and Stanze. "I see what good they could do. But they are bad things in themselves. Which choice overrides the other? That's what you must decide first."

"A wise consideration," Stanze nodded. "How far beyond our moral standards are we prepared to go in times of war?"

"You're a good being," I smiled at Stanze. "You both are. You'll make the right choice."

I left Stanze and Mardoch to their debate, heading for the healing rooms. Chia had given me the task of helping him with the new arrivals. Right now, he would need all the help he could get.

Chia had already handed out healing rods, and several Anumi were already tending to the worst wounded when I arrived at the healing rooms. With most of the new arrivals already being attended to, I approached the section that housed only the most badly wounded. This was where Chia worked.

I took a deep breath. In front of me was a screen. Not just any screen, but one made of a beautiful, luminescent kutu tapestry that had been moved from the temple. Despite the object's beauty, it made me worry to see it used. Chia only used it to give privacy to a kutu with particularly bad injuries.

I will not faint, I told myself, bracing myself to enter.

Suddenly, I heard a voice from behind the screen.

"Do not you think you are going to come in here and mess up this pretty face of mine, little Tachra," the voice said.

I was sure I recognised that voice.

"Peniva?" I gasped. Peniva, that big, hulking, wonderful Anumi leader whom I had witnessed so badly wounded on Eden1, was alive!

I rushed through. Chia was leaning over a terrible sight of war-wracked ripped flesh, bleeding energy and blood. Peniva was barely recognisable as a kutu, yet alone any specific kutu. His wounds were worse than anything I'd ever seen. But he was alive. I fought back the tears and kissed the one small area of cheek that was not wounded in his terribly disfigured face and crouched, holding his one remaining hand to my cheek.

"I cannot retune you fully just yet," Chia told Peniva. "You have armour embedded in your chest, hip and head. I will have to remove them first."

"Just do it," Peniva confirmed. "It is irritating me."

"Irritating? It must hurt like Eskah's oblivion."

I made a sharp intake of breath as Chia removed a large piece of metal from Peniva's face. It clearly pained Peniva, but he did not let it show. To see the one kutu that I'd witnessed so badly injured and seemingly doomed on Eden1 now lying here alive and soon to be healed again was a miracle. And it was symbolic. If this kutu could survive such odds, then others might survive other atrocities that I'd witnessed. I held onto Peniva's hand as if it was hope itself. I was so happy to see him alive.

"Careful with that hand," Chia instructed, as he removed another piece of metal from Peniva's face. "His fingers are broken."

"Oh," I suddenly froze. How could I have been so stupid? I knew I didn't have my true vision any more to tell me such things. I should have been more careful.

I gently let go of Peniva's hand, placing it next to his side. "I'm really sorry. Should I leave?" I asked, mortified that my presence could make things worse.

"No," Chia replied. "You promised to help me, remember?"

Peniva was flexing his fingers. "They feel better," he remarked.

Chia stopped what he was doing and checked Peniva's hand.

"They are mended," Chia said, looking at me. "What did you do?"

"Nothing," I replied. I really hadn't.

Chia picked up a read-out panel, inspected and showed me the screen, pausing on one image. A three-dimensional representation of Peniva's left hand rotated in the centre, beside it a list of injuries; all the phalanges on that hand were listed as broken.

"You healed it," Chia stated, putting the screen down and continuing his work.

"Impossible," I shook my head. "You must have fixed them."

"I have been too occupied with the severity of the head injuries to start tending anywhere else. You healed them."

"I cannot do such things anymore."

"Tachra," Chia sighed while he worked, "I know that you have severed your link to the Old One. I am a sensitive; I knew straight away. Now it is time to stop feeling sorry for yourself. You are still you. You still have your own skills. Now put some of those skills to use and help me heal this friend of mine."

Suddenly, realisation hit me. Of course there were still things I could do! I had convinced myself that I had become worthless. My sense of grief had made me believe I had lost everything. Yes, my link to the Old One was severed; yes, that would always make me feel a certain emptiness; yes, I was changed. But I was still me. I was still made up of the same things. I could still manipulate energy. That was what I was; it was not just something derived from another source. I had wanted Peniva better. And here, without realising it, I had healed his hand.

The realisation was like lifting a veil in my mind. I quickly examined Peniva's lower arm. Two gashes were particularly deep, both down to the bone. I concentrated on those gashes, pouring as much of my energy into them as I could. It took a great deal of effort, making me feel exhausted. Nevertheless, once I had sensed that these were mending I moved onto the next wound, a hole though the arm above the elbow, and then the next, a shattered shoulder.

"Whoa, slow down," Chia suddenly intervened. "You are close to collapse. You must slow down."

"But I've only just started!" I protested, seeing multitudes of injuries that needed tending.

"Tachra, it seems that the energy you use now is your own energy. You do not have the Old One's endless supplies any more. You will eventually learn to draw from the energy around you, but right now give yourself time to recharge. Just stop for a moment."

I did indeed feel weak. Chia picked up a healing sheet, recalibrated it to suit my human needs, and then wrapped it around my shoulders.

"This will help," he said. "Just remember that you now use your own energy, so you must learn how to control it. I can give you healing tools, but you must still learn how to do it for yourself."

"Did you purposely ask me to help with the wounded so that I would discover this?" I asked.

"Of course," Chia tutted.

"Why didn't you just tell me earlier?"

"Because, young Tachra, grief does not have ears for reason."

I nodded at that, and leaned over Peniva's shoulder to continue to heal it, monitoring my own energy levels as I did so. Chia was right: as I worked, I felt my own energy levels depleting. I learned to stop when necessary, allowing myself to rebalance, and then continue. It took longer than I was accustomed to, but I managed to heal that shattered shoulder and heal it well.

Having helped Chia to remove a particularly deeply embedded fragment of metal from Peniva's head, Chia told me that healing sheets could do the rest. I had just finished covering Peniva with several layers when I heard shouts.

"Chia! Chia!"

Chia was already rushing past me. Two Anumi were running towards the healing room, carrying a limp kutu. I quickly pushed a recliner into position. The Anumi ran in, placing the wounded kutu down.

It was Mardoch. All down one side, from his chin to his hip, Mardoch's body was missing. In his one remaining arm he was clutching his missing arm, the edges of flesh shredded and damaged.

Energy flowed out of Mardoch's exposed flesh. There was so much coming out. I didn't know what to do first. I put my hands onto an area of mangled tissue, concentrating with all my might to stop the energy flooding out.

"Good, keep it there, keep doing that," Chia insisted as he laid the most potent healing strips on Mardoch's ruined body. "Move your hands so they are directly over where the shoulder would protrude. Keep the energy flowing; *be* the flow."

I did as he asked, holding my hands over the gaping tissue, trying not to touch any of the hanging shreds of flesh and skin. I pushed my own energy out, linking with Mardoch's. He had lost a lot of energy and my own was quickly draining away.

"Hold it. Hold it, Tachra. You can do it. Breathe in the energy from the air. See it. Keep focussed. Come on."

Chia worked with a speed I had never seen before, weaving strips of healing in with strips of his own energy. He worked on the neck and the area of Mardoch's chest that was missing, leaving the large shredded area where I held my hands. I breathed deeply, keeping focussed, concentrating.

Chia finished binding the upper hip, flexed his shoulders, and then rubbed his hands together. Streams of his violet energy moved through his fingers. He picked up the severed arm, having to wrench it from Mardoch's unconscious grasp, and put the arm in place as I moved my hands away.

"Hold it there," Chia indicated. "Keep his energy flowing. Push energy into the arm."

As I pushed my energy out, Chia fused the connection with his own energy. The edges were messy, very messy, but now Mardoch at least vaguely seemed the right shape. Only a curved gaping hole in his side was now left.

Behind me, somebody passed something over my head. It looked like a piece of white metal body armour. Chia held the armour over Mardoch's torso, and suddenly the metal seemed to melt, oozing over Mardoch's body, wrapping around him, recreating the shape of his torso. It looked like Mardoch was wearing a perfectly sculptured white metal vest.

Once the substitute torso was in place, Chia quickly placed a retuning disc on Mardoch's forehead. Mardoch's outline blurred as he tuned to pure energy, and then he solidified as he took flesh. Once both extremes had been worked through, Mardoch rebalanced, his flesh and energy now equally matched.

"That should do it," Chia breathed a sigh of relief, stretching his back. He looked exhausted. He pulled up two stools, and we both collapsed down, waiting for Mardoch to gain consciousness.

We both sat in silence, too spent even to move.

I think I sat there for a while, my exhausted state unable to focus on anything.

"Well, what wonders be. I do believe I am alive," Mardoch suddenly whispered. He started laughing, making him cough.

"Keep still," Chia told him. "You were badly injured."

Despite Chia's protests, and despite threats of constraints, Mardoch slowly eased himself upright, looking down at the cladding around his torso, nodding to himself with bemusement.

"You put it back," he said, looking at the limp, re-attached arm. "Do I need to check that you put it on the right way?"

"I did consider giving you a tendril from a Lemur squid," Chia replied. "How in Eskah's oblivion did you manage that? Were you on a mission?"

"Sort of," Mardoch replied. "Stanze does not know. We decided that it is morally questionable to actively seek more time crystals, but I have already done many bad things. My morals are more questionable than those of the others." He started laughing again, trying to hold the metal around his torso as if the movement hurt. "I decided to try and steal more time crystals anyway. There was only one guard. Just one little guard looking after that big vault of time crystals. I made sure I appeared on the side of the vault so the guard could not see me. I stuck my arm in and grabbed a handful of crystals, and something inside the vault bit me. It bit me. Twice! Damn big teeth, too."

Mardoch tried to get up from the recliner. "I must tell Jychanumun. They must have a Nar beast. Nars were once native to the Gatherer clan, who were slaughtered. They had them as pets: placid with their clan, defensive with others. I did not think there were any left."

"You must stay resting. I can pass on a message. Your wounds still have to finish healing," I said.

"I have had worse," Mardoch replied, insisting on getting up. I tried to hold him back. He needed to heal.

"Let him go," Chia nodded. "He will be alright. Sore, yes, but alright."

"I'll go with him," I said, forcing my aching flesh to stand. "He cannot even walk properly yet."

Mardoch stopped in his tracks and turned around, looking at Chia and me.

"Oh yes, I nearly forgot," he limped back towards us.

Mardoch stood in front of me and started gagging. For a minute, I thought he was going to be sick on me. But, instead of being sick, he gagged into his hand. He looked around for something to wipe his hand on. I held out a towel and he wiped his palm on it.

There on the towel were ten spittle-covered, glowing time crystals.

"For you, Chia," Mardoch indicated towards the crystals. "So you can get your friend Orion back. Nine required, plus one for Eskah's luck."

I handed Chia the crystals. Chia stared down at the little crystals in disbelief, and then up at Mardoch with gratitude. "Thank you," was all he could think of to say.

Mardoch started chuckling to himself, limping off awkwardly down the corridor. I went with him, although he refused any help. "See," he said, "I got some. They had a Nar beast and I still got some."

Chia quickly caught up with our slow, ambling gait. He had selected one of the Anumi to oversee the healing room, clearly anxious to make plans for Orion's rescue.

The hub was as hectic as always. By the central console I noticed Stanze, Jychanumun and Kraniel, deep in intense discussion. They stopped talking when I approached and looked at me.

"There has been a change," Jychanumun stated. *Be brave,* he told me with his mind.

Be brave? That meant something was very wrong. "What is it?" I hurried.

"The Nigh-kutu have started collecting people," Kraniel replied. "They tried emptying an entire village. Many of the villagers put up a fight . . ."

"No!" I exclaimed in horror. "Show me," I demanded.

Kraniel adroitly moved in, touching areas of the control panel, indicating a specific screen. The blank screen flashed an image.

It looked like there had been carnage.

The tattered remnants of a small village lay sprawled out under the dawn sky. I recognised that area well. It used to be Meadsins.

Only a few of Meadsins' huts remained intact. Several blackened patches billowed dark smoke where huts had once stood. Others had doors ripped off, broken walls and charred areas. Bodies, human bodies, littered the ground. Several young children wandered aimlessly, some crying, some just looking confused. A wounded man knelt over another, the village carer, trying to give him aid. Two more carried an injured man into one of the remaining huts. The injured young man's bloodied red face and sandy-red hair stood out against the charred black ground. I would recognise that hair colour anywhere: it had to be Ren.

I scanned the rest of the scene.

"What is that?" I asked, pointing to an area. It looked like a person walking, but the figure lacked substance. "And that?" I asked, spotting another.

"What?" Kraniel strained his eyes. "Where? I do not see anything."

"There," I said, moving up to the screen and touching the area where a figure walked. "And there," I pointed to another. "And there are two more there, but they're not moving. They all look like people, but they're translucent."

"Really, Tachra, I cannot see anything," Kraniel shook his head. "Are they kutu in energy form?"

"No," I replied. "It's just like a person but made of a dull light. It doesn't look like the remaining people see them either. Am I just hallucinating?"

Jychanumun had walked forward, looking through my eyes. He could see what I saw.

"You are not hallucinating," Jychanumun said aloud. "What you see are some of the dead. Their consciousness has not yet been destroyed. Kraniel," he stated, "It appears that humans have begun to develop souls."

I picked up Jychanumun's thoughts. Souls were beings that had died, but retained a consciousness. A soul could exist without form. A soul could not die.

"What will happen to them?" I asked Kraniel.

"For the moment, I have no idea. This is a first, Tachra. Kutu have souls, but never have I come across a bio with a soul. I would imagine that for now, these souls would simply remain in the place familiar to them. How many are there?"

"Four that I can see," I replied.

"There are forty-three dead and eighteen injured," Kraniel gravely stated. "Only the young children and the wounded are left. We have an access point, not too far from the village. Dragun is already tunnelling through to rescue the wounded."

"Why did we not see this as it happened?" I asked.

"I was overseeing rescues. I am sorry," Kraniel replied.

"It's not your fault. It's the Nigh-kutu. And we are living like moles who dare not see the sky anymore," I fumed.

"There is more," Kraniel added. "The others from the village have been taken."

"Taken where?" I asked.

Kraniel changed the screen again.

I saw a field of Nigh-kutu. They had made a camp. Among them were humans.

There was so much going on in that scene that at first my eyes just scanned the entire image. But then I started picking out individuals and groups. Some men and women walked the edges of the Nigh-kutu camp, gathering wood for fires. I was sure that I recognised one of them as Ren's mate, Dinah. Other women were serving food, dozens of them, their postures indicating fear and servitude. A group of men sat cleaning armour. A Nigh-kutu walked past them, stopped, and began watching one of them. He pointed at something, and then hit the man. The man was flung backwards, picked himself up, and immediately started cleaning again, despite his swollen face. In another area, I could see young, part-naked women being pulled and pushed around, Nigh-kutu all around them, laughing. One woman tried to run away, but didn't get far before a Nigh-kutu brought her back to the fold. At the centre of the camp was a huge black object, bigger than a large hut, with smooth, angled, flat sides. Next to this object a Nigh-kutu held a woman down, forcing himself upon her.

"Slaves," Kraniel stated. "They have taken people to act as slaves, to do their will."

I was so angry. I was furious. But with this anger came a new feeling, a cold, focussed clarity.

"How do we rescue them?" I asked matter-of-factly.

"We cannot strike the camp yet. Our numbers are still too few. We would lose quickly."

"Why can't we rescue one at a time, as we did the Anumi?"

"The Anumi were in hiding," Kraniel replied. "The humans are exposed."

"How many more Shaa-kutu do you need to rescue before you can do a full strike?"

"We need to be sure of our odds. We need eight hundred more at least."

"But it will take years to attain those numbers."

"It will," Kraniel nodded.

"How many?"

"Without time crystals, and with the remaining hiding Shaa-kutu so scattered, anything between twenty and one hundred years." He glanced at me, expecting a reaction, but my emotions were distant. "We must take solace that this is the most plausible plan to ensure we are rid of the Nigh-kutu forever," he added.

"I accept your reasoning and see the sense," I nodded, "but it does not agree with me." I looked at the screen. "Nor, I imagine, does it agree with them. How long, if you had enough time crystals, until you could arrange a strike?"

"Two to four weeks," Kraniel replied.

"And how many time crystals would you need?"

"Not many, perhaps eighty, ninety."

Chia held out his hand, showing his newly acquired time crystals.

"I was hoping to use these to get Orion," he looked to the others. "But it must be a joint decision how they are used."

"I think they *should* be used to rescue Orion," I intervened, before anyone else could say anything. "Yes Orion is far away and, you say, secure. But can you be sure that Arrunn's skills will not locate him soon? Orion needs to be in a safe place."

"Agreed," Stanze nodded, and then looked at me. "You approve of using time crystals, Tachra, considering what they are?"

I glanced up at the scene of the Nigh-kutu camp and the human slaves being beaten and abused. Seeing that was all I had needed to convince me.

"Yes, Mardoch was right," I decided aloud. "Kutu have already been murdered to make these grisly time crystals. I do not like what they are, but they already exist; I cannot change that. Better that they are used for the good than for the bad. But we will need more to attack that camp and rid ourselves of these black-winged ones. How do we get them?"

Kraniel gestured towards the screen on the wall once again.

"You see that huge, black, faceted thing in the centre of the camp – the polyhedron? That is Arrunn's personal vault of time crystals. It arrived here a short while ago. The guard that brought the vault has returned to the temple."

"So there are no guards?"

"If you don't count the five hundred highly trained Nigh-kutu warriors all around it, no."

"And there is a Nar beast in that vault," Mardoch added. "A ferocious beast."

"So first someone has to pass through five hundred warrior Nigh-kutu, and then they have to overcome a defensive Nar beast," I stated. "That is not so bad."

"It would be suicide," Kraniel replied.

"For one of you, yes," I nodded. "You would be spotted straight away, caught and tortured for information, or your life turned into another little shiny stone. But for a woman fetching wood or cooking food, a woman who knows caution, a woman who has some vision of energy . . . such a woman could use her knowledge and skills to invisibly enter and exit via your closest access points. For a woman like that it might be possible."

I could feel all the kutu looking at me.

"You?" Kraniel asked in horror.

"Me," I confirmed.

"And the Nar beast?"

"One step at a time," I replied. "Anyway, I like animals."

TWENTY-TWO

"Yes, these creatures are merely animals," Arrunn stated, "but they also have uses other than as slaves, uses the benefits of which will span several thousand years. Do you know what they are?"

"No," Deimom replied. How he now wished that his warriors hadn't talked him into making the request to conquest more human villages.

"No, of course you do not," Arrunn replied. "Is there any point me explaining something to you that you would not understand?"

"No," Deimom stated.

"Then your request is denied. You will have no more of the human animals just yet. Your warriors are restricted to the spoils of that one village, for now. But if you succeed in finding the locations of these underground light-lovers, then you will have more. Would you say that is fair?"

"Very," Deimom nodded. "My warriors and I will not let you down."

"Of course you won't."

Arrunn waved Deimom away. Deimom bowed obediently and immediately left him in peace once again. Arrunn considered that had been a good decision to give Deimom and his warriors a village. It would keep their spirits high, increase their willing obedience, and heighten their focus on locating Jychanumun and the hiding light-lovers.

Arrunn knew that it was only a matter of time before those few light-loving kutu reared their heads from their underground hiding places. He could wait far longer than they could, thousands of years if necessary. Eventually they would run out of supplies. Eventually they would need to breathe in the light. Their patience would break before his did. Arrunn was on the right path. The best those remaining Shaa-kutu could do was defend their dying corner.

"A moment of pleasure," Arrunn said aloud.

The central chamber was empty except for his guards. His guards did not reply.

Arrunn held a small communication device in his hands. It had been made by the Shaa-kutu, specifically for the human, Soul. It had presented a potential short-cut for Arrunn, and one he could find mildly entertaining. Arrunn had sent one of his guards to get that device. He had tried activating it, but it was configured for Soul only. He had even tried using her unconscious body to activate it, to no avail. But it wasn't necessary to have the device activated. Used with shrewd creativity he could bring the Shaa-kutu from hiding, the human Tachra straight to him, and his victory over life itself even closer.

He closed his eyes, allowing his mind to access Soul's memories. He had not destroyed those memories after assimilating them, as he usually would have. These ones he would hold onto for a while and enjoy. And the human, Soul, he had left alive. Arrunn had shown caution when leaving her body, so that it did not diminish. But would she wake from her coma? She might regain consciousness, or she might not. It would be interesting to see whether or not she survived. If she did, she would require a second, more persuasive visit.

Although Soul had no knowledge of Tachra's exact location, she had known that the kutu and this human had underground accommodation to cower in. Armed with Shursa's and Soul's knowledge, Arrunn now had all the relevant data he required on the human Tachra: her ignorance, her weaknesses, her naïve use of energy and of knowledge that was beyond her own comprehension. She was the perfect example of how to waste the one and only link to the heart of all things. Her primary potential threat to Arrunn was her ability to use the Voice from the heart of all things, the Voice of command. That he would need to avoid. And her bond with some type of beast? That he would need to investigate.

Arrunn looked up at his guards, stood and stretched his limbs, rolling his shoulders.

"Dark," he commanded, drawing darkness in all around him until he stood invisible in the shadow.

"I wish to venture out, in anonymity," he stated. He did not expect any more meeting requests soon, but Arrunn would never let his protection slip. He would always stay more than one step ahead of fate.

Three guards walked forward and into the darkness to stand with Arrunn, concealed within the shadow. Two of the guards took a watchful position, their backs to him. The other stood in front of Arrunn, unwrapping his face covering.

Arrunn took the face covering, binding it around his own face. The exposed guard knelt to the ground, assuming the same position of meditation that Arrunn had just been sitting in. If anyone were to see, they would never know the difference. They would never know the difference because there was no difference. Arrunn studied the guard's face, which was his own face. The guard's long brown hair and focussed dark grey eyes were the exact image of his own. They were one and the same; the guard was a part of him. To split himself in this way had always been the obvious choice; one can only trust oneself. The guards were splinters of his own essence. They were the twelve from one.

Arrunn let the darkness drift back away from him and, clad like one of his own guards, walked through the temple and out into the cool night air.

Arrunn avoided proximity to the lake as much as he could. That small expanse of water was foul to his senses. It embodied everything that he despised: life, light. He felt the same way about the adjoining forest. But he did not need to venture in. He was just going to look.

Arrunn found the place where the forest floor showed the remnants of a human trail. He crouched, holding his hand over the area of ground where the trail began. Yes, this was the right one. This was Tachra's trail. He could almost taste it. He crouched silently, waiting, watching, listening.

The subtle rustle and movement from Earth animals in the forest convinced Arrunn that he was in the right place. He used his inner vision, straining to see the brightness of individual life, but still the vivid energy from the planet itself blinded him and concealed all other life-lights, even more so in this foul-tasting place. The taste of so much life sickened him. He cut off the sensation, not allowing himself to feel disgust. He didn't need to feel it again; the memory would never leave him.

During the course of that night, Arrunn waited and watched with just his eyes. He saw animals, many animals. They all ignored his silent, passive presence, carrying on their own nocturnal business, all except one. A pale, sand-coloured female wild cat, with tufts on its ears and watchful eyes, had spotted him and stopped, returning his silent observation. That creature had growled a low, deep warning, and then cautiously moved further into the thickness of the trees.

Arrunn stood up, laughing to himself. What a small creature! He had half expected another Nar beast. This posed no threat. But, it was another link to Tachra, an emotional bond. That too could be utilized at the right time.

TWENTY-THREE

The Nigh-kutu were attacking the land, throwing bolts of energy randomly everywhere, deep into the ground. I assumed that they now knew that we were somewhere underground. Fortunately, it seemed that they didn't know exactly where.

"Tachra, you must get lower underground. You are not safe here," Jychanumun told me.

"Just a moment more," I said. "I must understand the patterns. This is my only opportunity. You go and I'll follow."

I watched the screens intensely. I had not moved from this spot all night, other than to use the washroom. I had to understand how these people who had been captured by the Nigh-kutu were acting. I had to be able to blend in with them.

The hub shuddered again. The Nigh-kutu were getting very close, too close to the hub's position for everyone's comfort.

Although the Nigh-kutu assail on the land grew ever closer, Jychanumun and Kraniel did not move from beside me. Kraniel scrutinized other screens, monitoring the proximity of the Nigh-kutu as they roamed the skies, flinging energy bolts sporadically, deep into patches of land.

Most of the Shaa-kutu had already been moved lower underground and were working their way through the tunnels into areas deemed safe. Dragun walked behind them all, just in case the tunnels collapsed. His skills of manipulating earth and rock were even more precious now. Chia oversaw moving the injured. With the attacks happening so quickly and without respite, he had to wait to retrieve Orion lest he made a distance-jump back to a demolished hub and they were both buried in the process. I sensed his frustration, even though he did not let it show.

"They are getting close . . ." Kraniel suddenly warned me. "Closer. Tachra . . . come on . . . we have really got to go. We must go. Now!"

I heard the urgency.

I leapt down from the chair and started running towards the one open exit. Jychanumun ran beside me and, although blind, knew exactly where he was heading. Just as I passed the threshold, I remembered I had forgotten something. My bundle! I would need my bundle!

I turned around, running back into the hub, diving towards the corner where my bundle lay discarded. I grabbed it just as a loud thud boomed through the air, directly above my head. The ground shuddered and dust billowed around me. I ran back towards the exit, but I could not see. There was too much dust. The air was dense with it. I could hear deafeningly loud cracking sounds. It felt as if my ears were ripping. The dust was so thick that I couldn't breathe. I groped the wall where I thought the exit was. It wasn't there. It should be there!

Suddenly a hand was on my wrist. Jychanumun. He was pulling me with speed. I let him pull me. I could not see where I was going. Something dropped from my bag. I had to leave it. I could hear the collapse of great rocks thundering above me. I was yanked forward and then heard Jychanumun close a door. The sound became muffled, but the air was still thick with dust.

I felt inside my bag. My communication device; I had dropped it. My one connection with Soul and my family was gone.

I have to go back into the hub, I told Jychanumun with my mind as he led me forward. *I've dropped the communication device.*

We cannot. I heard the ceiling collapse, he replied. *When it is safe enough we can ask Dragun to retrieve it.*

I had to concede. That little device was now buried somewhere under stone and earth. Only Dragun could get through such a mass. Anyway, where I was going, I couldn't take it with me.

"Control your breathing; keep it shallow," Jychanumun instructed me as he guided me on.

"I can't see where we're going," I said, my words sounding muffled.

"We are the blind leading the blind." Despite the chaos, Jychanumun sounded amused. "I know my way."

Several sealed exits later and the air started to clear. I could make out the form of Kraniel, waiting for us.

"By Eskah," Kraniel frowned, looking at the bag I clutched in my hands "You cut that close. All for a bag?"

"Where else would I find an earth-made dress around here?" I replied. "If I entered the Nigh-kutu camp wearing a Shaa-kutu tunic, I think I would neither blend in nor last long."

"Point taken," Kraniel nodded, as he led us further down the tunnels.

It took a great deal of walking until we traversed tunnels that the dust had not contaminated so much. The air here smelt stale and heavy, but I was glad to be breathing it. Finally, Kraniel guided us through the tunnels to where several connected together and made one large space. Standing in small groups, looking resolute yet tired, were the kutu: dozens upon dozens of kutu. They carried weapons and healing equipment, anything that might come in useful. To see such strong, glorious beings reduced to this displaced state made my heart heavy.

I noticed that Dragun and Mardoch were standing to one side with only Chia and a few of the Anumi – the ones they had worked with since their arrival. Many of the other Shaa-kutu seemed to be segregating themselves from their new colleagues on purpose. I understood their reluctance to accept any black-winged ones, but I did not agree with it.

"You must all be united," I suddenly said. The thought had entered my mind and I did not want to stop the words. "If there is to be peace, then it must start right here, right now, with everyone who stands for that peace." I looked towards the Nigh-kutu and then towards the Shaa-kutu. "We do not fight against the black-winged ones on principle. We defend our right to peace, truth and freedom. If a Nigh-kutu fights for that too, is he not your brother?"

I stopped. All eyes were upon me. And yet I did not feel conspicuous. It was the truth, and I might not get another opportunity to say it. All these brave, wonderful kutu needed to learn to work together.

"Hear, hear, Tachra green eyes," I heard a frail voice call from behind the kutu.

Behind the kutu were humans: the remnants of those rescued from Meadsins. Between them all, kutu and human, they carried the wounded. I scanned the gloomy figures, walking towards the one who had spoken, now supported by another, a healing sheet draped around his shoulders.

"Ren," I said, hugging him. "It gladdens my heart to see you alive." As I hugged him, I noticed a large bundle on his back. I glanced over his shoulder. The babies!

"The skies saw fit to save them," Ren smiled weakly. "But Dinah . . ."

"I have seen her," I interrupted. "She is alive."

Ren pushed away the man who was supporting him, trying to stand on his own and stand straight. "Where?" he asked. "I must find her."

"It is already in hand. I will get her," I smiled.

"I'll help," Ren said determinedly.

"No, you must leave this to me," I replied. "But if I need your help, may I ask it of you?"

"Of course," Ren replied. He looked at me and grasped my hand. "Please hurry, Tachra. The babies need her. I need her."

"I will," I nodded.

"We will wait here until the attack to this land has finished, and then we will return to the hub and assess the damage," Chia told the others.

"It sounded bad. It sounded as if the roof caved in," I replied.

"We will fix it. We will have to."

"I am ready," I told Chia. "Take me to the access point."

"Now?"

"Yes. With half the warriors occupied with their assault on the land, I cannot think of a better time," I said with conviction.

I threw my bundle over my shoulder and smiled to myself. Chia looked at me questioningly, but I didn't say anything; he wouldn't understand. The familiarity of that action, taking my bundle, preparing for the unknown; they were things that I had thought I had left behind. It seemed that my life really would be a never-ending cycle of walking to new places. All I needed was a nice gnarled walking stick to accompany me and the setting would be perfect.

Chia, Dragun and Jychanumun escorted me through more

tunnels, moving slowly up to the surface, towards the correct location. There were no lamps in this place. Instead, Chia lifted his hand and sent energy from his palm. It lit our paths with a pale violet light and, as I walked through his dissipating energy, it filled my head with a clarity that I sorely needed.

I was hot from so much walking and breathing in the stale air. Sweat dripped down my face, congealing with the dust and grime. I took a long draught of water from my own pots, grateful that I had thought to fill them. Finally, after what seemed an age of walking uphill and hundreds of twists and turns, we were at the end of a perfectly smooth tunnel. I noticed what looked like a hand print, deeply embedded in the stone. This was it. This was the exit that Dragun had prepared.

On the other side of that tunnel was a natural fissure in the land. It was the very same fissure that had concealed a trapped Anumi for four days. For my plan, it was close enough to the Nigh-kutu camp, and close enough to where the human slaves ventured to collect wood. We had reached the end of the tunnel and the access point to the surface.

I quickly stripped off the kutu dress, discarding it to one side, and pulled my old choosing dress from my bundle. Then I took the rags from the bottom of the bag and wound them around my head and face, after the fashion of the Meadsins women, and replaced my boots with my cloth slippers.

"We really should wait until the hub is operational again," Chia fretted, as I finished dressing. "We will not be able to monitor you until then."

"I have my connection to Jychanumun," I replied. "That will suffice."

"And you must keep our connection open at all times," Jychanumun said. "Do not block me."

"I won't block you," I nodded. I looked at Jychanumun, his

eyes now uncovered, yet still blind. His empty, dark sockets were a stark reminder of everything that I now fought for. "I am sorry that I could not heal your eyes." I had to tell him now, in case I never got another chance. "I tried. I don't understand why it didn't work."

Jychanumun bent to me. "My sight will come back," he whispered. *I think perhaps I choose to remain blind at this time,* he silently told me with his mind. *Your sight has become my balance. You are my focus. You are my choice.*

Without thinking, I touched his cheek, and then I kissed him. I held that kiss, and for a moment I forgot about everything else. In that moment I felt our minds connect as one; not two shared thoughts, but a singular, joined thought. It was beautiful. Perhaps this was the type of love that Soul had talked about.

I heard Dragun clearing his throat, and I pulled back. Oh what cruel tricks fate plays. To have finally found an emotional place with Jychanumun, only for it to be at the most terrible time, a time when I had to walk away. Yet, even standing in a dusty tunnel, wearing a tattered dress, with congealed sweat and dust all over my face, it was still perfect. For I now realised that in facing difficulties, we all would realise our priorities.

"Are you sure you have everything you need?" Chia asked.

"Yes," I replied, tying my bundle over my back. "I can't take any kutu items. It wouldn't be safe."

I looked to Dragun and nodded.

Dragun pushed his hands through the rock barrier, walking through to stand in the fissure. He held out his cupped hands to lift me.

I took a handful of mud from the bottom of the fissure, rubbing it on my arms and face, pulling down my head covering and rubbing it through my hair, and then smearing it on my dress.

Once my head covering was replaced, I put one foot in Dragun's cupped hand.

"Be safe," Dragun whispered, as he lifted me up.

With my feet in Dragun's large, steady hands, and raised high from the floor of the fissure, I waited, crouched. Slowly, I lifted my head up, just enough to peer over the edge of the fissure.

It was daybreak and the land was still gloomy. I could hear the crackle of fires and Nigh-kutu talking and laughing. I could see them in the not-too-far distance. Several people were already out collecting wood. Perfect.

I pulled myself over the lip of the fissure as stealthily as I could, slid nimbly across the ground, belly down, and then pulled myself to a crouching position, slowly standing up as if I had just been attending to something. I quickly picked up two pieces of wood, the closest broken branches that I could see, and, carrying them in my arms, walked towards another figure who was already collecting sticks.

I caught up with that figure, walking alongside her, matching her pace.

"Do not look at me. Keep walking and collecting wood while I speak," I instructed her under my breath.

There was a slight falter in the woman's step, but she regained herself admirably, bending to collect another broken branch.

"Tachra?" she asked, her eyes darting momentarily up to my face as she arose and continued walking.

"Shh," I said. "Dinah, just listen and keep walking and working. Listen carefully."

I picked up a stick myself.

"We are going to walk together to an area. When I turn around and head back towards the Nigh-kutu camp, you keep walking. Ten steps ahead of you will be a natural fissure. Go down that fissure. Shaa-kutu will be waiting. They will take you to Ren and your children. I will be taking your place."

I heard a small gasp from Dinah at the mention of Ren and her children. She had clearly thought them dead.

"Where is . . . ?"

"Shh, just walk," I said. I had noticed a Nigh-kutu glance in our direction. I felt very exposed. My dress was only thin and my arms unsuitably uncovered.

"As you walk to that fissure, drop your cloak," I stated. "I shall be turning in a second. Keep walking, straight ahead. I have you covered. Don't look back."

I did not wait for Dinah's reply. I had to hope that she had her wits about her. I knew the girl well. She had worked for three years in the temple, helping Nana in the kitchens, before Ren had stolen her heart. We had spent many happy hours in the kitchens together. I hoped by the skies that she trusted me.

I reached a specific point on the land and suddenly turned around, heading for a large broken branch that I had left in the direct visual path of Dinah and the Nigh-kutu camp. From the corner of my eye, I watched Dinah keep walking. She dropped her cloak before disappearing into the hole in the ground.

Satisfied that I had no Nigh-kutu eyes upon me, I picked up the stick, turned around and casually walked to the cloak, picking it up and wrapping it around me while I walked, using one hand to fasten ties around my waist, and rearranging the fabric to bulk out my small frame. As I picked up more wood, I dug my fingers into the moist soil, wiping more layers of dirt on my face. I had to be as inconspicuous and unappealing as I could. It would not serve me well to be deemed fit for the Nigh-kutu circle of women.

Satisfied that I had as much wood as was appropriate, I headed towards the Nigh-kutu camp.

I was scared now that the Nigh-kutu camp loomed in front of

me. I had to keep my eyes focussed on the women who were busy preparing and serving food. I fixed my gazed on an older woman. If she had not had such a miserable, demoralized expression, she would have reminded me of my mother. I had to keep focussed on that face. If I did not, my quaking insides and weak legs would surely let me down.

For a brief moment, I almost faltered. What on earth was I doing? How, by the skies, had I convinced myself that I could do this? These were not gentle, life-loving Shaa-kutu. These were hardened, cruel warriors. Had I let my brief acquaintance with Dragun and Mardoch make me believe that these were also good beings under their brutal façade?

A part of me wanted to run back to that fissure, climb in and bury myself away from this terrible place. But I could not. As much as I didn't want to enter that Nigh-kutu camp, my quaking legs still carried me forward. It was that woman's face that made me do it; her expression was one of defeated misery. Perhaps I was the only person who could possibly help her right now.

It was too late to turn back now. I was there. And I had been spotted.

A Nigh-kutu started to walk towards me. I had witnessed this type of movement on the screens. He thought I was either loitering or not working hard enough. I bowed my head and quickened my step in response, aiming directly for the wood pile. The Nigh-kutu lost interest, turning to jest with one of his fellow black-winged ones. I dropped the wood on top of the pile and took a stool to sit and prepare food, making sure it was the same stool that Dinah would have sat on.

I picked up a portion of the strange, moist, dark-red Nigh-kutu food and started scraping away at the white sections around the edges. On the view-screens I had seen Dinah do just this, but she had made the job look quite easy. Now, when I tried it, the unfamiliar food seemed to want to bend in every direction except the one I wanted it to. I had no idea what type of fruit or vegetable this was. I'd never seen anything like it. As I worked at scraping off the white substance, which was like some sort of pith, my hands became stained with red liquid.

I gasped. The red liquid was blood! I felt myself start to retch.

"Don't you be sick," the woman to my right scolded me worriedly under her breath. "We'll all get a beating if you are sick."

I made myself focus on something else, repeatedly swallowing hard to stop myself retching. I managed to convince myself that this really was no different to a vegetable, making myself picture a potato in my hands.

"What is it?" I whispered to the woman as I continued scraping. What poor animal was being hunted to feed these beasts?

"At first I thought it was boar," the woman whispered as she worked. "But then I found something . . ."

She tossed the kutu food onto a tray already laden with the stuff, and then went to pick up another piece that needed scraping.

"Look," she whispered.

Continuing to work, I cast my glance to one side. The woman had moved her foot. Under where her foot had been was what looked like a large, severed finger.

"Is that . . . ?" I began in horror.

"Shh, keep your voice down," she hushed. "Yes, it's a finger. But look at the size of it."

She moved her foot again, nudging the horribly familiar thing. But it was far too big to be a human finger.

"A kutu finger?" I whispered, the nausea rising once again. "Kutu?"

"Uh huh," the woman nodded, covering her foot over the object once again and not pausing her scraping. "Although I have no idea whether it's from one of those black ones or white ones. It makes no difference. Let's hope they all eat each other into extinction."

"But the Shaa-kutu are good beings," I protested under my breath.

"Tish," the woman hissed. "This is their fault."

I could not reply. I was angry at her, even though I had no right to be. Of course this woman needed to allocate blame. This whole thing was something she had no control over. She had suffered losses and now sat, a slave, cleaning kutu flesh for more kutu to consume. It was indeed grisly. Once the anger had subsided, I felt sad. My brave kutu friends; how could their courageous actions and sacrifices be so easily disregarded?

But I had no time to dwell on how I felt. A Nigh-kutu had walked up to us, using a stick to poke us in the back. I followed the lead of the other women, picking up the tray of scraped flesh in front of me and walking out into the midst of the Nigh-kutu camp.

The sunrise was casting long shadows on the ground. The Nigh-kutu who had been out flying, bringing devastation to the land, were returning. I watched the other women bring trays forward, offering food to the Nigh-kutu as they arrived. I kept my head low and my eyes cast down as hands came from every direction, grabbing pieces of food. I was suddenly grateful to have this tray. It seemed that the Nigh-kutu were far too focussed on the food to notice any of the subdued women who were carrying it.

Once our trays of flesh emptied, we would run back and get more. The appetites of these kutu were ferocious. Each time I would refill my tray and head deeper into the centre of the camp, my downcast eyes designed to hide my true purpose: to observe the huge black vault at the centre of the site.

By the fifth tray of food the Nigh-kutu were at last getting too satiated to eat any more. The kutu who had returned were settling down to rest, and those who had stayed behind were now readying to leave. It seemed they were working their assault on the land in shifts. I hoped my kutu friends would be safe in their underground tunnels.

With most of the Nigh-kutu full with food and wanting no more, most of the serving women returned to their stools, preparing the next batches of kutu meat. But two of the women, with their trays still half full, remained standing, holding up their trays. They seemed to be waiting in case the Nigh-kutu called for more food. As if in response, a Nigh-kutu lifted his hand and shouted. The closest woman hurried towards him, her posture lowered in subservience, holding out the tray towards him. The kutu took a piece of meat, and the woman hurriedly returned to a more central position, her eyes scanning for any further requests. I noticed her face was badly bruised and swollen. The poor woman clearly had already had endured more than one run-in with these black-winged beasts.

Following the example of the two remaining serving women, I held my tray up and slowly picked my way towards the centre of the camp, towards the vault. The ground beneath my feet was flattened and muddied, the grass buried by multitudes of footsteps. There were flies, lots of them, all gathering on the small pieces of discarded food. The camp smelt and looked awful.

Having furtively made my way to the centre of the camp, I stopped by one side of the vault, loitering there. The site was growing still as the last of the second shift of Nigh-kutu had left, while the others settled into a satiated rest. Only a few fires crackled in the morning breeze; all was relatively quiet. As I stood, holding up my tray, I was sure I could hear movement from inside the vault.

The crystal vault was huge, taller than a hut and twice as wide. Its smooth, flat sides had regular holes, large enough to get an entire arm into, but not quite big enough to get my whole body into. And the holes seemed to have some sort of energy barrier warding them. The energy barriers did not worry me too much: I had probably rediscovered enough about my own skills to overcome them. But, I fretted, those holes were far beyond my reach. I could just about touch them, if I strained, but I could not see how I could climb up the perfectly smooth, sloping sides to enable me to get my entire arm in to grab any crystals. I might be able to do it, but to do it without being noticed by the Nigh-kutu? That I could not yet imagine.

As I stood there, I slowly became aware of a sensation of heat on the back of my head. I scanned the area, ensuring no one was looking, and cautiously put my hand behind me to touch the smooth wall of the vault. The vault felt cold, ice cold. The heat was not coming from there. And then I suddenly realised I could hear breathing. Something was breathing inside that vault. It had to be the Nar beast.

I glanced up to the holes around the edge of the vault. Condensation dripped from one of the openings; the one directly above my head. The Nar beast must have sensed my proximity. It was as if it could smell me.

I touched the black object again, ignoring the coldness, trying to sense the animal inside. Straight away, the feeling was overpowering.

By the skies! That poor creature was starving! Its hunger was so intense it was driven near to madness. Without a second thought, I grabbed a handful of flesh from the tray, made sure no one was looking, and, standing on my tiptoes, pushed it through one of the energy barriers and into the vacant hole.

I heard a muffled commotion inside that vault, and quickly

took a few steps away in case the Nigh-kutu had heard it. I saw one Nigh-kutu lift his head and glance towards the vault, but he just raised his eyebrows before lying back down again.

Once the way was clear again, I took a few steps backwards, posting more flesh through a different hole in the vault. I hoped by the skies that the Nar beast did not have jaws that could snap my hand through those holes.

Over the next few moments I secretly posted every last morsel of flesh into that vault. That poor creature! It did not matter if it was wild or aggressive: nothing should be kept in horrific starvation like that.

Knowing I would look conspicuous if I was seen holding a tray empty of food, I walked away from the vault and headed back to the food preparation area. I could still hear the heavy breathing of the beast contained in the vault. It was still hungry. Very.

I sat back on the stool that had been allocated for Dinah, and which was now my working place, and started the ritual of cleaning more flesh. My own section only had a little meat remaining, but behind the stool there was a pile of vegetables, obviously for human consumption. Each time that I picked up another piece of flesh to clean I would also pick up a vegetable and stuff it into the fold of my cloak, held in place by the ties around my waist.

Jychanumun? I called out silently with my mind.

I am here. I am with you every step of the way, seeing with your eyes, Jychanumun immediately replied.

Does a Nar beast eat vegetables? I asked.

All knowledge of the Nar beast was wiped out when the Gatherer clan was massacred, Jychanumun said. *No one knows what they eat.*

Has Chia got Orion back yet?

It is happening as we speak.

That is something to rejoice in. Are you all safe?

Yes. Now stop concerning yourself about us. You must keep your focus on your own actions.

Jychanumun was right; I needed to stay focussed. I withdrew our conscious connection, leaving him invisibly watching through my eyes, picked up the tray of meat, with the scavenged vegetables hidden inside my cloak, and then headed out to the centre of the camp once again.

I felt very conspicuous. I was the only human carrying out a tray of food this time. One resting Nigh-kutu lazily raised his arm as I passed, moving to grab my ankle. I shuffled to one side, placing the tray of meat under his grasp instead. He took a piece of meat, stuffing it into his mouth. A few steps later and another kutu tried the same thing. Again, I satisfied his attention with food. It worked, although this one was more hesitant. I walked on, but now I ensured that my footsteps did not fall within Nigh-kutu reach.

I approached the black vault in the centre of the camp. The Nar beast had clearly smelt me coming. I saw its hot breath moving around from hole to hole as it followed my progress. I stood on the other side of the vault and backed up a couple of steps, vigilantly watching for any Nigh-kutu eyes that may be upon me. A Nigh-kutu arose and walked towards me. I bowed my head, trying to make myself as unnoticeable as I could, and the Nigh-kutu walked straight past me, heading to the area where the part-naked women were held. A few moments later and I heard a woman's protests and a thud. This was terrible. I really did have to hurry up, get the crystals, and get these poor people out of here.

Standing on tiptoes, I glanced around, pulled a large root vegetable from the concealed folds of my cloak, and posted it through one of the holes in the vault. The way was clear. I quickly posted another two, and then three, up to six. I hoped this creature would eat vegetables, too.

I put my hand behind my back, touching the vault. "I'm sorry it's not more meat," I whispered quietly in Nigh-kutu. "It's all I could get."

I knew the beast would not understand my words, but it didn't matter. My heart went out to it. Once, this mad creature may well have been the beloved pet of a good Nigh-kutu clan, like Jychanumun's or Dragun's. This poor creature was just as much a victim of Arrunn's deeds as the people now trapped in this camp.

I suddenly heard a clunk on the ground and something hit my feet. I looked down.

There by my feet was a small, bright-orange time crystal!

I surreptitiously glanced around, bent down, and quickly picked up that crystal, tucking it into my cloak. The glow penetrated through the fabric, making a shining spot against my stomach. I had to quickly move it to right inside my dress, pulling fabric in to wrap around it and conceal it.

The Nar beast must have accidentally pushed out a crystal when it was moving around to get to the food, I thought. I decided to stay where I was, quickly removing the last of the vegetables from the concealment of my cloak and, at the first opportunity, posted them all through the holes in quick succession.

Clunk. Clunk. Clunk.

Three more bright orange time crystals had landed by my feet!

I quickly picked up the time crystals, tucking them into my dress along with the other, anxiously checking that the glow wasn't showing through the fabrics. Was that a coincidence? I wondered if the Nar beast had dislodged a large section of time crystals. All four had seemingly fallen from the same hole.

I noticed movement at the edge of the camp. Some of the women were moving from the food preparation area to pick up wood. I knew I had to be with them and stay in line if I were to remain concealed among them.

"I'll be back with more food very soon," I whispered.

I turned to leave. And then, from the corner of my eye, I saw it; it was the Nar beast, or at least a part of it. Two large nostrils on a long snout were breathing condensation against one of the vault's holes. This definitely was not a small beast. The nostrils lowered until I saw a single dark orange, reptilian like eye, looking straight at me. The head of the beast moved and I caught sight of a large jaw and jagged, irregular teeth pressed against the hole. Held delicately between the front teeth, as if it were a fragile egg, was another time crystal. With a small flick, the crystal was thrown out.

The little crystal landed exactly at my feet. Exactly! Not a few inches away, or off to my side, but right between my feet. The creature had purposely thrown it to me.

"Thank you," I muttered under my breath, quickly picking up the crystal, my eyes roving to ensure that no one else had just seen.

I wanted to give this Nar beast more food. I knew it was still hungry, but I had to play the part. I had to be out there collecting wood with the other women.

I headed back to the food-preparation area, leaving the dirty tray just as the other women had done, and headed out to collect wood.

I have five time crystals, I silently told Jychanumun as I walked, picking up pieces of wood.

I saw what happened, Jychanumun replied, *although I do not fully understand it.*

I'm going to drop them into the fissure. Make sure they don't just sink into the mud. I may not get more quite as easily.

I am ready. Are you coping? Jychanumun asked.

Yes, I replied. *I need to keep my wits about me, although this place is enough to scare the wits from anyone.*

Take no chances, Jychanumun instructed.

I picked up two particularly large branches and headed towards the fissure, dropping the crystals into an up-stretched hand before turning around to carry the large branches back to the camp.

After three more trips to collect wood, I had spent adequate time on the task to satisfy the Nigh-kutu who was monitoring the wood pile. I'd made sure I'd picked up the biggest branches that I could, and had carried as much as I could. My arms were a mess of embedded splinters.

Settling back on my stool to hurriedly catch up with the preparation of more kutu meat, I noticed that at the far end of the line a woman was staring at me through squinted eyes as she worked on her food. I suspected that she was not sure if she recognised me or not, but I recognised her. It was Mags, Ren's mother.

My first instinct at seeing Mags was that I wanted to walk up to her and tell her that her son was well, and that so were Dinah and their two children. But I could not risk it. I had to stay invisible. I dare not take the chance of anyone recognising me.

I pulled my head covering down further over my face, right down to my eyes, and pulled every last strand of my hair away from my face, ensuring it was all tucked in. Some hair had stuck to the mud and grime near my mouth, and I pulled it away, my fingers having to prise the hair from my lips. As my fingers brushed my lips, they tingled, and my heartbeat started to race with adrenaline. I suddenly felt stronger and taller, and my mind had an intense clarity.

I glanced at my fingers. They were stained with the luminous blood of the kutu. I had just put kutu blood in my mouth! I was horrified at myself.

Without touching my cloak with my hands, I rubbed my bottom lip against the shoulder of my cloak until it was dry and raw, and then I rubbed at it some more. The thought of consuming even the tiniest amount of kutu, even accidentally, sickened me.

Did you sense that? I asked Jychanumun as I concentrated on filling a new tray with meat. *The Nigh-kutu eat the flesh of other kutu. I think it gives them strength.*

It is not something that Nigh-kutu did when I existed with them. I am appalled beyond words, Jychanumun quietly replied. I could feel what he was feeling. He suspected that some of this flesh could be his friends. He thought it the most despicable, hideous end that any kutu could endure. *I have told the others,* he said simply.

As I worked in the Nigh-kutu camp, adding more scraped meat to the pile, I cautiously tucked more of the root vegetables into my cloak. I noticed that the woman who was currently walking the Nigh-kutu camp with a tray of food was returning. I hurriedly scraped at more meat, wanting to be the one who took her place. It seemed that I did not need to hurry. The other women willingly let me go. They looked relieved that the task would not fall to them.

I stood up, pulling out the bulk of my cloak, hunched over a little and then began to walk with a slow, subservient gait through the black-winged ones.

A group of around thirty Nigh-kutu sparred together at one side of the camp. They had arisen from their rest and were now more full of life than ever.

Please don't call me over, I thought, as I tried to work my way, unnoticed, to the centre of the camp.

They called me over.

My heart sank.

I hurried in the direction of the beckoning Nigh-kutu, knowing that any delay would result in a hard strike about my face. As I walked, three resting Nigh-kutu beckoned for food in quick succession. Each time I speedily carried the tray of meat directly to their hands, willing that they would not delay me. Frustratingly, each one seemed to be feeling choosy about which piece of meat they should select.

The group of sparring Nigh-kutu impatiently called for meat a second time.

I glanced to the row of other women preparing food. None of them moved to attend the sparring Nigh-kutu, choosing to look even more engrossed in their tasks. It didn't surprise me. The Nigh-kutu's aggressive, buoyant spirits just smelt of trouble. Once the reclining kutu had selected his meat, I rushed towards them, holding out my tray, refusing to pause for any other hand that rose from its slumbers to request food.

Thump.

I felt a hard strike to the side of my head. I hadn't seen it coming. The world spun around me. I stumbled. Half the meat fell from my tray. I tried to regain my balance and hold out the tray. I didn't need to pretend to take a position of cowering subservience, because I was already in one.

One of the sparring Nigh-kutu stopped his activity and picked up a large piece of the meat I had dropped from the ground, inspecting it for dirt. He looked at me, his eyes narrowing.

Thump. That one was right next to my mouth. That hurt. That hurt a lot. My entire head pulsated with pain. It made my head spin so much that I thought the ground was rising up. I couldn't focus. I didn't know if I was falling over or not. For a moment, I didn't know anything.

I think I swayed on the spot for quite a while. In my giddy state, I was aware of hands taking meat from the tray in my grasp. One of them suddenly gave me a shove away from them, hitting me around the back of my head as I stumbled. I unsteadily tottered away, not sure what I was doing or where I was going.

Another call for meat started to bring me to me senses. Like an over-disciplined animal, I handed out more food.

Think straight, Tachra. Jychanumun calmly told me. *Breathe deeply. Head towards a quiet place; go to the side of the vault that faces the fissure. There the least number of Nigh-kutu will be able to see you and you can gather yourself.*

I did as he suggested and my thoughts slowly began to clear, although the dizziness wasn't passing and the pulsating pain remained. I was really scared. I wanted nothing more than to return to the dark safety of the underground tunnels.

Please remind me that this is all worth it, I told Jychanumun. *Right now, I feel very alone, scared and everything hurts. I need to hear my objective from someone else.*

We have Orion, Jychanumun told me. *He is weak but alive.*

Jychanumun's words were like a ray of light. They were all that I needed to hear and a symbol of my objective. Orion, my friend, was safe. Such good news made my eyes drop tears. This was what I was collecting crystals for, to save kutu and human lives. A few cuts and bruises were insignificant in the scheme of things.

Thank you, I said.

As I grew near to the vault, happy with the news that Orion was safe, I could hear that the Nar beast was restless and snorting. I couldn't tell if the creature wanted more food or had sensed my disarray. I couldn't give it more food yet, though: I was too light-headed, and it was taking all my concentration to stay standing. Reaching up would certainly send me tumbling over. So I just stood by the vault, hoping the giddiness would soon pass.

Clunk. Clunk.

I glanced down. Two more time crystals had fallen by my feet. Again, they were orange.

Clunk. Clunk. Clunk.

Three more! It was as if the Nar beast had been waiting for me.

I quickly put my feet over the crystals, nervously waiting for the opportune moment to pick them up.

I couldn't tell if the Nar was throwing out crystals because it expected food in return, or because there was some sense of a higher thought process occurring. My mind told me this was nothing more than a programmed response, that the Nar sensed my presence and knew I would give it food, so gave me in return the only thing it had access to: time crystals. But my heart told me something else. My heart told me that this was not entirely a senseless creature. Was it driven to near madness with starvation? Yes. But was it a mindless beast, capable only of violence? No, I did not think it was.

At the first opportunity, when no Nigh-kutu eyes were upon me, I picked up the crystals, now hidden safely under one foot, and tucked them safely into my dress. And then, as soon as my way was clear again, I turned around and, stretching up as far as I could, posted every piece of vegetable and every piece of kutu meat into that vault.

Much to my surprise, almost instantly, the kutu meat came back out of the vault, landing back, albeit untidily, on the tray.

By the skies! This creature may be starving, but it still knew the difference between foods. And for an animal, its aim was surprisingly accurate.

I took a strange gamble.

"Do you understand me?" I whispered in Nigh-kutu.

Clunk, another orange time crystal fell on the floor. Did that mean yes?

I hesitated, thinking of how I could decipher this. "If you understand me, pick out a . . . blue crystal," I suggested quietly.

In truth, I did not expect this to work. I knew Meah, my

wildcat, did not perceive colours in the same way that I did. I certainly did not expect this Nar beast to recognize colours, yet alone understand my communication.

The Nar beast went still.

Oh well, it was worth a try. In truth, I had not thought that it would work.

Clunk.

I looked down. Sitting by my feet was a bright blue time crystal. I was speechless.

I quickly picked up the little stone, tucking it into my dress with the others. A Nigh-kutu was calling for meat. I had to go.

"I'll be back. I'll find a way to get you out," I hurried under my breath. "My kutu friend Jychanumun is of the Weaver clan. He will help me get you out and when we do, please don't eat us."

I started to walk away.

Clunk. Another crystal hit my foot. I had to quickly step on it to stop it rolling to one side. This one was not orange; it was colourless; inside was what looked like a tiny, luminous pearl. The colours of the pearl looked very similar to my own colours. That was when I knew: the Nar beast was not only intelligent, it could see more than its orange eyes perceived.

I quickly delivered meat to the waiting Nigh-kutu and then returned to my stool, ready to prepare more food. Someone else could do the next tray serving. I needed to think and I needed to think fast.

You got all that? I silently asked Jychanumun with my mind.

Yes, everything, he replied straight away. I could feel the concern in his thoughts, even though he was straining to conceal them from me.

Jychanumun, the clan that the Nar beasts were bonded to and killed long ago, were most of them orange in energy?

The Gatherer clan, yes, most of them were. Jychanumun knew what I was thinking. *Orange energy has the ability to absorb and combine things, both were necessary for the Gathering skill.*

I think that the Nar beast still recognises its own clan, even if it's just their life energy. Jychanumun, I do not know why yet, but I have this terrible feeling that those life crystals are still considered alive by the Nar beast.

Jychanumun paused. *The implications of that are great,* he said gravely.

I know, I considered, sensing the significance of a possibility I'd not foreseen. *What if some part of the dead kutu are still alive? I've seen the souls of dead people walking through the devastated village of Meadsins . . . could these time crystals be like kutu souls? Could it be that every time we use one we are killing the very soul of a kutu?*

Do not fret, Jychanumun told me. *I have travelled the Death Paths. I will look into this myself. We will use no more until we are satisfied we are not destroying good souls.*

I nodded to myself, satisfied at that, and then continued scraping yet more meat. I had a plan. I would collect wood at the next opportunity and pass these additional crystals to Dragun or Jychanumun. I would study that vault, and while collecting every crystal the Nar beast deemed appropriate to give me, I would figure out if there were a way to set it free without causing damage to anyone. It was a loose plan, but right now, it was the best one I could think of.

Tachra? a quiet, distant voice called to me. It was not Jychanumun's voice.

Did you hear that? I asked Jychanumun.

Yes, Jychanumun replied, *but it was very faint.*

Shh, I'll listen.

I tried to focus my thoughts on the unknown voice. There was only one other person who I knew could call me with their mind – Soul. I concentrated on Soul, bringing an image of her to my mind. And then it hit me, loud and clear, it was a voice shouting in my head.

Tachra, Tachra, Tachra.

I recognised the voice. It was not Soul. It was her daughter, Iris.

TWENTY-FOUR

"Tachra, Tachra, Tachra, Tachra," Iris chanted under her breath.

The little bead necklace her mother had given her was now clutched in her hand. She was sitting on the edge of the bed, rocking herself back and forth to try to stay calm.

"It's bedtime, come on," Ellen called. The old lady shuffled into the room, her face drawn and grey.

"I'm going to sleep here again tonight," Iris replied, "Keep mamma company in case she wakes up."

"Alright," Ellen replied, shuffling away towards her own room. "You know, little Iris, that your mamma might never wake up." Her voice was gentle.

"I know," Iris swallowed hard. She would not let herself cry again. She had to be strong. She had to make her mamma well.

And she didn't think Ellen looked very well, either. She was worried about the old lady. Ellen hadn't looked very well since old man Dannel had ceased, the same night her mamma had not woken up. Iris was very, very sad about Dannel. She had loved him very much. Now mamma still wouldn't wake up and old lady Ellen looked ill. Iris was frightened. No one was helping.

If only Tachra were here, she would help, Iris thought. Tachra had promised that she would always help when called for. And mamma and Tachra had decided to give her this bead necklace. Tachra had said it was special. Tachra had said that it meant she would know when help was needed. Mamma had said it was true, so it had to be.

As soon as Iris heard Ellen close the door to her room, she picked up the empty mug and quietly stole into the washroom. She had to stand on tiptoes to reach the wash pail on the ledge and get water into the mug. There was a clean towel too. Good.

Iris quietly walked back into her mamma's room. She knew exactly which floorboards made noises, and she made sure she didn't step on them. She climbed up onto the bed, careful not to spill any of the water. It took all her strength to lift her mamma's head from the pillow, and her hand shook as she tried to trickle water into her mouth. The water filled up in her mamma's mouth, spilling out from the side and onto the blanket. Iris carefully mopped it up. She couldn't tell if mamma had swallowed any of the water, or if it had just all come back out. She hugged her mamma around her neck, putting her mouth next to her ear.

"Wake up. Please wake up. Wake up. Please, please, please, please, please."

But mamma still didn't wake up. She didn't even stir.

Iris put her little hand over her mamma's mouth. She could feel she was still breathing. She took the towel and dipped the corner in water, wiping it over her mamma's brow, just as she had seen old lady Ellen do.

Iris sat as close to her mamma as she could. Even if she was asleep, it felt better being next to her. She put her mamma's hand on her lap. That made her feel better too. Her little legs dangled over the side of the bed, and she held onto the little wooden carved bead necklace around her neck.

I've got to think loudly, Iris thought. She remembered hearing Tachra and her mamma talking one day. They had thought she was not listening and that she was busy playing with Meah. But she always listened, even when she was playing. Tachra and mamma always had lots to say, and always liked to laugh. It was nice to listen to them talking and laughing. Tachra had told her mamma that maybe she thought too loudly – that was why Tachra could hear her. Mamma had thought that was funny, and agreed.

Yes, I've got to think loudly, Iris decided. *If Tachra is not helping, it's because I am not thinking loudly enough and she can't hear me. I've got to be grown up and think very loudly.*

Tachra, little Iris called with her thoughts, as loudly as she could. She held her breath when she thought that loud. *Tachra, Tachra, Tachra.*

And she kept thinking as loudly as she could and for as long as she could. She didn't want to sleep, but she must have fallen asleep. The next thing she knew, it was dark, and someone was carrying her gently down the stairs.

"It's alright, I've got you. You're all safe," the voice said. "Tachra sent me."

TWENTY-FIVE

It was a miserable morning, raining again in the Nigh-kutu camp, and I was cold and wet. But Jychanumun had told me that he had retrieved Soul and Iris, and that Orion was safely with his Shaa-kutu friends and healing. Those things made me feel a great deal better.

Dawn was breaking. I had made it through the first night in this awful place. I hadn't minded sleeping out without covers while it rained. I hadn't minded going without food, as I'd given all my own rations to the Nar beast. I hadn't even minded being given a sharp hit on the back with a stick because I was not preparing food quick enough. But I had minded that the same Nigh-kutu had continued to hit me so many times, and for no good reason, that I had missed going out on the wood collection. I knew that Dragun had been waiting for me to drop off more of the time crystals, but they were still concealed inside my dress.

I was sent out on my second run of handing out food on trays. I really disliked having to do this chore, but each time I started to see red at another hand grabbing at my ankle, or saw the expression on a Nigh-kutu's face as he gorged himself on kutu meat, I thought of the other people here. I thought of the women now huddled together with barely any clothes left, each desperate to be invisible to a roving Nigh-kutu's eyes. Or I thought about the men they held captive apart from the women, the ones they used for sparring practice and who were now more dead than alive. So I kept my subservient stance, knowing I was here to help them. I could do this. I had to.

Having just been ambushed by multitudes of hungry Nigh-kutu, the camp had started to settle once again. I went to collect wood, but the Nigh-kutu who had beaten me earlier just pointed with his stick, indicating that I should get back out with my tray. I made my way to the centre of the camp. Being near the vault of crystals and the Nar beast actually gave me a modicum of comfort.

"I can't give you food yet," I whispered to the Nar beast, moving my mouth as little as possible, "there are kutu looking."

The Nigh-kutu who had beaten me was watching me standing in the rain, my tray held high and head bowed. I didn't look at him directly, but I could feel his stare.

The Nar beast snorted. By now, I was convinced that this creature could understand me.

"When I get you out, you must promise me that you won't eat anyone," I whispered. "And if you promise that you'll not eat her, too, one day I'll introduce you to Meah. She is my bonded animal."

The Nar beast snorted again. I was sure it liked the sound of that.

Tachra, it is Jychanumun, I heard Jychanumun gently call with his mind.

I hope you are in a dryer place than I am, I replied.

We have Iris and Soul.

I wanted to feel relief. I had asked Jychanumun to personally ensure that they were both alright, but I sensed something was wrong.

What is it? I asked. *Do you have my parents, too?*

Now you listen carefully, Jychanumun said firmly. *I will fill you in fully, but first you are to get out of there, fast. Go to collect wood, come to the fissure and jump in. Do it as invisibly as you can, but if it means you are seen, so be it. Dragun and I are both waiting. He will seal the entrance as soon as you have entered. You need to get out of there.*

What's going on? I asked. *We still need at least another seventy crystals. I can't leave yet.*

Trust me, Jychanumun replied. *Get out at the first opportunity. I will tell you everything when you get here.*

Very good, I told him. But it didn't feel very good. Not at all.

I dropped as many pieces of meat on the floor as I dared without being noticed, and with a near-empty tray, started to head back to my food preparation area. The night-shift Nigh-kutu who had liked beating me so much was in the process of changing shifts with another. There were still women out collecting wood. If I timed this well, I could slip out to join the wood collectors unnoticed, and get to the fissure unseen.

I put my tray down. The woman who sat next to me smiled consolingly.

"Bruises or not, you should cover that pretty little face of yours," the woman said under her breath.

The rain. It must have washed the mud away.

I felt a tap on my shoulder and spun around, expecting a hard hit to the face again.

"I knew it was you!" the woman who had tapped me said loudly. It was Mags, Ren's mother. She had recognised me.

"Shh, please," I begged her under my breath.

"Shh?" she exclaimed. "Shh! Don't you 'shh' me. This is all your fault."

"Please lower your voice, please," I asked, trying to make her calm.

But Mags was having none of it.

"All this!" she exclaimed, throwing up her arms. "Everything. This is all your fault."

"Please be quiet," I hushed. "You'll attract attention. We'll get beaten again."

"I don't care. I would be happier dead!" Mags shrieked. "It's all your fault. It's your fault that my boys are dead. It's your fault that I'm here watching my daughters get raped by monsters. It's your fault that the kutu are here full stop. All this," she pushed me, goading me, "Is your fault. Your fault!"

"Please, I'm trying to help. Really I am. And I've seen Ren; he's alive and . . ."

"Arrrhh," Mags' rage exploded. She lunged into me, sending me flying to the ground. Trays and meat clattered around me and on top of me. Before I could scrabble to my feet again, Mags leapt on top of me, hitting me with her bare fists, crying out again that this was all my fault. I struggled to push her off, but Mags was not a small woman and her sheer weight held me firmly pinned down as she yelled and hit me.

Suddenly, what felt like a long metal rod hit my shoulder with such an intense force that I could only think of the pain searing through me. I felt Mags' weight roll off me as a Nigh-kutu bearing a long metal pole hit her repeatedly. I heard her arm crack with one hit. I pushed myself backwards to get clear of the blows, but the Nigh-kutu struck me again, and this one found my legs. A second Nigh-kutu had joined him, and crack after crack came down until Mags was reduced to a whimpering huddle.

I am coming to get you, I heard Jychanumun tell me.

No! Stay there. I'll get through this, I replied.

One of the Nigh-kutu looked at me and smiled. My head covering had come off. The cloak was ripped from my shoulder. I really didn't like the look on his face when that Nigh-kutu smiled. It made me think he was going to eat me alive.

The Nigh-kutu's expression changed as his gaze moved from me to the ground beside me. The smile disappeared. He looked horrified.

"A time crystal!" I heard him roar in his own guttural tongue.

I glanced to my side. There on the floor was a small, brightly glowing, blue time crystal.

Several Nigh-kutu now surrounded me. All were looking at the time crystal next to me. They seemed very wary of the little object.

The Nigh-kutu who seemed in charge scanned the ground around me, clearly looking for any more. He picked Mags up, slinging her to one side as if she were nothing more than a rag, looking at the ground she had been lying on. He then reached forward, picking me up by the collar of my dress.

I hung from the Nigh-kutu's grasp on the neck of my dress, my feet unable to touch the floor. I cast my eyes to the ground I'd been laying on. No more crystals were there, thank goodness.

As the Nigh-kutu searched the ground, still holding me up, the neck of my dress was tight around my throat, almost choking me. I couldn't breathe. And then I felt something slipping down the inside of my dress. The ties of my dress had loosened. I clutched my arms around my stomach, trying to stop the rest of the time crystals slipping any further down. Some of the little crystals started easing down though the folds in the fabric.

Clunk. Clunk.

Oh by the skies, please no.

My heart sank.

I didn't need to look down.

I closed my eyes, imagining the little crystals sparkling in the mud. Could this get any worse?

The Nigh-kutu dropped me to the ground and took a step back, as if even holding someone who had a time crystal was forbidden. He didn't pick up the time crystals that had fallen from my dress, and didn't even touch them. He made the others back away as the crowds of Nigh-kutu continued to gather behind him.

"Move back, Deimom is coming," the Nigh-kutu commanded.

There was a hushed silence. The Nigh-kutu suddenly pulled himself stiffly upright, standing to attention.

And then I heard the sound of the sway of energy wings moving closer. For a moment I considered making a run for it. It was a stupid idea. This was the one time that all Nigh-kutu eyes really were on me. I wouldn't manage even one measly stride.

I can do this, I told Jychanumun. *Don't you do anything silly. I can still make this work.*

I am here and ready, Jychanumun replied. And I knew that he was. I could feel the closeness of his physical presence. He was anxious to come for me, but I knew this was the worst possible time.

A huge Nigh-kutu, one as big as Stanze, his long black wings rippling all around him, landed directly before me. He was a fearsome sight, with a rugged, hardened face marked with scars and the cruellest eyes. His armour was immaculate, and all down his arms were black marks pitted into his skin. The black marks looked like Nigh-kutu writing. He had his hands on his hips and was staring at the little glowing crystals on the floor.

This formidable Nigh-kutu looked very angry indeed. He turned to the kutu who had been beating Mags and me.

"How did they get there?" he demanded.

"The human had them, High Warrior Deimom, sir."

"And how did the human come to have them?"

"I do not know, sir."

At this, the one they called Deimom looked even more furious. His eyes flashed with darkness and he flexed his jaw, rolling his neck as if forcing himself to stay composed.

"I leave you in charge of a simple camp of five hundred warriors and a handful of feeble slaves and you cannot manage?" Deimom fumed. "You bring me shame. Shame, you hear me? Your weakness looks like my weakness."

The High Warrior leaned forward, ripping off an embossed section of armour from the Nigh-kutu's chest plate.

"I strip you of all rank. You are now the lowest form of soldier."

"Yes, sir."

"Will you let me down again?"

"No. Absolutely not. Never, High Warrior Deimom, sir."

Deimom turned his attention to me. He leaned forward, grabbed a handful of my hair and picked me up, until I stood teetering on tiptoes. Then he released my hair so that my feet took my own weight, and in one swift movement pulled the cloak from my shoulders, grabbed the neck of my dress and pulled it downwards. The fragile fabric gave way, ripping down to my waist. The remaining hidden crystals tumbled onto the floor around my feet.

Deimom looked both horrified and angry.

"Where did you get those?" the Nigh-kutu asked me.

I looked at the huge Nigh-kutu and then lowered my eyes. I knew better than to answer. I was human and not supposed either to understand or speak the Nigh-kutu tongue. I gave it my best wide-eyed, scared and stupid look. It wasn't difficult. Right now, with this huge angry Nigh-kutu leaning over me, that was exactly how I felt.

Deimom picked up one of the crystals, holding it up to my face, forcing me to look up.

"Where?" he roared, sweeping his arm around the camp, thrusting the crystal closer to my face. "Where?"

Even if I did not understand the Nigh-kutu language, any one would have got the gist of what this hulking beast was asking.

I picked up another time crystal, and then another from the ground. I heard several Nigh-kutu gasp that I dared to touch them. I held the crystals towards the High Warrior.

"Pretty," I said in my native human tongue. I did not know how much these Nigh-kutu could understand of my human language. I pointed to one of the crystals in my hand, and then pointed to an area beyond the camp, away from the fissure. I pointed to another crystal, and then another area. I was trying to indicate that I had just found these on the ground when collecting wood.

The Nigh-kutu seemed to follow what I was hinting at and immediately sent over half the warriors out to search the land.

Jychanumun, I called, *close the tunnel up, just temporarily. I've pointed them in the opposite direction, but just to be safe.*

Jychanumun didn't reply. He didn't need to. I could sense he was already doing as I suggested.

One of the Nigh-kutu who had remained standing next to the High Warrior started to speak. I could never forget that Nigh-kutu, because he was the one who had beaten me so vigorously earlier that day.

"I have not seen that human out there," the Nigh-kutu said. "She spends much of her time by the vault."

"Is that right?" Deimom considered. "Have you seen her put her hand in the vault?"

"No," the warrior replied. "If she had, the Nar beast would have had her hand."

"Unless the creature has finally expired," Deimom frowned. "Arrunn would not be pleased at that."

The High Warrior looked at me, picked me up by my arm and started marching through the camp towards the vault, half carrying and half dragging me next to him. My feet couldn't touch the ground properly to take my weight, and the pain seared through my bruised shoulder as it awkwardly took my weight.

"Any sign of any more crystals?" he called to his searching warriors as he walked.

"None," they all shouted back.

He kept marching until we were poised directly in front of the vault. He touched a section on one side of the vault with his palm, and I saw the energy barrier over one of the holes disappear. Holding me up, Deimom grabbed my hand and stuck it into that hole. He shoved me forward, holding me hard against the side of the vault, so my entire arm was now inside.

And then I felt something: warm, rough skin against my hand, and then I felt the heat of the Nar's breath against my palm.

I held my breath, waiting for the jaws to close around my flesh and for the inevitable pain.

But the Nar beast didn't bite me. I felt the side of its head as it leaned its cheek against my palm. It seemed to be nuzzling my hand. I moved my fingers, stroking the face as if it were my cat. It nuzzled harder, as if relishing the contact. The Nar beast had known it was me.

The next thing I knew I was being pulled away. My arm shot out and the High Warrior dropped me to the ground.

"The Nar must be sick," he stated, and peered into one of the holes. "It's too dark. I can't see it."

He called over to another Nigh-kutu, the one who had just been stripped of his rank.

"The beast is either sick or dead. Put your arm in and tell me if it's dead or not."

The Nigh-kutu hesitated, but Deimom narrowed his eyes and put his hand on the hilt of his sword, drawing the blade a little from its sheath. "Now," he commanded.

The unfortunate warrior took two steps forward, peered into the unprotected hole, and then nervously slid one arm into the vault.

There was a dreadful pause, then the sound of something moving, and all of a sudden, the Nigh-kutu screamed. His screams were so loud and full of pain that it made my back shiver. He tried to pull his arm from the vault but could not. Something held him firm. Inside the vault, the Nar beast was snorting angrily. The warrior was struggling to break free. Suddenly, the warrior hurled backwards, impelled by his own force. He landed sitting on the ground, staring at the bloodied stump of his arm.

"Well, it is not dead," Deimom shrugged, ignoring the screaming kutu.

He looked at me and picked me up once again, forcing my arm and shoulder, right up to my neck, into the hole.

But once again the Nar beast didn't bite me. Again, it sniffed my hand and rubbed its face against the entire length of my arm. I looked at the Nigh-kutu holding me, unsure of whether I should start screaming for the sake of it, but decided that coming out without any injuries may give me away. So, I just looked at the intimidating warrior holding me, not sure quite what to do.

Deimom pulled me out, dropping me to the floor once again. I sat in the mud, my mind trying to figure out what I should do next.

"Bring me another slave," the High Warrior directed. "Perhaps these humans taste too bad."

Oh no, please no. The Nar may well injure the next person, I thought. What do I do now?

Tachra . . . Jychanumun called me with his mind.

But I couldn't focus on Jychanumun trying to talk to me. My mind was racing. Do I let someone else get injured, an innocent human? Perhaps, oh perhaps, the Nar beast would not injure another human? But what if it did? Do I tell the Nigh-kutu the truth now, to save that person? If I told the Nigh-kutu the truth, they would eventually figure out who I was and try to extract information about the Shaa-kutu. If I didn't do anything and the Nar did chew a different human arm, they would see me as different anyway and that would lead the same way. But what if I told them the truth and then killed myself? That would be keeping the Shaa-kutu safe, but it would not be helping the rest of my fellow humans. Whatever I did, the result would be bad for everyone.

Tachra, listen . . . Jychanumun tried to call me again.

Jychanumun, what shall I do? I asked. Already, one of the Nigh-kutu was carrying the bruised and helpless Mags towards the vault.

You have got to run. Run as fast as you can and get out of there. We are going to strike. Do you understand me Tachra? Focus. Get out of there, now. Run!

I had to get out?

I had to get out!

My body seemed to take over in response. I was so desperate to arise as quickly as I could that my feet slipped around on the muddy ground underneath me. Most Nigh-kutu eyes were on Mags as she was carried forward. I managed to shuffle backwards, find my feet and start running as fast as my legs would carry me.

"Bring her back," I heard the High Warrior say as I ran. He didn't even sound angry. He sounded strangely uninterested, as if I were yet another escapee who had no chance of getting away.

I wove through the outer layers of Nigh-kutu. I was running fast now, ducking and diving as hands reached out to grab me. I was small and they didn't see me until I was running right past them.

"Get out!" I shouted to the humans as I ran. "All of you. Get out now."

I saw many of the people take the opportunity to run, heading for the nearest way out of the camp. A hand caught the fabric of my dress. I spun and ducked, releasing the half-ripped dress from the loose ties around my waist, leaving it behind me. Another Nigh-kutu caught my arm. I twisted my arm around, bending like a fish in water, slipping from his grasp. All those forest runs with Meah were paying off. My instincts had taken over.

I had nearly reached the outside of the camp. The way ahead was clear of Nigh-kutu. I just had to cross the grassland and get to the fissure. Naked, muddied, running as fast as I could, and with adrenaline coursing through me, I felt the wings of a Nigh-kutu behind me. He was drawing closer, preparing to swoop down and pick me up. I wasn't going to make it.

And then I heard a roar, a distant, muffled roar.

I felt a wind on my skin, rushing past me, as if a storm had erupted.

Suddenly, from points in the ground in front of me, dozens of Shaa-kutu began emerging from nowhere. Their faces were set in determination. Their Anumi weapons and golden armour flashed under the morning sun. It was an awesome sight, as if the earth itself was birthing the ultimate courageous defenders.

The lone Nigh-kutu above me faltered, his sights now firmly fixed on the approaching Shaa-kutu.

I heard shouts from behind me. I heard the bulk of the Nigh-kutu drawing their weapons, launching into the sky, howling like animals.

A mighty clash of weapons suddenly raged above my head. The scent of burning, the ferocity of intent, was heavy in the atmosphere. Cracks of conflict raged so loud that the air felt like it was splitting. The heat became intense. The earth suddenly dried and grass shrivelled from the heat. The ground tremored beneath my feet. As I ran, a shadow came over me and I felt hands under my arms. I was being lifted into the air. I kicked as hard as I could, but the hands held me firm.

Don't struggle. It's me.

Jychanumun!

Clutching me in his arms, Jychanumun made a swooping dive towards some trees. Suddenly, he propelled himself to one side. A splatter of blood and energy sprayed my cheek and we both went tumbling, hitting the ground hard. Three Nigh-kutu were directly behind us, walking forward as their feet touched the soil, odd-looking rounded swords in their hands, their faces snarling.

"Get behind me," Jychanumun growled. He was crouched on all fours, his back arching, his blind eyes turned directly towards the three Nigh-kutu.

I crouched behind Jychanumun. I could see a wound in his side that had destroyed a large section of his body. I could feel the energy bristling off him like fur standing on end. He'd retracted his wings, and a cloud of shadow and light gathered around him.

Jychanumun suddenly leapt forward, abruptly stopping short of the Nigh-kutu. His energy kept moving, surging in front of him like a cloud of sheer force. It hit the Nigh-kutu, sending all of them reeling backwards, one with half his face and body disintegrating, his body falling like ash in the wind. One of the Nigh-kutu gathered himself quickly and flicked his arm forward, sending an energy bolt from his fist. Jychanumun leapt back, grabbed me and rolled.

I heard a commotion above our heads. Four more Nigh-kutu were approaching. Stanze was quick to intercept them, sparring with all four at once. Behind him, three more Nigh-kutu threw shafts of energy that sped through the air towards him. Stanze moved in a flash, weaving past some of the oncoming shafts, deflecting others.

I heard a ringing sound, building up like a multi-layered chorus. A flash of light caught my eyes. I spotted Chia in the distance. Next to him crouched another; his head and body obscured by a cloak. But I spotted a single tendril of red hair protruding from the hood. Orion! It was Orion! But I had no time to rejoice. Both of them held sonar rods, roughly pointing in our direction, aiming for yet another group of approaching Nigh-kutu.

"Cover your head!" I shouted to Jychanumun, forcing him down with all my weight.

Suddenly, a flash of light temporarily blinded me and my ears rang so I could hear nothing else. The sonar explosion had hit quite close.

Run, Jychanumun silently instructed me. *Run anywhere. Find a hiding place.*

I couldn't see properly. The sonar blast had nearly blinded and deafened me. I half ran, half crawled away from where I thought the fighting was. My shoulder hit the trunk of a tree. I held onto that tree, crouching low, forcing my sight to clear.

As my eyes adjusted, I could see chaos. Power raged in the skies and on the ground. Everywhere there were explosions and flashes of light. The Shaa-kutu were outnumbered, but they were fighting with a conviction I had never seen before. It was terrible wrath against controlled aggression in the fight: booms, flashes, blazing cracks, crackles, thuds, howls and roars ripped the sky as the two sides of kutu directed their force against each other.

To one side I noticed a group of around thirty men from Meadsins, Ren included. They had been given long-distance weapons and now crouched behind rock piles, firing at selected Nigh-kutu. Their position was tenuous, but I couldn't concentrate on them or the central chaos, as my eyes were drawn to Jychanumun.

Stanze was trying to reach Jychanumun, but was fending off several large Nigh-kutu, including the High Warrior Deimom himself. Jychanumun was surrounded. It looked like he had a binding rope wrapped around one leg, anchoring him to the ground. He flung energy out around him as the Nigh-kutu approached. Kutu went flying. Clumps of earth exploded as some of the shards hit the ground. Suddenly, another binding rope hit Jychanumun, catching his hand, wrapping around his wrist, melting through his energy and fusing his arm to the side his body. I could see Jychanumun divert most of his energy to release that hand and, as he did, two metal shards caught his unmoving leg.

"Kill them all except the Death Walker!" I heard the High Warrior shout.

Another two and then three shafts hit Jychanumun. I saw him falter. He could not release himself from the bonds that ensnared him. Stanze could not reach him. This was it. Jychanumun was not going to make it. If something did not change, my mind-bonded one would be captured.

I had to do something.

I had to do anything.

But these Nigh-kutu were fearsome and strong. They seemed to fear nothing, only Arrunn their leader.

They feared Arrunn. Suddenly my thoughts became focussed.

They had a weakness.

As if in slow motion, I let go of the trunk of the tree I was using for cover and stood up. I walked forward, taking deep breaths, hoping my nerves didn't make my voice come out as a quivering squeak.

"I speak for Arrunn, your leader," I shouted in Nigh-kutu. "I speak for Arrunn."

I kept walking forward

"High Warrior Deimom, you are commanded to stop this fight. Arrunn says you must listen."

Deimom had indeed stopped. Not only did I speak in Nigh-kutu and know his name, the mention of Arrunn had made all within earshot hesitate.

What are you doing? I heard Jychanumun ask.

I have no idea, I replied. I kept walking, glancing at Jychanumun as I passed him, making sure I walked tall and looked like I'd summoned some sort of confidence, which I hadn't. *But I will not let you be captured or die,* I told him. *I will buy some time.*

"High Warrior Deimom, Arrunn has sent me," I lied as I approached the huge Nigh-kutu.

I could sense that Jychanumun was working himself free.

Jychanumun has released his bonds. He was up.

Before I could say another word, Jychanumun had dived forward, grasping me and swooping into the air as his wings took form. Deimom leapt to one side and caught hold of one of my wrists. Jychanumun tried to rise higher, kicking the High Warrior away, but the huge Nigh-kutu would not let go of me. He was pulling so hard I could feel my arm wrench from the shoulder. I screamed with pain. My arm was being stretched to agony. Another Nigh-kutu seemed to come from nowhere, catching a hold of my ankle. Jychanumun was pulling one way, trying to fight them off, trying to hold me. The Nigh-kutu were pulling the other way.

The pain of my flesh was overbearing. It felt as if I were being pulled in half. My body was reaching its limits. Much more of this and my arm and leg would be wrenched from my torso. I couldn't even scream; the pain was too much. I was about to die by being ripped apart.

I could only feel pain and think one thought.

You must let me go, I told Jychanumun.

I cannot, he fought back.

You must! I am ripping apart. Let me go. Let me live to fight another day.

Jychanumun knew the truth of it. He could feel my pain. He could feel my body about to break. He did not want to let go, but if I was to live, he had no choice.

I felt Jychanumun reluctantly loosen his grip around my waist. I looked at him, our minds locked. That mere moment seemed to go in slow motion.

It's alright, I told him calmly. *Jychanumun, let me go.*

I slid from his hold.

I am sorry, I heard him say.

And then I was gone, flown fast and hard through the air, away from Jychanumun, above the battle that still raged at the Nigh-kutu camp, away from all the kutu that I loved.

I knew it was Deimom who carried me. I could see the black markings on the arms that held me. I struggled to break free, I kicked and I wriggled as much as I could, but his hold was as solid as a rock and one arm and leg would not function properly.

I had no idea of where I was being taken. And then I saw it. We passed a series of familiar rolling hills. The image before me was unmistakable. Set against a backdrop of deepest green trees stood the huge, golden Shaa-kutu building.

Deimom was taking me to the temple.

The huge Nigh-kutu set down on the grass in front of the temple, throwing me to the ground, standing on my back with such weight that I could not breathe. I kicked and yelled as he took a length of something and then bound my hands behind my back.

I could feel what he was using to bind my wrists. It wasn't made of any material substance. It was made of energy. *Perhaps I could break through this*, I thought.

I slowly tried to push through the energy that bound me. It took all my concentration, but I could feel it slowly slipping away. Deimom pulled me to my feet and started walking towards the temple entrance. I stood unmoving, pain seared though one of my legs, making me concentrate on keeping my weight on one foot as I kept pushing my energy to release me from the bindings.

My concentration suddenly faltered.

There, in front of me, at the top of the temple steps, now stood a group of around a dozen kutu, and although they did not wear the familiar armour, they were clearly Nigh-kutu. I hadn't heard them move there and I hadn't seen them only moments before. But now they stood watching me, only their cold staring eyes visible from within their black bindings, arrayed in perfect formation, each an exact distance apart from the next, each dressed in the same black, loose attire.

From behind the plain-clothed Nigh-kutu, Arrunn walked forward.

Being in Arrunn's presence made my insides feel as if they had frozen. I was suddenly unable to think straight. I was cold, paralysed to the spot. He *felt* wrong.

Arrunn paused at the top of the steps, watching me like a hawk eyeing its prey. There was something about his presence; I did not want to look at him, yet I felt compelled to. It was as if I had to, as if something terrible might happen if I didn't.

Arrunn did not have his wings showing, and his clothing included no armour, just simple fitted black attire. His long, dark hair glistened, contrasting with his creamy complexion. His physical presence depicted someone very fast and very clever. He did not look so terrible in the flesh, but I knew my eyes were deceiving me. Something within him was indeed powerful. His inner strength and intent were so palpable that I could taste them on the air. They did not taste good.

Arrunn stood and watched me for what seemed an eternity. My fear grew until I felt terrified. I thought I had known fear, but suddenly I knew that I'd never truly known it before now. This was a being of true dread.

Arrunn tilted his head to one side, as if contemplating me. "Cut out her tongue," he suddenly announced. The words sounded like thick cream and gravel. They almost hypnotised me.

I snapped to. Cut out my tongue? Cut out my tongue!

Get away. Run Tachra, I told myself.

Instinctively I started running, running as fast as I could and as hard as I could, ignoring the pain searing through my body, managing to shake off the loosened bindings from my wrists. I was aiming for the lake. I was aiming for anywhere that wasn't here. I ran as fast as my shaky legs would carry me. Run girl. Run. Run. Run. Run like the wind. Run as fast as your legs will carry you.

I didn't get far. Suddenly, twelve black-clothed Nigh-kutu guards descended in a circle around me. I ran straight into one of them. He didn't even flinch.

I tried to run again, to push past the guards.

The guards didn't move. Their circle grew ever tighter, ever closer around me.

Through the narrowing gap between two of the guards, a flash of sandy gold fur stood out against the trees in the background.

Meah?

Meah!

She was watching the guards, watching me, crouched low and getting ready to attack.

"Meah no! No! No!" I shouted.

But Meah had already launched herself from the depths of the forest and did not turn back. She was charging at full force towards the guards, her eyes set in sheer determination and with death on her mind.

"Turn back, Meah! No," I screamed.

But she would not turn back. She would kill to protect.

I saw Meah leap, aiming for the guards, her claws outstretched, her teeth bared and jaws ready to bite. One of the guards turned to face her just as she attacked. I pushed forward as the guard went to knock her aside, but another stepped forward and put his hand on my face.

Everything went black.

Silence.

Nothing.

N-o-t-h-i-n-g . . .

My mind felt foggy. Vague ideas of what had just happened washed through my thoughts, refusing to define themselves as dream or reality. But the pain was real. I could feel pain. Pain was good: it meant I was alive. I was lying down and in pain. I didn't know how long I had lain there, but I knew I was alive.

I tried to call Meah's name, but I had a gag tight around my mouth and my mouth didn't feel right. I tried to move to push myself to sit up, but my hands had been refastened, this time around my front, with something tight and secure.

Something, someone, pulled at my arm, forcing me to sit up.

I sat, my legs awkwardly bent. I couldn't move them, as if they were fastened to the ground.

A light dazzled my eyes as I felt a hood being slowly lifted from my head.

I squinted to adjust my vision. I was sitting outside on the grass. Sitting directly in front of me, cross-legged, was Arrunn.

Arrunn smiled at me and glanced down at a short dagger in his hands, carefully wiping the blood from the blade with a small cloth that was stained dark red.

"There is no point trying to loosen your bindings again. These ones are simple rope; far more effective against your skills," Arrunn said calmly.

He took the blood-stained cloth and carefully wiped my chin.

"Do not worry Tachra," he continued. "I have removed your tongue myself. I . . ."

Removed my tongue?! I started screaming, trying to scream, the gag around my mouth and the wrong feeling inside my mouth making the sounds come out as loud gurgling noises. My tongue! That's why my mouth felt so wrong. My tongue was gone. I tried getting up, but could not. I pulled against the binds holding me, but they were firm. I couldn't move, although I shook and I writhed and tried to break free with every effort that I could. I could not break loose. I couldn't even scream properly.

Arrunn just sat with his brows raised, watching, waiting, until my thrashing had stopped and my screams had been reduced to an exhausted whimper.

"As I was saying," he continued, once my noise had quietened enough for his satisfaction, "I could not have my High Warrior, Deimom, doing a poor job of removing your tongue. I have taken care of it. It will not cause you pain or become infected. There is no point in your suffering unduly." He looked at me. "Removing your tongue was necessary. I could not have you using the Voice on me, could I?"

I desperately shook my head, trying to indicate to him that I no longer had the Voice, that I no longer had such powers from the Old One.

Arrunn just smiled patiently.

"It is strange for me," he said, "to see this creature that has the link to the heart of all things. Such a small, weak, insignificant creature. Of course, I knew what you looked like, but still, I expected something more imposing. You see, such a thing as the link to the heart of all things was not destined to be yours. You were never destined to exist. But here you are. You exist and fate has led you to me, as much as he has tried to protect you. You told Deimom you spoke for me, so he saw fit to bring your body to me. He had no idea what you were. So, a bad choice of words for you perhaps."

I tried connecting to Jychanumun. I sensed he was alive, fighting for his life. The Nigh-kutu and Shaa-kutu war still raged. I didn't call to him. I needed him to stay alive.

I tried turning around to see if I could spot Meah, but my legs were firmly pinned to the ground by simple, human-made rope. "Meah?" I tried asking through my gagged, tongue-less mouth.

"That is quite an ugly sound," Arrunn mused. He leaned forward, ripping the gag from my mouth.

I automatically tried to lick my dried lips and swallow, suddenly realising the absence of my tongue and the impossibility of such a simple act.

"Meah," I desperately mouthed the word.

"She is quite fine," Arrunn replied, "and she will remain so, depending on you. I simply require information. You see, we have a discrepancy. Your existence has pushed fate onto a different path. I have looked into your mind for your memories, but there is merely an endless white void with no discernable information. Your link to the heart of things renders you quite unreadable."

"No," I shook my head. I tried to say, "No link," but the words didn't sound like words at all, just a gargle of blood.

"If you had memories like a kutu or like any other human, such as your father, all this would be easy. It would be over and done with by now."

"My father?" I tried to ask. "What about my father?" But again the words would not form. Sheer frustration made tears stream down my face.

Arrunn looked at me. It was a strange look, a look of composed superiority, his lips in a wry smile. He took from behind him what looked like bound papyrus book. It was my own personal journal with its attached writing tool.

I looked at my diary in horror. I had made notes about all my family in this book. Arrunn would know about them, about my friends, about me. My mind raced. I knew Soul and Iris were alive, because Jychanumun had told me as much. And I had seen my mother via the kutu's monitoring screens, so I knew she was alive too. But my father? With both my hands still bound together, I snatched that book and stylus. Arrunn let me take it.

My father? I wrote in Nigh-kutu. The words were untidy, but they were clear enough.

"He did not survive," Arrunn shrugged.

A scream gurgled from my mouth. I tried to lunge forward to hit Arrunn, but the bindings held me firm. I hit the ground with my bound fists and hit it again and again and again, as if hitting that ground could take away just a little of the pain. Not my father. Tears fell from my eyes as I pounded the ground, my legs, my head, but I could not divert the pain. Not my beloved father, the man who had guided me, taught me as a child, and had always made me feel safe. That strong, wonderful, caring man? I loved him so much. My father had to be alive and safe; he just had to be. No, not my father dead. Please, no.

I hit at myself and I hit some more. Suddenly, I felt defeated. The defeat passed over me like a great enveloping wave.

I can't do this anymore, I thought. I slumped forward, my head hanging in front of me, my muddied hair sticking to my wet face.

"He had lived his full life. He was old," Arrunn stated matter-of-factly.

I couldn't even look at Arrunn. I didn't want to fight anymore. I couldn't do this anymore.

"Now, now," Arrunn lifted my chin. "This defeat is pointless. Let us talk about you, Meah and this information. Concentrate, Tachra," he snapped his fingers in front of me. "Concentrate. I want to know only one thing. When did you attain your link to the heart of all things? I want a specific time."

It wasn't his question that pulled me from my dulled thoughts; it was the mention of Meah. I was suddenly filled with dread. Where was my Meah? He must leave her alone.

If Arrunn wanted to know just one thing, and then would leave Meah alone, I would give him whatever he wanted. I had no fight left in me any more, but Meah was my heart; her I could focus on and fight for.

"Uh? Uh?" I shrugged my shoulders.

Arrunn nodded calmly. "When exactly did you acquire your link to the heart of all things?" he asked again.

I still wasn't entirely sure what he meant. I picked up the notebook, clasping the pen in my fist, wondering if I could reach far enough to drive that pen into Arrunn's eye, but then wrote 'Old One?'

"Yes," Arrunn nodded. "When did you acquire the link to the Old One?"

I scribbled on the pad again, showing him the answer.

"Before you were born?" he raised an eyebrow. "I think not. Try again, and let us make it the truth this time."

I nodded, indicating that it was. It really was the truth.

"We both know that is impossible," Arrunn smiled. "The link must be to a consciousness. You would have no consciousness before you were born."

I took the notepad, scribbling as fast as I could. I had to correct two or three words. I showed him my writing. I told him again that it was before I was born and that it was the Old One who had done it; I hadn't chosen it.

"Tachra," Arrunn sighed. "Why try to misguide me? This entire charade will make no difference to me in the end. If you do not tell me what I wish to know, I will still succeed in all that I aim for. By telling me what I need to know, you will save me time and effort, that is all. And for that, I will spare you and your 'loved' ones. I am giving you an opportunity to help yourself."

I pointed vigorously to my scribbled notes, shrieking in frustration. *It's true!* I tried to shout. That's exactly when it happened, before I was even born. It's true!

"We could have kept this so simple," Arrunn shrugged. He stood up.

"Deimom," he called out, "summon twenty of your warriors."

"They are still fighting," Deimom replied from behind me.

"Did I ask what they were doing?" Arrunn said, his voice menacing.

I heard the movement of air behind me as Deimom left. Arrunn crouched in front of me once again.

"You still have the opportunity to tell me by choice," Arrunn said, the sound of threat in his voice.

Again, I pointed to the notebook. "True!" I tried to scream, but the word came out as just a sound. Arrunn didn't seem to believe me. Could he be so used to lies and treachery that he couldn't see the truth written on a piece of paper in front of him? I kept pointing to what I had written. "True," I said, over and over again.

"It is a shame you do not choose to tell me. I do not like forcibly extracting information. It is messy and time consuming," Arrunn shrugged. "Why does life always have to put up such a fight?"

Arrunn was carefully removing some of the bindings from my legs. I straightened my legs, trying to release them from their cramps. My ankles were both still tethered individually, tied firmly to metal hooks in the ground. I heard Nigh-kutu approaching. They landed on the ground behind me. Arrunn pulled me up, and I looked around.

Meah!

Meah was tethered to a huge plank of wood. She was alive and looked uninjured, but was lying on her side, ropes binding every part of her, holding her firm. I tried to run forward to her, but the length of the ropes around my legs stopped me after only two strides.

"Meah," I tried to call, holding out my arms to her.

Meah tried to struggle free to reach me, but the ropes held her firm. I went back to the metal hook in the ground, pulling at it with all my might.

"One last chance to tell me by choice," Arrunn stood beside me, watching my frantic attempts to escape. "If you do not, your beloved Meah will be only the start of this. Once I have finished with your creature, I will do the same for every last one of your family, and then Soul, and then your beloved Death-Path-Walker. I will work through everyone and everything that you care about until there is nothing left."

He held my notebook in front of me. "One last chance," he said, putting the stylus in my hand, pushing my fingers around it.

With my sight firmly fixed on Meah and Meah's gaze on me I crouched down, balancing the book on my knees, and wrote as fast as I could. I wrote so hard and so fast, my hands still bound together, that the writing instrument kept ripping through the paper, my tears smearing the marks.

I held the paper out to him, beseeching him. He looked at the notebook.

I am telling you the truth. Please, not Meah. She is my heart. I will do anything. Let her go. The link was made before I was born. It is the truth, I had written.

"Kill the beast," Arrunn nodded to the Nigh-kutu, "and do it slowly."

One of the Nigh-kutu walked up to Meah, slowly drawing a short dagger from its hilt. He placed the dagger on various points of Meah's body as if figuring out where to cut.

I ran forward. I tried prising my ankles free from the ropes that bound them. I was screaming. I was clawing at the rope, clawing at the flesh of my feet to break free, trying to rip my feet from my legs. Tears were running down my face. I ran back to the loop, pulling furiously, hitting it, kicking it, but it would not come out. And then I stopped. I felt Meah trying to reach my mind.

I faced Meah. My arms outstretched to her, tears upon tears. I could feel that she did not understand the violence. Her wide amber eyes were fixed on me, questioning, filled with loyalty and with love.

My heart stopped.

My world stopped.

I could feel nothing except the entirety of our bond. I could see nothing but her, her eyes, her beautiful amber eyes.

Watch me, I told her with my mind, pointing to my own eyes. *Do not stop watching me. I have you. You will feel nothing, only my love,* I told her. *I am yours. You are mine. Watch me, my heart. We are bonded. Watch me, look at me. I have you. Watch me. Stay with me.*

The Nigh-kutu slid his knife across the pad of Meah's paw, cutting deep into the flesh. I took the pain as her precious blood pooled onto the ground, her amber eyes fixed firmly on me.

The Nigh-kutu moved on to the second paw, and then the third and the fourth.

Stay with me. Watch me, my heart. You feel nothing, I told her as her pain seared through me instead.

The Nigh-kutu now looked at Meah's torso, placing his dagger over the centre of her chest. This was it; they really were going to kill her.

Nothing else mattered anymore. Meah was my heart.

I saw the connection that bound us, like a line of purest white energy that ran from my tethered body to hers, glowing against all else. Forever we were entwined.

My heart, my bond, I am going to take you away from this, I told her. *I am taking you to a safe place, a place where you will be happy, without fear, without pain. You and I, we are one. We will be free.*

I saw the dagger placed over her chest and the tiniest trickle of blood start to run down her side.

As the dagger slowly slid deeper, I left my body, moving my consciousness down the line that connected us, and then joined with Meah's mind. I pushed the entirety of my consciousness into hers, covering her fear with my love. Meah embraced my mind; I would not let her feel pain. And I felt no pain now. I would not let her endure the humiliation of this ugly death. We would leave these cruel memories behind. We would go somewhere without this suffering.

Taking our bonded minds and every morsel of strength that I had, I propelled us both away from this place, leaving my body falling unconscious to the ground.

Our joined consciousnesses were gone in an instant.

We were bonded, as one: one mind, one heart, one spirit. We had both left our bodies behind. Hers dying and mine just breathing, empty flesh. And I left the fear, hatred, grief and every terrible memory that I had come to know with that body; I didn't need them, we didn't need them. We could forget our past. This was all that mattered. And we knew exactly where we wanted to go.

Meah and I were cub and girl again, playing the game that we loved to play so much, the joining of spirits, running as one, thinking as one. Two spirits joined in essence. We were free.

TWENTY-SIX

"NO!" Jychanumun suddenly roared. The sound was filled with so much anger that it made the air oscillate around him.

The sky darkened. Thunder rumbled above his head. A crack of lightning sparked down to the ground below him.

"NO!" he roared again. In one move he effortlessly cut a line through the bodies of the three Nigh-kutu that fought him, severing them clean in half, sending their dead bodies tumbling down to the ground.

The sheer force of his energy lifted Jychanumun further into the sky. He breathed in the power of the storm that gathered, drawing in the energy and then flinging it down, raining spikes of force mixed with lightning and metal blades. Below him, the kutu still fought. The shards rained down on them all.

"NO!" he cried out a third time, his anger building. He would contain his hate no more. He would rip this world apart. He would make a storm so great as to consume this place.

He spread his arms wide as the darkness gathered around him. He breathed in the darkness, *made* the darkness, its potent power growing with every moment, deflecting every weapon and energy bolt thrown his way. He would no longer hold back. Tachra was gone! This world was now fated to die!

Suddenly, a lone spectral figure appeared within the darkness, hovering in front of him, unaffected by the warring or Jychanumun's potent fuming energy. The figure's energy shone with the love that only a clan brother could show.

It was the spirit of Cranun, no longer the Nigh-kutu warrior, but wearing his robes of peace as Jychanumun remembered him.

"Jychanumun, my brother," the spectral figure spoke.

"Get out of my mind Cranun. You are already dead," Jychanumun raged.

"Brother," Cranun smiled. "I am dead, but I am not gone. Do not wreak the final death on all life. Not yet. Hope is not lost."

"All hope *is* lost," Jychanumun fumed in despair. "I feel it, brother. She has gone. Arrunn took her innocence, took her heart."

"But," Cranun smiled, "she is not dead. You can sense that she has not walked the final death path. You and she are intertwined and you are still here. She still has one last tie that binds her."

"One last tie that binds?" Jychanumun roared, his anger mounting even more. "If she has made her choice to leave here, how could I validate bringing her back to this? To hatred? To pain? To hurt and loss? Even if I knew where her spirit was, I cannot do it. I will not do it. She deserves peace. She has made the choice to leave!"

Cranun tilted his head to one side, a surreal spectre of peace within the raging storm, untouched by the lashing anger around him.

"You would not bring her back to hatred and pain. Instead, you would bring her back to life, to love, and to peace," Cranun smiled. "All is not lost. Yes, she has now known pain and loss, but it is that knowledge which will be her balance. Just give her another choice."

"I do not want you to be right," Jychanumun fumed, now angry at himself. "That way has too much pain."

"I know. Your pain is my pain," Cranun held out his hands. "But you must not rain the power of death on all others when Tachra would not wish it. She alone, as the voice of the Old One, has that choice in her hands; not you."

Jychanumun bowed his head, his shame engulfing him. Cranun was right. Tachra would not choose death for all others. Tachra considered all life as precious. He had almost ended all life. He had almost lost control.

"I see that. But let her spirit be in peace, Cranun," Jychanumun shook his head. "I love her."

"It is because you love her that you will bring her back," Cranun smiled. "You will know where to find her."

The winds lessened. Jychanumun hovered high above the ground amidst the dying storm, black clouds enveloping him like the heaviness in his heart. He felt crestfallen.

The image of Cranun faded. Behind him, his blind eyes could make out the energy form of a flying Nigh-kutu, his black wings tipped with gold. It was Mardoch. Mardoch was flying towards him at a phenomenal pace.

"Come," Mardoch shouted. "We are to regroup before the next attack. Your red kutu, Orion, has requested we gather. Dragun has prepared a bolt hole."

Jychanumun did not move.

Mardoch swooped towards Jychanumun, catching hold of his arm, pulling him with him.

"That was a close call. You nearly did it, didn't you?" Mardoch laughed. "I thought you were going to obliterate everyone. By Eskah! This is exhilarating."

"Your humour is misplaced, but welcome," Jychanumun replied. He pushed his wings into action, looking back for any sign of Cranun. There was none. "If you ever see me displaying hatred again," he said simply, "you have full permission to try to stop me, using any means."

"What happened?"

"Much," Jychanumun flatly replied.

Mardoch guided Jychanumun down with speed and force, heading straight towards a sheer cliff face. Neither slowed their approach as they neared the wall of solid stone. At the exact point of collision, a fissure opened up and a hand reached out, pulling them both inside the opening.

Inside, the rock opened up into a narrow tunnel. Dragun indicated they should walk to the end while he waited for the others.

Jychanumun withdrew his wings and began walking the narrow space, letting his senses guide him. He had to stay focussed. He had to stay in control. He had nearly let his hatred overpower him. And Tachra did still exist. But she was not here, and she was not in the death paths. So, where was she?

"Are you sure you are still blind?" Mardoch asked as they traversed the constricted space.

"I still have my sense of energy. Only my eyes are blind, brother," Jychanumun replied.

"Who were you talking to out there, before I got to you?"

"Cranun."

"I thought so."

"Are you mocking me?"

"Never," Mardoch replied firmly. "I wear their spirits in my hair. I know they can show themselves when necessary. What did Cranun want?"

"In short," Jychanumun considered, "he wanted to remind me: All fates have a choice and all choices have a fate."

The tunnel opened up to what Jychanumun sensed was a small cave. Immediately to one side, the few remaining storage flasks of Ochrah had been placed, ready for the returning kutu. Jychanumun sensed the energy fluid, its pale glow penetrating through its holds. He could go without; let one of the other, needier kutu have some of their limited supplies.

Exhausted and injured Shaa-kutu were everywhere in the small space, sitting and lying in various positions. Jychanumun sensed that most had removed their golden armour, now giving off a subtle energy glow next to them. The unwounded were tending to the wounded. He scanned the space. There, in the far corner, was Orion. He had clearly just shaved off all his hair and now wore Chia's protective suit, but Jychanumun could still tell it was him. He was sitting, undertaking more healing on his badly damaged forehead. The crystal embedded by Arrunn had long been removed by Dragun, but the gaping wound still would not heal. He, Chia, Stanze and Kraniel were in deep discussion about something.

"Jychanumun, my friend, could you and Mardoch join us," Orion spoke through his HOTS.

Despite everything, it was good to hear Orion's voice.

"Come," Jychanumun indicated to Mardoch.

He stepped over a resting Shaa-kutu, picked up a spare healing rod and headed towards his team-mates as he started tending to the wounds on his side.

"Jychanumun, I owe you more thanks than I could ever say," Orion said aloud. "I am coming to understand the sacrifices you have made to help us, to help all kutu. No words are enough for my respect."

"Yet I have not effected any changes for the better," Jychanumun shook his head. "For that, I am regretful."

"Yet we still need your help," Orion considered. "We are

looking at the possible inevitability of our demise. We are hiding like criminals in our own world."

"I have seen such things before," Jychanumun shook his head sadly. "This is exactly what happened to the Nigh-kutu clans."

"For the second time in my life, I am finding it difficult to find a new plan," Orion admitted. "We must get Tachra back. Her Earth-sight is sorely needed."

"Tachra," Jychanumun bowed his head, "is gone. Did you not feel it?"

"Dead?" Orion gasped, his eyes flashing scarlet like a flickering fire. "No, tell me it is not true!"

"She is not dead, but she has gone. She has removed her spirit and mind from this world."

"If she is not in the death paths, then where? I must formulate a plan."

"I do not know," Jychanumun replied. "Wherever she is, it is beyond death and beyond this place. She could have chosen anywhere. All I know is that I must find her."

"What can we do?"

"This is my task alone," Jychanumun said gravely. "You can do nothing. Me? I must think."

"As must I," Orion nodded. "And quickly, before there are no options left at all."

Orion made a small gasp as Chia placed a glowing substance over the wound on his forehead.

"How are your eyes?" Orion asked through gritted teeth.

"Blind," Jychanumun shrugged. "I will cope. Your own wounds?"

"As you said, my friend," Orion replied, "I will cope." He laughed to himself. "A mere blip in the grander scheme of things."

Jychanumun nodded and glanced around the small space, looking for somewhere to sit. He found a small gap close to his team mates, and settled down to finish tending to his own wounds and remove the healing pads from his eye sockets for a while. Mardoch sat beside him, having claimed a flask of Ochrah for them to share. He handed Jychanumun the flask, instructing him that he should have some, even just a small amount.

"You said Tachra could have gone anywhere?" Mardoch pondered. "If I could choose anywhere, I would choose our planet Assendia, at the time of the two suns, when the land is brisk and energy condensed. You would be standing their philosophising with Harnun and Cranun, talking about life and fate. And I would be goading you to come fly with me on the south winds while they were there, just as we did that day so long ago."

"I remember that day well," Jychanumun nodded.

"As do I. I hold onto that happy memory," Mardoch said wistfully. "It has helped me through many difficult moments."

Jychanumun suddenly sat up straight. "Mardoch, my brother, thank you. I think I know where Tachra would go. I know of a time and place that she loved most of all. I have not forgotten. I know where she is."

"What do we need to do?" Mardoch asked, poised, alert and ready for action.

"I, not we," Jychanumun shook his head.

"You will not go anywhere without me. Not now I have finally found you again. Do not even think to argue."

"You cannot come to this place," Jychanumun insisted, "for I may not come back. If Tachra chooses not to return, I will be stuck between worlds."

"Then you must tell her that," Mardoch stated. "Then of course she will come back. She would not cause you any harm."

"Which is why I will not be able to tell her. She has to make the decision from the pureness of her heart."

"But what if she chooses not to come back?" Mardoch objected.

"Is there not another way? You cannot be lost too. Without you, we have no chance against Arrunn and his destruction."

"And without Tachra, there is no other fate anyway. It has to be both Tachra and me together in order to change the course of things."

"I understand," Mardoch nodded. He looked at Jychanumun. "Do you still have the keeper crystal I made for you all those millennia ago?"

"Yes, I still have it."

Jychanumun rolled his shoulders, looking at the wide, inscribed black armlet around his upper arm. That single item was the one thing that he had never stopped wearing. He traced his fingers over the ancient text engraved into the armlet and, as his fingers moved, the text glowed a pure white. When the last letter was completed, the text lifted up from the armband and floated in the air. Jychanumun slid the armband down his arm. There, embedded into the flesh and energy of his upper arm, was a small, green, glowing keeper crystal.

Jychanumun returned the armband to its position on his arm, the energy from the text settling back into the inscription, fusing to his arm once again.

"I never want to have to carry that in my hair," Mardoch frowned. "I will not lose you too, do you hear me? You must find a way to come back."

Jychanumun did not reply. He just handed back the flask of Ochrah to Mardoch. Mardoch took a sip. For a while, they both sat in silence.

"Then, if you might never come back, I suppose I should ask you all the questions I have always held my tongue about, shouldn't I?" Mardoch asked.

"It would seem an opportune moment."

"Why do you not talk of what you see in the future?"

"I do not see everything, only certain fragments. Even so, in short, such knowledge can corrupt. Arrunn is a good example."

Mardoch sat in silence again.

"Was that the only question?" Jychanumun eventually asked.

"Your answer has made me unable to ask anything else, lest it corrupts me," Mardoch frowned. He started laughing. "I had a whole list, all about me and my future. You have spoilt it now."

Jychanumun looked to Mardoch and smiled.

"Your eye sockets just had a spark!" Mardoch exclaimed. "The first sign of healing is there."

"Faith can heal many things," Jychanumun nodded. He put his mouth close to Mardoch's ear. "It will be alright," he whispered.

He put his hand on Mardoch's shoulder and stood up. He could say no more, much as he wanted to. He went off in search of Dragun. He had an idea. He would need a concealed place to work. He would need quiet and solitude, and all the peace that this earth could give him if he was going to locate Tachra and get her back.

It took the best part of the night for Dragun to complete the concealed space for Jychanumun. He could have completed the small cavity in the rock in no time if it were not for the constant requests from Kraniel to reopen the cave, bring another kutu into the fold, and then seal the rock once again. His skills were sorely needed and he was happy to be able to use them for the good of life and honour. It had been a long time since his life had had such a worthy purpose.

Dragun showed Jychanumun the small, isolated space he had made for him.

"Is this what you meant?" Dragun asked, after their long walk through the tunnel.

Jychanumun felt the opening with his hands. It was big enough to stand in, yet not big enough to move around in. It was a hollow buried in the deepest part of the rock mountain, surrounded by nothing but solid stone. Here, if it all went wrong, Jychanumun could do minimal damage. He had never tried to enter the private memory world of another before. He had to act with caution. Anything could go wrong.

"It is perfect," Jychanumun nodded. "And you must ensure the entrance is fully sealed. It will take me seven days to do this, and then I can last no more than two days away from my body, so keep it sealed for nine days. After that, come. If I am dead, bring Mardoch to me. He will know what to do."

Dragun went to walk away, to lead them both back to the bulk of the Shaa-kutu. They were preparing for a long-haul rescue of more Shaa-kutu around Eden1 without the use of time crystals. There was much to do.

But Jychanumun did not move.

"I will do this now," Jychanumun stated.

"Now? Do you not wish to speak to your friends first?" Dragun asked.

"It will only cause more dismay," Jychanumun replied. "You know what is to be done."

"Yes," Dragun nodded. He looked at the black and white kutu in front of him. Such a noble kutu.

"The Weaver and Walker clans work well together once again. You honour them both," Dragun said. He put his fist to his chest and bowed.

Without another word, Dragun took a step back and sealed the entrance to the cavity, walking backwards, replacing the shifted rock as he moved.

Jychanumun knelt in the centre of the space, using his sense of energy to see the place in the only way that he now could. He had not noticed the place darken; his blind eyes still could not depict such things with any clarity. But he had heard the movement of stone and the silence descend all around him. This was it.

Jychanumun breathed in the calm and tranquillity of the earth and bent his head, drawing his energy and consciousness into one central point. He had not done anything like this before, not to a place beyond his own familiar realms. He had to trust that his link to Tachra would guide him to the right place.

Slowly, all light drained from him. He felt the movement within him stop and his flesh solidify around him. His instincts tried to pull him towards the death paths, but he would not let them be his fate, not yet, and not if he could help it. He focussed his final thoughts on Tachra, reliving the words she had spoken of her favourite memory, picturing the sun, the light breeze, the smell of the trees and her, Tachra, happy in her valley, Elysium.

He had to hope that he knew her well enough.

He only had one chance.

TWENTY-SEVEN

Meah and I stood together, our spirits entwined as one. The forest smelt beautiful, and the morning dew enhanced the scent of all growth. A clump of wild blossoms at the forest edge gave out a sweet perfume, as if welcoming us back. The early sun rippled through the dense foliage overhead, casting speckles of light on the forest floor. The leaves at the top of the trees swayed gently in the spring breeze, making the most wonderful sound, and the sunbeams seemed to dance to that sound. I could smell the lake beyond and the purity of its water in the air. We were home.

Shall we run as one? I asked. *Or race each other separately?*

The tree, that tree, Meah indicated. Together. Oh, it had a lovely fat trunk and lots of sprawling branches to leap along. That tree looked so enticing. It needed to be climbed and clawed and conquered.

We were off, racing together, four legs and speed. The branches made paths to the next tree, and then the next. *Oh, look, that leaf looks like it's alive! Play with it. Make it move even more. Hey, what's behind you? Ha, nothing! You fell for it. No, you did. Alright, I'll race you separately, but my legs aren't as fast as ours together. Yes, thank you, treat me like a sluggish human.*

We were off again. My essence was in the form of my body, now a multicoloured light spectrum with eyes and hands and feet, and Meah was even more beautiful than ever, her golden essence sparkling like the fizziest kutu drink, her striding legs leaving trails of gold as she ran. And she could run so fast.

You won, you beat me, I told her, nuzzling her neck. *You would have won by even more if you hadn't stopped to chase that squirrel. Yes, you're right; it was a fat squirrel. It did need the run.*

I had an idea. *Let me take you swimming,* I suggested. *You take me leaping through trees, but you've never been swimming with me before. The water's not scary when you're in it, really it's not. We'll be as one. I'm a good swimmer. We can always try to chase a fish . . .*

That got Meah's interest. The idea of chasing a fish was far too appealing to let the prospect of scary water get in the way. Those pesky fish had always managed to escape her fishing attempts from the banks. We merged into one, an action so much better than when we had mind-shared in the flesh. That used to be so limiting. This way we could change form at will. I moved into Meah and from our merged four-legged, wildcat form we slowly rose, standing on two legs, taking the form of me, Tachra two legs, and not a bad swimmer.

We got to the forest edge and paused. Oh, the valley was so beautiful – not a building, kutu or human in sight. This was how it used to look, how it should always look; a pure, innocent, wondrous place full of the marvels of the earth. Tall flowers stood proud in clumps around the forest edge, their blue and purple petals a beautiful contrast to the greens around them. Their energy was even more beautiful, glowing around them and between them where more flowers were destined to grow. The Punni bushes in the valley were all in blossom, and some already had early berries. They shone with happiness, wellbeing, and the laughter of sunshine and rain. The grass looked soft and welcoming, as if made to be rolled on. And the lake glistened under the sunlight, its energy radiating far above it, transparent yet opalescent.

Come on! I laughed, running at full force towards the lake. I dived in, rising to the surface, swimming to the centre, and then lying on my back in the water. Meah loved it. It made her feel so relaxed that she wanted to go to sleep there. Sleep was suddenly much better than chasing fish.

We climbed out of the lake after a while and found a particularly inviting section of grass that caught the warmth of the morning sun. Meah and I separated, lying down on the grass, her head on my stomach and paw on my face.

You know you're squashing my nose, don't you?

Meah flexed her claws, telling me that her leg was far too comfortable to move.

I know, I smiled, putting my arm over her. *We can stay here as long as we want. I'm happy, too.*

TWENTY-EIGHT

Arrunn, his twelve guards, the warrior-physician he had brought from Eden1, Deimom and the twenty Nigh-kutu who had witnessed the event, now stood in the central chamber of the temple, looking at the naked human female heaped on the floor.

Arrunn had to assess the situation. He was now faced with a dead animal and a human whose body appeared more dead than alive. When Arrunn looked into Tachra's mind, he saw only darkness. When he looked into her energy, it was nothing more than insignificant sparks maintaining her basic flesh functions. This was not something he had expected.

Arrunn looked at the warrior-physician.

"Well?" he asked.

"I am not entirely accustomed to the mechanics of this species," the physician replied. "My first assessment is that this particular one is as good as dead. Evidence says it should be dead. It is in an unresponsive, comatose state. I would deduce that the mind and spirit, if such creatures have those things, have left the body. It may regain full functionality, but it could be in this state for days, weeks or even years. All likelihood is that it will die in this state. Do you require me to make it cease?"

"No," Arrunn replied. "She is to be kept alive, but secured. If she wakes, she still has something I want from her. This creature here could still save me a great deal of time."

"Would you like me to erect a containment area with monitors?" the physician asked.

"Energy containment will not suffice," Arrunn stated. "She will need to be kept somewhere with strong physical barriers, somewhere we can monitor her visually, too."

Arrunn glanced around the room. There in front of him was the perfect place. It was naturally segregated from anything else, physically secure, and, as Arrunn was going to be on this planet for some time, in easy visual access. It was the kutu-made water-well.

In the centre of the temple chamber stood the well, its perfectly smooth edges lined with layers of Uana, Memorite and Mazium. It was deep enough that Tachra's presence would not affect him while he worked, but if she did wake, she could see nothing and could not possibly scale such a smooth vertical incline. And from his position up above, Arrunn could oversee her every move.

"Drain the well. Create an entrance at the bottom with three high-security doors for our access. We will keep her there," Arrunn instructed. "You warriors will arrange the confinement and be assigned as her guards. And you," he indicated towards the physician, "will keep her alive and do everything in your power to make her wake."

The Nigh-kutu wasted no time beginning their tasks, working with speed and meticulousness. Arrunn disliked such movement and commotion around him, but he deemed it necessary. He stood at the back of the chamber, with his guards behind him, watching the Nigh-kutu work, issuing precise commands regarding the access point and the equipment required. The messiest task was the emptying of the well, but the Nigh-kutu worked surprisingly quickly, efficiently blocking off the water's natural access points and clearing the deep hole using a variety of equipment left by the light-lovers.

"It is complete," Deimom informed him, after half a day had passed.

At the side of the huge room, the Nigh-kutu had made a new entrance that led down and eventually joined to the bottom of the well. It would allow them easy access to Tachra. Arrunn walked to the side of the room, where the new doorway now stood. Deimom started walking with him, but Arrunn held up his hand, indicating that he would go alone.

Immediately through the door, there were three wide steps downwards and then a sheer drop. Arrunn walked over to the edge of the drop, letting his energy lower him at leisure. He landed at the bottom, where a small space opened up, the perfect size for storing immediate supplies, and now faced another door.

Good, Arrunn thought, they had used both Uana and Mazium from the temple for this first door. The multiple layers fused together into the hinges and surrounds, making a powerful barrier.

Arrunn opened that door, only to be confronted by a second door with just enough space in-between for a Nigh-kutu guard. He smiled. This second door was made from the metal of their home planet; even Deimom could not break through this.

Beyond that door was a third door. This one was made of simple, earthly wood. It was far less sturdy than the others were, but suitable considering where they were and still far too sturdy for any human's limited strength. Arrunn appreciated the unintended irony. Tachra's journal showed that she loved all the ridiculous living growths. So now when she awoke, she would have the remains of one to stare at day and night. It was appropriate.

Arrunn opened that last door and walked into the bottom of the pit that had once been a well. The glistening Uana that covered the outer layer of the well was invisible here. The layers of sediment from the water had dried and solidified, giving the walls and floor a chalky finish. From his position at the bottom of the well, Arrunn looked up. He could see nothing, only the distant covered dome. It was adequate.

"It will suffice. Place her here and set up a guard at each door," Arrunn instructed, once he had returned to the chamber. "And physician, I want her awake and conscious."

The physician rubbed his brow, unsure if such a thing was even possible.

"Go," Arrunn waved his hand. "I do not want to be aware that any of you are here."

The physician picked up the human and made the descent to the bottom of the well, placing her unceremoniously on the dirt floor. This seemed a great deal of effort for just one of an insignificant species. As he did so, he wondered why hadn't Arrunn picked one that was in good health? And why such strong security? Nevertheless, he was not going to question Arrunn. He valued his life too much.

And so the physician checked the human creature's condition and covered her flesh with a blanket he had found in the light-lovers' building. The first thing he would need to do was find out what nourishment these creatures required, and then find some healing tools.

The Nigh-kutu, Shemya, took guard at the first door, closing and sealing it once the physician had left. He stood to attention, alert and poised, yet his mind felt troubled. He had not enjoyed what he had witnessed with this creature and her bonded animal, even though the other warriors had revelled in it. He loved to fight as much as the next Nigh-kutu; he relished the contest of a battle of might and wit. But the taking of an innocent life had felt wrong. He felt no honour in that. He had seen the bond between those two very different creatures, and something in that bond had stirred the very core of him. It was something from his distant memory, familiar to him, but hidden in the back of his mind, unexplored. It almost felt as if he, too, had once loved a creature like that.

TWENTY-NINE

You want to go swimming again? I laughed. *But I thought you did not like the water. Yes, I know, lying in the lake is very nice. Come on then.*

Meah and I ran through the trees, only stopping to paddle in a puddle of rippling blue energy. It made Meah's paws turn blue and she had to run even faster, sporadically shaking her paws at the same time. It looked very funny. I chased after her, trailing my own line of bright blue from the puddle as I ran.

We both stopped. *Yes, I smell it too. He has come to see us!*

Meah had already darted off towards the scent, wanting to be the one to welcome him first. I ran after her. Jychanumun had come to visit.

Jychanumun was waiting in the very same place we used to meet. He looked wonderful. His energy swirled gently around him, wrapping around Meah as he bent to nuzzle her.

"Would you like to come swim with us?" I asked as I approached.

Jychanumun stood up, "Tachra," he smiled, "Yes, I would. I would like that very much."

"Do you think those long legs can race us?" I asked, smiling back. "Or don't kutu do such undignified things?"

Jychanumun laughed, looking down at his legs. I didn't think he would, but he suddenly started sprinting, heading out of the forest and towards the lake.

"That's cheating, you have a head start," I shouted as I ran after him. "Go Meah, don't let him win."

As Meah ran ahead, I joined with her energy, running on four legs with her once again. We overtook Jychanumun just past the half-way point and, as we approached the last few strides towards the lake, took the form of Tachra, diving into the water. Jychanumun dived in shortly later and we all, three minds and two forms, paddled lazily on our backs.

It felt so good being in the valley, lying in the water with Meah and Jychanumun. Nothing mattered here. We could all be carefree.

We stayed in the lake for some time, until a breeze started to stir and rustle the leaves on the trees. Meah decided that she wanted to go and run: a cool breeze on a warm day always made her energetic and mischievous. I climbed out and lay on the grass with my hands behind my head and the sun on my face, listening to Meah's escapades in the background as she chased invisible winds. Jychanumun came and sat in front of me, watching the lake. It was good to have him here too.

"How did you find us?" I asked.

"You brought me," Jychanumun smiled, turning so he faced me. "Once you told me of a spring day, here in Elysium, just before you heard the call from Soul, before you had met any kutu. You had said it was the most beautiful day of your life."

"It is beautiful. Nothing bad can happen here, ever," I smiled. "I am glad you're here too. Now it's perfect."

"I am glad you did not choose to forget me."

"On no, you are a good memory. Does that mean that you're

not real? That you're just something I have decided to imagine here?"

"I am very real, my Tachra. I left my body to come and search for you. I need to talk with you," Jychanumun's tone was serious.

"I don't want to talk about horrible things," I replied. "I left all those behind."

"I am sorry that I was not there to stop them."

"It wasn't your fault. Anyway, like I said, I left them behind and you're here now. That's what matters."

"Other things matter, too."

I sat up and crossed my legs. "Are you going to get all serious again, Jychanumun? Look around; it's beautiful. Just be happy here."

Jychanumun stared at me. In this form he had his eyes back. They were darker and more radiant than ever.

"Do you know who you are? What you are?" he asked me.

"Of course," I laughed. "I am me, Tachra, a human."

"You are much more," he shook his head. "Tachra, there are things I must tell you. I will only tell you once, so if you choose to forget them, that is your right. But you must know. If you are to make the choice to stay here, then it is my duty to tell you what else you are choosing."

"I'm all ears," I shrugged, nonchalantly running my fingers through the grass.

Jychanumun nodded. "When the kutu were formed . . ."

"Oh, just show me," I interrupted him, "like you used to."

I stood up and let my energy swirl around me, pale multicoloured strands winding through and around the form of what was once Tachra the girl. It felt wonderful again. It was how I should always feel: no pain or limitations of the flesh, just the entirety of who I was in a vague containment of form.

Jychanumun stood in front of me, his beautiful black and white radiance, the clarity of truth, past and future, in the form of a beautiful kutu. I held out my hand and my energy wove out towards him. He stepped forward, walking into me, wrapping his thoughts around mine.

And then Jychanumun showed me things that made my thoughts spin. Things about him, about me, about all beings. Things that I knew I could never forget.

No one kutu is the same, Jychanumun showed me. When the universal consciousness split and created the kutu, each acquired different aspects of that consciousness. Some took the parts that could dream, others create, some analyze, some the passion for dance, some a dislike of solitude or love of change; the list was endless. I saw them all flowing before me, kutu upon kutu, each very different in their skills, their ideas, their thinking and their motivations.

Part of that balance, Jychanumun explained, meant that there was also one kutu who retained the memory of the split. That kutu remembered how wholeness had once felt, and now was fully aware that it was no longer whole. That kutu was conscious of its own differences and saw them as imperfections, and bore witness to the imperfections and incompleteness of all kutu. And yet, instead of embracing the differences among all kutu, that kutu chose to see those imperfections as wrong. He grew to despise the life that now was so imperfect. That kutu was Arrunn.

I gasped when Jychanumun showed me Arrunn, struggling not to let my memories of him surface. This was not a broken kutu, or a kutu who had been wronged or damaged in any way. This was a kutu who chose to despise life for all its differences. His hatred had festered so much that his sole aim had grown to end all life and consciousness, including the Old One.

I tried to pull away.

"Look at me, Tachra," Jychanumun beseeched me. "I once saw the inevitability that Arrunn destroys all life and links to the Old

One, spreading his festering thoughts like a disease that eats at the flesh. But that has now changed. You exist. The Old One listens to *your* choices regarding life. He could not make such a choice, as an eternal being what he could never understand is the value of living a limited life. You represent his choice as to whether or not all life should go on. He hears your choices regarding life, and yours alone. But you, you understand life, and you find it precious. Already, when the Nigh-kutu first attacked Earth, your choice saved all kutu and human lives. That was *your* choice. Yours Tachra; no one else's. He listened.

"Your choices create change and fate. I did not foresee Arrunn's interest in you until he came here. I believe even Arrunn did not know. He had thought he needed to find Orion, to find me; we were part of his tools. We still could be, but now your existence and your choices have made another possible future. The future is in your hands. Your choices can change the outcome. That," he pulled me close to him, "is something only you can do."

I pushed Jychanumun hard, pushing him away from me. I wanted to hear no more.

"I can change nothing," I told him. "Look at me. I could not save my link to the Old One, save my father, save Meah. If I could change things, I would have changed those!"

"Those things are not gone," Jychanumun replied. "You did change them. Meah will never die. The love and bond between you both will always exist and you two will always be joined. The evidence is right over there, chasing leaves, squirrels and the wind. Only her flesh is no more; her consciousness still exists. You severed your link to the Old One, but he is still part of you and always will be. All you severed was your choice to use his direct power in that mortal life. And your father? Let me show you something . . ."

Jychanumun held out his hand and pushed his energy out. It drifted from his fingers like silver-speckled smoke, creating a wall of reflective light in front of us. Within that wall of energy a picture slowly formed.

Now I did not want to look, or even think about such terrible things as my father's demise, but the vague glimmer of hope that my father could possibly be alive overrode my fear of seeing something that I might not like. So, I looked.

"What is it?" I asked, straining to see the picture as it finished forming.

"It is your old hut in Threetops, right now, in the world of substance and linear time," Jychanumun replied. "Your mother refused to come into hiding with Soul and Iris."

I peered closer at the image. In a dulled room, my weary looking mother sat on the edge of her bed, her head in her hands. She looked so tired. I wanted to reach into that image and hold her, to give her some sort of comfort and tell her that she would be alright.

And yet, within that image, my eyes were drawn to something moving behind her. It was as if someone were pacing the length of the room. It was a spectral figure in greens and golds, not flesh like my mother. And, other than the unusually bright luminescence of the energy, that figure was unmistakeably my father.

"Your father passed away in the flesh, but not spirit. He has a soul," Jychanumun told me, "just like those humans you saw in energy form wandering around Meadsins after it had been attacked. If a human has developed the capacity for true love, that love-bond creates something that cannot die - a soul. He may not have flesh and body, but your father is as much alive in energy and consciousness as he always was."

"But it's obvious that my mother cannot see him!" I was vexed to the point of anger. "What is the point? That must be so frustrating for him."

"Your mother does not know how to look," Jychanumun

replied. "You would be able to see and speak to him. Your mother could be taught."

"What will happen to him?"

"I do not know," Jychanumun shook his head. "This is something I have not foreseen."

"Because I exist?"

Jychanumun nodded.

"Then I would think it best that I stayed here and stopped causing so much trouble," I replied vehemently. "Everything I try seems to end up hurting those I love."

"If that is your decision, then I understand. But I must tell you this," Jychanumun paused, looking at me. "By removing yourself from the world, the world has only one inevitable outcome: the end of all life. You are inadvertently choosing that fate by staying here. And so I am here, the emissary of whatever outcome is to be, to ask you to make one more choice. Will you stand by your choice to stay here, knowing that it would be the inevitable end for all life and all consciousness? Or will you return to your body and help me to create another path?"

"You are telling me that this huge thing, something bigger than me, something as big as all life, comes down to my choices? That's ridiculous."

"It is true," Jychanumun nodded. "The Old One linked to an innocent, with no history and no predetermined ideas on life, so he could understand life. He listens to your choices. Your choices for life, or death, become his choices. Because of that, your choice can create change. Those changes affect the outcome. I am a pure mixture of black and white, life and death. I could be either fates. You are the Old One's awareness of choice, and because of that, your choices are my fate. And," he paused, "you are *my* choice."

I wanted to argue with Jychanumun. If what he said were true, I didn't want such a burden on my shoulders. I was too small, too stupid, and too weak for my choices to affect anything. But I heard the truth in what he said, as much as it made little sense. With that, the reality and consequences of Jychanumun's words started to sink in.

So, the Old One listened to *my* choices on life itself? Just the idea of it made my head spin. Was that all I was? Did I have any personality of my own? Did I choose who I was? And what about the effect of my choices on others; how would I know if a choice was critical or just part of everyday life? How would I ever know if I was making the right choice? It made my thoughts reel with endless possibilities that looped around and around, and it all brought me back to the same thing: why, oh why, did this have to be my burden? Surely any kutu would do a far better job.

Jychanumun smiled, hearing my thoughts. "You are an innocent. You came into this world with no pre-formed memories, no preconceived ideas of what life should or shouldn't be, no bias, no ties to bind except those that you chose to make. You came into a perfectly balanced environment and balanced surroundings, with an upbringing that did not force choice upon you, but allowed your own to develop. And you were formed right within the heart of all things, in a world that swayed neither one way nor the other. An innocent such as that would discover the value of life without prejudice or bias."

"And now, with all my stupidity – for isn't that what innocence truly is – you ask me if I choose to end all life. Well, of course I don't," I frowned, crossing my arms. "So, no, let the world go on. There, does that suffice?"

"I wish it did, my brave Tachra . . ."

"Oh, don't you call me brave!" I interrupted, pointing my finger at him adamantly. "I've learnt that brave is just another way of saying that something is going to hurt."

"You are here," Jychanumun waved his arm around my beautiful valley. "You have created your own private place. A space between worlds where only you, and those you are bonded to, could ever come. Here time stands still. You are not part of life here and your choices will have no consequences on life. You must be in the real world, within moving time, for your choices to be felt."

"So you are asking me to go back there?" I asked horrified. Please, I thought, let there be another way; any other way except having to return to the flesh body. I do not, I cannot, go back to that. Not now.

"Yes," Jychanumun nodded.

My heart sunk. "But that body is a tattered mess. Arrunn had me. And what about Meah? I cannot leave her."

"Meah will always be with you now, in spirit, consciousness and energy, wherever you are. If you chose to return, I would do everything in my power to get you from Arrunn's clutches.

"But there is more," I told him, feeling a wave of anxiety. "I am no longer the same person. I've learnt emotions that I don't want and so I left them in that body of mine. I'd learnt fear. Fear is a horrible thing. And worse, I had discovered hatred. I cannot go back to that."

I sank my head, ashamed. "If I go back to my body, I will remember that hared and fear in full. What if such feelings make me evil? I am scared I will do terrible things."

Jychanumun walked forward and wrapped his arms around me, enveloping me with the strength of his energy.

"You will never be a bad person," Jychanumun told me. "Yes, you understand hate and fear. You see they are destructive things. But you also understand love and courage. They are constructive things. Together they are balanced and whole. They are the perfect ingredients to make a balanced choice."

"So I have to go back to pain and suffering to save life, or at least to give life a chance? This is not a happy choice." I sighed.

I looked up at my beautiful, black-eyed one. I decided that I now rued the day when I told him that not all choices have good outcomes. I should have kept my mouth shut.

"If I did return, what would happen? How long will Arrunn have me? How will I get out?" I asked.

"In truth, I do not know," Jychanumun shook his head. "For we are walking paths now that I have not seen. I see only fragments of a future, far, far in the distance, and in that I see us both."

"I have dreamt that, too," I agreed. "But in my dream the world looks very different. It looks like a terrible place."

"You must embrace your courage. I do not think this will be an easy task. It may well be fraught with problems to overcome."

"Must I go just yet?"

"Are you saying that you choose to return?"

"Do I have a choice?" I frowned, and then laughed at my own answer. "Yes, I think I choose to return," I nodded. "You say that if I do not, then all life will inevitably end. I choose to love my family, my human and kutu friends, the animals and even every last plant on this planet. So yes, as much as I want to stay here and be happy and free, for them and for life itself, how can I not return? It is not a nice choice and I do not wish it, but I have to."

Jychanumun put my hand to his lips and bowed.

"My flesh will live only two days without my essence," Jychanumun said. "The sooner we return, the better. I know not what Arrunn does with your flesh while we are here."

I nodded and pulled away, bending to nuzzle Meah, who now brushed against my legs.

"Then, if I can have just a moment of time, I shall run with Meah and remember the things that make us both happy."

And with that, I ran. I ran not for the need to escape from fear or pain, but from the sheer joy of running and feeling the wind in my hair and having Meah beside me. For one more brief moment, I savoured the joys of existence. I remembered what it was to be happy.

THIRTY

For Arrunn, the days passed slowly on this stinking planet, teeming with life.

Arrunn watched the change of Nigh-kutu guards, watched Tachra's motionless body from the top of the well, and watched his incompetent warriors constantly fight with light-lovers of far fewer numbers. He did derive mild satisfaction from every kutu slaughtered, replaying the memory in his mind, but it did not satiate him. How he longed for the end of all life. That would be the perfect moment. That moment could not come soon enough.

Time, he told himself. All he needed to do now was bide his time.

He relaxed with an inner smile, maintaining his stony façade, carefully planning every possible eventuality, every aspect he may need to take into account.

Suddenly, a high-pitched wail, a human cry of pain, snapped his concentration. It was a horrible noise, revolving around the entire room, echoing off every wall. It was a scream so full of emotion and suffering that it vibrated through to the very core of him. Wail after wail waved through the entire building.

Tachra was awake.

One of the Nigh-kutu hurried forward, bowing. "We cannot get the human to quieten," he stated.

"I had guessed as much," Arrunn raised his eyebrows. "Where is the physician?"

"Trying to sedate her, without harming her."

"Very good. Tell him to hurry up," Arrunn replied.

The Nigh-kutu hurried away again.

The physician came and went, each time carrying new equipment and new sedative potions, and each time bearing new scratches and bruises on his own flesh. But the wails continued, lapsing for mere moments only to start again.

The sun began to set, casting darker shadows in the gloom of the chamber, and still the female screamed.

In the distance, a lone Jychanumun, now released from his crevasse in the rock, concealed himself, watched the temple, and listened.

Wail after painful wail sounded from the building. A sound so heart-wrenching he would give his own life to help she who made it. He looked for every way to get to her, but the quantity of guards, and the presence of Arrunn and the Nigh-kutu, all made his chances impossible without harming Tachra too. But he would find a way. He would have to.

This was what Tachra had feared and had always dreamt of. It was the very same image from her dreams that she had told him about so many times. It was her worst nightmare. And here he was, watching the story become a reality, just as she feared it would, and unable to stop it.

Here, now, set in the darkness of night was the magnificent, glowing, golden building, set against the backdrop of darkest trees, and the beautiful doorframe that now looked so ominous, with its huge, snarling statues either side. And from that doorway, screams filled the air. The screams were full of agony, memory, and loss. It was a sound so painful that it made the air taste of blood. A sound so painful that its intensity lit up the land with sorrow and anger. But what Tachra had not realised was that it was he, Jychanumun, who would be the one to witness this scene from her nightmares. She had dreamt her dreams through his blind eyes.

He tried to connect to Tachra's mind. He wanted to send her comfort. But Tachra would take none: she needed to do this; she wanted to do this. She had returned to the entirety of her emotions and memories. She had to exorcise her pain. Jychanumun felt like his heart was bleeding.

THIRTY-ONE

I wanted my screaming to make me feel better, to rid me of the shadows that festered in my heart. But no matter what I did, or how loud I cried and screamed, that shadow was still there, darker than ever.

I had returned to my body. The reality of every terrible thing that had happened had hit me with such force that I could not control myself. I did not want to control myself. I hurt and hated too much.

I felt Jychanumun try to connect to me, to calm my rage and my pain. I wanted none of it. I loved him, yes, but this was for me, for Meah, for my father and for every good being that had suffered for no good reason of their own. I had left a part of my essence with Meah in the forest, but that only served to remind me of the injustice that had been done to such a beautiful, innocent creature. Nigh-kutu had stood and watched Meah be killed and had not done anything to stop it or help her.

I hated those who had done that to her.

I was in a hole in the ground. This is what they had done to the glorious water well in the centre of the temple. The purity of the glistening, clear Earth water had been removed, and my rotting, hateful flesh had been put here instead. The well was now my prison. They contaminated every good thing that they touched. They had made this beautiful place into an ugly one.

I hated them.

A repulsive, manipulative looking Nigh-kutu, with tendrils of weaving dark energy, kept trying to enter the well through a thick wooden door. I went for him every time he opened that door. I leapt on that kutu, hit and kicked at him until he either threw me aside or dropped what he was carrying and left. I then broke every piece of equipment he dropped until my hands were dripping with blood. He got in once, managing to get close enough and quickly enough to administer a potion into my arm as I tried to squeeze his throat. I had ripped out that needle with one hand and lunged forward, biting the Nigh-kutu on the neck until I felt my teeth meet. He was spineless and vile.

I hated him.

My body was a mangled mess. I couldn't talk without my tongue, and couldn't even properly swallow the spit that collected in my mouth. My ankles were raw with claw marks from my own fingers, and my feet a mass of cuts and bruises from running barefoot on sharp stones. My entire body was black and blue under the dirt from so many beatings at the Nigh-kutu camp. And my hands were so badly damaged, now a mangle of ripped skin and flesh hanging off the bones that they no longer felt anything. My body was fit to die, but my pain was my power. They had left me nothing to wear and nothing to clean myself with. This place was vile. My body was vile. They had done this to me.

I hated them for that.

I screamed for the duration of the night. I could sense Arrunn's presence in the room above me, and I could sense that my screams disturbed him. Good. Arrunn may detest all life, but what I felt for him was greater than anything he could ever feel. He was the worst of them all.

Hate was not a strong enough word for what I felt for him.

Though my prison remained dark, I sensed morning come. I had grown silent due to the weakness of my flesh, but my vehemence had not lessened, only increased. I stood in the centre of the chamber, just waiting for a Nigh-kutu to walk through that door, flexing my hands as the blood dripped on the floor around me. I felt wild and I did not want to stop it.

My eyes scanned for a way out or any point of weakness that I could utilize. I could see none, only the large wooden door in front of me. I heard a distant noise above my head and looked up, catching a glimpse of Arrunn as he moved away from the edge of the well.

How dare he watch me like a slave for his entertainment? I would stop that!

Crouching down, I began writing on the hard sediment on the floor. I wrote using the blood from my fingers, and when my fingers started to dry I picked up a piece of broken metal from the floor and bored those words into the hard, chalky residue that now covered the bottom of the well. I bored so deep into the residue that the golden Uana underneath glowed through the letters. I wrote large Nigh-kutu letters and words; from the depths of my mind I found the memory and understanding of the origins of all kutu words. All words had three-dimensional meaning to kutu. All words brought about a thinking and feeling response in them. I would use that.

I would write curses. I would curse them all. I would make Arrunn see and feel those curses and suffer pain every time he looked down into the well.

I wrote feverishly, moving up to the walls, concentrating on the area directly in front of the door. I would have none of them entering here unless they felt pain. They deserved pain. They deserved worse than pain.

After writing several strong curses that would evoke agony, fear and sickness, I heard the locks on the door move back. I crouched down at the far side of the well, my back against the wall, my matted hair stuck to my damp face, and watched.

A kutu entered, throwing a flask of something and piece of food in my direction. He looked at me and laughed.

I glared at that kutu. I would have lunged forward and bitten him too, if he had not been sub-consciously drawn to the curse on the wall behind me. Immediately he began convulsing. I saw fear in his eyes. He rushed backwards, slamming the door and quickly slotting the bolts back into place as I heard him being sick. I picked up the shard of metal and continued boring more curses into the sediment around me. It was still not enough.

I hated them. Their choices reviled me, repulsed me. They did not deserve to live. I should kill them.

A calm washed over me, just for a moment. It was a calm that I thought I'd forgotten.

Yes, kill them. Murder would make me feel better.

I did not need to lunge and kick at these Nigh-kutu to hurt them. I could do so much more than that.

I pushed the blanket away that they had left for me. I wanted nothing from them. I would rather be cold and naked than touching something they had given me. They deserved to die.

Yes, murder would most definitely make me feel better.

Tachra, do not . . .

Jychanumun tried to connect to me. I shut him from my mind. He deserved better than to feel the hatred that now consumed me. Perhaps he should have made me stay in the other place where I was happy and could do no damage. I had warned him that I might now be a bad person.

I saw my own energy swirling angrily around my body. I held my hands out in front of me, pushing the power outwards from my finger tips until the tendrils of light wound around each other, forming a loop. I closed my eyes and concentrated, feeling my surroundings. I pushed my energy forward, touching the door, caressing the door. On the other side was a short tunnel before another door. In the small space between doors stood a Nigh-kutu guard. He should be killed.

I pushed my energy through the locked wooden door of my prison and straight into the Nigh-kutu's body. I went carefully, slowly easing into his body. I felt him shiver in response. I wanted to kill him. I was going to kill him. And he would never even know I was there.

I pushed my energy up into the Nigh-kutu's mind, gradually linking with his consciousness, taking a dormant role. I wanted to kill him, but I faltered. A brief thought occurred: should I be doing this? Should I kill any being, no matter how bad they were? And then, as if in response to my lapse in anger, I saw something in this Nigh-kutu's mind: his memory of Meah's slaughter. This kutu had stood and watched as another Nigh-kutu had killed my beloved Meah and he had loved it. He had loved it so much he wished he were the one holding that dagger!

I was furious. My hatred soared back into place, consuming me. I wrapped my energy around that kutu's mind and I squeezed. I squeezed and I squeezed, feeling energy pop and sparks collapse, enjoying every moment of destruction. I squeezed as I felt that kutu collapse to his knees, and I just kept a hold of his hateful memory and squeezed even harder.

Suddenly, something in the Nigh-kutu collapsed, one last squeeze and I had shattered his mind.

The Nigh-kutu fell down, dead.

I pulled my energy back to my body, breathing hard.

That had made me feel much better.

Once I had caught my breath, I made myself even more comfortable on the floor, crossing my legs and sending my energy out once again. I felt a little better yes, but it still wasn't enough.

I pushed my energy through the wooden door, past the dead Nigh-kutu, only to be faced with yet another door. This was made of something I had never seen before, but it didn't matter. The mass was no obstacle. I pushed my energy through the door. Beyond the second door was another short tunnel, another door. And, oh perfect, there was also another guard.

The second Nigh-kutu guard seemed more relaxed than the first, even bored. It was as if he was just waiting for me, waiting for his unavoidable end, waiting for death.

I pushed my energy straight into the Nigh-kutu's mind, immediately searching for a memory to fuel my hatred. I found it straight away. It was right at the front if his thoughts. This one had also watched Meah die. And what was this? He had thought it was funny! He had found my desperate attempts to reach Meah and release her amusing! He wished that her death had taken even longer!

Now my hatred was really in full force. I took all that hate and squeezed that kutu's mind as hard as I could. *Look who's laughing now!* I screamed inside as I squeezed at his mind. Not so funny now, is it? Go, on; laugh at your own death!

Suddenly, pop.

The Nigh-kutu's mind collapsed.

The Nigh-kutu fell down, dead.

That's not so funny now, is it, I thought again, hovering, seething over the Nigh-kutu.

I was so incensed at the thoughts from that Nigh-kutu that I did not go back to my body this time. That death had not satisfied my anger, but only made it rage even more. I saw another door. I felt another guard's presence beyond that third door too. I needed to kill again.

Tachra please . . . Jychanumun tried to reach me again.

I pushed him away. I did not want to stop.

I moved my energy forward and straight through another door and into my next victim. I didn't want to be careful. I wanted this one to be aware that he was about to die. Straight away I knew where to look for the memories that would give me enough hate to kill him. And oh, did he have memories: memories of the enjoyment of Meah's death, memories of planning to do the same to other animals and humans at the first opportunity, memories of torture that inspired him. This one was despicable indeed.

Squeeze that mind. Squeeze. *I hate you.* Let him feel pain, just as he wished for others. Squeeze.

Pop.

Ha, one less Nigh-kutu in the world.

I could do this forever, I thought. But I pulled back. I had to pull back, forced into my own body once again. My energy was waning. As much as I wanted to rid this world of all the beings who would do such terrible things, to my frustration I realised I had to pause. This body would die if I did not stop. I did not want to die just yet. I wanted to live for vengeance. I would have to rest for a while, rest so I could kill again.

As I sat catching my breath, I did not hear any commotion denoting the discovery of dead kutu beyond my prison's door. I guessed that they would stay there until a change of guard occurred. That was a shame. I would have liked to have heard their reaction. I would also have liked to have new, fresh, live targets right outside my prison. But all felt quiet. It did not matter:

it would take a little more energy, but I could push out further than the immediate doors of my prison to find my next victim. Just a few more minutes and I would be ready to go again.

While I waited, I picked up the shard of metal from the floor and began writing on the walls again. As I bored those shapes into the wall, my mind began to soothe.

"Why don't you give up?" I heard a voice from above my head.

I looked up and could see no one watching me, but I knew that voice now. It knew it very well. It was Arrunn.

Arrunn had a way of speaking that threw suggestions into the mind. As he spoke, I could feel him coercing me to give up, insinuating that giving up was the best option.

"Why don't *you* give up?" I angrily shouted back, but the words came out merely as loud, angry gurgles.

"I do not choose to," he laughed.

What? He'd answered my seemingly unintelligible noises? He understood the gist of my noises! That vile, hateful creature understood the seemingly meaningless noises I tried to make with my tongue-less mouth.

"Can't you do anything good?" I shrieked. The sound came out like a whining scream, but I now guessed he would understand.

"Oh, my dear Tachra," Arrunn's voice echoed down from above me. "It is not that I cannot do good, it is that I choose not to. What you consider good does not taste so to me."

I heard Arrunn laugh to himself. My anger rose once again. I hated the sound of my own voice; the ugly gurgles that now left my mouth. He had done that to me with his own hands. And if he understood me now, why did he pretend that I needed to write down my words before Meah had been killed? He was taunting me then and was still taunting me now. I feared him and I hated him. He wanted my fear to break me. Well, it would not! I would just hate him even more. I embraced that hate, gathered my energy and pushed the core of my energy upwards.

I had aimed to find Arrunn. I wanted to try to squeeze his mind and rid the world of him. My energy surged upwards, up into the room above my prison, the room that use to be the beautiful central chamber. I made sure my energy was as invisible as the air in the room. I would not be detected.

Straight away I found a Nigh-kutu. He was in the same room as Arrunn.

I suddenly stopped.

What was this?

This one had nothing to kill?

This Nigh-kutu had no consciousness of its own!

My energy hovered invisibly in the room and I looked at the creature that stood, presented in the form and embodiment of a Nigh-kutu. I tried to sense what it was. I saw a line that ran between him and Arrunn. And then from Arrunn more lines threaded out to other kutu around him. There were twelve in total.

They were all Arrunn's guards!

I sensed that that these guards were not alive in their own individual right. They were extensions of Arrunn himself. Somehow, Arrunn had spilt himself, with one central consciousness attached to twelve identical parts of himself. Arrunn was one from twelve, or they were twelve from one. My energy spun around. I could not possibly kill one, as Arrunn's consciousness could just move to any one of the others to which he was attached. The only way to rid this world of Arrunn was to kill him and his twelve guards at exactly the same, precise moment. But that was impossible. I was only one, alone and maimed.

Perhaps I could kill these guards in quick succession, I thought. But how far did Arrunn's skills go? What if he could just move to inhabit another body, any body? He could go anywhere. It might take me forever to find him, and he might damage good beings as a result. I could not kill him like this.

I spun my energy around. Arrrgh! I was so frustrated. I hated him. I wanted him dead.

The frustration in me grew. I was so angry. I wanted to kill, I *had* to kill, but I could not kill the one I wanted to. I pushed my energy further out, determined to be satiated, lunging forward out of the chamber and into a different room, where I sensed three Nigh-kutu. All were preparing to take over from guarding the doors outside my prison, unaware that I had already killed their loathsome colleagues.

I thrust my energy forward, passing over the Nigh-kutu, lightly touching their essences like the wind moving through the trees.

Oh perfect. I sensed that all three had been present at Meah's murder. I would have to work quickly.

I jumped into the closest Nigh-kutu mind, not bothering to conceal my energy, immediately finding his hateful memories. Another evil being. Another who deserved to die.

Squeeze his mind. Squeeze. Take all that rage and give him what he deserves.

Pop. The Nigh-kutu fell down dead. There, he got what he deserved, even if it was far too quick for such an evil being.

As his fellow Nigh-kutu both bent to him, unsure as to what was wrong, I acted quickly, jumping into a second mind, feeding off his malevolent thoughts, letting his abhorrent acts fuel my rage, squeezing his mind, squeezing, squeezing, squeezing. Dead.

No time to hesitate; onto the next one. It's your time to die now. Oh yes, you are a particularly vicious one. And what is this? You held the knife that cut the flesh of my beloved Meah. You, I particularly hate. You deserve more than a quick death. You deserve to feel intense pain. You cannot scream or make a sound, no you can't. You will think this pain lasts for eternity. For you, I will let your thoughts freeze on the pain and suffering you've inflicted to others, all reflected back at you a thousand times, and that last, single thought will be all you remember.

Squeeze that mind. Shape it into everything that it fears. Your fear tastes good to me. Squeeze out every morsel of your despicable life, just like Meah's precious blood as it dripped to the ground. Squeeze. I hate you.

Dead.

That was over far too quickly. My energy seethed above the three dead Nigh-kutu. I should return to my body now, but I could not. I had relived Meah's death through their minds and my hatred was as great as ever. I still was not satiated. I had to do more.

I thrust my energy from that that room, knowing the guards had not made a sound and my presence had not been detected, moving into another, the other side of the corridor around the central chamber. Here I sensed a different Nigh-kutu about to exit the building. Oh yes, killing this one might ease some of my frustration.

I leapt into his mind, straight away seeing that he was another Nigh-kutu who had witnessed Meah's murder. I wrapped my energy around that mind and got ready to squeeze, looking for the memories to stir my hatred.

What was this? I hesitated.

This was not what I was expecting.

I let my consciousness become still in this Nigh-kutu's mind, slowly easing my grasp around his thoughts.

From the depths of his memory I could see that this Nigh-kutu had disliked watching Meah's flesh murder. He had felt compassion for Meah, and for the bond Meah and I had shared. I delved deeper into the kutu's mind, taking a passive role as he walked from the building, absorbing what his memories had to say.

This Nigh-kutu's name was Shemya. He wished that he had been able to save Meah and me. He had seen our bond and felt it as something good. He did not think it right to destroy such a beautiful thing.

As I examined this Nigh-kutu's mind, I became aware that he was walking outside in the dark. He was walking towards my forest, by the side of the temple. I picked up a strange mixture of emotions as he walked: trepidation, hope, and something more familiar. A bond.

Shemya, unwittingly carrying my consciousness in the back of his mind, walked quietly into the trees. I could feel him trying to make sure that his footsteps were not heard. He looked around regularly to ensure no one was following him. He wanted to keep his coming here a secret.

In the midst of a thick clump of trees, Shemya stopped and bent down, taking some items out of his pocket.

"Valiant," I heard him gently call. "Valiant, come on."

From a hollow in the natural slope of the land, a beautiful young cub stuck its head out from the darkness. It hesitated for a moment, spotted the Nigh-kutu and happily stumbled forward towards him. As soon as the cub reached Shemya he leapt clumsily, nuzzling the Nigh-kutu's face, just as Meah had once done with me.

I knew straight away that this was Meah's cub. She must have given birth before her death. Seeing the small creature made my own hateful thoughts freeze. I remembered love.

Shemya cuddled the cub, hand-feeding it small pieces of food, sometimes chewing a piece first if it was too tough for the cub. The cub was at ease and happy, even joyful to be with this kutu. I watched them play together, tumbling on the leaves. This kutu loved that cub already. I could see the line between them, a perfect line of energy that bonded them now and forever. It made me happy and sad at the same time. I knew that my body, back in my prison, was shedding tears.

I stayed and watched the wonderful scene between kutu and cub until I felt my energy wane to dangerous lows. I then pulled back into my body, sitting quietly in the dark confines of my prison as the tears streamed down my face. They were tears of happiness that Meah's cub was alive and loved, tears of sadness that the cub did not have its mother, and tears of shame for my hatred and my terrible acts. That lone Nigh-kutu had stopped my murderous spree. I had seen that he was a good being at his core. As much as his existence had somehow been misled and manipulated to enjoy the barbarism of war, this was a kutu who valued life above death and compassion above cruelty.

I laid my head against the wall. I was so tired. Tired in my body and mind. What had I done? I had done a terrible thing. I had taken lives. I avowed there and then that I would never use my skills to kill another being again.

And so from my huddled position I did not feel hate when I heard the Nigh-kutu guards change and their gasps at discovering three dead bodies. I did not feel hate towards the next guard who threw food into my prison. But I also did not rub off the curses on the wall. At least with those still there I would be left alone. My hate had been firmly put in a box in my mind, and I did not wish to look in that box ever again. I was weary now. My body was falling apart and now my mind felt like it was falling apart too. I had to find something to hold onto.

Jychanumun, I called.

Tachra, he immediately responded. I sensed his relief. *You have been blocking me.*

I've done terrible things, I told him.

Jychanumun was silent. He was probably as ashamed of me as I was of myself.

I'm so tired. I can't fight anymore. I am a bad person. I understand if you want nothing more to do with me, I told him.

Oh Tachra, Jychanumun sighed. *My silence is not condemnation, it is understanding. I have understood hate too. We share a hatred of injustice. Does that make me a bad being?*

No, I replied. I hesitated, not because I didn't think Jychanumun was a good being, but because of what he was indicating. He was trying to make me feel better about myself.

I felt what you did, Jychanumun continued. *To take a life is wrong. That cannot be undone. But you have made sacrifices and saved thousands. And now, when you could have stayed in Elysium, you returned to help save others yet again.*

And killed several Nigh-kutu instead, I told him.

And I have killed many more in this war, Jychanumun said vehemently. *Do you feel like a bad being?*

I carry guilt and remorse.

I nodded to myself. I understood that.

Are Soul and Iris alright? Are they safe?

Yes, Jychanumun replied. He paused for a moment, and I felt his uncertainty about telling me something. *They are in a safe place. Soul has lost nearly six years of her memories. She is relearning about her life; she and the child bonded immediately.*

Nearly six years? But she will not remember me. My soul-sister . . . My heart felt heavy.

She has not changed. Such friendships as yours can always be rebuilt. Iris tells her all about you.

This offered me little comfort. I didn't want to cry again, but I could feel the tears down my face. Was I going to lose everything over time if I couldn't get out of this place?

I don't know how I'm going to get my body out of here, I sighed, feeling desolate.

I am working on it, Jychanumun replied. *We just tried an attack to rescue you, but were fended off and lost several Anumi. We had to retreat and regroup. We will try again.*

An image from Jychanumun's mind suddenly entered mine. It was the very same image from the beginning of the dreams that I had never told Jychanumun about. In those terrible dreams, I had seen Jychanumun and my friends try to rescue me from something. I had seen them try again and again, each time losing more good kutu to death. The conclusion of those dreams had been terrible. They had showed me that, in the end, even Jychanumun would die trying to save me. This was the very thing I had decided to try to change. Yet here it was, happening anyway.

No! I suddenly exclaimed. *Jychanumun, listen to me. You must not try any more rescue attempts. You remember those dreams that I would never tell you about? They are here. In them, I dream that you will try to save me. While trying to save me, you and all the Shaa-kutu eventually, one by one, will be killed. You must not try another rescue. Promise me. Please.*

Jychanumun hesitated.

Jychanumun, Promise me now! I tried shouting into his mind. *For you, me and everyone. You said yourself that fate and choice must run together. This world will have no place for me if you are not with me. Do you hear me? Please, I beg you, this is important. You must not attempt any more rescues. We will find another way.*

I hear you, Jychanumun slowly replied. *I feel the truth of your words. But it greatly reduces my options.*

Aren't I supposed to be the one with options? I asked him.

Then you must promise to hold on, Jychanumun replied. *I will find another path if you promise not to give up hope.*

You strike a hard deal, my black-eyed one, I replied, but a sense of relief washed over me. *I will find a way out of here.*

I felt his mind quicken. He was watching something.

I have to go, Jychanumun quickly told me. *Nigh-kutu close. Must concentrate.*

I felt Jychanumun shut off from me. I had to hope that he had truly heard me. I had to hope that, by telling him about those dreams, he would not attempt any more rescues. He couldn't, or it would be disastrous. It would be the beginning of terrible things.

From my position leaning against the wall of the well, I could feel emanations of energy moving closer. I recognised that energy. It was Shemya, the one who had tended to Meah's cub. He was obviously on food and water duty today. Maybe here was one who could help. Could he be trusted?

I quickly looked around the room. There was barely anything in this place that could be of any use: a few broken pieces of equipment that the Nigh-kutu physician had left behind in his hurry to get out, a thin blanket, and an empty water container. I ran to the blanket, crouching over it so no prying eyes could see what I was doing, took the shard of metal and ripped off a small corner. I stuck the metal hard, a bit too hard, into my already raw finger, making it bleed much more than I expected.

On that piece of pale cloth, I quickly drew a cat's head. Well, it was supposed to look like a cat's head; it was more the type of picture that Iris would draw with her eyes closed. But it was the best I could do in a hurry, in the gloom, using my finger. I grabbed the empty water flask and, as the bolts drew back from the wooden door, stuck the piece of fabric inside the top of the flask, resealing it as I stumbled forward.

A hand came round the corner of the door, throwing in some pieces of fruit. The hand went out again before I had a chance to act. And then that hand came around the door again, this time throwing in a full container of water. I grabbed that hand, thrusting the empty container into it. The hand dropped the container and quickly shot back from the door.

As the empty container fell, I deflected it. It rolled on the floor, landing on the other side of the door as it closed.

I hoped by the skies above that it would be Shemya who picked up that flask. I hoped by the skies that he would check inside the stopper before refilling it with water. And if he did, I hoped by the skies that he would communicate back with me.

I felt Shemya walking away. He only paused to pass through the three locked and guarded doors, and then he stopped. He pushed out his energy wings to rise straight up to the steps, to reach ground level. It seemed to take him a great deal of energy to rise straight up, without movement in either direction. As his energy coruscated around him, I noticed something. What I had taken to be predominantly russet-coloured energy was actually a deep, rich orange, overlaid with black. I felt my heartbeat quicken. He had orange energy.

Jychanumun, I called out silently with my mind. *Can you talk now?*

Yes, Jychanumun replied. *Flying; reconnaissance.* It sounded as if he was flying fast.

The old Nigh-kutu clan that had Nar beasts, you said they were all predominantly orange energy, I hurried. *Were many other Nigh-kutu predominantly orange?*

There were a few, although not many. Why? Jychanumun asked.

I don't know, just a hunch, I replied. *Probably nothing more than hope. Did you pick up my thoughts about the Nigh-kutu who was looking after Meah's cub?*

I did. I am monitoring him.

He's got orange energy; it's just overlaid with darkness.

That explains much, Jychanumun replied. *It could explain why there is a Nar beast still alive and also why he could bond with Meah's cub. Either he has turned his back on his past, or he has forgotten.* I felt him change direction as he flew. I felt that he needed to concentrate. *Tread carefully, Tachra,* he added. *Take no chances.*

I sensed that Jychanumun needed to concentrate, and so I disconnected from him once again and sat back against the side of the wall, surrendering to the cold and pulling the torn, thin blanket back around me. I sipped at the water, savouring it. It was good water, taken straight from the lake in my valley: pure, wonderful Earth water. I could sense its purity. At least they had not tried to contaminate this lot. I could see a piece of fruit close by. Shemya had thrown in what looked like a large pear. Seeing it made my mouth water but, as hungry as I was, I was not going to chance eating any food they provided. I could sense that they had put something in that pear. And even if that pear was not contaminated with potions to make me unconscious or pliable, it just made me think of the meat that they ate. That fruit may have remnants of kutu blood on it.

I knew I had to figure out a way to get out by myself, and do so as soon as possible. I could not survive here for long. I was already close to the limits of my bodily endurance. I did not want to eat the food they provided, lest they had put some sort of poison in it. I did not want to sleep for anything longer than a few breaths, lest they came in and did something to me. And I did not want to relax my mental barrier, lest Arrunn found some way of getting into my mind. I was exhausted and my body was weak. I knew I could not endure such things for much longer.

Looking around the small area, which was now my temporary home, the prognosis of my chances of escape looked bad – very bad. The vertical, smooth walls of the well were unassailable for any creature that could not fly, and even a bird would become stuck this far down such a deep, narrow drop. Unless I suddenly developed the skill of levitation, that route was impossible. I could not pound my way through the walls of the well, as not only were the well's walls made of layers of kutu materials far stronger than my flesh, but only solid rock lay beyond them. Even Dragun's tunnelling skills would be of no use: the well had been built fully lined with thick layers of metals and other substances, including Mazium, which the kutu found unbreakable. That left the route that the Nigh-kutu took to get here as the only other option for escape. There were three solid doors, two of which were made out of unbreakable elements, and then yet another sheer, smooth tunnel up to the surface. No human could scale that. So that was impossible too. The prognosis did look dire indeed.

From my huddled position, I thought deep and long. How had my simple choice to leave my hut, the safety of my family, and my bountiful home village to go exploring come to this? My body was a mess. My heart was aching from so much loss. I struggled to keep hold of any shred of sanity. And I struggled even more to hold onto hope. This was far removed from what I had intended.

I must have sat thinking for some time. Either that, or my sense of time had become misplaced. I heard the latches on the door slide back again and sensed that someone was bringing more fresh water from the lake.

I warily watched the door open, sensing it was Shemya. I held my breath, wondering if he had found the image I had left for him. And, if he had, would he communicate back. Or would he openly accuse me of something? I didn't sense that Arrunn was with him; that much was good. He did not walk in, but threw a water bottle and an apple into the cell.

Once I had felt Shemya exit through the three doors, I cautiously reached out and picked up the new water bottle. I hunched over it, concealing my actions, and tentatively unstoppered it. At first I thought that the fabric that I felt inside the stopper was just the same one I had placed there earlier. But I soon realised that the bottle was now full of water while the fabric was still dry! This piece of fabric must have been put in place after the bottle had been refilled with water.

I pulled out the piece of fabric, barely daring for any feeling of hope. I could hardly see anything in this gloom, yet alone make out any image. I held the fabric close to one of my carvings, allowing the subtle glow that filtered from the Uana to light the fabric enough to see. There, on the same piece of ripped blanket, I could just make out another drawing. Next to my badly drawn cat's head was a second, smaller one. I looked closer at the smaller image, holding it right in front of my eyes. It looked like the face of the smaller cat had a smile on its face.

Shemya was telling me that the cub was well. It made my weary heart glad.

I was about to scrunch the fabric up to keep it in my hand when I noticed something else on that fabric. On the back was written a single Nigh-kutu word: *sorry*.

Then and there, I knew my senses had not been failing me. Even if it was only one lone solitary being, goodness could still exist amidst the Nigh-kutu. I had hope.

THIRTY-TWO

Mid-skirmish, Orion had sent a message to all that they were to regroup immediately, and had given them all new co-ordinates.

Once again Dragun had been the gatekeeper, bringing them all into yet another confined space embedded into a rock. This one was set into the side of a small, stony hillock, covered in thin grass and a single, leafless tree. At first it seemed an unusual choice, but as soon as they had traversed the very long, narrow tunnel, going steeply downwards, deep underground and only recently constructed by Dragun, the choice was clearly a good one.

When Jychanumun walked into the space, he knew exactly where he was. This was Kraniel's secret underground laboratory, the one that Tachra had mentioned many months ago, the one that Kraniel had used to idle away his free time and overactive brain. Its location was close to the temple. Dragun had been painstakingly working on a long, winding tunnel from the hillock to give them access to this place.

"Impressive," Mardoch nodded approvingly, as he squeezed into the small space beside Jychanumun. "Rather small, but it has more equipment than I have ever seen in one place. This is Kraniel's laboratory?"

"Yes, although we were not supposed to know anything about it until now," Jychanumun nodded.

"I am not surprised," Mardoch chuckled. "On Immorah, even having just one of the pieces of equipment around here would warrant death."

"Had things become that bad?"

"Worse," Mardoch frowned. "After Arrunn had destroyed all books and taken away the right to learn, he began setting his own laws and belief systems. Do you remember the death chamber, where Arrunn wanted you to work?"

"I cannot forget it," Jychanumun frowned.

"It is now called the Inner Shrine. He would have the kutu believe it is the gateway to some personal ascendance."

Jychanumun was suddenly furious. "He makes them cease willingly, using lies? We have to stop this, lest all Nigh-kutu become condemned in death or in life."

"It may be too late to save them in life, my brother," Mardoch sighed. "I do not believe I am evil, but purely because I come from the darkness I see the wariness in others' eyes."

"No Mardoch; you are one of the most honourable beings that I have ever known. This will be stopped," Jychanumun stood up. His voice was raised and he knew it. He wanted all those around him to hear.

"Both shadow and light are capable of good and evil," Jychanumun declared. "You must all see the beauty of what the shadow truly is: honour, valour, loyalty, passion and so much more. Arrunn corrupts the truth of it. Arrunn chooses evil; it is not inherent in the darkness. The shadow once had many great beings: Nigh-kutu who loved life and valued each other. They were slaughtered. Will you all fear or hate everything of shadow origin just because of him? Will you believe that from the shadow only hate and fear are born? Open your eyes. See that darkness has beauty and greatness, too."

The small room had fallen silent. None of the kutu had heard so much, and with so much passion, from Jychanumun in one speech. They were shocked to silence.

Jychanumun sat down, "I may be blind, but I must make them see," he spoke through gritted teeth. "If shadow and light cannot co-exist, there is no unity." He buried his head in his hands. "I do not know what else I can do," he sighed.

Mardoch put his hand on Jychanumun's shoulder. Jychanumun did not pull away.

Orion walked up to them both. Jychanumun had sensed him coming. Orion was a good being, and Jychanumun would even call him a friend, but he did not wish to hear his sophistries, not now.

But Orion did not rebuff Jychanumun. "I see the truth of what you say." He bowed before him. "As I always have. When we have peace, I would be honoured if you would show me your home-worlds. I would be honoured to see the beauty of true shadow."

"As would I," Stanze remarked from the far side of the room.

"And I," another echoed.

"And I," another voice spoke up.

One by one, every Shaa-kutu in that small, confined room agreed.

Jychanumun felt a change in the air move like a wind around them. They understood. They truly understood. There was hope.

Jychanumun leaned back and shut his eyes. Hope was a wonderful and a necessary thing, but he still had to free Tachra from her terrible prison. But she had made him promise not to attempt any rescue, and he would not break that promise. He no longer had any options remaining to him. He truly did not know what else he could do to affect the outcome of things.

The last of the Shaa-kutu were now safe in Kraniel's old laboratory. Dragun had finished resealing the entrance and had returned, tired yet resolute, dusting the grit from his arms. Jychanumun sat straighter, sensing Orion's tentative presence, sensing that Orion had something very important to say.

Orion walked to the middle of the small opening, clearly very animated about something. His red energy swirled around him, moving out to touch the others that surrounded him.

"Everyone," Orion announced, waiting a moment for their chatter to silence. "We have a new option. It may not be the best solution, but it may just work and buy us time."

That caught everyone's attention. The silence became absolute. Only the ragged breaths of those newly arrived could be heard over the hushed anticipation.

"Kraniel has told me that there is a way to close the bridge between the light and the dark." Orion announced, and then held up his hand, shaking his head. "And no, I am sorry to say that we have not stumbled upon it yet. But there is a way, and our great kutu minds could find it if we had more time. But Kraniel has discovered a way to create a time fissure and give us that much needed time. Kraniel, I shall hand over to you."

Kraniel bowed, standing up. "I shall keep this simple," he began. "I have discovered a way, using the foundation energy of the essence that we kutu have at our core, to project all kutu away from this place and from any place, to be trapped within time, in pure energy form, for a while. We would be alive and conscious, but unable to affect any aspects of the physical world. During this time, Earth and non-kutu life would continue. A time fissure of this kind would draw all the Shaa-kutu who still existed back to the light, even those trapped and in captivity, and all Nigh-kutu would return to the shadow. That would give us time to heal the injured, devise a way of overthrowing Arrunn's hold on the remaining Nigh-kutu, and design a permanent barrier to the shadow. And when the fissure collapses and all kutu are released, we could put that barrier in place."

"That sounds extreme," one of the Anumi spoke up. "Can we not continue as we are?"

"As we are, we cannot win," Orion shook his head. "We are outnumbered, and more Nigh-kutu arrive daily from Eden1. And while we fight, Arrunn still progresses in his plans. Captured Shaa-kutu are disappearing at an alarming rate around Eden1, and here, the Old One . . . well, you have already seen what results from disturbing his slumbers. We need another way."

"Can we not use the time crystals to help us?" one of the kutu asked.

"No," Orion replied. "We now know that each time crystal contains the condensed energy and consciousness of a kutu. Could any of us justify sacrificing an unknown kutu, perhaps a good kutu, a friend, a potential friend, to aid us in war?" he asked. "I cannot! I would be as bad as Arrunn! I do not know how to release these consciousnesses from their bonds, but we could find a way."

"You say we will be trapped within either darkness or light for a time. How long exactly?" Mardoch asked Kraniel.

"I estimate we would have enough energy for perhaps fifteen thousand years at most. There would be plenty of time. It would allow us to regroup and find a more permanent solution. If we find a solution sooner, then I can undo the fissure sooner. Fifteen thousand years is the maximum. It may take far less."

Mardoch had suddenly gone quiet. It sounded like a plan. It sounded like a plan that could work. But he was suddenly looking at his own inevitable doom.

"So you are saying that we would be caught in time, conscious and alive, in pure energy form, held by the power of either light or shadow?" Mardoch asked.

"Yes," Kraniel confirmed.

"And for that duration we could not be physical at all, or affect anything physical."

"Correct," Kraniel nodded.

"And the shadow could not bleed into the light, or vice versa."

"Confirmed."

"And by doing this," Mardoch asked tentatively, wanting to ensure he had got it right, "All Shaa-kutu would be trapped in their light origins, and all Nigh-kutu in their shadow origins? And all Nigh-kutu could still interact with each other; but only in energy and consciousness? They would still be capable of harming each other?"

"Oh," Kraniel suddenly paused, looking at Mardoch, and then Jychanumun, and then around at Dragun: all three of the Nigh-kutu who now sat among them as friends. "My mind saw you as one of us, not Nigh-kutu. I think you have found a flaw in my plan."

Mardoch sighed deeply. "I am Nigh-kutu. I would be slaughtered by my own kind now, whatever form I was in. I would be treated as the ultimate traitor. But," he looked at Kraniel, "I came here knowing that I may need to sacrifice myself for a greater good. I still stand by that. If I am to die among my own kind, then so be it. They need to see the truth of what they have become."

Dragun walked forward, brushing the dirt and dust from his hands. "I am with you," he nodded. "I treasure life. It is a worthy cause to die for."

Jychanumun raised his head, in his blindness sensing the courage, the hope, the sadness. Both Mardoch's and Dragun's words, linked with Kraniel's brilliant idea, had just presented him with the choice he had been searching for.

"There is something I could do to help," he said, "if help is required, but it is not an easy task."

"Please speak," Kraniel said. "If you know of any solution, then we wish to hear it."

"I am the Death-Path-Walker," Jychanumun said. "I guide beings through death, when they wish it. Between life and death there are paths, my paths. Those paths are neither life nor death; they are between existences. If, when the time comes, Mardoch and Dragun wish it, they could choose death, but I would then guide them along these paths, holding them there, not letting them walk to their end. They could wait where these paths meet until the time is right, and then I could guide them back to life."

Jychanumun sensed the energy of his brother and Dragun. "It would mean taking your own life at a specified time and, once you arrived at the paths, waiting for me to come," he told them. "Waiting in the paths can be difficult."

"And what about you?" Chia asked.

"I would choose to do the same in order to guide them and to stop my own energy being flung into the darkness. I too would wait in the paths."

"And Tachra?"

Jychanumun considered this. "If she would agree, I would hold her in the death paths too. She would have to take her own life and leave this mortal flesh behind. It would be different for Tachra; in the future she would have to be reborn if she was to live again."

"It would be asking a great sacrifice of her to leave all the human bonds she has made. Would she do such a thing?"

"I do not know," Jychanumun replied, "But where she is now, I do not know how we can rescue her. Her situation is dire."

I would . . . Tachra silently told him. She had been listening all along. *If there is just one plan, it is one more than I currently have. I see no clear way forward and this stupid body won't last another month in this stinking place. If you think you can devise something to change the course of things, I will do what is needed. Let me make this decision while I still have some stability of mind.*

Are you sure of this? Jychanumun asked.

I'm not sure about anything, Tachra replied. *I don't even know if I'm me any more. I need to trust you. I sense you feel it is the right thing.*

I think it is the only way, Jychanumun told her. He tried to send her soothing thoughts. He tried to send her the same good energy that she gave out so willingly to others. Her energy felt weak, yet she tried so hard to hold onto the good in things.

"Tachra would do this," Jychanumun nodded to Kraniel. "How long do we have?"

"I will be ready with the right material in five days," Kraniel replied.

Jychanumun nodded. Five days? He hoped that Tachra could survive that long.

Once everyone had finished asking questions, they were requested to stay within that cramped space while Kraniel worked. Now that they had a plan, they wanted to keep everyone safe and away from the Nigh-kutu. Most of the kutu took the opportunity to rest. Orion and Chia paced and organized. Dragun and Stanze ventured out to gather the last of their rations from various bolt holes. The Anumi did what healing they could on the wounded. Although still tense, it was the most relaxed state they had been in for weeks.

The hours passed and Jychanumun grew restless. He needed to stretch his wings. He sensed that Tachra was trying to rest her mind without sleeping, and so he did not disturb her; she needed to find respite wherever she could. Her fragile body and mind could not endure much more. Kraniel said the fissure would take five days to arrange.

He leaned his head back and shut his mind, trying to block the loud thoughts of the kutu around him. He needed to find his own strength, so he could give strength to Tachra. It would be the only way she could endure another five long days.

"Old One," Jychanumun whispered under his breath. "If you have ears for my words, listen now. Please do not forsake Tachra at her time of great need."

THIRTY-THREE

Believing that I was going to die a long and painful death was one thing, but now, being in the midst of that time, feeling my body decline and my mind grow fragmented, was more difficult than I had ever imagined.

Jychanumun had told me that I had to last out another five days in this prison. I think a day had passed since then, maybe more. It was getting difficult to tell. I know I'd been here for many days already, but I'd lost all track of time. My emaciated body and wounds that wouldn't heal were a clear indication that I'd been here perhaps a few weeks. It felt more than that. It felt like I'd been here forever.

Jychanumun had told me that when the time was right I would have to make myself cease in body. Once I'd done that, I was not to walk to the Old One. Instead, Jychanumun would take me to the death paths where we would wait, watching time move. He said that waiting in the death paths was the only possible chance of changing the fate that Arrunn wanted for all life. He said that we might have to wait for quite a long time before we could come back. He said it was the only way. I knew this. I'd listened through our connection to everything Orion and Kraniel had told him. My death would have to coincide with Kraniel activating the results of his experiments to send all kutu back to their origins. I would die in body yes, but not spirit. And when the time was right, we would all be coming back to fight for life itself.

Choosing death so save life? It was an irony that even in my broken state I could see. I also saw the balance of it. Perhaps, I wondered, the kutu's sacrifices of so much of their own life-time, my own sacrifices, these were the balance of things too.

Waiting five days hadn't sounded so long when Jychanumun had said it. Back in the temple, when times had been easy, five days would have flown past with little more than holding classes and playing with Meah in the forest. But now, when every moment was a test of endurance, five days stretched far ahead of me. I didn't know if my body would last that long.

The thought of death seemed like a relief from my physical pain, yet it also scared me. I'd spent so long fighting to stay alive that the notion of allowing death now felt wrong. It was made worse knowing that I would have choose not to go to the heart of the Old One. I knew I would be drawn to go there. I would *want* to go there. Right now, sleeping for eternity with the Old One and feeling the peace of his endless dreaming, sounded quite wonderful.

My body was a mess. The gloom showed my flesh to be a mass of dirt and damage. My mottled blue and white skin clung to my bones. My body already looked dead. Trying to move around was an almost impossible effort. And when I did muster the strength to move, the pain was unbearable.

And yet, as agonizing as it was, the pain of my flesh didn't worry me. What worried me was my mind. My thoughts had patches where I couldn't think straight. Sometimes I simply drifted into a numb mindlessness. Sometimes I battled with myself to keep any clarity of thought. Sometimes I forgot where I was. Sometimes, I even forgot who I was.

I vexed that even if I did manage to keep this weak body going for another five days, I might not die at the end of it. What if my mind collapsed before then, and I became too mad to remember how to cease? What if my mind became too numb to hear Jychanumun, and I missed him telling me when the time was right? If ever I needed to find any additional inner strength, it had to be now.

It took a great deal of resolve not to find escapism in my in-between world, the memory of my valley, which I had created for Meah and me. I knew that time meant nothing in that place. If I went there I may not be able to focus on keeping my body alive and I'd surely cease before those five days had passed. So, I had to stay awake and stay focussed. It was not easy. It was even more difficult than the walk I'd done over the mountains when I was a girl. Then, at least I had walking and looking for water to concentrate on. Here in the gloom, with little other around me than more gloom, and unable to endure the pain of moving at all, I could find little to focus my thoughts on.

Struggling to retain any clarity, my mind regularly drifted. It was in such moments that I was repeatedly drawn to the same thing: my father, or rather, my father's soul. In those fleeting moments, I found that I could connect to his conscious energy. He knew that his body had died, and yet he also knew that he could still think, move, and have feelings. He still *felt* very much alive, but could no longer interact with the world as he did in life. He was lost, unsure of his path.

The first time I'd managed to push out my energy far enough to make father to see me, he had become very upset. He thought that I too had ceased in flesh. But, I told him I was well. I even tried to tell him I was happy. But, in his true state of beautiful gold and green energy, he could see that wherever I was, I was suffering. That made him angry. His anger made me love him even more.

I could not have my father's soul lost, invisible and wandering here forever.

There is a place that I can take you, I told my father. *It's a beautiful place where you would be safe and happy. It's a place in space and time that is precious to me: my valley. I can come and go from that place at will. And when mother dies, I can take her there too. And Soul, and Iris, and any good beings that know love and have developed a soul. You would be happy there.*

Father was hesitant.

So I then took a great risk, depleting my own waning energy levels still further, and brought father to Elysium to see it. I wanted to see if it was somewhere that he could be happy while he waited for mother.

When father had walked into that hole in space and time, the memory of my valley, he had fallen in love with the beauty of the place. He saw it slightly differently to me. Through his eyes I could see over the lip of the valley to an image of my old hut in Threetops, surrounded by beautiful apple trees. He saw the valley as his own place of beauty, filled with small changes that were special to his own memories.

It was a wonderful moment of realisation. That was when I knew; although this place was my special place, everyone that I brought here would see what *they* considered special in their own hearts. It was the very essence of what this place was.

Oh, what wonders! How full of love and content such a place could be, I smiled to my father. *You too see it as beautiful.*

It is beautiful, my father replied. *And you, my daughter, are beautiful too. You say that only good souls can come here?*

Yes, I smiled. *It's the bond of love that creates such a place; the love of life, love of another. Only those who know love and possess inner beauty above all else have souls. Only they can access this place after death.*

And, with my assurances, my father had chosen to stay in Elysium. He would stay just a while, he said. He would wait for mother to join him.

I told father I would visit him soon. I knew that time was not significant in this place. Time would not drag or hurry, but exist as he wished it. And, as this was my special place, born from my love of my wild cat and my valley, it was as safe and unbreakable as the bond Meah and I would always share.

I kissed my father on his cheek and he went off to pick apples. They were mother's favourites. I watched him walk happily away and I did not want to leave. But I had to.

Coming away from that beautiful place to the harshness of reality was one of the most difficult things I'd ever done. I returned to the pain of my flesh, the grim reality of my situation, and a new overwhelming worry: What if I'd stayed away longer than I'd realised? What if I'd been away too long and the kutu had already gone? What if I had missed the specified time? Mere moments in Elysium could be any time to the flesh: seconds, months, even years. Had I just done a very stupid thing?

Jychanumun, I called out cautiously with my mind. My heart thumped with trepidation.

I am here, Jychanumun replied.

Relief flooded through me at hearing him. I had not stayed away too long.

How long more? I asked him.

Three and a half days, Jychanumun replied. *Kraniel is working fast. You must be strong and hold on a while longer.*

I didn't reply, letting my mind calm.

Can you hold on until then? Jychanumun tentatively asked.

I felt the emaciated, damaged state of my body. In truth, I did not know how it would last another three days.

I don't know, I replied.

I mentally disciplined myself; I had to be strong.

Yes, I can hold on, I added, with more conviction.

Jychanumun let me drift from our connection. I sensed he was anxious about my mental and physical state, but I didn't want him to know how weak I really was.

I ignored the pain of my flesh and took solace in thinking about my father, happy in Elysium. If only I could give such happiness to all the wonderful human souls who had experienced death, but had not died? My mind circled around on my thoughts, trying to focus. But why couldn't I? Surely all human souls could go to Elysium if they wished? Yes, I realised, although I would have to be careful that I didn't stay away from my flesh for too long, it was possible. I could offer all the human souls a place in my Elysium. Not only would I be doing something worthwhile, I would have something to focus on. Having something to focus would also help me to stay alive for a few more days.

For two days and two nights I did not rest. I pushed out my weakening energy as much as I could, one by one finding the humans who had ceased yet could not die. Each time I found one, I told them what I had told my father, about souls and about their loved ones, and then I gave them the option of staying in Elysium.

Every single one of those beautiful human souls chose to stay in that in-between world. There they were safe. They would be happy. Each one saw it as a place of beauty drawn from their own memories. At last something warmed my heart and gave me hope that I could do something right.

Relaxed with the knowledge that I had found every human soul wandering the planet, I found rest in the darkness of my prison and let my depleted energy settle. I was exhausted. I had pushed myself beyond exhaustion. I barely had enough energy to keep breathing any more.

My breathing became slow. Slower still. Breathing made my chest hurt.

It would be so easy just to stop breathing now. No more.

I could no longer be bothered to draw another breath. I found myself relaxing into a comfortable numbness, my eyes half open but unfocussed. I knew the fragile state of my body. My body wanted to fall into a deep slumber and never wake up.

Breathe, I told myself. *You must breathe.*

But not moving is so much better.

Breathe!

I didn't want to take another breath, but I thought of my friends, I thought of the Shaa-kutu, and I thought of the endurances Jychanumun must have suffered in his life. I had to breathe and stay alive for a while longer, for him, for them.

I mustered every morsel of willpower that was left. I took a sharp intake of breath. It made me cough violently into the dirt on the floor. That really hurt.

Breathe again. Once more.

Another deep breath. More shooting pain.

I forced myself to move, clumsily twisting around and pulling at the blanket beside me. My numb fingers awkwardly fumbled with the cloth, which had started to rot with damp. I began feebly tearing strips of rags to wrap around my hands and feet. Some of the cuts kept bleeding, but binding them would give me something to do, which in turn would stop me sleeping. I must not sleep. I did not know what they would do to me if I slept. And even if they did nothing, I would stop breathing and would never wake up. I had to stay awake to stay alive for just a while longer.

Nevertheless, half-way through binding one ankle, I found myself drifting into sleep again. It was so nice. For a moment, everything hurt less.

Wake up! I scolded myself. *You must not sleep. You will never wake up if you do. Wake up!*

I dragged myself forward and picked up a half-full flask of water, pouring it over my face and belly. I was so tired. Even the cold water wasn't helping to keep me conscious. A part of me even hoped that Arrunn would start one of his taunting sessions. That always made me more alert; at least, alert enough not to sleep.

Arrunn taunted me regularly. He would stand away from the well's edge, speaking to me. He was trying to break me. He offered me healing, comfort and beautiful things. He threatened pain and death to everything that I loved. He tried lulling me into giving up. He told me that it would make no difference to the end result, that I would just be saving myself a great deal of pain. He taunted me that my body would soon break and was already breaking. He said that once I had died, the next time I saw him it would be from the heart of the Old One, when he would finished all life, including me. He said that I could stay in that pit and die, knowing that I had only another death, an eternal death, to look forward to. Every time he spoke, he gauged my reactions, trying to find a way to break me. But I learnt more about Arrunn from his questions and taunts than he did about me.

Arrunn still believed that I knew the time when I acquired the link to the Old One. He could not see that the first time I had answered him I had given him the truth. I understood why. He believed that such a link would only be given to one of strength, intelligence and power. He thought that I must, at some point in my life, have done something amazing or unique to make me distinctive. His own arrogance made him think that. If only he could see that the opposite was true.

The worst thing that Arrunn did was to bring humans to that well, making them come and look at me. They would line up and take turns at the edge of the well, just standing, staring down at my broken body, fascinated, horrified, until led away. I felt their pity. I felt their revulsion. I even felt their anger at me. It made me miserable. That very nearly broke me.

Arrunn must have sensed my distress at having people watch me, for he made those people come and stare more and more often. Sometimes the people came several times a day. It didn't get any easier to cope with.

"Come and see what Tachra's teachings lead to," one of the Nigh-kutu would announce as the humans arrived.

And those people would come and stare, and then leave, often thinking that Arrunn's way must be a better way to live. They did not want to end up like me.

It made my heart heavy to think that Arrunn was already starting to corrupt some of the people. I had started to sense changes in their reactions. At first, most of them had felt pity when they'd seen me, and I'd had the impression that they had been forced to come. But those compassionate people were growing fewer as time passed. Most now felt disgust, viewing me like a dirty object. But even worse than the disgust were the people who felt loathing. They blamed me for bringing the kutu here, and they didn't contain their anger, throwing insults and accusations at me whenever they could. I tried to shut my ears to them, but couldn't. Every one of those insults hurt more than the sharpest stone.

Now, from my crumpled position on the hard floor I could feel the presence of humans nearby. I think they were gathering to see me again. I'd hoped that Jychanumun would tell me it was time to leave here before I had to endure another round of these watchers. But I still had hours, maybe even as much as half a day, to wait. It seemed I would have to endure at least one more session yet.

I wanted to move from my crumpled position, but I couldn't. My body was too weak.

Anyway, I thought, *nowhere in this well offers sanctuary from prying eyes. I may as well just stay here.*

So I stayed on the floor, naked and broken. I couldn't even manage to pull the remnants of the blanket to cover me. I mentally braced myself for the onslaught of emotional hurt. It didn't take long to start.

"Oh, look. There she is. She doesn't have such big ideas now, does she?" the first one said.

"You should be ashamed of yourself!" another spat over the side of the well.

"Is that really her?" someone whispered. I felt their horror.

"Poor creature."

"Really, though, is that her? It could be anyone."

Silence. The next person just stared. I felt their anger. They were too angry to speak.

More people. More anger. More pity. More abuse. More horror.

I tried to shut my mind from the barrage of words and feelings. I could not. More and more came forward. One threw something heavy, a stone. It bounced of the wall of the well, thumping hard into my back. I was surprised that it didn't hurt, but my body was quite numb.

The Nigh-kutu had brought many people to the well this time. Or perhaps, my thoughts cruelly suggested, people enjoyed coming here to see this, to watch my broken body lying on the floor. Perhaps they asked to come.

After a torrent of abuse and yet more pity and anger, I thought the last of the humans had finally left. I felt a wave of relief. In my relief I became aware that someone was still watching me. Someone was still there, someone whose thoughts were desperately sad and concerned.

Suddenly, there was a voice in my head.

I'm going to help you, the voice said in earnest. I got an image in my mind of what I looked like from the top of the well.

I forced open my eyes and glanced up, without moving my head.

Iris!

No! Get her out. Don't let her see me like this. Don't let the Nigh-kutu see she is something special. Get her out of here.

Iris, go away! I screamed in my mind as powerfully as I could, pushing all that I could of my depleted energy towards her.

I'm going to get you out, she told me.

No Iris. Go! I growled.

I'll find a way. I promise, the child told me. She knew that I could hear her.

GO! I shouted into her head with all my might.

I felt a woman pull Iris away from the edge of the well. "Come on, child," the woman said. It was not Soul. I did not know who this was.

I felt horrible at being so harsh to little Iris. The heart of me wanted nothing more than to hug her and tell her how much I'd missed her and her mother. But I couldn't. I couldn't escape this place. I couldn't move. I didn't want her to see me like this. And the child needed protecting: she was too precious to be recognised as something special by the Nigh-kutu. If that meant speaking harshly to her and making her hate me, I would have to bear that.

I had thought the people had stopped arriving to watch me, but then I heard more people approach, followed by more cruel and pitying words. I did not hear these clearly – they just blurred away into the background. I was worried for little Iris. I strained to contain that anxiety.

Stay calm, I told myself. Do not let Arrunn sense your dismay or he will harm the child to get to you.

Jychanumun, I called.

I am here, Jychanumun replied. *Not long now. Hold on a little longer.*

Iris, I said, *was here. Must be kept safe. Special child, born from the first love on Earth.*

The child will be safe, Jychanumun replied. *She has her own role to play in the future. As does Soul. Both are safe. And they will look after Meah's cub. They already know. It is the perfect match.*

I sighed inwardly; Jychanumun had picked up my concerns about the cub.

The Nar? I asked. *She is a good creature really . . .*

My brave, compassionate Tachra, Jychanumun replied. *I would not forget anything that has touched your heart. A Nar is an extension of its bonded Nigh-kutu. If a Nar still lives, then so does the Nigh-kutu it is bonded with. When the fissure is created, the Nar will be with that kutu.*

I felt my mind drifting towards unconsciousness again.

Hurry up, please, I begged him. *My will is strong, but all else is failing.*

Be ready, my beloved, Jychanumun instructed. *I am readying myself now. I have to do this all at once. I have others to lead into the death paths; all must follow at the same time.*

I'll be ready, I replied,

I closed my eyes. I think I was ready to leave here now. I was ready for death.

I felt my breath slowing. Yes, I was ready to go.

Iastha Tachra, Jychanumun called, *Stay with me. Just a moment more.*

I tried to force myself to sit up. I kept tilting over. I leant against the wall of the well. I couldn't lift my head.

If I concentrated, could I make my heart stop? Could I use the last of my strength and will to bring this death about? What if I could not? What if, no matter how much I willed it, my heart just kept on beating past the time when Jychanumun was ready? I had wanted to be able to simply allow myself to die. But now? To bring death to my body at an exact time? I did not think I had the strength to be sure of this any more. I would have to find another way. I would have to bring about my death some other way.

I blindly scraped my hand in the dirt around me, trying to find the shard of metal. There, I had it.

I am with you, Jychanumun told me. *Wait just a moment more. I am here.*

It really is you? I asked. *Are you tricking me?* I was afraid that I could no longer tell.

Just feel my essence, Jychanumun replied. *I am me; you will feel the truth of it.*

It was true. It was Jychanumun. It felt like Jychanumun.

I drifted off into my own subconscious dreaming again. My mind drifted around on itself, aware of the shard of metal in my palm. The drifting felt nice. It didn't hurt anymore. I was ready.

THIRTY-FOUR

In a dark corner of the kutu's last waiting place, Kraniel's old laboratory, Jychanumun knelt with his two Nigh-kutu friends, Mardoch and Dragun. It was their time.

Behind Jychanumun, Orion spoke encouraging words to the remaining Shaa-kutu as they stood in rows, waiting. He spoke of strength, love and courage. Jychanumun did not hear the exact words, but he let their energy wash over him like a soothing balm.

Kraniel touched his shoulder. "We are ready," he whispered.

"Very good," Jychanumun replied. "Wait until all light has left my body. It will not take long. We will meet again in our futures, my friend."

Kraniel walked away. He was ready to activate the time fissure that would return all kutu back to either the light or shadow energy, all except Jychanumun, Mardoch and Dragun. Those three Nigh-kutu could not return to the shadow without endangering themselves. Instead, they were to die and wait in the death paths.

Orion's voice changed. He was still speaking to the Shaa-kutu, but pushing his courage and strength to the three Nigh-kutu. Without turning, Jychanumun saluted the Shaa-kutu salute. He had said his farewells already.

Jychanumun nodded to Mardoch and Dragun. "Just remember, do not fight this. And when you get to the paths, do not move, not even one step, until I return with Tachra."

Mardoch and Dragun said nothing. They didn't need to. They trusted Jychanumun. Each held out his right hand.

Jychanumun wound around their three wrists a length of his hair that he had cut. It would help to keep them grouped together until they were on the paths. He relaxed and opened his mind, feeling the essence of his two fellow Nigh-kutu.

"Let go, let your energy move into me," he told them smoothly. "This will not hurt. I will keep you safe. Let me guide you," he began to sing.

Mardoch and Dragun let go willingly. Slowly, the light from their flesh moved down their arms, connecting with Jychanumun. Jychanumun took their energy and their consciousness deep into his own mind. Once all essence of them was with him, he opened a path to death.

THIRTY-FIVE

My love? I heard Jychanumun call. His voice sounded different, wonderful. He was singing.

It is time. I am with you. I will not let you feel pain. This is not death but just a pause before another life.

His words were soothing, calming my mind.

It's time? I asked.

Yes, it is time, he sang.

It was time. Time to leave this life.

I forced open my heavy eyes, trying to focus on my hands. My eyes would not see through their blur in the gloom. I blindly clasped the shard of metal, digging it deep into the thin flesh of my arm, dragging the shard up my arm, and then, before my fingers grew too numb, I swapped hands, scratching a gash in the other arm. I didn't feel any pain.

I'm coming, I said. I could feel the life slowly flowing from me. I could feel the warmth of my own blood on my skin.

From my draining stupor, I saw the door of my prison flung

open. I saw the Nigh-kutu Shemya run in. He tried to reach my arms to cover them and stop the bleeding, horrified at what I was doing.

No! I told his mind, struggling to pull my arms away. *Shemya of the Gatherer clan, remember who you are. Find your Nar beast. She waits for you. Help the Nigh-kutu to see the truth of things. Remember you are a Gatherer; that is still your path.*

Shemya's mouth dropped open. He had heard me, not just with his mind, but with his heart. He had heard and understood. It was as if I had awoken a dormant memory in him. He remembered. I saw him stagger backwards, stumbling.

Another kutu barged in front of him.

Arrunn shielded his eyes from the curses on the wall, suddenly stopping.

I do not fear you anymore. I thought, my mind becoming vague. *I do not even hate you anymore. I wish for only peace for you.*

But Arrunn could not hear me and he could not move any closer. Something was happening. The dark tendrils of his energy began to move away from his body. Like smoke being drawn in a breeze, the darkness of his inner being was pulled away, pulled to something greater than the containment of his form. He stood, frozen to the spot, unable to move, watching his essence depart from his flesh. It trickled from his eyes, his skin and his hair. He had a look of shock on his face. He had no control over this.

Kraniel had done it.

He and all Nigh-kutu were being pulled back to the darkness. He was going home, to his origin. All kutu were going home.

My eyesight was dimming like a candle slowly dying. Arrunn's form was growing vague. I didn't feel frightened any more.

As my sight of the physical world faded, in place of my prison walls the brightness of Meah's bonded consciousness now sat next to me, gently nuzzling my face.

My heart, I smiled, *always together, forever. Our bond can never be undone.*

The energy all around me moved in a beautiful, hypnotic sway. I saw all colours and forms, blending and merging beyond the physical walls around me.

So this is what death felt like.

I felt a ripple of awareness, a familiarity that I knew so well; a familiarity that I thought I had lost forever. Feeling it gave me peace. It was the Old One.

I thought I had severed my link to you, I said weakly. I felt drawn to him, drawn to his inner peace. I so wanted to go to him. But hadn't Jychanumun told me that I must not?

Little one, the Old One whispered. His voiced moved around me and through me, like part of my energy. He sounded wonderful to my ears, like a multi-layered chorus of the most beautiful sounds, all merging to make one voice. *You severed your link to me. But I did not choose to sever my link to you. You are part of me, such things will always be.*

I am dying, I told him. *I want to come to you, but still I cannot. I must go to where I can come back to the flesh in the future. I must help save life itself.*

You have choice, the Old One said. *I hear you.* The words were gentle, as if he were smiling.

I wanted to stay talking to the Old One. I wanted to hold onto every moment in his presence that I could. But I felt my body in its last moment of life. I felt the Old One's presence pull away. He was letting me go. He was valuing my choice. He would always be part of me and with me, but he valued my choice. I was both as he had shaped me and I had shaped myself.

I could still hear Jychanumun singing. The singing was growing louder now. It was a beautiful song. It made me feel safe just to hear it.

Meah and I both saw the spectral image of Jychanumun at the

same time. He was crouched in front of us, his light and shadow radiating around him. He leaned forward, tenderly brushing the hair away from my damp, dirty face. He smiled and stood up, holding out his hand.

I stood up, feeling no pain, feeling no hurt, feeling only the love that creates a strength beyond any mortal flesh. I looked back at the slumped body that used to be mine, now a pale image of death reflected in Jychanumun's light. That was no longer my body. I had no body. I no longer wanted that flesh. What I had been was dead. My energy now flowed around me, vaguely resembling the form of the girl I once was.

I took Jychanumun's hand.

Iastha Tachra, beloved, he said.

My black-eyed one, I smiled.

It is done. It is your time.

And with those words, I left all remnants of my body behind.

Meah and I walked a death path that felt velvety under foot – a soft, dark, inviting path. I rested my hand gently on Meah's head as we walked, embracing her closeness, the feel of her fur so real to my spirit. I saw the spirits of Dragun and Mardoch walking too. We walked towards where Jychanumun guided us, a door not far ahead. It was a sombre walk, yet a joyful walk. Sombre because we had chosen to leave the lives we had valued so much; joyful because we would return, and when we did return we stood a good chance of saving all life.

We would return to make our final stand for life itself.

We would return when it was time.

Coming Soon

The third novel in The Chronicles of Fate and Choice trilogy.

The future is here.
All worlds collide into our world. It is the final stand
for life. It is the battle of wills, minds, hearts, and
souls. It is the battle to control time.
This will be our fate.

Available for pre-order:
www.rubyblaze.com

About the Author

KS Turner

Kate Sarah Turner was born in the suburbs of Norwich in the UK. She trained and worked as a designer and artist in London, and now lives and writes in Somerset. Kate's passions range from music to sculpture, maths to science and philosophy. The novels in The Chronicles of Fate and Choice series were inspired by a series of dreams.

τumulτus is the second book in
The Chronicles of Fate and Choice trilogy.

To find out more about Kate, visit www.rubyblaze.com